DETRITUS:

The SIP Initiative to Stalk Hitler

Tom Depperschmidt

PublishAmerica
Baltimore

First printing

This is a work of fiction set in a background of history. Public personages both living and dead may appear in the story under their right names. Scenes and dialogue involving them with fictitious characters are of course invented. Any other usage of real people's names is coincidental. Any resemblance of the imaginary characters to actual persons, living or dead, is entirely coincidental.

At the specific preference of the author, PublishAmerica allowed this work to remain exactly as the author intended, verbatim, without editorial input.

ISBN: 1-4241-4422-1
PUBLISHED BY PUBLISHAMERICA, LLLP
www.publishamerica.com
Baltimore

Printed in the United States of America

Dedication

To Bert; to our children and their spouses:
Susan, Mark, Tracy, Joel, Noelle, Andrew,
Lisa, Amy, Joan, Joseph; to all our grandchildren

To Dorothy,
I hope you continue to do well and enjoy life.
God bless you.
Tom

Acknowledgments

My wife Bert for her moral support, her forbearance with my early morning writing habit, and her ever sage advice.

Daughters Amy and Susan, for their careful manuscript reviews and stellar technical support and assistance.

Sons Joel and Mark, for guiding me through the mysteries of computers and cyber space and offering their helpful critiques of the manuscript.

Daughter Joan, son Andy, brother Don, and sisters Marilyn and Marcy for their good ideas and encouragement.

University English Instructor Julie Hoffman for her insight, corrections, and suggestions on an early draft.

My colleagues in several venues over my lifetime for their (mostly positive) influences on me, especially classmates at St. Joseph Military Academy, Hays, Kansas, and my comrades in army ranks at Ft. Bliss, Texas and in Alaska.

Any errors or omissions remaining are mine.

CAST OF CHARACTERS

Major Characters

Hayden Brooke, Captain, U.S. Army.

Sarah Spurges Brooke, wife of Hayden Brooke.

Everett Giles, Director of the top secret Special Intelligence Program (SIP).

Frederick Penner, German Jew, immigrant to U.S., best friend of Hayden Brooke.

George Spurges, father of Sarah, peace philosopher

Public Figures

Folke Bernadotte, humanitarian, Head of the Swedish Red Cross.

Winston Churchill, British Prime Minister.

Anthony Eden, British Foreign Secretary.

Adolf Hitler, German Chancellor.

George C. Marshall, General, U.S. Army Chief of Staff.

Joachim von Ribbentrop, German Foreign Minister.

Franklin D. Roosevelt, President of the United States.

Minor Characters

Barnard Alexander, Lieutenant Colonel, U.S. Army, Commander of special SIP team, which includes Major *Bill Driver*, Captain *Frank Tobias*, and Lieutenant *Keith Raymond.*

Wyatt Baxter, Lieutenant Colonel, U.S. Army, Deputy Chief of Intelligence, 82nd Airborne Division

Braxton Belleau, Colonel, U.S. Army, Paris Chief of Army Intelligence.

Lester Choles, Corporal, U.S. Army, cryptographer in Paris office of Army Intelligence.

Jerry Connelios, Captain, U.S. Army.

Hans Eberer and Matthew Kleine, German cover names for two U.S. Sergeants.

Josef Feldern, German Prisoner of War (POW) from Cologne.

Jimmy Hartage, Corporal, and *Phil Merchant,* Sergeant, U.S. Army aides to Hayden Brooke at Ft. Bragg, North Carolina.

Eric Klaysa, Lieutenant, German Army, captured near Strasbourg, France.

Julius Osbert, German Army Lieutenant on a train.

Martin Pake, ex-U.S. Army Air Force bombardier.

Liam Paulding, British intelligence agent in Paris.

Jackson Pendler, Major, U.S. Army, Director of U.S. Army Intelligence, Strasbourg, France.

Lion Tamer, code name for Lawrence Teegarden, German mole in British Intelligence.

Helmut Schwartz, Lieutenant Colonel, German Army, Frankfort office of Military Police.

Beatrice Spurges, mother of Sarah Spurges Brooke.

Hugo Valerian, Major, U.S. Army, Judge Advocate General's Office.

Chapter 1

The White House, Friday morning, October 27, 1944

"Good morning, General," President Franklin Roosevelt called as General George Marshall was ushered into the Oval Office. "Pardon my failure to get up. That little task seems to be more difficult these days."

"It is good to see you again," the General said as he circled the desk to shake the President's hand. He took a chair on the other side of the desk. There was nothing appropriate for him to say about the President's health.

It was 8:30. The President and General Marshall, Chief of Staff of the U.S. Army, were meeting for their regular Friday morning conversation on the state of the war and war planning.

The President sighed. "General, I wonder at times what possessed us to get involved in this European war."

Expressing a doubt of such gravity after almost three years of the conflict itself demonstrated the trust Roosevelt had in Marshall. The President valued the general as his closest adviser. He recently had said of Marshall that he could not sleep at ease when Marshall was out of Washington.

The General's strong command of history and diplomacy in addition to his excellent military background allowed the President to discuss international political and military matters in confidence that his views would be understood. He told the General on one occasion that he would make a great Secretary of State or Defense some day when his military prowess was not needed so desperately. In turn, General Marshall needed the ear of the President without layers of bureaucracy filtering their conversations.

"Our historic friendships with Great Britain and France would have forced us to do something, sooner or later, something more than spouting rhetoric against the growing evil of the Axis influence in the world," Marshall said. "I think it was inevitable that we would get drawn in at some point. The German declaration of war against us four days after Pearl Harbor and our war declaration in response simply sealed the direction in which we were already moving."

"That is sadly true," said Roosevelt. "Still, I can't help but think of those countless political agreements, pacts, alliances in the 20's and 30's among countries, many of them involving us. People had reason to think that all those formal understandings for mutual defense, non-aggression, and declarations of friendship would help to settle past and current disputes among countries amicably."

Marshall saw and heard that the President was speaking tired this morning. The color in his face was not good, more pasty gray than usual. His visage was melancholy, even grim, reflecting his depressed message. There was little today of what Marshall privately had described as the President's famous "political smile."

"One could argue just the opposite, I suppose," the General said. "Those agreements were formal expressions of new political and military alliances being created. There probably was as much mutual offense contemplated by the signatories as there was defense."

"Good point, General. Germany's declaration of war on us was due to its own 'Pact of Steel' with Italy and Japan. No one seriously doubts that Pact was designed for hostile purposes. And despite Hitler's claims that we committed aggressive acts against Germany and its partners, we had to defend our interests in view of the new alliances being formed. Despite some criticism now, this country's leadership has never doubted for one minute that we were on the right side of this fight."

General Marshall was not sure how much moral support the President needed this morning, but offered some. "I know this country's political and military decisions have been grounded in that conviction. Our willingness to help our Allies with Lend Lease, even before our active military involvement, and at some risk to our neutrality then, proves our moral commitment."

"I regret most that many inter-war agreements lulled the Allies into complacency," Roosevelt said. "Maybe that was the real intent of the dictators. Of all belligerent countries in this war, the Axis powers obviously went into battle far better prepared. They had been planning aggressive actions for some time. Western European countries hoped appeasement would soften the warlike posture of Germany and Italy. Indeed, they often avoided military preparations of their own for fear those efforts would be construed as hostility by the Axis powers."

The President warmed to his point. "Critical diplomacy lessons have to be learned from the inter-war negotiations, General. One is that an agreement is only as effective as the good will of the contracting parties. There is no international court strong enough, and not enough concerned nations who will band together, to enforce the agreements reached.

"If any militarily weak or unprepared country enters into an agreement with an intention other than to buy time with a dictator, it is in for an awakening and disappointment. The aggressors use those agreements as strategic political and military tools to achieve their ends at an opportune time. The agreement starts when the aggressor starts it, and ends when the aggressor ends it. Anyone who thinks differently is being duped. Good intentions of the weaker country don't mean anything."

The President sat back in his chair. His body language did not exude energy. He grasped the mahogany arms of his chair regularly for support. Marshall knew he needed to end this session soon to avoid wearying the President even more.

Marshall sought to summarize. "The grim reality is that the only treaty that has binding effect for a weak country is the one following its destruction or surrender. I don't know how the world community will handle this problem in the future. We have had stronger countries bullying the smaller guys all along. The German treatment of Poland is a classic case. The fact that Germany's invasion was the trigger for the European war makes it even more important to study. It is the model for the futility of verbal condemnation of an aggressor."

The President nodded. "National lawlessness was rampant between the wars. Back on the playgrounds when I was a boy, some brave soul would occasionally challenge a local bully. 'Why don't you pick on someone your own size?' Maybe the reason no country offered resistance was the follow-up. 'Yeah?' taunts the bully, 'how about you?' and bloodies the nose of his antagonist."

General Marshall smiled at the image of Roosevelt in a playground brawl. "Propaganda was driving diplomacy," he said. "Hitler's pretexts for breaking agreements were often of the flimsiest sort, as if he were taunting the other signatory or the world at large to challenge him. Even his apologists in other countries had trouble parroting those pretexts. They had to see finally that Hitler's objectives went beyond allegedly 'German territories'."

The President suddenly leaned forward on his desk. "The Allies must win this war, General! The alternative is too horrible to imagine. The world would see more than genocide of the peoples the Axis call 'undesirables.' It is clear from the chilling reports of Axis conquest that the Fascist dictators envision themselves as masters, as superior to other races and peoples. Dominated peoples are not only losers in battle. They lose all their rights. They become slave peoples, worked and starved to death. If they resist in any way they are tortured or killed.

"And this is the twentieth century, not the middle ages! God must see the democracies and benign kingdoms victorious! Continuing ascendancy of totalitarian regimes is unthinkable!"

General Marshall had never seen the President so passionate in defense of the cause. He sensed as well the message of urgency the President was delivering. *Win the war in Europe soon!*

The President and British Prime Minister Winston Churchill had agreed shortly after the U.S. entry into the war on a "Europe First" strategy. That meant the defeat of Germany and Italy and the minor European Axis countries was to be given Allied resource priority over the Pacific Theatre. Now the President made explicit the message Marshall had anticipated.

"General," he said, "we were not attacked by Germany or Italy. Pearl Harbor was the Japs' doing. Our major effort needs to be directed primarily against our attackers.

"Even though they weren't provoked into war by attacks on their mainland or colonies, the British don't see it that way. They have their own European alliances. They feel honor bound to live up to them."

The General did not disagree. The President had been insisting for some time that the United States needed to put more effort into the war against Japan. The war planners had not been starving the Pacific Commanders, General Douglas McArthur and Admiral Chester Nimitz. However, those leaders could use more manpower and material. Victory soon in the European Theatre was the most expeditious way to effect re-allocation of both to the Pacific Theatre.

The President continued. "God knows, if all these reports of atrocities against Jews and others are true, the Allies have some real maniacs in Europe to take down. But our main task is defeating Japan. We can't count on much help in the direct assault on Japan from any of our Allies. Nothing from the French. They're still getting back on their feet after being liberated. And from the British and Canadians and Australians and the British empire troops...well, they'll fight in India and Burma and the Malayan Peninsula...where the British empire has been threatened. But where else can they be plugged in against Japan?"

Marshall knew the President admired Churchill personally and as a wartime leader. Churchill's doggedness and confidence infused the President with new energy whenever they met or corresponded. Roosevelt's essay on the current state of the global war was mildly critical of his closest ally, however.

"I don't think they can do much more now. They're spread even thinner than we are," the general said.

"I know, I know!" the President said, suddenly excited. "And that's my point entirely. You know, General, Churchill was most effusive in his praise of our Navy after we whipped the Japs at Midway. He has been most complimentary in all our victories in the Pacific.

"But do you know what? He might just as well have been saying—and maybe he was saying—'keep up the good work, Yanks. We're thrilled to see you can handle the Japs by yourselves in the central and southern Pacific, because that's the way it is going to have to be. We'll do some cheerleading, but cheerleaders dance on the sidelines'."

Marshall chuckled aloud at the President's analogy. He suspected the put down of the other Allies was prompted more by weariness with wartime demands on his time and energy than dissatisfaction with Churchill or other leaders. He offered to continue the assessment.

"I know we can count on only a little help from the British in the island-hopping battles. That's our show. They will have some troops in certain spots in Asia, but not side by side as we are in Europe. As for the material resource supplies…well, that's going to be almost entirely our show the rest of the way."

The President nodded agreement as he sank back in his chair again. Marshall saw that the conversation had to come to an end now.

"I'll look right away into what we can do to get things cleaned up in Europe," he promised as he rose to leave. "We do need to get focused more on the Pacific."

"Thanks ever so much for your time and good counsel," the President said, extending his hand.

While being driven back to his office, General Marshall reviewed the state of the American armies in Italy and Western Europe. The American Fifth Army in Italy had come close to breaking completely through the final, difficult-to-penetrate German mountain lodgments along remnants of their Gothic defense line south of Bologna. That defensive line was four miles deep. Now the Fifth Army was exhausted and had gone into winter operations status.

There was no significant progress of Allied armies in Western Europe recently. All appeared to be buttoning up for the winter, adopting a defensive posture. General George Patton's Third Army was about to open a winter offensive along the central-southern front in France. That effort offered the only promise for some immediate movement of American forces.

Marshall was bothered by the recurring thought that, after all these years in power, Hitler was still largely an unknown quantity in many ways. Hitler had made some serious military mistakes recently. However, his direction of the initial phases of the war from a German political and military standpoint had been effective.

Allied intelligence services were unanimous that Hitler continued to exercise direct, total command of all German military forces ever since the surrender of his Sixth Army at Stalingrad in 1943. He apparently was setting tactical plans as well as overall strategy.

Marshall had the uneasy feeling that the Western Front was too quiet. Hitler might be brewing up something nasty for the Allies. General Bradley was taking some risk in having American divisions of the First Army cover longer lines than usual. Some of those divisions were manned with green, untested troops.

Marshall could not conceive of any dramatic initiative that would accelerate resolution of the European conflict. He would sound out Everett Giles on the whole matter shortly.

Chapter 2

Washington, D.C., Friday morning, October 27, 1944

"Colonel Giles," General Marshall greeted his old friend on his office phone. Marshall had had many conversations with Giles since the war started. Marshall told Giles that he treasured the relaxed conversations they could have together, however serious the topic. Giles knew that Marshall was not just buttering up an underling. He believed that a man in Marshall's position needed someone to talk to without formality or pretense, more a friend than counselor. Giles was happy to serve in that role.

Everett Giles was not really a colonel. In fact, he was a civilian, now head of the top secret agency, the Special Intelligence Program (SIP) that General Marshall had created in early 1944.

Giles had served in the Signal Corps in World War I, gaining the rank of captain. He and Captain Marshall had frequent contacts while Marshall served as Chief of Operations for the First Infantry Division in France.

Giles left the army in the late 1920's, finding military life too dull in peacetime. He had taken a position at a small Midwestern university teaching mathematics and logic. Although not connected by military service during the 1930's, Giles and Marshall continued their friendship.

At the outbreak of hostilities in Europe with Germany's invasion of Poland on September 1, 1939, President Roosevelt promoted Marshall to full general and appointed him Army Chief of Staff. Shortly after, Marshall appealed to Giles to return to the Army Intelligence service. Giles was then over 60.

Giles had quibbled with Marshall only briefly and good naturedly about Giles' rank. Marshall first assured him of permanent civilian status. "You're too old a dog to be drafted," he said.

They agreed that his pay rate and benefits would be that of a full colonel. It was the rank they thought Giles would have obtained as an intelligence officer had he remained in the Army Signal Corps in the inter-war years.

In the four-plus years of service since his return, Giles had done his duty at the personal expense of a suppressed imagination. He finally asked for a meeting with the general.

"Military intelligence is more than the technical kinds of things I have been doing," he told Marshall. "I do feel an obligation to continue serving in wartime, of course. But I no longer want to be part of the 'invisible ink' crowd setting up minor deceptions and designing Marx Brothers caricatures for agents' disguises. There is more to intelligence than deception.

"And intelligence is more than interception of enemy information, or even gathering and interpreting it. We find very few gold nuggets in those interceptions. Practically all of the daily intercepts are routine, housekeeping kinds of things. At most it is information of a tactical nature, hardly ever strategic."

Giles told Marshall that his most important intelligence contribution could be in marrying intelligence to operations. The strategic planning he envisioned would require approval from a very high level of political and military authority, of course.

Giles' request to Marshall to use his talents differently coincided fortuitously with the General's own thinking at the time. He told Giles in response that he had recently conceived the model of a new intelligence group. The Special Intelligence Program would be more suited to intelligence needs for the military at this stage of the war in Europe.

SIP would be a new strategic think tank. The grist for its deliberations would be the intelligence already gathered by all existing agencies. It would then consider strategic and some tactical uses of that knowledge. Even consideration of "blue sky" ideas to shape military and political decisions was within its purview.

Moreover, the SIP office would be an agency answerable directly to General Marshall. It would thereby be free of pressure to spin information to suit tactical commanders.

Marshall directed Giles' new SIP agency to serve three critical intelligence purposes. It would be General Marshall's eyes and ears on site for major Army campaigns and missions. It was to collate and interpret highest level intelligence. It would plan top secret projects using that intelligence.

Those tasks were a heavy responsibility. Giles thrived in them. He was on hand at General Dwight Eisenhower's headquarters in England during Overlord, the Allied invasion of Normandy in June, 1944. Although the immediate military requirements for intelligence were more tactical than strategic, the invasion was the first practical exercise in SIP's oversight mission.

Giles was deeply troubled by plans going awry early on the morning of June 6. The drops of three Allied paratroop divisions had been widely scattered beyond the planned drop zones. There was heavy loss of troopers. Many units were behind schedule in securing their objectives as a result.

Equally troubling were reports that the Allied bombing of German coastal defenses had yielded limited success. Weather and poor visibility caused the bombing attack to hit too far inland. Many powerful German gun emplacements on the bluffs commanding invasion beaches were undisturbed by the bombings. Giles relayed to General Eisenhower the concern shared by many of the intelligence staff on hand that the price to be paid in casualties by units struggling across beaches under hostile fire would be very high.

Eisenhower already had the same information and also didn't like it. Somberly, the Supreme Commander pondered the few options he had. There was no reserve paratroop division to send. He turned down Giles' suggestion for several hours' delay in landing the main invasion force to allow the bombers to re-load for a low-level, precision attack to complete the reduction of German beach defenses. He decided that the momentum of the massive movement of men and material already started forced its continuance despite the hazards.

Giles and his group learned bitter intelligence lessons at Normandy. Brilliant invasion planning can be compromised by much less-than-perfect execution. The timing of intelligence offered to commanders is critical. Fate can always override planning.

Disaster for the Allies at Normandy was averted by employing their strengths: air superiority, the sheer volume of manpower and material that was poured into the attack, and the will of commanders to win the objective.

Three months later, Giles was in Paris in the week preceding the Market-Garden campaign which began on September 17, 1944. This combined air and ground invasion was the brain child of British Field Marshal Bernard Law Montgomery. It was designed to punch a major hole in the German defenses in the Netherlands. The offensive would proceed along a 65-mile, hard-to-defend corridor from Neerpelt to capture Arnhem near the German border.

Montgomery then envisioned the decisive stroke to end the war in Europe. The 21st Army Group would open the corridor from Arnhem through northern Germany for quick seizure of Berlin. General Eisenhower approved the plan to get the Allies moving against the strong enemy defenses on the French-German border.

The Market-Garden plan called for dropping over three airborne divisions along the invasion route to secure vital bridges, neutralize German defenses along the way, and allow Allied ground units to cross rivers and move without delay to capture Arnhem. The operation was supported by giving Montgomery top priority access to military equipment and supplies. It drew resources away from the rest of the Allied combat units in France. The resource shift effectively halted the hitherto fast-moving American Third Army of General Patton in its drive toward the main German defense line behind the Rhine River in southeastern France.

Giles believed the strategic objective of Market-Garden was flawed on the drawing board. Even assuming the operation's success in capturing Arnhem, the subsequent attack through northern Germany toward Berlin would draw Germany's military forces like a magnet. The Allies' ability to exploit the shift of German armies to defend Berlin, presumably from behind the West Wall, would be limited in the short run by the paucity of resources left to the American armies by the provisioning of Market-Garden itself.

Moreover, in its reliance on an extremely narrow invasion route, Market-Garden was a high risk operation under any circumstances. A heightened risk was discovered in photographic surveillance several days before the operation's beginning. These photos revealed previously undetected, strong German defense units. They included elements of the German *Schutzstaffel* (SS or blackshirts) Ninth and Tenth Panzer Divisions being moved from the west coast of the Netherlands to a rear area for rehabilitation. Those units had been moved directly into the planned path of the Market-Garden advance!

Here was a situation that could be controlled much better than Overlord. There was still time to change the plan or delay its beginning. Alternately, the stronger than anticipated German defenses could be neutralized by concentrated air attacks before the Allied operation began.

Giles and other intelligence officers were quick to discourage continuing the operation as scheduled. They were dumbfounded at the refusal of the operation's commanders to adjust the tactical plan in light of the recent intelligence gathered. The power of military commanders' egos, impatience at the progress of the war in Western Europe, and blind faith in the surprise, boldness, and size of the operation generated a different kind of momentum for its continuance than at Normandy. Those factors overwhelmed the common sense of postponing or canceling the operation.

The price of Market-Garden's failure was high. The operation cost the Allies over 17,000 killed, wounded, and missing. The pivotal strategic objective, Arnhem itself, was not taken. The threshold for Montgomery's planned decisive invasion of Germany was not crossed. The attacks initiated a serious struggle as Allied units fought for several weeks to hold the perimeter around their narrow salient.

Giles and the rest of the intelligence community pondered still another critical war-planning lesson learned. Personalities and ambitions of military leaders can override carefully considered judgments, even when those judgments are supported by unequivocal intelligence.

"Are you clear?" The General's question was standard, determining if Giles was alone and that the phone line was secure from any eavesdroppers.

"Clear and secure," Giles responded as he recognized the General's voice. "SIP is at your service."

"Good! Everett, I know it's late for a meeting today, so let's just chat a minute. Are there any developments I should know about?"

Giles knew that the General's question was simply an invitation to open discussion, without a lot of formality or background needed. It was also superfluous in that Giles had often assured the General that SIP would inform him immediately of any important intelligence it learned.

"Where should I start?" Giles asked. "First the defensive. The British reading of German radio traffic by cracking their Enigma coding process has revealed high level communications about German Army movements that we were already aware of. There is some speculation about future Allied deployments, but nothing that should alarm us. Hitler continues to exhort his field marshals and generals to be more aggressive, of course. Those intercepted communiqués are so vague about their immediate plans that they also are not worth much. Certainly they do not seem to warrant any special response on our part.

"There are also routine discussions about war planning and war games, but nothing we detect that is immediately and specifically important. There is the first mention in the last few days about something called *Wacht am Rhein*. It translates as 'Watch on the Rhine.' It sounds like a purely defensive plan someone has developed. Maybe the Germans are also shutting down offensive operations for the winter. But its mention in our intercepts of Enigma transmissions hints that it might be something more important."

"Okay…keep an eye on that. And the offensive?"

"You know that I've felt all along that our distinct advantage strategically is air superiority. We sustained serious losses in aircraft and personnel to establish it. Now that we have paid for it, we ought to use it. I can't see anything in our arsenal that can be deployed decisively more quickly. Our Eighth Air Force and the Royal Air Force should continue to mount massive bombing raids to further reduce German industrial capacity. When we finally eliminate their ability to produce the basics, oil and ball bearings and steel, we should follow up by hitting their production of aircraft, tanks, and artillery pieces, and on down the line to paper clips, if needed.

"Our tactical air support can continue assaults on their military forces in the field. Their manpower losses have already been severe, and Hitler is scraping the bottom of the barrel for replacements.

"Nothing we have studied in our intelligence gathering seems more promising now than stepping up the air effort. The ability of Germany to provision its military is waning. Our production of aircraft is greater than ever. We ought to throw everything we have into that effort."

"I don't disagree with your appraisal and recommendation at all, Everett. However, it will still be necessary to take and occupy the German mainland to force their surrender."

"General, the problems left by Market-Garden are severe. Montgomery's 21st Army Group is still locked up in serious struggles to hold the ground within the perimeter of the invasion route. Why not a major winter offensive by the American armies all along the present battle line?"

"The Germans have toughened up their defenses since we're that close to their homeland," the General warned.

Giles thought the strategic opportunities were too compelling to divert his suggestion. "If the four American Armies in central and southern France, the Ninth, First, Third, and Seventh, in order, north to south, were now given priority in supplies, the odds are good they could close to the Rhine in a month or six weeks of hard fighting, and probably force some crossings."

"Montgomery would scream at being put on the back burner with resource priority," Marshall said.

Giles did not want to annoy his good friend, but he thought the argument had to be pressed. "Montgomery had his chance to shine in Market-Garden. The plan, especially its reach to the final objective, was not well thought out. He did not account well for enemy manpower and its disposition. He ignored the intelligence available to him. We are still on hold while he cleans up that mess."

"I am bothered by the virtual stalemate there and all along the Allied front," the General said. "The British have held Antwerp since September fourth. But it is still, to this day, of no use to the Allies as a port. A supply port that size and that far forward is critical to our logistics. The Schelde estuary needs to be finally cleared of enemy troops so the Antwerp port can be put to Allied use.

"Here it is almost two months after taking Antwerp and we're still pushing supplies from the Atlantic coast 300 miles across France by land. You'd think Monty would understand that priority, since his Army Group is arrayed around Antwerp."

"We can't reverse Market-Garden, General. But we can ensure that something like that won't happen again by putting the next major effort in the American sector, in General Bradley's hands."

"A major winter campaign," the General said to try on the idea. "That would certainly keep our armies from passing the winter around pot-bellied stoves."

"With a major shift of resources to them, and increased tactical air support for each of the four armies, I suggest it can be done," Giles said.

Marshall paused before continuing. "As you know, Everett, there are major political issues among our Allies to confront in all these initiatives, especially with Churchill and Charles DeGaulle. Those issues are very troublesome now, given what has happened in the last few months. Thank God I don't have to deal directly with those things."

Giles was pleased to be the sounding board for Marshall's venting frustration with the Allies. The disappointment he expressed was not something he could tell many people.

The General paused a while before addressing Giles' proposal again. "I appreciate all you have said, Everett. You are definitely on the right track. As always, logistics will control what we can do offensively in both combat theatres. We are already pressing to get more done with what we have. We're at our peak effort pushing supplies across two oceans and into effective and immediate use."

Marshall paused again. Giles did not think it was appropriate to break the silence or suggest an end to the dialog. Marshall asked suddenly, "Anything special your unit is working on?" He went on without waiting for an answer. "Everett, I can't tell you all of what this is about. I need to know if you have any special projects on your shelf that could be used in Europe to good effect, and rather soon. You know, of course, that we have not made much progress on the ground in the last month or so. Most of the commanders in the field seem to favor closing up shop for the winter. We need all army commands to review their options."

Giles realized he did not have much to say here. "Do you really want to know all that we are working on, or just considering? All the dirty tricks, grand deceptions, mis-directions, half truths?"

Marshall replied quickly and firmly. "Heavens no! I really don't need or want to know all your plans or projects, especially those only in the idea stage, for several good reasons." Giles knew that the volume of intelligence and derivative planning that needed to be managed was the reason Marshall chose to establish SIP in the first place.

"Everett," he said finally, "all army commands are going to have to be more innovative and aggressive to get some resolution in Europe soon. That is urgent. Supplies permitting, the air war can be intensified. A major winter offensive all along the front would take some doing.

"I don't have to know all of what SIP does. You have good people and resources at your disposal. If you need more, let me know and I'll do what I can. It is essential that we do not hibernate over the winter. You and your unit need to be thinking about decisive projects that can help end this European war soon."

"I understand," Giles said. He was already pondering the tone of urgency in Marshall's voice and language, the specific "more innovative and aggressive" message, and what "decisive projects" really meant. The General, Giles believed, was urging SIP to use intelligence for more than military operations.

What extra-military options can SIP initiate, he wondered? For example, can the Allies hope realistically that German leadership and/or war policy can be changed? And what actions by SIP are allowed or would be required to effect such changes?

Giles knew that G-2, the official Army Intelligence staff department, had just a month ago called for another sweep of all army personnel to identify special skills available. Would SIP's use of special assassination teams or individuals against German leaders be an appropriate option to consider now?

The SIP Director's search for answers was interrupted by General Marshall.

"Have a good weekend, Everett," he said abruptly. "I would appreciate your work on this directive soon."

Chapter 3

Ft. Bragg, N.C., Friday afternoon, October 27, 1944

The formal message had glared at him from the middle of his desk for several hours.

Captain Hayden Brooke is ordered to meet with Lt. Col. Wyatt Baxter in his office at 16:30 today. He is to keep this order secret. Baxter's signature was above his title, Deputy Intelligence Officer, 82nd Airborne Division.

Several features made the message curious to Hayden. Baxter sent the message by courier this morning. It was hand written. A message so simple not trusted to a typist? Hayden knew that most division clerks were being released from Friday afternoon duty. Baxter's staff likely would not be around to observe Hayden's visit.

Hayden called to his company clerk. Cpl. Jimmy Hartage popped into view at the office door almost immediately.

"Get me Capt. Jerry Connelios, Corporal. Try his barracks first."

"Yes sir," the Corporal responded.

"And you take the rest of the afternoon off. You probably have things to do." Hayden did not want to give a phony excuse to the clerk for his own early departure.

"I really have a lot of paperwork left to do and…" his clerk started. Hayden shushed the protest. "It's never finished, today or next week or ever."

The Corporal had been Hayden's company clerk since Hayden took command of C Company of the 2nd Battalion, 505th Parachute Regiment, two months before the Normandy invasion. Jimmy had a sense of responsibility greater than his nineteen years would suggest. He recognized from the day of his assignment as company clerk that a company commander is foremost the leader of fighting men engaged in the deadly practices of war. The company commander also has administrative duties that daily range from the trivial to the somber.

Jimmy had been valuable to Hayden as the clearinghouse for the information flows into and out of the company. He had learned to deliver to Hayden the subtle nuances picked up in phone and face-to-face conversations, allowing Hayden to solve problems before they developed into crises.

"Captain Connelios is on," Jimmy said shortly at Hayden's office door. Hayden motioned Jimmy to leave as he picked up the phone. The Corporal, seemingly resigned to the order to leave his work unfinished, gathered up a few belongings, waved a goodbye at the door, and left the office.

Hayden hadn't spoken with Jerry Connelios since Monday, one of the few times in two years they had not talked daily.

They served together in combat, most recently in command of their companies, side by side in line in the same battalion since the Normandy invasion. Jerry had been rotated back to Ft. Bragg on October 2, a week before Hayden's return.

"Jerry!" he called. "Bad day?"

"I'm ready for the drink now," his friend replied.

Hayden regretted postponing their 16:00 meeting without being able to give a good reason. "That's why I called. I've got an appointment coming up that I can't shake. I can't even say how long it might run."

"Oh?"

Hayden was annoyed that Jerry prodded when he should have just accepted Hayden's word. He didn't like being evasive. Evasion to a friend was deception. Being officially secretive was the surest way to arouse the wrong kind of suspicion about his meeting.

"Tell you what. If you're free, let's have drinks and dinner about 19:00 at the Officers Club. I should be free for sure by then and I'll fill you in as best I can."

"Fair enough," Jerry said. Hayden was relieved that Jerry wanted to be a good sport, after all. "I'll see you then."

"Damn," Hayden said under his breath as he cradled the phone. This Baxter meeting had better be important, important enough to compensate for an awkward relationship with a friend.

He glanced at his watch. It was 15:15 on the last Friday afternoon of

October, 1944. At 15:30, Sgt. Phil Merchant would deliver to Hayden the observations he had been collecting on a variety of topics from combat veterans back from the Pacific Theatre. Those observations would be part of a manual to familiarize paratroopers who might be jumping into Japan in a year or two. It would introduce troopers to the climate, a little language, and the enemy they would confront. Hayden assumed that the task for Sgt. Merchant and himself was simply army make-work, something to keep them both officially busy for a while.

Hayden gazed out the window at the bleak surroundings. Everything on an army post is in muted colors, as if to emphasize that military life is most often joyless and hard. The olive drab of uniforms is relieved only by the beige drab of conformist barracks with no personality as buildings.

A light rain had been falling all day. The tail lights of a steady stream of lumbering two-ton trucks and jeeps and vans passing the office stretched into cruciform stars reflecting against the wet asphalt. Hayden snorted aloud at the thought that the only real color outside his window was provided by the tail lights of army vehicles.

A little over four years ago he was just another young man with no life plan or special ambition. In May, 1940, in Texas, he had signed on with a wheat "custom-cutting" crew. After a few weeks of getting equipment readied, his crew in the first week of June began following the wheat harvest north into the plains states. The crew hired out to wheat farmers without equipment or the ability to harvest and haul their own crops. The job took them into Canada in the late summer. It was hard work but good pay.

Along the crew's route, he met Sarah Spurges one evening at an outdoor concert in Wichita. She was pretty, thoughtful, and considerably less shy than the girls he had met in high school. He later began to send her notes from the temporary bases the crew set up in their northward trek, telling her the towns ahead where they planned to stop. He began to anticipate her letters. It made each long, hot, dusty day of work bearable.

On September 17, 1940, his twenty-first birthday and the end of their harvest work, Hayden learned of jobs available at Boeing Aircraft in Wichita. President Roosevelt had begun to get the U.S. armed services prepared for possible war. The President proposed building enough new ships for a two-ocean Navy. In the middle of May he had called for production of 50,000 planes. Boeing would produce a big percentage of that total in the years ahead.

It was at Boeing that Hayden met and became close friends with Frederick Penner. Frederick was twenty-five, a recent émigré from Germany, and a Jew.

Hayden learned to speak passable German from him, while Hayden helped Frederick with his English. They worked well together, played chess, hunted and fished on weekends.

When a larger group of Boeing workers got together in spring and summer, softball hilarity reigned as they all tried to teach Frederick the game. The slower they pitched to him, the more difficult it was for him to get bat on ball. A chorus of "ahs" built the anticipation with each high arching pitch to him, followed by widespread "oohs" and laughter as Frederick's feeble attempts to hit it failed.

Frederick took it all in good humor. His satisfaction came in the fall soccer games when he took his turn as teacher. He smiled at the inept footwork of his American friends trying to learn this strange sport. He cried "foul" often and loud as they illegally swatted at the ball with their hands.

Hayden began dating Sarah shortly after his return from his wheat harvesting job. They drove one Saturday morning to Hutchinson, northwest of Wichita, and spent the day at the Kansas State Fair. While they walked the midway hand in hand that evening, Sarah asked him suddenly. "What do you want in life?"

"You mean now?" he teased, squeezing her to him as they walked.

"I like your straightforwardness…I think. Goodness, is there such a word?"

"That word is close enough. Thank you. I can't say anything for sure about a career. Nothing specific. I'd like to be able to look back at the end of my days and believe that I accomplished something in my life, and was happy doing it. How about you?"

"Oh, I hope for lots of important things," she said. "I want to love and be loved, have good friends. I would like to think that in my lifetime the world will achieve a lasting peace. My family is Quaker. The influence of their belief and example has been very strong on me."

Hayden would have liked her to add, maybe just hint, that he might have a continuing place in her life. He felt that way about her. Had he hinted something like that, however, he felt he might rush her. Her impish unpredictability might cause her to say something he did not want to hear.

Even as he held the thought, she pulled him toward the Ferris wheel in a change of physical and verbal direction. "There's lots of time for this serious stuff later. Let's have fun now."

At the peak of the wheel they rocked their seat, high above the flat land, lights, town, and the outlying dirt roads marked by the moving headlights of ever more cars coming to the Fair. They were about to touch the stars above them on this perfect evening. Hayden knew then that he loved Sarah and would tell her soon.

The year beginning in late 1940 had been the happiest of his life. He was settled, with new friends and a stable job.

The war news was increasingly ominous in late 1941. Hayden and his friends were deeply troubled by the expanding international tension. They feared the United States could not preserve its nominal neutrality for long. The German *Wehrmacht* had occupied Austria and Czechoslovakia and rolled easily through Poland, The Netherlands, Belgium, Norway, and France. It had nearly bagged the entire British Expeditionary Force at Dunkirk.

Italy had attacked and conquered weak countries in its neighborhood and North Africa. Japan's aggression in China and French Indochina threatened the security of Southeast Asia and the Western Pacific. In September, 1940, Germany, Italy, and Japan signed the Tri-Partite Pact, the "Pact of Steel," pledging mutual aid if any of the three countries went to war with any country not then a belligerent.

The German invasion of the Soviet Union on June 22, 1941, looked at first to be a repeat of Germany's quick conquest of France. The U.S. had already introduced the novel concept of Lend Lease to assist Great Britain and the Western democracies, and now extended that assistance to the Soviet Union.

President Roosevelt nationalized Philippine armed forces under the command of General Douglas McArthur on July 26, 1941. In August, 1941, Congress passed the second Selective Service Act, extending draftee service to eighteen months. Hayden had registered shortly after the passage of the first draft Act in September of 1940, the first peacetime draft in U. S. history.

He realized now that world events were limiting his options. He was not ready for marriage, although he and Sarah had talked of it. He would not seek or accept a draft exemption for work in an "essential industry," recognizing the humbling truth that a machine would someday do the work he did at Boeing.

Hayden asked for Sarah's input. Her answer was calm and firm.

"I agree with all of your assessment about your concerns and our lives together. But there is a critical issue that will not go away. War is evil. It solves nothing. I have serious misgivings about your contributing to war." Her hesitation before continuing was her fear of his answer. "Would you consider filing as a conscientious objector?"

"No!" Hayden responded quickly and emphatically. "Sarah, I'm not moved by the bravado of war movie heroes and martial music and pep talks. But I will not shirk my responsibility!"

Hayden called the draft board in his Texas hometown the following week and asked to be moved up on the draft list. He reluctantly and somberly said goodbye to Sarah and Frederick. He left by train in early October, 1941, for induction at El Paso, Texas, and basic training a few miles away at Ft. Bliss.

He adapted to army life easily. The routine and physical activity suited him. He was distinguished as a marksman. His personnel file noted his German language ability.

Toward the end of basic training, and after the United States was at war, he was encouraged by the training cadre to apply for officer training. In the process of agreeing, he wangled a week's leave for early January, 1942.

The realization had come quickly to him during basic training that almost all of his private's pay was being used for long distance calls to Sarah. He thought constantly of her. Depressed on Christmas Eve, with no relatives to call, and while many of his barrack buddies ventured across the Rio Grande to the low-price bars and fleshpots of Juarez, Mexico, he called Sarah and asked her to marry him. She agreed instantly, any reservations she might have entertained remaining unspoken. He then talked with her father George, with whom Hayden had had several long, thoughtful, and friendly conversations at the Spurges' country home. Sarah's mother Beatrice asked only if he loved Sarah, but she already knew the answer. Hayden told her he would always treat her daughter with love and respect.

Hayden arrived in Wichita January 8, 1942. Sarah and he were married three days later after very impromptu arrangements and honeymooned in Kansas City.

His next stop was Ft. Benning, Georgia, for the officer training program started there in 1940 by then Brigadier General Omar Bradley. Upon completion of the program in May, 1942, he was commissioned a Second Lieutenant. His request to join the 505th Parachute Regiment was approved. The regiment was activated in early July, 1942, and soon would be part of the 82nd Airborne Division scheduled for further training at Ft. Bragg, North Carolina. He became a platoon leader in the second battalion of the regiment under the command of Col. James Gavin.

Hayden liked his new life. Even during the constant changes—experiments, accelerated training schedules, assimilation of new recruits into the division—he found the lower and middle grade officers of the regiment and division with whom he most came into contact to be dedicated and professional. Most of all, he trusted them. That mutual trust became the foundation of the division's *esprit de corps* maintained during its most intense engagements throughout the war. There was also a distinct swagger among troopers in the division. That confidence, Hayden believed, grew out of two things: completing the hard and demanding schedule of training; meeting and conquering a primal fear on their first jump.

Before moving to Ft. Bragg in early 1943, Hayden got another week of leave. Sarah's recent activities were very troubling to him. She had become active in a peace group. She was speaking out forcefully at church and social meetings against the war.

"Why don't you come along with me to my meeting? You need to understand my feelings." Her comments stabbed directly at the heart of the issue that had grown to divide them in his absence.

"Can't you skip just one meeting?" he countered. "We have only a few days before I have to get back."

"Absolutely not!" she replied. "My friends expect me to be there. This work has to go on." She tried to measure the depth of his stern visage before venturing her trump card. "There's no reason you can't go along with me. You would not have to wear your precious uniform."

"No!" he shouted. "I deplore your sarcasm. You are mocking who I am!"

Hayden regretted that their conversations were never the same again. Her comment about his uniform was the breaking point. The intimacy that had been so natural between them became strained and awkward.

The principles Hayden learned in a year and a half of basic, officer, and paratroop training guided him through several major campaigns. He led a platoon through Sicily and was a company executive officer as a First Lieutenant at Salerno. As a Captain, he commanded a company in the Overlord and Market-Garden invasions.

By the second week of October, 1944, the Market-Garden operation in the Netherlands was winding down. After the 82nd Division came under the formal command of the British XXX Corps on October 8, Hayden asked for leave back to the States. He wanted to work on reconciliation with Sarah. He really did not expect to get the leave and was very surprised when it was approved quickly.

He flew home and called Sarah as soon as he could, the first live conversation he had with her since the movement of the 82nd Division to North Africa in the Spring of 1943. His welcome home a day later was cool. He picked up more disquieting talk of Sarah's continuing peace group involvement.

The Stop War Now group had become officially unpopular. The U.S. Attorney General's office, under the aegis of the Smith "Alien Registration Act" passed by Congress in June of 1940, had conducted a preliminary investigation of the group.

While nominally aimed at aliens, the Smith Act's reach was extended to include domestic subversion with the outbreak of war. Official scrutiny of Sarah's group was even more intense.

The Spurges family had been on the unpopular side of public sentiment before. They had been toughened by that experience to resist what their consciences told them was wrong. The "overthrow of government by force" was never part of their agenda, however.

Hayden tried with all his power to persuade Sarah and her family to soften their rhetoric. There had been bad blood between the family and their neighbors for some time. Sarah told of new rumors about her family in their rural community southwest of Wichita. They were accused of using a short wave radio to communicate clandestinely with "Germany." "Strange visitors" were among the arrivals and departures at the Spurges farm home reported breathlessly by townspeople. Some of the gossip poison had begun to follow Sarah to her job in Wichita.

Hayden's attempts to persuade had little effect. Sarah and her family were cordial to him, but adamant in their stand against war. Hayden had returned to duty just this past week, despairing that his relationship with Sarah could ever be salvaged.

His reverie ended as Sgt. Merchant emerged out of the rain, jogging up the sidewalk, dodging water puddles. The Sergeant shook off his poncho as he entered Hayden's outer office.

"Good afternoon, Captain," he saluted.

"Hello, Sergeant. Your timing is exquisite. Come on in here," Hayden said, leading the way into his inner office. "Let's see what we've got so far."

Hayden took folders from his aide and did a quick scan of each in turn. He asked an occasional question and was satisfied with the answers.

"Great job, Sergeant. This is a good start." He handed the folders back. "File these. We'll start the next round on Monday."

Sgt. Merchant took the comment as his dismissal, bundled up the files, and disappeared into the outer office. He reappeared in a minute.

"Anything else, sir?"

"Thanks again, Sergeant. I'll see you Monday."

Hayden collected his hat and poncho. After only a week, he was already tired of paper shuffling. He was ready for something different, maybe some action again. But he couldn't imagine what it might be. Maybe the meeting with Lt. Col. Baxter would give him some new direction.

Chapter 4

Ft. Bragg, N.C., Friday afternoon, October 27, 1944

Hayden arrived for his meeting to an empty reception room. He called out, "Hello? Colonel Baxter?"

"Come on in, Hayden. Put your things on the table there," he said as he came into the outer office. They shook hands perfunctorily as the Colonel passed him on his way to the front door. He locked the door and pocketed the key. He turned to see Hayden's wrinkled brow and said "precaution."

Hayden had a moviegoer's image of an intelligence officer as an old, graying, distinguished looking man who would constantly re-light and suck on a pipe before delivering a well-considered thought. Lt. Col. Baxter owned none of those trappings. He was young, probably just a few years past thirty, crew cut, athletic looking. He neither smoked nor fidgeted. He was also a combat veteran and had been rotated home right after Market-Garden. The Colonel folded his hands calmly on his desk and got to the point quickly and officially.

"Captain, whether or not your involvement in this project continues after this meeting, or after next week, or after however long, you are to keep this meeting totally and permanently secret. Okay?"

Hayden felt a little prickliness on his neck. He thought of not being able to tell Jerry anything, nodded once, and said, "Yes, sir." There might never be "Hayden" or "Wyatt" between the two again.

"And," Baxter continued, "the things discussed in this meeting or following from this meeting will have to be evaded or denied if they ever arise in conversation."

Hayden thought his vow of secrecy obviously covered conversation as well as the fact of their meeting but was willing to accept Baxter's protocol for the meeting. He thought also that now his concocted story to Jerry would somehow be an official evasion or denial, less a lie. More like duty.

Baxter waited for Hayden's second agreement and got it.

"Now I'll have to tell you first of all that I don't know all the details of your possible involvement in any operation. I'm a go-between, really." He fumbled a bit for the right words. "I'm under orders from way up"—he motioned in the general direction of the Atlantic Ocean—"to swear you to secrecy, to clear you, and to start processing you if, well, if things work out so that you become involved in some project outside the division."

He held up his hand to stop a question Hayden was forming. "Not yet. You'll probably have a lot of questions, some of which I'll bet I can't answer. I'll tell you what I can first."

There was only a hint of Baxter's smile as he went on to describe the Army protocol they both knew well. "It seems there was a gigantic screening of Army personnel of all ranks recently. You are one of just a very few whose card, or ID number, or whatever, popped out of this sorting process." The smile suggestion was totally gone as he continued.

"You've kept up your German?"

Hayden volunteered that he had served regularly as interrogator on the front lines in the processing of German prisoners of war.

"You're a trooper. You've had three combat jumps. You have experience operating alone and also leading units behind enemy lines. You shoot a rifle better than anyone I've ever known." Baxter clicked off the qualifications as if they were on a laundry list.

Hayden nodded again as the prickliness on his neck came back. He thought he knew where this whole business was going.

"And you've got the brains and are physically fit. No wounds that would keep you from performing some strenuous work?"

"No, sir," Hayden said.

Baxter waited a moment before delivering what he thought to be an original observation. "It's remarkable how few people in this man's army have that combination of skills…"

"But there it is," Hayden finished for him, and Baxter smiled again.

Baxter now did something the stereotypical intelligence chief of movies would do. He stood up, clasped his hands behind his back, and began pacing back and forth behind his desk.

"Captain, I'm not going to blow smoke up your skirt," he said after three passes. Hayden cringed inwardly at the corniness. "I suppose every intelligence man in service who has had a hand in getting an important project moving has told the people going out that this project, if successful, would end the war, shorten the war, save thousands of lives." His voice trailed off. "As I said, I don't know what this one is all about. I can't even make a good guess." He stopped and leaned his knuckles on the desk. "I do know this. I have never sensed the same secrecy and evasiveness when I was told to talk with you about this...about your possible involvement."

Baxter changed directions abruptly. "You know, of course, how sluggish our progress has been in Italy. We've barely moved there lately. The Germans have skillfully organized their withdrawal along the Italian boot, moving from one natural defense position to another. They have bled us of manpower and material.

"Market-Garden sucked enormous resources away from Bradley's 12th Army Group. It stopped Patton cold in his tracks. And then the whole damned operation did not reach the conclusion that was planned.

"Now we've gotten indications that the Germans are not nearly as close to being finished as a lot of people thought just two months ago. I, and a lot of others, thought our division wouldn't be needed for another jump in Europe. Of course, that is part of the reason some of us were sent back here. A lot of the higher brass think we are too costly to employ there for what can be gained. I just don't know."

Hayden couldn't understand the reason for the Colonel's recitation, but guessed it might have been the prologue of a message someone higher up had delivered in backgrounding Baxter for this meeting. Baxter looked at Hayden but did not stop for a reply to his comments.

"Something decisive has got to go our way pretty damned soon or we'll be fighting this war all our natural lives."

The question that followed surprised Hayden by its suddenness. Pointing to the folder on his desk, Baxter asked, "Do you have any hunches, any thoughts on this? No one else has talked to you? No, I guess that's not likely."

Hayden knew Baxter's reputation from North Africa, Sicily, and France as a hard-nosed, courageous soldier. He was probably as honest as an intelligence operative could be in wartime. It was clear to Hayden that Baxter had been left out of the intelligence loop on the essence of this mission. The only piece of arguably inside knowledge he obtained and let slip was that Hayden's involvement, if any, was to be in Europe. Hayden did want to confirm the hint.

"Well, if the qualifications they've set fit me well enough, how about my leading a team dropped behind enemy lines for fact finding? It would seem to follow that if someone's going to use me, the project would be where I have some experience, language and all. A test run for a Pacific Theatre jump by the division maybe?"

Baxter was quiet for a moment. "Well, I don't think it has anything to do with the Pacific just yet, not for another year or two. I have a gut feeling this project is European and has been brewing for a couple months.

"Just my hunch on Europe, you understand. Nothing official. Your assessment sounds okay. Fact finding maybe. But that would suggest the division would be involved again and there is no indication in any recent events that that is the case."

They both went quiet. Baxter did not ask Hayden to speculate further. Hayden thought Baxter maybe knew a little bit more and was not going to reveal it. Implicit in the way Baxter had rejected Hayden's team suggestion was a further hint that Hayden might be groomed for a solo task. However little Baxter knew, Hayden concluded, he was not going to speculate any more. He was wrong.

"And intelligence gathering," Baxter suddenly went on, leaning closer to share the dirty little secret that everyone knew intelligence officers knew, "well, we've got experts all over the place doing that—code breakers, people in the resistance, army intelligence, navy intelligence, allied intelligence…"

Hayden wanted to say that "All God's children got intelligence," but immediately thought better of it. His attempt at levity would be misunderstood in this setting.

"Nah, Captain. I don't think they need you for that. You know, this thing is so secret I may never know what it's all about, whether it ever took off, whether it worked, unless you get picked and agree to do the job and then tell me." He laughed. Nervously, Hayden thought. "And maybe," Baxter admitted almost in a whisper, "maybe we're not even supposed to speculate this much."

Baxter was quickly all business again. "I said you could ask questions. I'll answer what little I can."

Hayden knew there was no purpose to be served in asking a lot of questions Baxter would answer "I don't know" or "I can't say." Baxter had been shut out of the inner loop and obviously chafed at the exclusion.

"Only one thing," Hayden said. How soon does this project get going?"

"First I have to ask you. Knowing what little we both know, Captain Brooke, are you willing to sign on for the next step? Is there anything you know about or can think of, any reservations that you have that you should announce before we proceed?"

Hayden was curious as to what the Colonel might be fishing for. He was reminded of the solemnity of wedding vows, with so many unknowns facing a couple and yet their willingness to agree to take the important step. And thinking of weddings, was Baxter probing into his relationship with Sarah? Or Sarah's relationship to the Stop War Now group? He decided to ignore the question, not comfortable with how far its tangle might lead the discussion.

"I take it you must have an answer soon."

The Colonel nodded. "Very soon."

Without asking, Hayden stood up and, pacing, began aloud his own list of weigh-in factors. "This is risky business, no doubt. All trooper jumps are risky. I am a soldier. An officer. I obey orders. And despite the option implicitly offered here, this 'invitation' takes on the character of an order to a soldier.

"I've faced danger before, along with countless thousands of others in uniform. Someone has to do these kinds of things. Some endure depth charges in submarines. Some fly bombing missions they cannot realistically hope to return from. Some paddle with their rifles across a river in a rickety canvas boat under intense hostile fire. Apparently someone up there needs someone with the particular skills I have."

Hayden admitted to himself that he knew ever since he came into Baxter's office that he was not going to say no. That decision stood despite the little information he had gotten and despite the unknown dangers that could surface.

"Yes sir," he said, sitting again. "I'll stick around for the next preview. I'll sign on."

He adopted the same conspiratorial whisper Baxter had used only minutes before. "Colonel, I had a hunch too. When my request for a leave was granted so quickly after Market-Garden, I thought there might be something more in the wind than the Army's need for my paper-shuffling skills or my ability to dream up things paratroopers should not do in Japan."

The Colonel's chuckle seemed to Hayden to be more tension release than appreciation of Hayden's comment. Baxter now very deliberately unlocked the upper left drawer of his desk, drew out a letter-size manila envelope, and opened it as he announced its general contents.

"Here are your orders, made up ahead of time, just in case." He carefully un-stacked and re-stacked the documents, calling them out one-by-one as if announcing the contents of a time capsule. "Your travel orders…a temporary duty transfer out of the 82nd Division…billeting information…a 'first available' pass for your plane transportation."

Baxter sensed Hayden's disbelief without ever looking up from the document he was holding. "Sorry, Captain," he said. "The answer to your question is that they want you right away. There is a cargo plane tonight to Camp Springs Army Air Field outside Washington. I reserved you a space on it about three hours ago. You know how these things have to be done."

Hayden did know. For soldiers, the appeal to wartime requirements made everything acceptable, however insensitive to soldiers' well being the procedures were.

Baxter slid the envelope across his desk and picked up a multi-copy form. "You'll need to sign to show you got all these things."

Hayden pressed heavily as he signed without reading the form, straightened all the copies and carbons, and handed the packet to Baxter. He sat back, not sure if he needed to ask something. Baxter gave him time.

After a few long seconds, Baxter said "Well..." He stood, reached in his pocket for keys. Hayden stood also.

"I'll send a jeep to your barracks in about four hours so you can catch that plane at 22:00. It's better that you don't tell your staff anything. I'll make sure some explanations are made."

Hayden gathered his hat and poncho on the way out. They walked like old buddies to the front door of the office. Baxter reminded him, "When you make your calls, well...you know about 'loose lips' and who all is listening." Neither smiled.

"And, by the way, Captain, your week here on the manual was not wasted. I'm looking forward to seeing what you've done so far. I know the operations people will be interested."

Hayden said a simple thanks. He paused at the door, getting into his poncho.

"Was there another set of orders for me if I had said no? And, if I had said no, would I still have been welcome in the 82nd?" He thought better of the questions immediately. "I shouldn't ask those things."

They shook hands. Lt. Col. Baxter said with obvious sincerity, "Do the division proud, Hayden. God speed wherever this takes you."

Chapter 5

Washington, Friday evening, October 27, 1944

Everett Giles knew all afternoon he had a spell of serious thinking ahead of him after his morning call from General Marshall. Finally free of the press of a series of high level meetings, he returned his attention fully to his notes of the general's call.

Only two questions raised in Giles' mind during the phone call were already answered. It was common knowledge that the President spoke with General Marshall every day and they met each Friday morning for war discussion and planning. It was reasonable to conclude that today's meeting had prompted General Marshall's renewed sense of urgency about ending the war in Europe.

The second question was whether Marshall was disappointed about SIP's relative inactivity recently. More likely, he was revealing that he was no longer interested in small ventures from SIP. He wanted something big to change the present course of the European war.

Other questions could not be answered so easily. To Giles, the fundamental European intelligence questions always focused on the strength of the German defensive commitment on the Western Front. That commitment was a composite of German military and political strategy. Moreover, to say "German" was to say "Hitler." Any American initiative would have to consider what it knew or could learn of Hitler's strategic thinking.

The conviction that Hitler would never surrender or allow surrender had become one of the bedrocks of American military thinking. It grew from piecing together intelligence from American and Allied intelligence services and the underground inside and outside of Germany.

There were three good reasons for that conviction. All had a connection to the July 20, 1944, assassination attempt by German military officers against Hitler at *Wolfschanze* in East Prussia.

The first was the distrust of his associates aroused in Hitler by the July 20 plot. American staffers had learned from defecting and captured German officers and civilian officials, documents, and radio interceptions that Hitler was now highly suspicions of almost all his generals and aides. Part of that suspicion was grounded in his need to fix blame for recent military setbacks. Hitler's disdain for the old German aristocracy and the aristocratic mindset of high ranking German officers was of longer standing. Their contempt for him as a "Bohemian Corporal" was no secret in German military circles. His discovery of the same group's involvement in the July 20 plot added to his distrust of them.

That distrust was now being turned to Hitler's advantage. The compliance of high military officials to strategic and tactical plans authored by Hitler would itself prove or disprove their professed loyalties to him and the Third Reich!

In this curious vein of dictatorial thinking, further military campaigns were required to ensure his officers' loyalty. Moreover, those within and outside the military who had spoken directly, but more often indirectly of surrender, were defeatists, the very ones whose loyalty had to be proven.

The second reason was Hitler's "war personality." Military victories early in the war were due to his brilliance and strategic insights. The more recent setbacks were due to his generals' failings, disloyalty, and not following his orders. An impartial observer would conclude that Allied preparedness at this stage of the war obviously contributed to the changed balance of power over five years. The size and power of the Allied military presence had increased many-fold since the early German victories in France and the Soviet Union. That fact would not dissuade Hitler from his conclusion on the source of the German military's rise and decline. Nor would an objective appraisal of the reduced strength of his military forces in both manpower and material convince him to surrender. Hitler's egomania allowed him alone to make the official, correct assessment of the German position in late 1944.

The third reason for the American intelligence community's conviction that Hitler would not surrender was the promise of new German weapons. Ironically, Germany's stalled weapons development could be traced to Hitler's own critical decisions early in the war. His publicly expressed hope, however much dampened by reality, was that production of great numbers of ME 262 jet aircraft, V-2 rockets, with the promise of V-3 and V-4 rockets to follow, and a new breed of panzers could yet be parlayed into victory. Surviving the July 20 plot strengthened his belief that Germany's destiny and his own were inextricably linked. His ordering more and better weaponry could prove that link.

All of these technical achievements, even in minimal quantities, had been made painfully clear to the Allies in recent months. In Hitler's optimistic assessment of Germany's power to make war, its delayed atomic weaponry program was not totally out of the picture.

The problem for American war strategists in Hitler's apparent determination to continue the war was his reputation as a "loose cannon on deck." There was concern on the part of Allied leaders that Hitler could easily go further off the deep end mentally. He was still very dangerous in large part because of his unpredictability.

The crime of genocide in territories under Nazi control was no longer in doubt. Its potential expansion to other groups was even more ominous to Allied observers. The possibility of an ever greater crime by Hitler, if a crime greater than genocide was possible, was an unknown calamity the Western democracies feared. There was also growing dread that Hitler in one of his wild moments or defiant last acts might execute Allied prisoners of war.

Given the profound nature of these military/political issues in the European Theatre, Giles was certain that his unit could not offer an inconsequential plan in answer to General Marshall's directive. He was confident that others in the American intelligence community would conclude the analysis of problems and solutions as he had. To bring a change in the political structure and direction of Germany, and thereby an end to the war, it was now imperative for SIP to plan to sever the head of the German beast!

Giles was not blind to the possibility that he was misreading clues or flawing the analysis. Was assassination within the scope of General Marshall's suggestions this morning?

He recalled that the General had not repeated his request for information on "offensive plans" when Giles sidestepped the question. Marshall did say that he did not need to know all of what SIP was doing. Was he simply emphasizing that he did not need to know the details of plans as long as the results were favorable?

Giles was convinced Marshall had given a go-ahead to SIP for any big operation. The General had asked him specifically about "special projects on your shelf," under the umbrella concern about ending the war in Europe, and that "rather soon."

Marshall had to know that assassination of Hitler and German military leaders had always been an option on the shelf within the Allied intelligence community. He would not publicly suggest an assassination attempt on an enemy leader under any circumstances. If asked directly for clarification of his intent to include the assassination option in planning, Marshall would necessarily have to be evasive, even though he might want to use it as a strategic weapon.

Therefore, Giles concluded, he could reasonably interpret this morning's phone conversation as authorization to proceed with a mission against Hitler personally. Giles knew also from his personal association with the man, both in how he said some things explicitly and inferred others, that Marshall expected Giles to reach such a conclusion. Because such a project was "special," not being assigned to other intelligence units, Giles logically came to believe that Hitler's assassination was a directive being given to SIP alone.

What clinched the case in Giles' mind was the American leadership approval given to kill Japanese Adm. Isoruku Yamamoto, the architect of the Pearl Harbor attack and Japan's chief military strategist. The attack on Yamamoto occurred after a de-coded Japanese message indicated the admiral would be visiting troops on the island of Bougainville in the South Pacific on April 18, 1943. The significance to the present plan against Hitler was that the attack on Yamamoto was approved by Navy Secretary Frank Knox and the President. Admiral Chester Nimitz gave the final order to proceed. Yamamoto's aircraft was attacked and downed, resulting in his death.

It was also apparent that the U.S. wanted the attempt on Yamamoto to be viewed as a "casual encounter" or an "accidental hit" by American P-38 pilots flying from Guadalcanal. That subterfuge was not established because of any political or moral qualms about the killing. Rather, it was designed to lead Japanese intelligence away from concluding that the Americans had learned of Yamamoto's visit to Bougainville by cracking the Japanese Navy's principal communication code. The Americans had in fact been reading some of various Japanese codes since before the outbreak of the war. In an ironic twist of fate, American cryptographers' breaking into Japanese codes was facilitated by their early wartime successes in intercepting communications to Tokyo from the Japanese Ambassador to Germany in Berlin.

The question of the propriety of assassinating an enemy military or civilian leader was intriguing to Giles. Why, first of all, should an enemy leader, presumably vital to the enemy's war effort, be exempt from killing? Was it because of the fear of retaliation? Obviously, high ranking officials in all countries were already well guarded against such attempts, often with units permanently and exclusively assigned to that task.

Second, how would the taking of an enemy leader's life be any different from the taking of any enemy's life, whatever his rank? How could Japan continue to conduct a war effectively if its top 100 military, political, and industrial leaders were removed from leadership? Given the potential impact such killings would have on an adversary's ability to prosecute a war against us, why would we not encourage their elimination by whatever means available?

Or was the reluctance a case of removing the devil we know compared to his successor? American intelligence had no way of knowing what person or persons would succeed Yamamoto as the primary Japanese Central Pacific strategist, however, or what the strategies of his successor might be.

In the case of Hitler, moreover, it was clear to Giles that he was the initiator, implementer, and guide of the German war effort. No one of his close followers or associates commanded the loyalty he commanded, for better or worse. Whether the cause of that loyalty was his personal charisma, his dictatorial suppression of opponents, or his appeal to national pride and honor, his status as the factual and ceremonial German dictator was pre-eminent among Germans. And despite his development of a hard-line cadre of think-alikes, without him the relationship of Germany to the rest of the world in the last decade would have been vastly different. Giles was more certain than ever that the course of history could be changed in an abrupt and salutary direction by Hitler's demise.

What did SIP have to offer specifically to carry out an assassination plan? Giles reviewed the plans on the shelf that could be used against any target, including Hitler.

The two general options under continuing consideration by SIP were a team or an individual effort. The most logical team approach would have a unit jump into the area around Berchtesgaden, Bavaria, to strike Hitler at his mountain chalet, Berghof. The alternate team approach would employ a jump along rail lines connecting Berlin with Berchtesgaden or with forward command posts. The team would sabotage the rail line or train carrying Hitler.

The other choice was a single sharpshooter dropped into Bavaria. The plan would situate the shooter to kill Hitler from an adjoining mountain or wooded area at Berghof with a long-range rifle shot.

An operation of either kind would amount to a suicide mission for any participant. Giles, after long discussion and private thought during development of the shelf plan, became convinced that using a single operator was the more expedient choice.

This operation would require complicated tactical preparations. There were critical problems of timing, cover, deception, mobility, and execution to be worked out in either scenario.

The personnel requirement was obviously the critical ingredient of a successful plan. Selection procedures had been in place for some time to identify military and civil service personnel for special missions.

The assassination attempt on Hitler would now be moved out of the realm of the shelf-plan hypothetical to a "planned probable." Its success would be a strategic, decisive stroke. It could lead to the end of the war in Europe as General Marshall and President Roosevelt were urging.

Some of the wheels for such a climactic project were already in motion as a matter of department routine. Giles picked up the phone to engage the rest of the machinery.

The team leader chosen would see the project through from its present planning stage to its conclusion. The first name Giles thought of to lead the effort was Lt. Col. Barnett Alexander of Army Intelligence. Alexander would lead a group of officers who would handle the nuts-and-bolts, hands-on oversight of the project's plan and execution.

"Colonel Alexander, Everett Giles here," he called out once he had the prospective team leader on the phone. "Sorry to bother you at home. And I hate to disturb your Saturday plans on such short notice. Can we talk about something special in my office at nine in the morning?... Thank you. I'll see you then."

The reality of beginning this momentous operation caused Giles to consider its implications anew. Marshall admonished him to "think big", and there was nothing bigger for him to undertake than Hitler's assassination. The rush of energy caused him unaccustomed nervousness. He stood, stretched, swung his arms and flexed his knees as he thought of the project that would bear his signature. It would forever be linked to him and SIP, even though only a very few people would know of it.

The same linkage would be even more true of the person selected for the mission. What personality, character, and motivation must a man have to conduct such a mission? He tried to envision the man. Out there was a list of candidates not yet known to Giles. No doubt all were already known for their wartime contributions, all of them with distinguished military or civil service. However, one of them would emerge out of that anonymity. That man was destined to have a new distinction, publicly or secretly.

He sat again with the memory of his own military service. He asked himself, what if I had been selected in 1917 to perform some intelligence chief's plan to end World War I quickly by undertaking such a mission? What would my feelings have been, assuming I had the skills, had I been asked to stalk and kill Kaiser Wilhelm or Chancellor Bismarck?

Why would they have chosen me? I was an ordinary Indiana boy. Now there are maybe thousands of ordinary youths who are eligible. Any one of them could be chosen. "But that's the point, isn't it?" Giles said aloud. Out of the long list of candidates, one will be chosen for the skills he possesses. He will be the one most suited to the task. Not a thousand are chosen for the job. Only one.

It was now almost frightening for Giles to consider the project's scope. Momentarily overwhelmed by the magnitude of the task, he tried to confront the emotions he was feeling—apprehension at its possible consequences, concern about the lives involved, uncertainty about the adjustments required as the mission proceeds.

He will have final responsibility in the whole matter. He will have to plan quickly and carefully. Lurking always in his philosopher-technician's mind is the compelling question. Can it be done?

Giles penciled notes on the qualifications Col. Alexander should look for in screening personnel for the mission.

(1) a marksman
(2) a paratrooper
(3) fluent in the German language
(4) intelligent, with an ability to adapt to changed mission needs and on-site circumstances
(5) able to operate alone in hostile surroundings
(6) ruthless
(7) familiar with survival techniques in cold weather

Giles knew that a group of prospects had already been screened by G-2 for possible use in individual projects. After processing by the intelligence people at Camp Springs, several should be available for special training in a few days.

Chapter 6

Ft. Bragg, N.C., Friday Evening, October 27, 1944

Back in his barracks room, Hayden tried to call Sarah to tell her he was changing locations. All long distance circuits were busy. There might be a line open in 15 minutes, and the operator would call him when it was available.

Hayden reflected somberly that the war had cast its smothering shadow on tens of millions of people around the world. Countless more millions of decisions had been forced by the war, most of them life-and-death decisions. In that perspective, a marriage that went dead did not amount to much. His admitting to the slight global significance of their problems did not make it any less painful to him, however.

Hayden knew that Sarah was faithful to him. He believed that intuitively. She was an honest, loving, and caring person.

Not all the secrecy claimed in his refusal to relate details of his military life was "official." He had found it convenient to use that excuse at times, however. Most of all, he did not want to raise with her the issue of his having to kill people. Almost certainly, the mission he was being considered for would require more killing.

There probably were some things she wouldn't tell Hayden. The inner council of her peace group might quail at the prospect of its own secret deliberations being made public. He would not ask her to reveal those. Asking her would sound retaliatory, forcing her to invoke a secrecy claim of her own, casting all of their future discussions into a distrustful, argumentative mode.

The unfortunate twist the war had forced on their conversations appeared most clearly in limiting what the two of them could talk about easily. Innocuous questions were inadvertently loaded with emotional tension. A simulated give-and-take came to haunt him.

"What have you been up to, darling?" she would ask.

"I've been making war, and associating with other people who make war. It is part of the attack mode we are always in. We do small unit killing mostly. And what have you been doing, sweetheart?"

"I've been publicly condemning killing every way I can, my dear. That condemnation extends to national leaders who decide to make war and includes those who kill when 'following orders.' I associate with people who speak, write, and organize against war."

So, was the marriage a mistake? He often asked himself that. It seemed insincere for both of them to blame their problems on time and events. Those circumstances should not affect the love they felt for each other. They did, however.

Hayden remembered fondly their early meetings when their love for each other grew. When his custom-cutting crew came to the Wichita area in June of 1940, Sarah had already left her parent's farm some forty miles southwest of Wichita for a job as a secretary-receptionist in the city. Hayden and his co-workers attended a Saturday night concert in a public park on the banks of the Arkansas River. Sarah was seated on a blanket with several girl friends close to Hayden. He noticed immediately her vivacious dark-haired beauty and utterly charming smile as she talked easily with her friends.

At the end of the concert, Hayden and his friends strolled closer to the girls' group. He stood alongside his friends in meaningless chatter with the girls. As the group shifted, his eyes ever on Sarah, Hayden unknowingly backed into a cooler of soft drinks, his heels soon fast against the cooler. He began to fall backwards. He windmilled frantically to keep his balance.

Sarah stepped forward quickly to grab his hand and steady him. While his friends and the other girls howled their laughter at his misstep, Sarah asked with a pretty smile if he was okay. He answered with the best smile he could muster that he would be all right if she continued to hold his hand.

"I won't do that for long," she replied, withdrawing her hand. "But if you still need support," she teased, "I will walk with you back to the parking lot."

With her second smile, Hayden was smitten. He was more than eager to accommodate her suggestion, to walk and talk with her, to learn her name and address. They corresponded through the rest of the harvest year.

On his return to Wichita that September to start his job at Boeing Aircraft, he called Sarah immediately. He learned that in her move from her parents' farm to Wichita earlier in the year she hoped to escape the hurt she bore at her neighbors' treatment of her family. That pain grew out of two incidents of hostile and rude behavior. Hayden encouraged her to voice her resentment at her neighbors' conduct.

It had all started in 1936, she said. The Spurges family had read about the depression-reduced prices of farmland in the Midwest. After preliminary inquiries, they sold their forty-acre farm in Pennsylvania and moved to Kansas.

Within a few days of their arrival, George and Beatrice Spurges and their fourteen-year old daughter Sarah Grace found several attractive farm properties and assessed their options. They began the process of purchasing a house on 640 acres, a full section of farmland. It was the nicest property for miles around. The previous owner had gone broke and had no choice but to sell. Their move from the East seemed justified in the bargain-basement price they paid for the property.

News of the Spurges purchase spread quickly through the farm community. That they were Quakers was mentioned also. His full name was George Fox Spurges, after the George Fox who founded the Religious Society of Friends, the Quakers, in England in the early 17th century. It was rumored that the new family intended to grow soybeans, not wheat.

The Spurges family soon was pleasantly surprised to receive an invitation to a late Sunday afternoon lawn party at the home of one of their new neighbors. In accepting, they did not suspect they were embarking on a stormy evening.

It did not take long for their new neighbors to tell George and his family that they did not like that their former neighbors "were taken advantage of." George sought to tell them that the farm purchase was really a blessing for the previous owners. They got something for their farm, the current market price. They did not have the mortgage foreclosed. Nor did they have to abandon their property.

Some of his new neighbors scoffed at George's use of "blessing." They called it robbery. Others went on to attack the pacifism of Quakers. They brought up news reports of German and Japanese atrocities as justification for their war-like stance against the Axis powers.

George responded that he was happy to learn his neighbors were on the side of Jews and Chinese. His neighbors were friends of neither, of course. They resented openly what they interpreted as sarcasm.

One asked pointedly if George had served his country in the Great War. George replied calmly that he had volunteered as a medical aide in a Philadelphia veterans hospital. His neighbors were not satisfied with the evasive answer they detected. George repeated that he had served as best he could, from April of 1917 to beyond the November armistice, until April of 1919. He did not tell them he had served without pay. The hospital had provided him room and board as compensation. He also did not tell them he was a conscientious objector, but he felt they suspected that already.

Sarah related to Hayden that her father now had enough. He would not be baited further. He rose to gather his family and leave. The host couple intervened to persuade him to stay, apologizing for any discomfort. Beatrice gave him a look of acceptance from across the table. The Spurges family decided to stay despite the whispers still drifting along the long row of tables.

Sarah vividly described the natural storm that was brewing at the same time as the verbal confrontation. Both were the first storms of their kind she had ever experienced. Both made indelible marks on her memory.

The farmers had noted the gathering, fast-moving clouds, quietly confirming their presence to each other as something of concern to their livelihood. The clouds turned steadily darker and ominous in the early evening. As the party ate, they saw the first muted flash of lightning in the distance, like a porch light flipped on and off. The flashes repeated, steadily brighter and wider, with louder rumbles of thunder.

The phone ringing startled all of them. It was a policeman friend of the party hosts twenty miles away. He reported strong winds and heavy rain, all of it heading their way.

The storm front was building fast, darker and uglier, standing higher on the southwest horizon. Its rapid approach was outlined by even more frequent lightning flashes and churning movement in the clouds. It looked like a weather czar had divided the sky abruptly and powerfully into dark and less dark along a sweeping curve.

Sarah admitted to Hayden she was afraid. She recounted also that, even in the face of impending disaster, nature gave out of both hands. The wind blew the warm earth-and-growth aroma of ripening grain at the assembled group. It reminded Sarah of the savory essence of yeast released in bread baking.

About eight o'clock the storm announced it was very near. A sudden, loud rumble followed a sky-splitting streak of brilliant light that brought troubled cries of "Oh!" from the party. Against the light they could see the depth of a dark, roiling front, perhaps two miles away. It would not spare any of them. It would strike all their lands and crops.

A new kind of wind moved through the yard...too cool, too sudden. The farmers as one knew its message. Many shivered. Almost in unison they voiced the four-letter word that carried threat, terror, and chilling of hearts. *Hail!*

The wind and driving rain might be enough to knock down the wheat crop. They force the maturing stalks with their heavy heads to bow, making it difficult or impossible for combines to pick up the stalks for cutting. Hail shatters the plants, however, heads and stalks indiscriminately. Its icy fists pummel the plants to shreds. The devastation is no less complete for being random. The crop is razed. There is nothing but a jumble of straw where neat, profitable rows of grain had stood minutes before.

The cold wind signaled the end of the party. There was orderly scrambling as neighbors picked up bowls and trays. Silverware clattered into boxes. Red and white squared tablecloths whipped, flapped wildly, and doubled up across table tops.

"Goodbyes" were hurried as people moved to their cars and pickups. Unreal, false hopes were exchanged as consolation to each other. "Maybe it won't be so bad. Maybe it will blow out or stay up higher."

A few big splats of rain hit car hoods and truck beds. Then came the sound they most feared, the blip, blip, blip, *ping*, as the first small hailstones mixed with rain began to move over the parking area, smacking the metal of sheds and vehicles. The ice pellets intruded on wood and cloth and human skin indiscriminately.

The downpour found the fragile food plants in the field just beyond. The contest between the driving, cold, dark force and the placid, warm, leaning golden stalks' power to resist was short. Insurance might be just enough to cover the costs of planting. Farmers had contributed their labor "free" again this year.

There wasn't much solace to give by anyone. Women joined hands with their men. Some wrapped an arm around their husbands' waists as they hurried to their vehicles. Here and there heads leaned against each other. Feelings were too deep for words, not just for their lost livelihood, but for the numbing helplessness they felt.

Sarah was sure that the pettiness shown by their new neighbors could not survive the reality of their shared vulnerability to nature's destruction. She was wrong. She recognized instead that the terrifying storm and the degrading questions their neighbors asked before it symbolized the enduring hostility they had to the new family. At her age, Sarah was unable to fathom any reason for their hostility.

Two weeks later, Beatrice Spurges persuaded George and Sarah, in the spirit of forgiveness and neighborliness, to invite the same neighbors to a party on their farm. No one bothered to reply to the mailed invitations. No one showed up.

The organized snub took a long time for the Quaker family to get over. Their capacity to forgive was tested more seriously when George was arrested for working on Sunday.

A year had passed. One Sunday evening the county sheriff showed up at the Spurges farm house. George was just returning from cultivating his first year's soybean plants. The sheriff asked George to confirm that he had worked his fields that day. George acknowledged that he had.

"There is a law against doing business on Sunday that is not of an emergency or philanthropic nature." The sheriff struggled pronouncing "philanthropic," but George understood immediately that the issue was not the letter of the law. Beatrice and Sarah had joined George and the sheriff in the yard and heard the latter's pronouncement.

"Are there exceptions to the law?" Sarah asked.

"Well, there is one. A person can get a written permit."

"And who issues the permit?" Sarah pressed.

"The county attorney usually handles that." The sheriff hesitated in stating it, seemingly not sure. However, the law enforcer quickly recovered his aplomb and would see his duty through to the end. "And you don't have one, do you?"

George Spurges disgustedly shook his head "no." "What happens now?"

"Well, I have to arrest you. You can spend three nights in jail or pay a $50 fine."

Sarah's father did not want to give the community behind this outrage the satisfaction of either choice. But he would not abandon his family in the face of this new hostility. He wrote a check for the $50 fine. In accepting the check, the sheriff wagged his finger and said that he better not catch George working again on Sunday or he would throw him in jail for sure.

George visited the county attorney's office early the next morning. He was very interested to observe that the clerk had trouble finding a blank permit. She said apologetically during the delay, "we never have reason to use these things."

George completed the form, taking care to fill in every blank as carefully and completely as he could. He was convinced from the nature of the information sought that the "Sunday Blue Law," whatever its merits as public policy, was not meant to apply to agriculture.

Four days later a short letter from the county attorney arrived.

Mr. George Spurges' request for an exemption from the Kansas law in order to conduct business on Sunday is denied.

Reluctantly and bitterly, George and his family complied with what they knew was a discriminatory, arbitrary, and hate-driven application of the law against them. They had observed many instances of tractors and combines moving in the neighboring fields on Sundays. During the June wheat harvest, all farmers or hired crews in the area were in the fields every day of the week until cutting was completed. If the observation of the county attorney's clerk was correct, none of those farmers had obtained permits. All were violating the law.

He asked his Quaker associates in Wichita for the name of a reliable attorney. The attorney drafted a letter to the federal district court in Kansas asking for a hearing on this important constitutional issue of discriminatory application of state law. The attorney pointed out that it would not be appropriate for the Spurges to pursue the matter in county court since the issue could not be handled impartially there. The county court would have to apply state law. The county attorney, as nominal prosecutor of the law's violation in that court, was a defendant in this matter.

The federal judge invited the parties to come in for discussion. The judge asked the county attorney, the sheriff, George's attorney, and the Spurges family to join him in his chambers. A court reporter was on hand to record the meeting.

"I prefer to handle this matter informally for now in the hope of settling it without a lot of bother and expense," the judge said. "If necessary, we will schedule a formal hearing.

"The issue today is not the validity of the state law or the sheriff's power to enforce it. The issue is discriminatory application of the law. The claim of the county that George Spurges has not exhausted his rights in a state court is not material to that issue."

In short order, the judge determined that the facts as alleged by George Spurges and his family were correct. The county attorney reluctantly admitted that no permits had ever been issued for agricultural work on Sunday. He admitted also that he knew of no other arrests ever of persons doing Sunday agricultural work in the county.

Sarah had researched back issues of the local newspaper in their county for the month of June. They reported on the progress of the local wheat harvest, listing day-by-day total bushels of wheat received by grain elevators in the county, including deliveries on Sundays. George's attorney presented the reports as evidence of agricultural work known in the community to be done on Sundays.

The judge did not probe into the motive for the officials' actions, but sought to gauge the intensity of the community's prejudice.

"Do you want to pursue this matter formally, Mr. Spurges?" the judge asked.

George hesitated. He knew that a court order resulting from a formal hearing or trial would establish a precedent for equitable enforcement of laws in other situations for other people. His attorney whispered to him that it was George's "call." George read in Beatrice's eyes a "no" answer.

Sarah admitted to Hayden that she had stared straight ahead, her jaw set, avoiding her father's search for an answer from her without asking aloud. She wanted to fight the injustice publicly. George turned to the judge and said "No, Your Honor."

The judge asked the county attorney and sheriff the same question and got negative responses quickly.

"Good," the judge said. "This is not a formal order, but here's what I recommend. I advise that the county attorney apply this law fairly in the future, without even a hint of discriminatory treatment. I advise that the county attorney and sheriff not allow any departure from this fairness standard. In so many words, if the law is applied to any one farmer, it has to be applied the same way to all farmers, all the time. It's as simple as that.

"If any future situation occurs like the one we are here for today," the judge continued, "we'll get together again, review today's conversation, and proceed from there.

"Two more things. I advise that Mr. Spurges be refunded $50 from the county with an apology. And his record should be wiped clean."

The judge paused and surveyed the faces of the small assembly. "We can't make neighbors love each other. We can insist that the law is applied equitably to all. Finally, this...this informal discussion has been beyond the hearing of the newspaper and radio people. This court won't compel any of you not to talk about it. But I recommend that it not be made a public point of contention to divide your community further."

In less than fifteen minutes justice had been done, informally but effectively. While the Spurges family had been vindicated, Sarah reported sadly that resolution of the matter wholly in their favor did nothing but increase the hostility of their neighbors.

Hayden was convinced that these confrontations with their neighbors had forever soured Sarah's attitude toward the community. She could not understand their hatred. Her Quaker heritage of bringing peace to the world had been challenged. Hayden felt she had been emotionally scarred by the incidents.

She needed to confide in people, share her concerns with them, and not consciously shut them out. She expected the same in return.

The principal outlet for her emotional distress was active involvement in the peace movement. Hayden regretted that he had not been available as a confidant to her, to dissuade her from the political danger her involvement contained.

The call from the operator told him to hold while she dialed Sarah's number.

"Sarah? Can you hear me okay?"

"Hayden! I can hear you loud enough but there's some static."

"The circuits are very busy again, Friday evening and all. We have only a few minutes, of course."

"I know," she said. "How've you been?"

"Well, this week dragged a lot. I don't take well to shuffling paper. I've missed you terribly."

"I miss what we had three, four years ago. We just ran…well, since then we developed our lives along separate tracks, like single people."

"I don't think our getting married was the wrong thing to do, Sarah. All those other things happening did not affect my love for you. And they still don't."

"What threatens our marriage is absence, with secrecy a close second. What have we had together? Three weeks total in three years? I feel shut out, all the time. I can't know what you are doing. I suppose I wouldn't be happy if I did know. I haven't known whether you were dead or alive for long periods of time. I dreaded the thought of a uniform coming up the sidewalk to deliver the government's 'official regret' message."

"Sarah, I'm being re-located. All I can tell you is that I'll be in the D.C. area for now. Then…I don't know."

"Or can't say," she said, with some anger.

"That, too. I'm sorry."

"See what I mean? For most of three years I haven't known where you were any day. It wasn't easy facing every day not knowing if or when you'd be coming back."

"I wrote when I could. If I had written more, the censors would have just cut it out and made you even more curious. And I lived for your letters."

"Damn this war! I hate the distance it creates between us. I have tried to understand when you would not talk or write about your war experiences, even though battles are reported in the newspapers and on the radio.

"I fear something fundamental has happened to you. Is there something you won't tell me because of your sensitivity to my Quaker background? Are there horrible wartime things you did that you can't bring yourself to put into words?

Not knowing, I can only imagine terrible things happening and that you are a part of them.

"I so hoped that the secrecy would be ending, along with your absence, on your return from Europe. But again you would not tell me anything in the week we just had together. I just can't seem to crack the wall of secrecy between us.

"What will you be doing now? No details, just generally. That's not too much to ask, is it? Can't you see how important your being open with me is?"

Hayden was tempted to tell her. He could not, however, whatever the cost. "I'll write you soon and tell you what I can. Uh, oh."

The operator was breaking in for emergency use of the line.

"I'll write soon. I love you, Sarah."

Hayden heard her sob as the circuit closed.

Chapter 7

Ft. Bragg, N.C., Friday Evening, October 27, 1944

Jerry Connelios was at the bar when Hayden arrived at the Officers Club. Hayden's mind was flooded with the events of the last several hours. He reproached himself for agreeing to this meeting. He was already tired and would have to make a special effort not to let the day's distractions affect this farewell meeting with his colleague and friend.

The club was a one-story building of wartime construction. It was a plain building, but spacious. It reminded Hayden of the pre-fabricated housing that was being used increasingly to speed up construction. The bar was the smaller of two large rooms and the main entry into the building. The larger room, entered through a wide doorway off the bar, doubled as a dining room and dance floor. A five-piece band of enlisted men was playing with only occasional dancer response.

Hayden and Jerry had been seated barely five minutes in the dining area when a young second lieutenant sauntered over to their table. He was handsome in a boyish way. He was wearing too much cologne.

"I didn't expect you to be here this evening, Jerry," he said, resting his hand on Jerry's shoulder. Hayden was so preoccupied with the day that he was asleep at first to the signals the lieutenant was giving. He awoke quickly to note that a second lieutenant did not call a veteran captain "Jerry" unless they were related. He was much too familiar with Jerry. Hayden could not shut out the image of what that familiarity meant.

Jerry hurried to cover his embarrassment. "Captain Brooke, this is Lieutenant Hanna."

Hayden did not want to shake Hanna's hand, but did. He knew the polite thing to do was to ask the Lieutenant to join them, and for him to make the offer. He couldn't bring himself to do so for several reasons, not the least of which was his disapproval of what he had witnessed. He hoped it didn't show on his face too much.

"Lieutenant," Jerry said, trying to force some resolution of the awkwardness, "Captain Brooke is in a big hurry tonight, and we have some really important things to talk over. Can we catch up on the news later?"

Jerry's attempt to find cover in his formal addressing of Hanna by rank did not fool Hayden. It only added to the distaste Hayden was experiencing. Too much had already happened right in front of him. Jerry was right about one thing and didn't know it, however. He offered his own closure to Jerry's suggestion.

"I really am short of time, Lieutenant. It was good to meet you," he said, and forced himself again to offer to shake the Lieutenant's hand.

Two ideas hit Hayden as one. Could Jerry have been sent back to the States so abruptly, without a reason given, or at least none that Jerry had told him yet, because of his sexual orientation? Could he be on indefinite hold awaiting assignment for a reason connected to that orientation?

He recognized also the wisdom of Lt. Col. Baxter's routine admonition on the secrecy of his impending re-location. If Jerry has a homosexual leaning, as Hayden now suspected, Jerry is vulnerable to someone's blackmail. He could be under threat of exposure to reveal important information at any time.

Jerry and he had soldiered together. The companies they led fought side by side in combat. They had partied with other junior officers of the regiment in Sicily and Italy, shared concerns, offered toasts to their lost friends. Jerry could ask about Hayden's future assignment as a right of friendship.

Hayden had put him off in his afternoon call to allow himself time to sort out answers to the questions he expected from Jerry. However remote the possibility that someone would get at him through Jerry, Hayden thought, he now had to be very careful about what and how to tell Jerry regarding his re-assignment to the D.C. environs.

Jerry would have to accept his reticence on his future doings. Having witnessed Jerry's reaction to the unexpected meeting with Hanna, Hayden decided he would be brief and non-committal.

After they ordered dinner, Hayden confirmed the accuracy of Jerry's comment that they did not have much time for talk.

"I've been ordered out of here. I'm being re-located. I have to leave in a few hours."

"Where to? Why the hurry? What are they going to use you for now?"

"All I can say for sure," Hayden said, "is that I have to hitch a ride on a cargo plane at 22:00 tonight. I wish I could say more."

"Sounds like important doings for you…official, secret, urgent!"

Hayden thought Jerry had encapsulated perfectly the boundaries for their discussion of his near future. He realized also that his own ignorance of the nature and timing of his assignment protected him from saying more than he should.

"Yeah, I wish I knew what it was all about."

"Ordered? Not consulted?" Jerry pushed.

"You know the drill. The army says 'we need a volunteer.' Brooke, you're it."

Hayden could see that Jerry wasn't satisfied. He cut off his friend's next question. "It may be as routine as reveille. The folks upstairs always get carried away with the secrecy tag." He sought to change the conversation's direction. "I had a hunch there might be something going on when my leave request was approved so fast after I got back to France from Nijmegen."

He threw out the next question without much thought. "How about you? Did you find out why you were rotated back here?"

Hayden had asked it to quell Jerry's questions about his new assignment and to re-direct the conversation. It came out wrong for Jerry. It was too direct and unexpected for him. From his friend's reaction it was apparent to Hayden that Jerry took it to be more than a show of interest in his well being. His eyes flashed anger briefly. He was flustered, taking too long to answer a simple question.

"No. Nothing solid. I really can't talk about that."

Although Hayden suspected that the "can't talk" was really a "won't talk," he agreed, "Oh, sure. Sure!"

They began their meal, silent for several minutes. Hayden had to be evasive about his orders. Jerry had thrown a veil of secrecy over the circumstances of his recent recall to the States, probably shielding a crisis in his personal life. The double evasions floated out there between them in the painful silence.

The dining room was increasingly crowded. A smoky haze was building. Practically all the uniforms were those of the 82nd Airborne, but Hayden did not recognize anyone by name. More couples were dancing. The band played mostly foxtrots and waltzes, accommodating the dancers' desires to dance close to each other. Hayden noticed several tables of unescorted women together, all of them wearing insignia of the Medical Corps.

Hayden wished desperately that Sarah could be here. She loved to dance. He would remind her of her own exhortation at the Kansas State Fair years ago to "have fun, and leave the serious stuff for later." If she were here, he would ask her to ignore the symbolism of military uniforms all around her and, for the evening, he would too.

The celebratory mood of the drinkers, diners, and dancers was not reflected at his own table. Hayden recalled that Jerry had never told him about a wife or sweetheart back home, as most men in military service do. Although he doubted that Jerry would be interested in his tale of marital woes, he offered conversation again.

"I'm sorry to say that my rotation back was probably too late for Sarah and our marriage. She was really upset when I called her earlier this evening. I suppose she thought I should have been back in Wichita for good a long time ago."

"Too bad," Jerry said without feeling.

"Yeah." For the second time today, Hayden regretted how the war was ruining conversation between friends. He saw no point in telling Jerry anything further about Sarah's Stop War Now group. He had once casually mentioned it while they were in Europe. Jerry responded, "Good for her! I hope she and her friends get this thing stopped soon." Hayden had answered that he didn't think that likely, and Jerry needled him, "You really don't detect sarcasm well, do you?"

Hayden was reluctant to ask Jerry anything else, or raise topics that would go nowhere. He shoved his plate aside and finished his drink. Jerry did the same. They made eye contact for a brief second. Hayden saw that Jerry was now viewing as a disaster what started as a get-together for old friends.

"Well, I should be going—get showered and packed and all." He tried once more to salvage their relationship.

"Look, Jerry. The only certain address I can give you is Sarah's. If you want to write, for any reason, send it in my name to her. I hope you do. We've been friends, for several lifetimes it seems. And we can't know what will happen in the next few months, to you or to me. I don't know what I'll be able to tell you. But I'd like to hear how you're doing."

"Thanks, Hayden. That's decent of you. I'd like to keep in touch."

"Going back to your barracks?" Hayden asked as they both rose to leave. Through the wide doorway to the bar they could see Lieutenant Hanna watching them.

"No, too early," Jerry said with a smile. "I think I'll have another drink," pointing to the bar.

It was a defiant, reckless gesture. It told Hayden that, after tonight, Jerry really didn't care what Hayden thought.

Hayden offered his hand. "Good luck. Be careful, Jerry."

"You too," his friend replied as they parted.

Chapter 8

Berlin, Germany, Friday Night, October 27, 1944

German Chancellor Adolf Hitler had spent most of the night considering two major issues. He was constructing a new political initiative to divide the British and Americans. He was also developing a backup plan for his armed forces, a major winter offensive on the Western Front, to do the same militarily.

The political initiative was known only to Foreign Minister Joachim von Ribbentrop and Propaganda Minister Josef Goebbels. As early as September, 1943, those trusted advisers had approached Hitler about a compromise with one enemy. Hitler trusted von Ribbentrop and Goebbels as efficient aides and loyal Nazi party members. Their intentions were good. They did not speak from an agenda of defeatism or surrender.

Hitler was not philosophically opposed to compromise as a political maneuver. The stipulation he had made to their suggestion in 1943 was that he would enter into negotiations only from a position of strength. Had things gone his way in the momentous battles at Stalingrad and Kursk, however, he admitted to them he would not have stopped the *Wehrmacht's* advances for negotiations. He wanted victory over the hated Soviets, not negotiated settlements.

Therefore, a truce negotiation strategy had to be more subtle. It required at least a position of Germany's relatively superior strength. It had to promise him an advantage that might not otherwise be achievable by political or military means.

He sensed that opportunity developing now. He was sure he had relative strength in the West. That assessment rested on two convictions.

The first was recognition that the British-American Market-Garden campaign into The Netherlands had been thwarted at great cost to the Allies. Allied strategic plans seemed to be in disarray ever since. There was also intelligence that the Allies' hunger for war against Germany had dissipated.

In addition, the British and Americans did not always agree on strategy or objectives. *Abwehr*, his principal intelligence service, was picking up strong indications that the two Allied army group commanders, British Field Marshal Montgomery and American General Bradley, had disagreed sharply on the advisability of mounting the Market-Garden offensive. The resource diversion to support Market-Garden, moreover, had stopped General Patton, Bradley's most aggressive commander, in his attacks in south central France.

The second part of his assessment of relative strength of forces in the West considered disposition of his own forces. His western defenses were strong since the German army had been re-deployed to a prepared defensive line at its border, the West Wall. He was convinced that front could be held.

His perspective on the *Wehrmacht's* condition generally was sobering but not hopeless. Any map would show immediately that his land armies were being challenged seriously on all fronts.

His once proud sea arm was in shambles. The loss of his naval showpieces *Bismarck, Tirpitz, Scharnhorst,* and *Gneisenau* revealed to the world the destruction of the image more than the reality of Germany's overall surface ship power. The steady depletion of his submarine fleet finished the picture of diminished German naval strength.

The *Luftwaffe* had been neutralized, its aircraft now being used almost exclusively to defend the homeland. Germany was less and less certain of fuel supplies. The promise of more new weapons—rockets, jet aircraft, tanks, even atomic bombs—was unfulfilled and uncertain.

That he would consider making a truce overture would surprise his senior political and military leaders. The idea made more sense to him now.

Although Von Ribbentrop and Goebbels had in mind *rapprochement* with Soviet Premier Josef Stalin in their 1943 recommendation of compromise, he now will make a peace overture, not to the Soviets, but to the British!

The logic of his plan has an obvious military advantage. A truce in the West will free much of his still sizable force there for re-deployment against the much more serious threat from the Soviets on the Eastern Front. Without the British on the Western Front, the Americans can no more defeat Germany alone than the British can alone. Neither country has the power alone nor the will to win the war.

The potential political gain is also significant. If the Americans eventually go along with the British in the truce, so much the better for his force re-allocation plan. If not, he will achieve a more serious political split between the major Allies without an attack. Churchill dragged Roosevelt into the European War. Roosevelt's "Europe First" strategy, with which Churchill eagerly complies, has shown all along the American impatience to get on with the war against Japan.

The fact that Allied leadership is not always on the same page strategically will continue to work to his advantage. His offer of a truce to Churchill alone is based in large measure on his belief that Britain is war weary. The British have been bled seriously of manpower and resources since their 1939 declaration of war. The rain of V-2 rockets on Britain since just before the Allies' Market-Garden offensive has weakened their resolve. He will offer to halt those attacks as a good faith cease-fire proposal.

Churchill will have to consider his proposal. Both the German and British peoples are Nordic. Both are anti-Communist. Surely Churchill can see the merit of Germany's hegemony in Europe, Italy's in the Mediterranean, the Middle East, and North Africa, with Britain keeping its colonies and empire.

However, if the truce initiative should fail, he can still energize his armed forces with his own determination and insight. His planned military offensive in the Ardennes is precisely the correct corollary to that political initiative.

Only a few trusted aides and technical staff are aware of the plan's existence on a "need to know" basis. His code for the operation suggests a defensive plan, *Wacht am Rhein*, in case anyone should get a rumor of it. The strategic objectives will be offensive, however. His plan is for thirty-eight divisions to attack along a fifty-mile front in mid-December. His technical staff reported recently that the odds favor bad weather during that time, grounding the Allies' tactical air support of their forces in eastern France.

The surprise attack will thrust through the Ardennes forest, repeating the pattern of the Spring, 1940, German invasion in the West, but on a smaller scale. Then the French and British armies were mauled by his *blitzkrieg* tactics. This attack will focus on the overextended divisions of the American First Army. Some of those troops are untested. There should be no difficulty for his Fifth and Sixth Panzer Armies to penetrate that weak defensive crust. Then, flanked by his Fifteenth Army on the north and Seventh Army on the south, the panzers will seize Northern France and the Low Countries. They will split the British and American Armies, drive north and west, and re-take Liege and Antwerp. The Canadian First, the British Second, and the American Ninth Armies, having recently pushed salients into The Netherlands and at Aachen, will be cut off and trapped in their forward positions. The success of his plan will force all the western democracies to sue for peace.

However, an attack in the West will require a substantial diversion of army divisions from other critical areas, especially the Eastern Front. That is the main reason he is adopting Von Ribbentrop and Goebbels' urging for a political alternative.

In the beginning and now, his most serious attention has been given to his ideological enemy, the Soviet Union. He sought in the 1930's to finesse the Soviet situation with his eastern ally, Japan. His diplomats tried to dissuade Japan from fighting the Soviets in the near arctic regions adjoining Manchuria. In fact, he was opposed to Japan warring at all with the Soviets. His armies alone were sufficient to subdue them. Instead, the Germans proposed to Japan the easier and more lucrative conquest of Australia, the Philippines, and Southeast Asia countries as their primary military objectives.

Early in 1941, Germany agreed to a historic, secret agreement with Japan. The first part contained Japan's promise not to war with the Soviets. He did not want the Japanese laying claim to any territory in Europe as payment for participation against the Soviets. The second part of the agreement incorporated his strategy to involve Japan in a war with the United States. He pledged Japan assistance in case of war with the U.S. With German support, Japan could move aggressively in the southwest and south central Pacific.

From his perspective, Japanese aggression against U.S. and British possessions in the Pacific would occupy American armed forces. Significant American resources would thereby be diverted from Europe to the Pacific. That manpower and material would not be available to other Allies in Europe, including the Soviets.

Ironically, the Soviets also realized an advantage from the 1941 German-Japanese agreement. They would not have to fight a two-front war. Since the Soviets considered Germany a real and growing military threat, they welcomed the Japanese pursuing military interests in the Pacific, not Eastern Asia. To that end, the Soviets signed an agreement with Japan in April, 1941, requiring neutrality by the other party if one of the parties went to war with nations in the region of their common interest.

Hitler knew that at the right time, those agreements would be as meaningless as the non-aggression pact Germany and the Soviet Union had signed in August, 1939. Obviously, the Soviets did not count on their eventual defeat by Germany as part of any advantage gained by its agreement with Japan.

His ultimate war objective in this political maneuvering is to face his

Wehrmacht eastward, to free the world of Bolshevism. As political amateurs, the Soviets do not realize that their own vast resources are the spoils of war he seeks. Poland in 1939 simply had been a piece of territory that divided the Soviets and Germany geographically, a block of land in his invasion path to the USSR. In the conquest of Poland that ensued, the German people had been reassured. Their long run political desire, to right the wrongs imposed on Germany by the damnable "Versailles Dictate" following the 1918 Armistice, was already being realized.

Despite military reversals in the East since 1942, he is still convinced that the Axis forces can pound the Soviets into submission. Surprisingly, the Soviets have demonstrated a willingness to sacrifice both territory and manpower in their military tactics to date. However, their military and political vision is all wrong. Their leadership is uninspired. Like their improbable, war-inspired political bedfellows, they have no understanding of what world leadership entails.

His efforts to date have vindicated his and Germany's struggles over two decades. The war experience of 1914-1918 was not a German loss. The winners, or those who fancied themselves as winners, got to write the history books of that shameful era. The so-called inter-war years were only a pause in that struggle. The temporary victors became complacent, satisfied with the Versailles Treaty restrictions on Germany. And now they tired of war. He will exploit their weariness.

The remedy for the temporary setbacks his country is now experiencing is to prepare anew. He will build a larger, stronger military machine. He will point the way to obtain and develop resources. He will continue to lead the German armies with his strategic insight. He will order all Germans to devote renewed energy to that effort. The German people can again be rallied to make sacrifices. He will rouse the people to see this epochal conflict succeed for the glory of the Third Reich.

He will direct von Ribbentrop to communicate with the British and propose a preliminary meeting. Churchill won't be bluffed or taken in as easily as Neville Chamberlain was at Munich in 1938. Most of the British people's fear of war displayed at Munich obviously has been overcome. He is confident Churchill will choose accommodation over sacrifice, however, just as his predecessor in office did.

Von Ribbentrop should make contact through a neutral intermediary with Anthony Eden, British Foreign Secretary, in utmost secrecy. He will instruct von Ribbentrop to begin immediate construction of the stipulations to be placed on the meeting itself and on the topics for consideration.

The British might raise the Jewish question on behalf of all the Allies. They are all hypocrites. They certainly were not innocents in their dealings with Jews over the decades. They also recognize Jews as trouble makers all along. He cannot imagine that the Jewish problem, and his "final solution" to it, is a truce-blocking issue.

He will keep his generals in the dark about his truce and military plans for a while. They are not trustworthy. If the truce succeeds, he will shelve for now his *Wacht am Rhein* plan for attacking the Allies through the Ardennes in mid-December.

With the truce putting the British on the sidelines, many of the thirty-eight divisions and all the armor he had slated for *Wacht am Rhein* can be used to crush the Soviets. He will direct his North, Central, and North Ukraine Army groups to adopt a defensive posture for the winter. With the shift of divisions from the West, the South Ukraine Army Group and Army Group F can be strengthened sufficiently for a late winter offensive.

They will then strike through Rumania, retake the oil facilities there, and press on to the Black Sea. The grain belt of the Ukraine and the oil-rich Caucasus lie just beyond.

His immediate strategy is to divide and conquer! Take Great Britain out of the war. He knows Churchill will drive a hard bargain this time. He will have to use equally hard-headed diplomacy to achieve the time and space needed to win Germany's ultimate victory.

Chapter 9

En route to Camp Springs Army Air Field, Friday Night, October 27, 1944

Hayden squeezed into the cargo bay of the Army C-47, fully loaded for its flight from Ft. Bragg to Camp Springs Army Air Field ten miles southeast of Washington, D.C. He sat on the floor against the bulkhead with three other soldiers. He was tired but too wound up to sleep. Too many weighty issues impacted his life too quickly today. He had not had time to digest all of them for their direction-changing implications on his immediate future.

He was most curious about his meeting with Lt. Col. Baxter. The deputy intelligence chief probably did not in fact know much about Hayden's possible mission. For all Baxter knew, Hayden was being recruited to interview German paratroop prisoners of war about their marksmanship training.

Hayden decided he need not worry about any service-connected responsibility. That would take care of itself. He probably could not easily control its direction in any event.

His call to Sarah had been painful for him and apparently for her. He was confident that their problems were not rooted in personal dislike for each other.

Looming now was a crisis that he alone could resolve favorably. It came down ultimately to his career in the army versus his marriage. His continued military service was virtually obligatory under the present circumstances. He could not now foresee any change occurring in his service commitment soon unless there was quick victory of the American armed forces over their enemies. He would try his best to explain the situation and his feelings in the letter he would write to Sarah soon. He hoped she would try again to understand.

He was very troubled by his evening with Jerry and the likelihood that Jerry was homosexual. Hayden loathed the thought. He had never known Jerry's professional conduct to be less than honorable. He could not recall that their personal relationship was affected in any way. Jerry was not stupid. He had to be aware of the dangers ahead for him. Hayden feared for Jerry's future in military service.

The war had already put a stamp on all aspects of his existence. As it ground on and on, he worried that it would grind him flat until he no longer knew himself.

He re-situated his legs to get more comfortable on the hard floor of the plane. The other three soldiers were quiet. It appeared they were dozing. The ability to sleep in almost any circumstances and surroundings was one of the soldier traits Hayden marveled at early in his service. He accepted the ability as routine now.

The war grinding on reminded him again of his father-in-law and friend, George Spurges. One Sunday in the spring of 1941, several months after Sarah and he began dating, she invited him to their country home to meet her parents. After dinner, Mr. Spurges and he sat on the front porch in a warm, comfortable southwest breeze. They talked casually about work and weather. Hayden knew of the Spurges family's encounters with unfriendly neighbors and the sheriff, but did not detect any bitterness in George Spurges' comments. The land, its location, his family, and his life work were all the happiness he could ask for.

Their talk drifted to the news. Under various pretexts and ruses, Germany had attacked its neighbors on all sides. It had extended its military control to a sizable segment of Western Europe. Japan had seized territory in China and Southeastern Asia. There was disconcerting talk of atrocities committed in the wake of both countries' military conquests.

George Spurges asked, "What do you think, Hayden? Is war the answer to these developing international crises, these atrocities, these countries grabbing territory?"

Hayden stated that the only effective way he knew to stop the aggressors was military action.

"Go to war with them?"

"When necessary, yes," Hayden responded firmly.

"I would disagree that war is ever necessary," Spurges replied evenly. "War is a horrible experience for everyone involved, directly or indirectly. A country that initiates war commits the major crime against humanity."

Spurges was emphatic on the question of war's evil. "Most of the principal

World War I leaders, and a lot of second-level political and military leaders could have been found guilty of crimes against humanity under even a minimal moral standard by an objective court."

"Even so, evil has to be countered," Hayden said. "Prime Minister Chamberlain's concessions to Hitler at Munich did not stop Nazi aggression, only encouraged it. Only armed force could have stopped Hitler then. The world can insist that something is done to stop aggressors. There are fundamental values that the world community must uphold."

Sarah's father stressed again the awful immensity and tragedy of war. "Nothing can justify the enormous loss of life and disruption that war brings. The results of war are never as decisive or as favorable as a country hopes for in the beginning. Hardly anything is changed except the disruption of lives that war causes in so many ways."

Spurges launched into a diatribe, his passion for his cause evident to Hayden in the cynicism and bitterness with which he stated it. "All countries have grievances of one kind or another against their neighbors at any time. Those grievances may carry over from past wars: humiliating defeats, a punitive war-ending treaty, lost territory. Or they arise because a country flaunts its differences: religious differences, different living standards, different languages and culture. Grievances unite countries in a war-like mentality just as fundamental values do, maybe more so.

"Because those grievances matter in the public psyche, a country's leadership has to do something about them. Indeed, a country's leaders often emerge because they can correctly identify the depth of those grievances in the public mind and promise resolution to them. Often, and unfortunately, that promise is couched in an appeal to military action. The public accepts that appeal when it harmonizes with its own attitudes about grievances, imagined or real, and using war to resolve them.

"Each of the national players and potential players in a coming conflict then constructs an immense grinding wheel. The wheel is built with a country's production capability, especially war material, its natural resources, technology, brain power, and the always essential manpower.

"Countries invite potential allies to join them to increase the size and strength of their wheel. Those prospective allies may think the same way politically. Allies often join in because promises are made about a share of postwar treasure, or territory, or power. The more troublesome allies nowadays are those who want to use war to re-make the world into their own vision of what is right and just.

"At some point the politics of war overwhelm caution. An insult is hurled against another country's 'national honor.' That's a very important war trigger, whatever it comes to mean in any country. The announced need to defend one's country against external or internal threats is often the subterfuge for offensive action. Maybe a political figure is assassinated. Or a hostile incident occurs, real or alleged. The incident routinely is exaggerated by fabrication and lies.

"The grinding wheels are set in motion. A thunderous roar erupts as opposing wheels engage. Sparks fly. The detritus of war begins to gather, the residue of the grinding. The best of a country's technology is left on the battlefield. The best of each country's youth is re-formed as broken and torn bodies. Brain power and physical prowess are no longer distinguishable among the dead.

"Once hostilities start, the unreal is real. War is touted as the necessary precursor to peace and progress. War-like bluster is re-fashioned in the guise of patriotism. Those who counsel peace are smeared and vilified.

"Lives are forever disrupted in countless ways by countries' resort to armed force. Sadly, it is not just the youth in their prime who are injured or killed, but children in their innocence as well. How can anyone comprehend their confusion and suffering?

"No country is ever guilty of starting a war, of course. The blame can always be placed on another country, typically the one first attacked. No side in war ever announces that its own purpose and actions are evil or ungodly, that it intends to debase values, or that it seeks other than noble ends.

"Each side gives demeaning names to its enemies to justify its killing of them. Enemies are 'mad men,' 'mad dogs,' 'brutes,' 'devils.' It is permissible, you see, even laudable, to kill mad men and devils.

"Even the language of war in public media, the propaganda both sides use, is tainted by the slanted view created of the other side. They make 'sneak' attacks. We 'surprise' the enemy. Side A mounts a 'stout defense' against an attack. Side B's defense is 'fanatical.' Their offensives are 'suicidal.' Our attacks 'show courage under intense fire and heavy losses.' One country's leaders 'throw away lives in a vain search for glory or empire.' The other country's dead have 'made the supreme sacrifice' in defense of their sacred land, or honor, or values."

Hayden insisted that some wars must be fought. "By any standard employed, there is evil. There are evil men who must be challenged and checked and defeated. In our communities, people have a right to defend themselves against murderers and burglars and rapists, and the same right exists against extra-national criminals."

"Defend?" Spurges responded. "Burn down your house to defend it against arson? How many members of the household, adults and children, are you willing to sacrifice to ensure that defense? What price will you pay? If you say 'we'll pay any price,' and the other side says the same, then the price of war simply increases. Under that slogan, both sides set about creating a bigger and stronger grinding wheel to keep from losing the war.

"The belligerent countries, and especially the side losing as the fortunes of war shift, desperately seek to replace their losses. More of society's resources are channeled into hardening the grinding wheels. That means fewer resources available to the civilian population. Thus, civilians are asked again—they are required, really—to sacrifice further to ensure victory.

"Civilians bear other costs. Many civilians in war zones who live through the battles become refugees as a by-product of the grinding. They swarm the roads, looking for food, shelter, medical attention. They overwhelm all public facilities by their numbers. Decent people facing starvation or death for themselves or their families turn to stealing and killing merely to sustain existence.

"And the wheels grind on, for months or years, sometimes for decades, until one side's wheel, its war machine, is destroyed or irreparably broken, or damaged more than the other side's wheel."

The C-47 lurched as it hit an air pocket. One soldier who had been snoring awoke, startled.

"Not there yet, Corporal," Hayden said softly, "just a bump in the road."

Hayden had interrupted his future father in law again.

"Despite the misinformation, even the duplicity that brings a country into war, most people want those announced objectives. They identify with national goals and are willing to fight for them. Even if national honor comes to mean only a simple will to survive against the overwhelming brutality of war, people are willing to sacrifice and die for it."

"Are they willing?" Spurges challenged. "The answer is really one of timing. Would there be a different answer if people really understood beforehand what the costs of war will be…that the son or brother or husband or father will be ground up in the process and never return? Or that their innocent children or grandchildren will be brutalized?

"The simple fact is that few people can know the horror of war before they experience what hostilities really mean. No one asks the farmer if it is okay to use his farm as a battlefield, to dig trenches on his farm land and rifle pits in his front yard. No one asks his permission to drive columns of horses or trucks or tanks over his wheat and corn fields.

"No one asks the shop keeper if it is okay to break down the walls of his shop and destroy his goods and his livelihood. No one asks the thousands of common people if they would like to see their homes destroyed, their children uprooted, or be forced to flee as refugees, wandering away from the battlegrounds to other unknown perils.

"If they all could know the damage, destruction, and carnage beforehand, would they be as willing to go to war to preserve some vague conception of national honor? Or to retaliate for the assassination of some unknown, distant archduke?"

Hayden interrupted. "Then what motivates and sustains people in the midst of war, in their wartime miseries, if it is not their belief in the righteousness of the cause?"

George Spurges was quick to respond. "All people hope, most of them vainly, of course, that the really serious consequences, the death and destruction of war, will be far away, that war won't touch them personally. They think they can have what they are told is national honor at no cost to them.

"And if there are direct costs, well, they are told that everyone must sacrifice to defeat the Hun, or protect values, or whatever.

"Slogans are trumpeted. Defend this sacred land! Protect our women and children from assault! Our cause is just! God is on our side! We must defeat the other side by whatever means we have, since the other side is always less moral, less worthy, and less righteous. When the war slogans are repeated often enough, each country's people are carried along on that created belief.

"All agencies of government are enlisted to ensure a favorable outcome. Propaganda, fabrications, lies…all can convince a society that the war it is pursuing is 'right.'

"Once into the war, whatever the provocation was or was alleged to be that brought a country to war, it is now necessary to support our brave fighting forces. Few suggest that the best support they can give is to keep those brave men out of harm's way in the first place. Few on either side stop to ask if it would be better for a country's farms and stores and women and children, even its national honor, if the war were not fought.

"Other haunting questions are asked but never answered. 'What is this war really about?' 'Are the benefits worth the costs?' The few who have courage to ask, even in the face of widespread death and ruin, are labeled 'defeatists' or 'treasonous'," Spurges said bitterly.

"The exultation when war is over is regularly confused with a sense of victory, that something useful has been accomplished. But victory is rarely clean.

Troublemakers exist as before. The exit from one hostile encounter is the threshold to the next."

"What do we do with these troublemakers, if armed force is not the answer?" Hayden asked.

"To be sure, we are a long way from a system of effective restraints on aggressor countries," Spurges said. "There is likely a long, difficult period of tension ahead, given the hostilities engendered in this conflict now brewing, before an international system of conflict resolution is developed."

Hayden persisted. "What, then, is your final answer?"

"Destruction of the war mentality!" Spurges responded eagerly, convinced that such a colossal change was possible. "The road to peace, domestic and foreign, in families and communities, has to start with each individual. Personal differences have to be resolved through reason and the rule of law, not violence.

"The world population has to be taught, one at a time as necessary, how differences can be settled peaceably. We have to begin at the beginning. Education of infants and children away from the idea of 'self' toward a concept of 'other,' away from self-centeredness toward other-centeredness, is a difficult but fundamental concept to instill as they mature. That goal is nothing more radical that learning the 'Golden Rule,' however. It is also the fundamental Christian social message. Peace, not war! Forgiveness, not condemnation! The essence of the Rule is found in all major religions," Spurges added with a bright twinkle in his eyes.

Hayden could not contest effectively the idealism of his future father-in-law's vision. But he argued that an imperfect world, unwilling to learn the lessons of peace, requires the use of force from time to time. Education of the world to peace being a herculean task, it is never to be achieved fully. It requires a much larger percentage of every country's resources than they would consent to give.

"More than is now being devoted to war and preparation for war?" Spurges asked. "Leave the money out of it for a moment, Hayden. It's impossible to get an accurate total of, or in any way comprehend, the billions spent on war anyway. Would peace education require the eight and one half million military deaths, another twenty-nine million soldiers wounded in battle, to say nothing of the five million civilian deaths and untold millions of injured civilians for all sides in the Great War 'to end all wars'?"

Hayden had responded civilly but staunchly to George Spurges' pacifist vision for world politics. He could not contradict his dramatic portrayal of the awful waste of war, however.

He dozed off finally, exhausted by the day and his review of its problems. The jolt of the plane hitting the runway at Camp Springs Army Air Field woke him an hour later.

Chapter 10

Camp Springs Army Air Field, Early Saturday, October 28, 1944

To Hayden's enormous surprise and pleasure, there in the small lobby of the airport control tower of Camp Springs Army Air Field sat Frederick, his best friend. Frederick had worked with Hayden from the fall of 1940 up to the time Hayden enlisted in the Army a year later.

Frederick was equally surprised to see Hayden hurrying to greet him. They shook hands and thumped each other on the back enthusiastically and for a long moment could only shout "Hayden! Frederick!"

As they sat at the small table for coffee, Frederick told Hayden he was catching a 1:00 flight out of the air field and was sorry he could not say anything more. It was then just a few minutes till midnight.

"I can't say anything about what I'm doing, either," Hayden said. "All I can say is that I am supposed to call for a jeep when I get here. But that can wait."

They had corresponded by letter three or four times since they separated when Hayden left for military service. Then, abruptly and with no explanation from Frederick, a letter was returned to Hayden. Hayden tried to call Frederick in Wichita and found that he was no longer at his old address. Again, when the 82nd Division was about to leave for North Africa from Ft. Bragg in early 1943, he asked Sarah to inquire locally. She came up empty on Frederick's location.

"Since we're each in a separate secrecy zone, what can we talk about?" Frederick asked.

"We can talk about old times, our work together, our friendship, the fun we had before the world got so dangerous," Hayden said. "I wish there was something other than coffee to toast that wonderful time together. That was the best year of my life. Maybe age twenty-one is always the best year."

"Age twenty-five was not so bad for me either," Frederick said. "Four years age difference seems less and less important as we get older. And we've gotten older much faster than the years would indicate, haven't we?"

Hayden nodded.

"I thought when I came to this country that, with my problems, my accent, my newness, my beliefs, that I would have trouble meeting people. But you and your friends…well, your kindness and good humor made me feel accepted."

"I had some of the same hesitation when I left home. Here I was, a small town Texas boy in a big city. Well, I thought Wichita was a big city. It was the biggest I had ever lived in." They both laughed.

"Well, my background was different, of course. Germany was changing so rapidly in the 30's, so tragically in the wrong direction. It wasn't a problem of big city or small, or of my leaving one for another. I saw a peaceful community go to a hateful community, hatred aimed at my people and me every day, every minute. It had nothing to do with any of us doing anything wrong, just for being Jews."

Frederick grew pensive, visibly sad as his recollection of a Germany dramatically changed. Hayden tried to turn Frederick back to the good memories of when they both worked at Boeing Aircraft in Wichita.

"The fun we had while all that machinery was screeching away right in front of us. It probably was criminal of us to accept the good pay while we were having such a great time."

He was referring to the production activity they were hired for. They had been trained at Boeing to operate drill presses. Their stations were side by side. It was monotonous work, noisy, and not very dangerous.

Routinely there were delays, sometimes up to several minutes, before the next partially completed engine components were passed to them for processing along a constantly moving conveyor belt. They were able to relax, talk, tell stories, and eat a snack in those brief interludes.

Frederick taught Hayden a lot of things, especially German. Hayden reciprocated with English lessons and the nuances of American idiom and culture. They alternated work days for speaking only German or English to each other. They went rabbit or pheasant hunting with their colleagues on weekends. Frederick often met Hayden and Sarah for movies.

One day Frederick brought a writing tablet to work and placed it on the stand between their work stations. He proposed they use it for chess notation. Hayden had learned the game as a boy from his late father and had played occasionally since.

Frederick was quite good at the game. The procedure he suggested was a severe mental challenge. Since it was not appropriate to have a chess set out in the open at their stations, they would play only from recall of their game moves. They visualized the placement of pieces and their moves on an imaginary chess board, as chess masters do when playing blindfolded. They alternately penciled in their moves, with the notation available to confirm where their pieces were on the imaginary board.

As they were developing their memory and skills, occasionally one would say, "You can't move there. You've already got a piece on that square." They would check the notation to retrace their moves, laugh at the mistake, all the while doing their monotonous work with an eye on the supervisor.

Frederick had just learned the Nimzo-Indian variation to the Ruy Lopez opening and taught it to Hayden. Hayden began reading more about the game in his spare time, replaying the moves of masters.

"The war of the chess board is nothing like this war, is it?" Frederick asked. "What can you tell me of your war experiences? I see you've been in several campaigns from the ribbons on your jacket. What combat jumps have you made?"

"Well, I suppose there is nothing very secret any more about those campaigns. I've made three combat jumps—in Sicily, Normandy, and Holland. The 82nd Division jumped in the Salerno battle, but my battalion went ashore in boats."

"All of them difficult?"

"Each of them was in its own way. There is always the uncertainty, the confusion, and the aura of danger that hangs over those big operations. The battlefield is never tidy. And the dead and injured…countless numbers of them all around."

"All for the cause," Frederick said.

Hayden had a fleeting thought of how George Spurges would respond to the invocation of "the cause" to justify death and injury but did not verbalize it. "Yeah, the good guys won in each of those battles, the ones who survived did. We remember that good result. It would have been a lot worse if we had lost any of those battles."

"And how is your beautiful Sarah?"

"I saw her just two weeks ago when I was rotated home from Europe. She was cool, tense, pressured. I felt so constrained in what we could talk about easily. In just a few minutes the small talk was exhausted. And the big issue… There is such a distance between us that we can't even get close to talking peace or war any more. It gets too personal. So, what's left?"

"The future, of course," Frederick said in sympathy and counsel. "We should think of all our friends together again after the war. We must plan for people in love with each other to work and build their families in peace and joy."

"When I called her this afternoon, she was bitter, angry. She hinted at a formal separation from me," Hayden said. "She really is upset at how things have been going—or not going—between us. I have told her many times that this war cannot go on forever. I have been trying to get her to look to the future."

"That's the direction for you to take," Frederick said with renewed enthusiasm. "Keep loving and caring uppermost in your talks, and look to the future." He laughed. "Here I am, hopelessly single, acting like a marriage counselor."

Hayden smiled. "I understand what you're saying. So far she has not been appeased by that approach. The future I promise is always too far out there, too much constrained by this war, too uncertain for her to hope."

Frederick let Hayden pause to gather his thoughts and talk out his concerns. "She frightens me at times. She has such a passionate, adamant belief in her vision of peace. Maybe after all this killing, and knowing I am a part of it, she is a little disenchanted about her group's chance of success. Maybe she is disenchanted with everything, even with me."

"I like to think I could be as passionate in promoting peace as Sarah is, even though her beliefs bring some danger to herself, and some threat to your marriage," Frederick said. "However, I admit on the front end that my peace wish is cast in my own terms. It is formed by my opposition to the evil going on in my country. Peace to me is an end to that evil. Only secondly is it an end to the violence that must be used to stop that evil."

Hayden said, "Deep down, philosophically, you and I both know that the peace option is the one we all have to take some day."

There was a somber, far away look on Frederick's face as he spoke. "Think of all the resources for social and economic good Germany had available. What if it had harnessed the intellects, the skills, the energies of peoples of all races toward the country's betterment? What if it had used the harshness of the Versailles Treaty to rally the German people to social and economic progress, to political democracy instead of war? What potential we had in Germany. Think of the progress we could be making. What waste! What a tragedy!"

"I can't imagine what this war has meant for you, trying to live with the evil that passes for political activity in your country. After all these horrible years, I still don't understand the intense animosity toward Jews."

"Hatred of Jews is centuries old, of course," Frederick said. "That hatred has been a rallying point for many nations' efforts in support of other goals. It is much easier to rally people to something a country is against than to identify what it is for. Demagogues usually prefer a threat for that purpose, an alien ideology, real or imagined. The dark tools of deceit and propaganda can be employed in constructing that threat."

Hayden was intrigued with the threat idea, one that George Spurges had articulated so well. "I find it interesting that Hitler has escalated that hatred of Jews in wartime, even though it is a possible divisive force inside Germany. He faces formidable opposition from the outside on all fronts at the same time."

"However, in Hitler's concoction of this rallying call to Germans," Frederick said, "Judaism is both an internal and an external threat. It has been easy for Nazi leaders to whip up public fervor against Jews as the cause of all of Germany's economic, political, and social problems. Postwar inflation and unemployment in Germany, the Treaty of Versailles restrictions, political instability—those are real problems. The common source of those problems, alleged Jewish machinations, become real also in the minds of most Germans through unrelenting Nazi propaganda.

"Hitler goes further to link Judaism and Bolshevism internationally to rouse more domestic political anxiety. Bolshevism is also a real problem. Selling the German people on the idea of a link between Judaism and Bolshevism establishes the external threat. National Socialism is offered as the only solution to both the internal and external threats."

Both men were silent for a long time. Fewer soldiers moved around the lobby. Several slept on the floor.

Hayden realized their remaining time together was dwindling. After these months of lost communication, there was a lot he wanted to know. He did want to find out a little about Frederick's recent history and his reason for being here most of all.

"When did you leave Boeing?"

"Not long after you left for the service. I felt I had to do something about the war. I took a government job of sorts too." He held up his hands to ward off Hayden's question. "I can't answer anything about that."

Hayden smiled. Unlike Jerry Connelios' secrecy about his career crisis, Frederick's position probably required secrecy. He could only speculate about the kind of job a German national could obtain in U.S. government service in wartime.

Time was short for Frederick to catch his plane. They both rose reluctantly.

"I have a good feeling about you and Sarah," Frederick said as they walked to the exit. "After this madness is over, and you both have a chance to talk freely again, without the pressure that war puts on both of you…well, you both are honest, caring, and reasonable people. I can't believe that two people with so much in common will continue at odds with each other once the source of your discontent has been removed."

Hayden was moved at the thoughtfulness expressed by his friend. "I hope the best for you now and after the war is over. I hope you can be proud of Germany again. I hope you can live free again in your country, restored to its place as a positive cultural influence in the world. And I hope to see you then. We'll get together again when this is all over."

The party boarding the plane was treated to the genuine affection of two old friends for each other. They hugged each other without embarrassment or a further word, then turned away, choked with the emotion of their parting.

Chapter 11

Camp Springs Army Air Field, Early Saturday, October 28, 1944

Frederick was surprised and elated to see Hayden in the airport lobby. Frederick was on his way out of the country, having been posted to recently liberated Paris. He had been a civilian agent of U.S. Army Intelligence for almost three years.

He could not imagine what new assignment or project would bring Hayden to Washington. He could not intrude on the confidence of his friend to find out, just as he could not reveal more that he did about his own service assignment. Hayden's move probably was just a routine shift in location. If so, however, why could he not say anything about it?

He was sure his own mission and agency identification had not been compromised in his meeting with Hayden. An agent's cover had to be protected, of course. He had learned, however, that security was not only to ensure that friends or relatives would be discreet. The security veil also protected the friends or relatives. They could not reveal under pressure what they did not know.

He had corresponded with Hayden for a while after Hayden went into the army. Frederick was aware of Hayden's selection for officer's training and his assignment to the 82nd Airborne Division. When Frederick went into Army Intelligence, however, his superiors thought it best for him to minimize correspondence with all contacts. Even his new address could tell more about his wartime work than others should know. Frederick regretted the secrecy requirement that forced him to break off contact with his best friend before he could give any reason at all.

Within days of the United States entry into war against Germany and several months after Hayden went into the Army, Frederick was contacted by two Army Intelligence recruiters. They learned of his leaving Germany in 1938 and were impressed by his strong anti-Nazi convictions that prompted his departure. The intelligence recruiters couldn't yet spell out how he might be needed, but they told him he could be very helpful to the Allied cause. His first-hand knowledge of German and Germany could be put to good use.

Frederick learned code and radio operation easily. The more difficult task was learning the feel of keyed radio transmission. Learning to send was not as important as the ability to recognize the "signature" of senders. In most coded radio transmissions, there are very subtle nuances of keying that identify who is sending, called the sender's "fist." By the end of their training, Frederick and his classmates were able to identify a sender's nuances regularly and automatically, a task they had considered impossible at the outset.

His trainers saw early on that Frederick's mental alertness could be used to handle radio interceptions. He showed a rare talent for making the fine transmitting distinctions among real agents. They assigned him to advanced training.

Working in close contact with veteran agents to de-code messages, Frederick became part of an effective intelligence team. He learned how to make immediate responses to agents in the field. The team came to rely on Frederick's native German language ability. His chess-playing skill provided him the ability to analyze combinations, to know where to look for them in military and political radio communications, and to see through and beyond them.

Of course, only a few, top-level political and military people in each country knew the big secrets, the overall strategy, the immediate and long run military objectives, and the disposition of armies and resources. Intelligence services on both sides could glean only hints of what those big secrets were. The job of analysts was to determine where the hints pointed and eventually suggest what, if anything, could be done about them.

The intensity of Frederick's intelligence training was relieved occasionally by in-field training. All team members of the several intelligence groups being developed were inserted into German prisoner of war camps in the U.S. beginning in 1942. U.S. military authorities were relocating German prisoners taken in North Africa, later in Sicily and Italy, to POW work sites in the U.S. POWs often were quartered near German-speaking communities in the Midwest. They could be hired out under guard at nominal wage rates to perform mostly manual labor in and around those communities.

The POW compounds provided good opportunities for testing language, cover, and deception abilities of new intelligence agents. Agents were inserted into a POW group for a month or so. To ensure their initial cover, several agents would be inserted into a compound along with a group of real, newly relocated POWs. That way, the intelligence agents would not stand out as plants. Typically, these agents made up no more than two percent of the POW group.

The instructor staff did screen the POW groups to ensure no prisoners were from the same German Army battalion or smaller unit the intelligence agents were alleging to be from. Otherwise the POW group could learn who the fake POWs were and isolate those agents, or worse.

The American guards were not told that some in the POW group they were overseeing were actually American agents in training. The agents were instructed in cover stories that the instructors had checked out for consistency. In addition to the training gained in these encounters, the agents were encouraged after their "release" to report to military authorities on the POWs they met.

On his first experience inside a group, Frederick learned of a POW named Josef Feldern from Cologne, Frederick's home city in Germany. His first reaction was to avoid Feldern. On second thought he decided that his encounter with the POW would be a good test of his ability to work within his cover identity.

"I heard you are also from Cologne," he greeted Feldern on their truck trip to a work site.

Feldern seemed genuinely pleased and not at all suspicious of Frederick's introduction. "Yes, I lived there with my parents all my life until I came into the service. And you?"

"The same with me. I'm Frederick Lehm. I left Cologne two years ago. I've lost contact with everyone there. I learned my parents and family were killed in a bombing raid last year."

"Too bad," Feldern replied. "Mine are gone, too. There are sacrifices we all have to make."

Frederick chose not to bite on Feldern's potentially political comment. "Did you hear much from home, before your capture, how things were there?"

"Not much. One of the men in my company was also from Cologne. He said his brother back home wrote him that our military comrades in the city were taking shelter close in to the cathedral because Allied bomber crews are apparently instructed not to destroy or damage the cathedral."

"How about that?" Frederick smiled. "Very clever."

Frederick was pleased that, in his first attempt at undercover work, he had learned a bit of information he could later pass on to his trainers.

Agents as POWs could also keep an eye open for German officers hiding their identities. They could expose diehard Nazis and identify other politically outspoken prisoners for special attention. POW organizers of revolts and escape plans or other mischief could also be spotted and reported.

Other politically conscious prisoners could be marked for observation, especially those with a leaning toward democratic systems. They might be groomed for U.S. citizenship, even for recruitment as agents.

What Frederick did not realize until after he had completed his training as a counterfeit POW was that these insertions permitted his military intelligence superior to scrutinize him. Shortly after his last stint inside a POW compound, he was called in for a meeting.

His intelligence superior first commended him for his progress and behavior. He then abruptly challenged Frederick.

"If you were a German agent in the U.S., wouldn't you try to gain credibility while you learned about the American intelligence system?"

"Well, I suppose so…if I were a German agent."

"Wouldn't your behavior be about the same as it has been during these testing periods if you were preparing to obtain and send confidential information back to your homeland?"

"That hypothesis is also valid, sir, since I have nothing to hide. But if I were trying to deceive, to work undercover for Germany, it seems I would have to raise suspicion about myself in one area or another to counter the image of my behavior as too innocent or routine. I would be damned if I did that, I suppose, and now damned if I don't."

His superior smiled and chose not to pursue the matter.

Frederick understood immediately what these "testing periods" meant. He was being observed and tested for loyalty. The senior intelligence officers could not check Frederick's background the way they did American nationals because he had grown up in Germany and lived a relatively short period of time in the U.S. His recruitment obviously occurred after some scrutiny. But the security people had to check him out on a current basis to determine if he was playing spy games.

This was not the time for Frederick to protest his innocence, however. His best course of action was not to look over his shoulder. He would continue doing his best.

Frederick's team of nine handlers now being assigned to operations in Paris was given the responsibility for five new field agents being sent into Germany. They would maintain an alert around the clock to serve and protect those agents in the field. Each shift would consist of one veteran of Army Intelligence and one newcomer. Each shift was nine hours, overlapping by one half hour the preceding and succeeding shifts to ensure the passage of current information. The extra three team members allowed all to take some time off and to change the composition of the two-man shifts regularly.

Frederick often considered the weighty responsibility he and his team would carry. Good intelligence was critical to the successful prosecution of the war against the Nazi regime. Helping to keep that intelligence untainted and valid was his new task. He welcomed the challenge.

Chapter 12

London, Saturday Evening, October 28, 1944

Ever since Foreign Secretary Anthony Eden had passed him the "eyes only" document from German Foreign Minister Joachim von Ribbentrop via the Swedish humanitarian Count Folke Bernadotte on late Friday afternoon, British Prime Minister Winston Churchill had thought about little else.

The document was titled:

Proposal of the German Government to the British Government to Enter into Negotiations to Secure a Truce Between Their Countries.

His first reaction on reading it Friday evening, and then studying the language more carefully on Saturday morning, was to reject the proposal outright. His continued strong suspicion of Hitler's motives kept him from changing his initial decision.

The tone of the document was clear. Hitler was suggesting discussions. While not coming hat in hand to request truce talks, Hitler clearly was asking for considerations, not demanding them.

What would be the harm in talking to the Germans in the interest of peace? He could always reject the proposal. With a heavy heart, and beset by doubts, in private he considered again the question he had confronted for several years: What is the best course for Great Britain? He began to review the background of his country's relations with Germany by considering first the state of international diplomatic relations over the past quarter of a century.

Seemingly good progress was being made in the post World War I period in the direction of permanent world peace. The Washington and London Naval Treaties promised reductions among major powers in the arms race. Most world powers eagerly joined in considering disarmament plans. Alliances of friendship were formed.

New treaties adopted seemed to address major problems among nations. The Dawes and Young plans had tried to relieve Germany's financial straits following its economy's war devastation.

Countries with sizable populations came of age in the first third of the 20th century. These peoples were searching for economic development and personal advancement. It promised to be a special time.

Where did it all go wrong?

Amid all the political, economic, social, religious, and ethnic issues among countries, Churchill identified two overwhelming forces that moved the world into the cauldron of World War II.

First were the remaining problems of World War I. Second was the rise of dictators and their demands for territory. It was not just coincidence that those issues were joined in time. Those dictators, especially Hitler, politically exploit unsolved problems. Territorial expansion is a natural expression of the ambition of dictators during this time, which might be saying simply that grabbing territory or treasure is what dictators do.

Those two difficulties, each strong enough alone to create insurmountable obstacles to world peace, are worsened by two other powerful forces. One is the effective use of propaganda by aggressor nations. Its essential message is "truth is what we say it is." The side that can practice deception longer is able to define "truth."

The other force has been the disposition of present Allies, in their weakness and lack of preparedness for war, to yield too readily to aggressors' demands. This weakness has been evident in volatile situations other than the 1938 debacle in Munich where Neville Chamberlain caved in to Hitler's bogus claims in Czechoslovakia in return for a promise of peace.

Exploiting that weakness of future Allies may have been the most clever propaganda strategy of all by the dictators, he thought. Militarily unprepared countries besides Great Britain were intimidated by aggressors' demands. They appeased through inaction. Belgium and The Netherlands, as good examples, strictly avoided any activity Germany might consider hostile, including self-imposed limitations on new defenses. Tiny Luxembourg did not even ask for Allied protection for fear that request would provoke Germany to occupy it.

Churchill admitted in the privacy of his study to three British diplomatic errors aiding the ascendancy of dictators in the interwar period. They too were sins of inaction.

Great Britain should have worked harder to make the Versailles Treaty address the problems arising from Germany's World War I devastation. Premier Georges Clemenceau of France adopted a much harder line on requiring German reparations and admission of German guilt for the war than the other Big Four leaders, Prime Minister David Lloyd George of Great Britain, President Woodrow Wilson of the United States, and Italy's Premier Vittorio Orlando. Clemenceau's position was somewhat understandable. Many Frenchmen were bitter since France was the battleground of the war started by Germany. The French suffered heavily in property and human loss. They wanted Germany to pay for that loss. Clemenceau voiced that demand forcefully. The other leaders yielded to him.

The humiliating terms the Treaty imposed on Germany were harsh and unwise. Germany had to disarm and accept restrictions on the size of its armed forces, give up its colonies, pay reparations set at $33 billion in 1921, and admit guilt for starting the war.

Churchill regarded those terms as unfortunate and unrealistic. The suffering German people, already reeling from wartime-induced shortages, had their very survival threatened by those added burdens. The country suffered serious unemployment, rampant inflation, and critical food and materials shortages in the 1920's due to the Allied blockade. It simply was unable to meet the reparations demands.

The second sin of inaction he thought Great Britain responsible for was its silence on the political re-structuring of Germany. This lack of guidance probably was the most serious weakness of the Versailles Treaty and a major limitation on securing peace in Europe. Revolutionary forces soon de-stabilized Germany further. Starting in 1918 with the abdication of Kaiser Wilhelm II, German government cabinets failed at an average rate of one per year until 1933.

Hitler's identification of the Treaty as the initial cause of Germany's ills had the ring of truth to rally the German people from their defeat in war. Hitler used it effectively, albeit ruthlessly, to build his own power and that of the Nazi party. He was able to lay the responsibility for accepting the Treaty on Germany's liberal, republican form of government in 1919, the Weimar Republic. Hitler thereby focused the liability for Germany's postwar problems, the staggering inflation and unemployment, on political factions other than the National Socialists. Added to the mix of guilt-laying was Hitler's alleging the alliance of Bolshevism and Judaism.

By directing the blame at others, Hitler could justify the Nazi Party's rearmament to re-build Germany's war-making potential in the name of the new Third Reich. German territorial ambitions could then be realized, both for past territories taken from Germany and those newly desired. Military power also facilitated the settling of scores from the past, especially against the hated Bolsheviks in the Soviet Union.

The third sin of inaction assignable to the British was the diplomacy of appeasement. Churchill acknowledged it was the most controversial impediment to postwar peace. Could the British have taken a firmer stance when Hitler made his first aggressive political and military incursions? Would Hitler have launched his belligerent ventures had he not received implicit encouragement in not being challenged for his actions? Could Hitler's aggression have been stopped with a firm condemnation backed by a united military resolve of the Western democracies?

Hitler achieved enormous territorial and strategic gains with only verbal protest from Great Britain or no opposition at all. He denounced the Versailles Treaty early on in the 1920's and then began to ignore it in the 1930's. As an adjunct protest against the Treaty, Germany left the League of Nations in 1933.

Hitler unilaterally terminated the Anglo-German Naval Treaty of 1935. The British had agreed to the Treaty as a concession to Germany to ease tensions. It allowed Germany to increase its surface ship tonnage to 35% of the British level, a departure from the Versailles Treaty provisions limiting Germany to six capital ships.

The British paid a diplomatic price for that concession. The 1935 Treaty caused a split in the Stresa Front, a 1934 pact among France, Great Britain, and Italy. Those countries were alarmed at Germany's pace of rearmament and formed the pact to discourage Hitler's aggression. The rift caused in the Front, especially between France and Great Britain, was the icing on the cake for Hitler in achieving the 1935 Naval Treaty with the British.

Churchill ground his teeth as he recalled Hitler's termination of the agreement. It was an especially galling affront to the British. As with their later attempts to ease tensions, the British effort was not good enough for Hitler. At the same time, Germany began to exceed the 100,000 man army limitation imposed on it, created a new air force, and expanded submarine production, all in defiance of the Versailles Treaty.

In 1936, German troops reoccupied the Rhineland, the demilitarized districts on the west bank of the Rhine, again in violation of an explicit Versailles Treaty prohibition. The ownership of that territory west of the Rhine had been disputed for many years by France and Germany. The move was a particularly significant transgression by Germany, marking the first overt military incursion of Hitler's Third Reich.

Churchill paused to re-light a cigar and pour another measure of brandy. His bitterness grew as he recalled the failure of France and Great Britain to challenge that German aggression, while Germany's military machine was not yet dominant. That failure marked a new era in Hitler's ability to repudiate with impunity the peaceful settlement of disputes.

From that point on, Hitler's own settlement technique of diplomatic/ military conquests continued against only verbal resistance. Hitler pressured Great Britain into the agreement at Munich, allowing him to seize the Sudetenland. In March, 1939, he completed the annihilation of the Czechoslovakian state, violating his pledge at Munich that the Sudetenland was his last territorial claim in Europe.

The pivotal, internationally explosive aggression by Hitler occurred in 1939. In March of that year he had, in effect, ordered Poland to cede to Germany the "Polish Corridor" linking Germany and East Prussia and to yield the city of Danzig to German rule. When Poland refused those demands, but offered to negotiate them, Great Britain and France announced they stood behind their pledges to Poland.

Hitler pressured the two Allies to repudiate their pledges to Poland to avoid war. Repudiation would have destroyed the prestige of Britain and France to intervene in any other international crisis. We were in a no win situation, Churchill thought, dispirited.

With Germany's invasion of Poland on September 1, 1939, Great Britain and France declared war on Germany, and World War II was set in motion. Germany invaded the Soviet Union in 1941 to "save the entire world from Bolshevism." More than an ideological victory, however, Germany wanted the USSR's storehouse of resources, especially food and oil.

In summary, Churchill mused, the policy of appeasement that Great Britain and France practiced in the 1930's was ineffective and ultimately dangerous. The two countries yielded to Hitler's demands as long as they could because they were not ready for a war over Hitler's Versailles Treaty violations and his theft of territory that followed. Their yielding to Hitler, however, only made him bolder in his next treaty violations and territorial encroachments.

Churchill rose from his chair to stretch and walk a few paces. He stirred the fire-eaten and crumbling logs in the fireplace absent mindedly for a while before he sat again.

He rested his head against his chair, wearied by his review of crucial events in the interwar period and the wartime decisions that followed. This peace offer from Hitler was forcing another decision that could lead to damaging consequences and increased turmoil within his country.

He took a note pad to summarize the pros and cons he saw in agreeing to truce talks. He believed first that the offer grew out of Hitler's recognition, finally, that his military position was tenuous. Hitler had to acknowledge that his armed forces were contained, in fact surrounded. His surface naval force was destroyed. Resources were no longer available to rebuild it after incessant Allied bombing of Germany's war production plants. The German *Luftwaffe* was neutralized. All of his armed forces were less certain of fuel supply after the Soviets took Rumania and the Ploesti oil facilities just months ago.

By mid-1943 the Allies had won the "Battle of the Atlantic." The convoy system providing food and materials to Great Britain and Allied military forces from Canada and the United States had survived after serious losses. The U-Boat strangulation of Britain, by severing its supply lines with the West and disrupting its ability to feed its population and sustain its war effort, was Churchill's greatest wartime fear.

Churchill's second note was an overall assessment of his country's current military status. He was cautiously optimistic. The Market-Garden campaign was a less-than-total success story. British losses were substantial, especially within the decimated First Airborne Division. The Allies were delivered a rather sharp rebuke because Allied intelligence about German strength in the general area of the Market-Garden thrust was ignored. Britain's fighting machine continued to be bled of resources and manpower.

The British homeland had been afflicted anew by aerial bombardment in 1944, this time by flying bombs and guided missiles. The impact to date of those German "vengeance weapons" on civilian morale was serious.

The positive side of the intelligence reports was that Germany's three-front strategy was all but defeated. Allied air power should be able to complete the task. Churchill believed he could, if necessary, bargain with Hitler from an overall position of strength with the British 21st Army Group virtually at the doorstep of the German homeland.

Churchill's third note admitted he was uncomfortable with a secret truce that excluded the Allies, especially the Americans. His encouragement to Roosevelt to move the U.S. toward war proved to be the decisive political stroke to defeat Germany. The Americans came to Great Britain's aid in its most desperate hour. They had been the best of allies. Starting in November, 1940, the U.S. allocated half of its annual aircraft production to the British. The U.S. had been a good friend to other allies as well, providing close to $50 billion of aid, half of which came to Great Britain and a fourth to the USSR. With U.S. help, after 1942 the Allied cause suffered no major defeat in battle.

At the Casablanca conference in January, 1943, Roosevelt and Churchill agreed that the Allies would demand unconditional surrender of Axis enemies. It would be difficult to keep the Americans out of the negotiations loop now. If the conditions of a peace agreement were ever set between Great Britain and Germany, any future surrender terms would no longer be unconditional. There was more than a hint in Hitler's truce strategy that he intended disharmony between the British and Americans as a secondary diplomatic gain.

Churchill acknowledged deep concern in his fourth note that he would be partner to a deal with a brutal dictator if a truce somehow were reached. He did not trust Hitler. He admitted immediately that he also did not trust his Soviet ally, Premier Josef Stalin. However, Hitler was the enemy, Stalin now an ally. The wartime agreement with Stalin to conduct war against Germany to the finish would have to be violated if a truce with Hitler were reached now.

If Hitler reached a separate peace with us, Churchill reasoned, it would free many of his army divisions in the West and in Italy for movement to the Eastern Front to fight an all-out battle with the Soviets. If successful there, he conceivably could plunder Soviet oil and grain and establish a defense line that could be held against massive Soviet manpower. Alternately, his Western forces could shift their focus to confront the American armies in Western Europe and Italy who would then be fighting virtually alone.

Since this peace overture obviously is a cynical move by Hitler, might it not be wise to agree to a truce for that reason, to free Hitler to take on the Soviets in a death struggle for both their armed forces? Churchill asked cynically.

As point five, Churchill asked his notepad, "And then what?" If Hitler should prevail in the East, or West, would he then turn back to his initial objective to defeat the British?

Or was German war-making capacity now so reduced that Hitler could not make a meaningful threat against the British? How ready would the British be to start over when Hitler reneged on the agreement? After snubbing their allies in an agreement, could the British then stand alone again, as in 1940 and 1941? What guarantee could Churchill obtain that would be more binding on Germany than the one Hitler gave at Munich?

Churchill noted point six. Since Hitler is asking for a truce, significant good faith action can be required of him as a condition to any agreement. Can

Churchill use the negotiations to achieve a major diplomatic victory as a price of agreement?

In a sudden surge of his combative energy, he thought of a pre-condition so immense in its implications, and so verifiable that, if accepted, the potential gain would overshadow any reservations the British people or any Ally might have. That gain would be great enough to justify keeping the talks secret from Roosevelt. He could achieve an enormous *fait accompli* that the Americans and other Allies, in the interest of humanity, could not easily reject.

The vehicle for his diplomatic victory will be the "Jewish Question!" He had been consistently outspoken against past atrocities committed by Nazis against Jews. He had been moved by each new report of atrocities to issue another public condemnation of Nazi policy. He had announced to his associates that punishment for the genocide and crimes to date against Jews and others deemed "undesirable" by Hitler could never be negotiated. Even without the truce, any negotiations on other serious end-of-war issues to be resolved between the Allies and Germany, he would insist, would be conditioned by his adamant position on punishment of those responsible.

Stopping future atrocities might now be possible. The condition for an agreement to a truce with Hitler, even agreeing to a second meeting, can be simply stated. Churchill wrote furiously now, a grand proposal being fleshed out as he composed.

> *(1) All Jews and political dissidents, meaning inmates of all nationalities, are to be released from concentration or "work" camps. Under joint British and German government protection, those inmates wishing to leave Germany will be transported to Palestine.*
>
> *(2) Germany will pay reparations at twice the value of property confiscated from all these inmates, deceased Jews, and political dissidents by the German government since the beginning of pogroms against them. These reparations will provide a settlement fund to finance shelter, food, medicine, and public amenities in Palestine.*
>
> *(3) The International Red Cross will be asked to oversee the evacuation of all camps and transportation of inmates, without hindrance from German officials. The German government will reimburse the Red Cross up to 100 million pounds sterling for that service.*

Churchill sat back, pleased that he had found the proper price he can extract for the truce Hitler is seeking.

He will ask Foreign Secretary Anthony Eden to undertake the negotiations. If Eden is agreeable, he will ask that the Jewish Question be established as a condition for another meeting and for any agreement that might be reached. That condition will be established firmly, adamantly. The release of concentration camp inmates will be the threshold to any further negotiations.

Eden's position with von Ribbentrop at the first meeting will therefore be simple. If the condition is rejected, so be it. If Hitler wants to reject the condition, the resolution of this essential human rights issue, nothing else is worth discussing. Churchill can then tell Roosevelt that he had approved Eden talking to the Germans, but that it had come to nothing.

Insisting on the condition will actually serve several purposes, Churchill thought. The most important is that Hitler will be forced to consider in good faith the price for a truce. If Hitler were to agree to the condition, and other negotiated peace terms were acceptable to both sides, the prospect for the agreement's acceptance by Parliament, the British people, and eventually the other Allies would be improved. Finally, any agreement would reveal to the world conclusively the unimaginable evil of the Nazi regime shorn of a propaganda cover for its crimes.

He will ask Secretary Eden tomorrow if he is temperamentally disposed to arrange a meeting with von Ribbentrop.

Chapter 13

London, Monday morning, October 30, 1944

Winston Churchill greeted his old friend, political ally, and fellow Cabinet member, Foreign Secretary Anthony Eden.

"Thanks for coming in, Anthony. I know you have a busy schedule. Coffee or tea?"

The two leaders settled into easy chairs and waited until the valet served them and left the room before Churchill continued.

"Knowing the serious pitfalls that could lie ahead, I have agonized over a proper response to the communication from Hitler via von Ribbentrop and Count Bernadotte. It is very important that we review our options. Germany has not respected its past agreements with us or with others."

Churchill fiddled with a cigar. "My first response Friday to the communication was that there are powerful, overwhelming reasons to reject a meeting out of hand."

"That is the same response I had, and have," Eden said. "It is a shame that we must even take the time to review a peace offer from an aggressor. Without his aggression, there would not have been destruction of the peace in the first place."

Churchill asked, "Should we, then, not agree to meet with the Germans? How would the British people answer?"

"Their immediate response likely would be what my own is," said the Foreign Secretary, "disbelief that Hitler would think we would be interested in listening to him, outraged at his cynical motives, repulsed by his past duplicity, and horrified at the atrocities which he presumably will be asking us to overlook."

Churchill sighed. "The trail of broken agreements by Germany is long and tortuous. All the major Allies know that and have felt the effects of aggression and broken promises by Germany."

"His communication forces us to consider the very real likelihood of German treachery in all of this, whether we meet with them or not," Eden said. "I doubt seriously that anything good will come of it whatever we do.

"Conscious of the past duplicity of Hitler, I must also confess to some ambivalence in my view of the whole matter. Risks have to be taken in any political action we consider. They certainly are present in a venture of this magnitude."

Eden paused and leaned forward in his chair. "I believe we share the conviction, Winston, that if there is even a small chance that a meaningful, enforceable agreement to end further bloodshed is possible, at least we are obliged to look at it."

"Anthony, that is precisely the attitude I hoped you would have. Another look at the offer is the reason for our meeting today. Since we are the ones approached, we can set conditions on the beginning and continuation of discussion, to determine how much good faith Hitler wants to exhibit."

"Before we get to conditions we should set, I see a questionable premise entered implicitly into this offer by the Germans."

Churchill nodded for Eden to continue.

"Hitler apparently believes that a piece of paper now has more meaning to us than previous pieces of paper had. I believe it was inevitable that, despite previous agreements he signed, he would have gone to war at some time, if not in Poland, somewhere else. He would have chosen some issue to use as a flash point for hostilities, regardless of any paper he signed with the victims of his aggression. He talked 'peace' to the world community at Munich and elsewhere as long as it served his war planning. Professing peace proved to be his best propaganda ploy, lulling future adversaries into believing that avoiding war with Germany was possible. I would be appalled if British acquiescence to his truce proposal led to promotion of Hitler's hostile designs in any way."

The Prime Minister responded with more passion than usual. "In the unlikely event we should reach a truce agreement, written assurances from Hitler would not be a sufficient guarantee of his compliance. Performance would be required before we would accept a truce. It would be absolutely necessary for von Ribbentrop to understand our resolve on this point, and convince Hitler of our resolve."

"Moreover, the strength of his compliance must be tested beyond your and my acceptance, Winston. In good faith, and through our own conviction, we would need to persuade our people that the peace promised is real, enforceable, and enduring. Hitler's guarantees would have to be equal in gravity to the sacrifices of the British people to date."

"That demonstration is absolutely essential. This time, Hitler's good faith can be shown only by immediate actions, not words," Churchill said.

"We need to consider also what is the minimum performance standard we will set for Hitler in our demands for a verifiable guarantee," Eden said. "If we intend to look seriously into the idea that this truce is being offered sincerely by Hitler, however difficult that is to comprehend, is it our strategy to spoil any deal on the front end by making impossible demands? Do we proceed as if the offer is real or not real?"

"My proposal, for us to consider today, may answer both your concerns," Churchill said. "I suggest we meet the Germans. I suggest raising the bar of our agreement so high initially that our questions about the sincerity of Hitler's offer and our pursuing further talks can be answered at the same time, with the same demand."

Churchill puffed generously on his cigar before continuing. "You know I have never considered the mistreatment and slaughter of Jews and other so-called 'political enemies' by the German state to be negotiable. Nor is the penalty negotiable for the perpetrators of those crimes when it comes time to settle up for this war. Those issues are not part of my proposal.

"We can demand that, under International Red Cross auspices, all Jews and others imprisoned in German concentration camps be released. Their release should be stated as a condition for a second meeting. We can set a date for compliance, monitor the progress, and resume negotiations if the Germans meet our demand. Compliance is verifiable by the project's very nature. We can test Hitler's sincerity immediately in his compliance."

"A proposal of that moment and potential effect is entirely worthy of your vision, Winston. It is grand, simple, and practical at the same time. I suppose there is not one chance in a thousand that Hitler will accept it."

"I doubt he will," Churchill replied. "However, recent intelligence that you also may have seen suggests that German deportation of Hungarian Jews may be ordered stopped by the end of 1944. There is a positive in that news. There is a remote possibility that Hitler will accept our demand.

"One chance in a hundred," Eden said dryly.

Churchill smiled. "Hitler's spurning our demand would yield the same result as our outright rejection of his truce offer."

The Prime Minister exhaled a large cloud of blue smoke. His look was far away for a moment before it settled soberly on Eden. "If Hitler somehow were to agree to our condition, and if there were no other serious obstacles to the agreement, I would consider worthwhile the trading of thousands of concentration camp inmates' lives for a truce."

Eden nodded. "I don't mean to be difficult, Winston. Hitler has made peace feelers before and we have never encouraged him. Why should we bite on this one? How is this one different?"

"I believe the present situation is different in at least three respects, Anthony. This time Hitler has requested talks—for his own purposes, no doubt—but he has requested, not demanded them. Second, we and our Allies now hold a position of military strength unmatched in the last five years. We can incorporate that strength into our bargaining position. Hitler has to know that already. And we have a trump card to play, the release of German concentration camp inmates, to ensure candor, verifiability, and enforceability in any agreement reached. Hitler does not yet know our uncompromising position on that."

Eden needed convincing on another issue. "I am troubled that our Allies, especially the Americans, are being excluded from the talks. We ought not offend the Yanks deliberately. Lend Lease by the U.S. to Great Britain in quantity and timeliness was of critical importance in 1941 when Great Britain stood alone against Germany. That was before the U.S. was even involved as a belligerent.

"A separate peace treaty by Great Britain with Germany might seriously compromise the Americans' plan to get on with the Pacific war. At a minimum, it would extend the time for the Americans to achieve resolution of their European involvement. At worst…" Eden shuddered to think of the consequences of an American-German stalemate, or of the U.S. being forced to abandon its own stated objective of Germany's unconditional surrender.

"I am not overly concerned about what present or future critics might say of our involvement in such an adventure," Eden continued. "No one in the future, or in different surroundings and circumstances, will be able to re-create the exact events, pressures, or motivations that we face now. However, would Great Britain be any more moral, or less cynical than the Germans, if we took this offer and violated our wartime agreements with the U.S. and Soviets? Could we, in good conscience, let the Soviets in the East, and the Americans in Italy and France, go it alone after all we have been through together? And how would that decision fare in the post war era? What new alliances could Great Britain call on, if it had to?"

"I concede the strength of your moral argument, Anthony. I admit my own moral justification for a separate peace is situational. Nor am I unaware that splitting the Allies politically, even if no truce is ever achieved in negotiations, could well be another devious ploy by Hitler."

Before continuing, Churchill puffed long and hard on a cigar that had grown old. "The consequences of a separate truce should not impact the arena of morality as much as the realm of trust. The hard feelings with our Allies that may result from an agreement, unfortunate as they might be, could be offset by the great moral good in freeing the inmates. If there is no agreement reached, any contention raised about our private talks with Hitler is no more serious than schoolboys keeping secrets from each other."

Eden thought there was more to it that that, and started to object. He quickly thought better of it. "I'll ponder that question, and answer, again."

Churchill smiled. "My instinct tells me that Germany is beaten, whatever the outcome of the truce offer. I devoutly hope that our country will never be subjected again to hostile confrontations. I shall do my utmost, and I am sure you shall also, Anthony, to ensure that this country never again faces an aggressor with less than adequate forces and preparedness."

"That preparedness certainly is the best answer to any potential threat," Eden said.

"You have asked weighty questions. I can think of no better devil's advocate than you to test the strength of our reasoning before entering into truce talks.

"However, I cannot help but note that the passion you display in raising these questions may have consequences for your participation in any negotiations. Can you undertake this mission? The British government cannot entrust this task to anyone but you. You alone have the experience, the skill, the understanding, and the resolve to articulate and defend this country's interests."

"Thank you. I am flattered by your continuing confidence in me, Winston. I have always put the security of this country and its empire at the top of my list of priorities. The answers you have given to my questions have been most helpful. They have assuaged my concerns at the same time they have helped prepare my responses if those issues are raised, even tangentially, by the Germans."

"Since you think the proposal is workable," Churchill said, "we ought to spend a few minutes on our meeting strategy. As desirable as it would be for us to see the end of those attacks, we should not now demand cessation of the V-2 rocket launchings by the Germans. That demand would suggest the V-2's are a priority negotiating concern for us, that they are hurting us more than they really are. In any event, if these talks fail to produce a ceasefire, we do not want to encourage the Germans to increase those attacks out of spite."

Eden knew that Churchill had already directed Field Marshal Montgomery to pursue destruction of the V-2 launch sites in The Netherlands more vigorously. The task proves to be very difficult since the Germans apparently have mastered the setting up and dismantling of launch stands and moving them to another site quickly. The sites are therefore virtually impossible to locate and attack by air in the short time a temporary launch site is used.

The British already know from information passed from the underground in France, Belgium, and The Netherlands, however, that the effective range of the V-2 is no more than 120 miles. The best counter to the threat, therefore, is to push the battle line aggressively toward Germany to put the English mainland beyond the reach of the launch sites. With the planned progress of the 21st Army Group, that serious air threat to the British homeland should be eliminated in a matter of weeks, especially since that is Churchill's stated priority to the Group, ahead of clearing the Schelde Estuary to Antwerp of German defenses.

"I suggest also that we say nothing about German U-Boat activity," Churchill continued. "I'll confess that the greatest fear I had early in the war was that this country would be starved of food and materials, that we would not be able to import those vital supplies in sufficient quantities to sustain this population and the war effort in the face of German submarine destruction of convoy ships."

"I'll confess that Luftwaffe attacks were my greatest concern," Eden said. "In my worst dreams I could see German bombers leveling all our great cities, destroying our factories, disrupting our transportation system. I feared at some point the spirit of the British people would break."

"There has never been a doubt in my mind on that score, Anthony. The British people are discouraged from time to time, of course. They are weary of war. But when I saw firsthand the spunk of the British survivors after the Luftwaffe raids on Coventry and several London districts, I was shaken to my core with pride. These staunch people, their homes gone, their factories and jobs gone, even their loved ones gone, simply refused to give up. And God bless the heroes of the Royal Air Force who would not let that destruction go unchallenged."

Both statesmen quietly mused about the wartime devastation and the British people's refusal to quit.

"In any event, we have those undersea scoundrels where we want them now," Churchill said. "They are on the verge of extinction due to our advanced submarine detection and destruction techniques. Any suggestion by the Germans that the cessation of their U-Boat attacks would be a meaningful bargaining offer should be dismissed out of hand."

Churchill asked, "Do we need to talk preliminaries or procedures?"

Eden said that he could handle both within the guidelines they had just discussed. "I will suggest a meeting date for sometime in the next three weeks and a meeting site. I will also propose procedural rules."

Eden continued. "The substantive issues have to be handled face to face. The Germans probably will guess our agenda, what we will insist on, and how they will respond, except for the grand proposal, of course."

Churchill thought again of the absolute necessity of keeping knowledge of this meeting from the rest of the Cabinet, the Allies, and especially from Roosevelt.

"Anthony, in preparing for this meeting, we have to insist on absolute secrecy in the meeting and in preparations leading up to it. We both know how powerful the German propaganda machine has been, and how shamelessly it can distort any facts. We have to ensure that no propaganda created by either party can emerge for partisan benefit.

"We would need to maintain secrecy for a while if the talks should happen to be successful, of course. We would need time to inform or negotiate with our Allies without the nuisance of conflicting public views on what has taken place. In the probable event of their failure, there would be less chance of blame-placing by Hitler. Insist to von Ribbentrop that any leak will cause us to stop the process immediately."

Eden added his own caution. "I recommend also, for similar reasons, that there should be no meeting transcript, no recordings, only a written declaration of any final agreement reached. We don't need critics parsing each word or phrase of meeting notes to detect hidden meanings that will emasculate an agreement."

"Agreed," the Prime Minister said. "I know you will keep me informed on all that happens on this matter."

They rose and began to walk to the door.

"What neutral meeting site will you propose?"

Eden pondered the question for a moment, then smiled. "A ship somewhere in the North Sea, I should think."

"How very British," Churchill chuckled as they shook hands in parting.

Chapter 14

Camp Springs Army Air Field, October 28 – November 3, 1944

After he watched Frederick board a plane early Saturday morning, Hayden called for his transportation. He was met by two officers who saluted. The leader was a first lieutenant who identified himself as "Lt. Jones" and asked, "Captain Brooke?" He had proper unit and brass insignia of an infantry officer. The other was a second lieutenant who answered to "Lt. Smith." His insignia showed he was in special services.

Lt. Jones produced an order signed by a Lt. Col. Barnett Alexander. They led Hayden outside to a jeep without another word spoken. The silence continued for the five-minute trip. Hayden did not ask questions and neither of the two officers volunteered anything. He suspected the two were having a little fun with phony names.

The jeep and passengers were checked through two control points. Armed guards patrolled a secure area with chain-link fence all around. Hayden was taken to a barracks. There was a guard at a desk at each end of the hallway, off of which individual rooms were located. The room arrangements were spartan. A bed, chest of drawers, a desk and chair, a closet, and a bathroom. There was no phone or radio.

Lt. Smith called Hayden's attention to the two uniforms hanging in the closet. They were standard army, olive drab, woolen winter uniforms. There were also a field jacket and cap. None of the clothing had unit or rank identification.

"You will need to wear one of these uniforms to all functions, sir." the lieutenant advised. "You should not wear your rank or unit insignia. We advise also that you do not identify yourself by name or unit to anyone here except those who have authority to ask. You will recognize them since they will call you by name. Someone will be along to show you to breakfast at 06:30. Good night."

Hayden was energized and did not sleep well. His nap on the plane had taken the edge off his drowsiness. He thought of his association and work with Frederick. While delighted to see his friend, he regretted that their paths might never cross again until after the war. He was most curious as to what brought Frederick here at this time. Why had he departed on a military plane with other civilians?

After breakfast, Hayden was given a thorough physical. His weight was within one pound of his enlistment weight. The doctors were satisfied that he was fit.

The afternoon brought tests that Hayden could describe only as "mental-psychological." The questioners sought to determine the intensity of his views of the war, his attitude toward face-to-face killing, and his reflection on non-democratic political systems.

He was then wired to a machine that looked a lot like a lie-detector test and was asked many of the same questions. His recorded emotional responses were no doubt going to be compared with his previous verbal answers. The optional high school battery of tests he took to identify possible career choices were the closest thing to the depth of these questions. The standard for passing the tests was not given to him, but he evidently had passed.

A series of meetings started Sunday at 11:00. A man in his early 60's who identified himself as "Colonel X, the Projects Director," provided background to the prospects seated in folding chairs in the two front rows of the dining room.

"You are a select group of twenty-six men who have passed the preliminary physical and mental tests. In the next few days we will determine if you are suited for any of several important missions we have in mind."

The "we" ostensibly scheduled to do the appraising were sitting on each side and behind the group of twenty-six. They stood out by their numbers, probably three times as many appraisers as prospects. Each wore his regular Army uniform with rank, insignia, medals and ribbons, but no name tag.

By contrast, the twenty-five other prospects Hayden saw around him were all in the same olive drab uniform as he, without any personal identification. Their identical uniforms furthered the prison-like atmosphere. These measures, Hayden thought, were an unnecessary precaution, even silly.

Colonel X seemed to read Hayden's mind. "You may think the secrecy, security, and anonymity being imposed on you are excessive. They are for everyone's protection. Since you do not know each other's names, units, past service, or possible future missions, you cannot be forced under pressure to betray others or inadvertently divulge classified information.

"These arrangements are designed also to suppress speculation among you. It is better that you do not know anything about each other, what skills each of you has, or what your family connections are. I recommend you maintain this attitude of confidentiality for as long as you are here, and beyond."

In the absence of normal military identification signs, there was de *facto* equality among the recruits, with no way to tell an officer from an enlisted man. In other circumstances, Hayden thought, he might be ordering one of these men into a confrontation that might cost the man his life.

"Some of you are from the several corps of the army. Some of you are from government civil service. Whatever your background, we feel you have the ability to perform vital service to this country.

"I need to tell you also that some danger, of varying magnitude, will be involved in each mission. We will determine your ability and willingness to take on a special mission. Some of you are likely to have missions in the Pacific Theatre, some in the European Theatre.

"You may wonder why you are being considered over intelligence agents who are already trained for special projects. That answer is easy. You have a special skill or combination of skills that regular agents do not have or cannot master quickly enough. There is a war on. We can teach you what you need to know about intelligence operations in a few weeks. It might take months or years to teach intelligence agents the combination of special skills you have acquired over your lifetime. And you are fresh faces. Some career intelligence staffers are known in some foreign countries."

Hayden felt that Colonel X's repeated references to intelligence agents confirmed the missions being contemplated were "spy business." That would be something new for him. His German language ability now seemed very important to his selection for a mission.

In the week that followed, no specific missions were identified to the men in group meetings. Indeed, it was soon evident that this was a week of further testing and screening. The prospects who gathered for breakfast on Tuesday had decreased to twenty-three. Two more were gone the next morning.

Had those who left already been selected for missions? Or had they been found deficient in some respect? If he were dismissed for any reason, Hayden believed he would feel unworthy, ashamed at not measuring up to some standard. Given the preliminary screening to bring these men here and the mental-psychological test battery that each recruit apparently had to take, he was sure that dismissal from the group would be due to attitude, not lack of skills.

Hayden had a lot of free time for resting and reading. He thought about the group meetings with the interviewers on Monday. Colonel X was not present. There were general philosophical discussions of competing political systems, updates on the progress of the war, and how intelligence operations fit in. Hardly any of the recruits had questions to ask when they were given the chance.

The pace and tone of the interviews changed for Hayden on Tuesday. The first meeting was in a small conference room with a table and six chairs around it. A lieutenant colonel, major, captain, and first lieutenant were already seated when he entered. The practice of no name tags was followed again. It was difficult to determine ages compared to Hayden's, given that faces seemed to age more rapidly in the stress of war. No one rose. They were all observing him quietly. Each had a folder in front of him. My personnel file, he thought.

The obvious leader of the group, a man Hayden came to know later as Lt. Col. Barnett Alexander, pointed to a chair and said simply, "Sit there, Captain Brooke."

The bomb dropped at the outset was unnerving to Hayden. The interviewers wanted to know about his Sarah.

"What can you tell us about your wife's meetings with a pacifist organization?" the leader asked. So they knew that Sarah had gotten active in the peace movement.

"She is Quaker," Hayden started. "She is passionate about putting her religious beliefs into action." Hayden realized that he knew very little about Sarah's doings, nothing about the peace group itself, and that these questioners knew much more about both than he did. The question also suggested that their information was quite recent.

"As an army officer, how do you feel about her association with that peace group, Stop War Now?"

"Sarah and I have had words about it. She once tried to persuade me to go to a group meeting with her, but I declined."

"Why did you decline?" The question came from the Lieutenant.

"I was concerned that someone in the group, not Sarah necessarily, might try to make an army officer the showpiece of an anti-war statement. 'Here is a combat veteran who supports the peace movement by his attendance here'...and so on."

"So you disapprove of what your wife is involved in?" the Major asked.

Hayden had never thought seriously that he might not be selected for a mission because of Sarah. He would not belittle her convictions, however, regardless of the consequences. He realized a careful, honest answer was needed.

"Well, sir, I certainly would not deny her the chance to speak out as she does, even for a cause that is not popular. I believe, as I expect everyone in this room believes, that that right is central to what this war is about for Americans. I feel a stronger distaste for those who would deny her that right than for those in the peace movement. It does create an awkward setting for an army officer, however."

All the interviewers made notes. The Lieutenant nodded almost imperceptibly. The Major looked stern, as if he might object to Hayden's answer, but asked again.

"What does she know about your possible new assignment?"

"She does not even know I have a new assignment, only that I am changing location."

"What does she suspect?"

"I don't know. I have no way of knowing. She's very bright. Any attempt I might make to learn about her reaction to my changing location probably would reveal more to her than from her. The questions I would ask might allow her to pick up more than she should know, or raise suspicions in her mind."

"Would your attitude be affected by any resistance she might have to your undertaking a killing project?"

"No, sir. She knows I am in the army, that the war continues, and that soldiers try to kill the enemy. Her beliefs oppose killing. That difference in our beliefs has been the source of disagreement—sometimes strong disagreement—between us. So my answer is no. My attitude would not be affected."

"We understand that you have discussed divorce." The Lieutenant Colonel made the observation somewhat casually.

Hayden was shocked to learn that they knew. A phone tap? Agents snooping around back in Kansas? Talking to whom? George Spurges? Sarah herself?

"I believe she despaired at one time of our living a normal life together because of my service commitment. I suppose divorce is something she might still consider."

"Can her silence be relied on under the circumstances?

"I am confident she knows so little of my army routine that there is nothing she could say with authority that would mean anything to a questioner, even assuming her natural discretion about personal matters were to change."

The interviewers' absence of questions on specific information from their investigation of Sarah provided Hayden some assurance that she had not said anything yet to put her, and by association, him, at risk of censure.

"What about her political beliefs generally?" It was the Major again.

Hayden forced himself not to smile as he framed his answer.

"I can state unequivocally that she has never stated to me a hint of a desire or intent to overthrow the government of this country."

Hayden saw that the thought seemed to amuse the Lieutenant Colonel, who changed the direction of the questioning abruptly.

"Are you aware that Capt. Jerry Connelios may be homosexual?"

"I suspect as much." Hayden felt uncomfortable, even somewhat disloyal to Jerry in admitting his suspicion. He was also annoyed at the interviewers for asking. He had decided at the beginning of the week to tell the truth and not evade tough questions. But if these men had a basis for believing what they did about Jerry, they did not need Hayden's affirmation of their belief. They had already demonstrated by their knowledge of his current standing with Sarah that they had the power and means to investigate people fully.

"How long have you suspected that?

"I was aware for some time that Capt. Connelios never talked about a wife or sweetheart the way most soldiers do. I never had a conscious suspicion about his orientation until quite recently, however."

"How would his being formally charged with 'conduct unbecoming an officer' affect you?"

"I would regret his being charged. He fought hard and led well and bravely in the four campaigns we experienced together. It would be a shame to see his fine career ruined."

"Did he ever make an advance toward you?"

"No, sir."

Hayden thought he should try to warn Jerry. Letting him know what Army Intelligence knows might cause him to be more discreet. Perhaps he could call him if he ever got off a military installation, away from the pervasive monitoring.

After the Tuesday meeting, Hayden and the interviewers met in think-tank settings and discussed wartime experiences. He had to consciously fight back his growing vexation with them over the questions they raised about Sarah and Jerry. He wanted to know how bravely these men had responded to their own calls to duty, their confrontations with danger and, most of all, how they defended their beliefs under pointed challenge.

Instead, the group talked about the mental toughness required to handle a clandestine mission. Hayden knew his readiness was being assessed constantly in the comments he made. After one long discussion, the Lieutenant Colonel surprised him again with a sudden and potentially revealing question.

"Captain, assume for the moment that your mission is to kill a high ranking German military leader with a special sniper rifle. This is not a combat setting, you understand. It amounts to stalking a man, and shooting to kill that man in cold blood. Can you do that?"

Hayden felt the stares at him more than he saw them. He was sure this question was not a topic for roundtable discussion. It was directed at him, for him alone to answer. Now. He suppressed a quickly growing sense of excitement at the first open mention of the possible purpose of a mission for him. He kept as much matter-of-factness in his voice as he could in his answer.

"I would treat it like any combat killing, a destruction of the enemy." None of the interviewers made notes.

In the guise of Colonel X, Everett Giles returned to the compound Friday afternoon. Giles wanted to know about personnel available for all the missions SIP was planning. The mission being overseen by Lt. Col. Alexander for an assassination attempt on Hitler was SIP's highest priority, however. Some of the information he would convey to the team of handlers as he sought its recommendation was forced by the weighty project.

In his opening comments to the team members on Monday, Giles implied that SIP had the approval of higher-ups to conduct this mission. The team knew from Giles' reputation that there weren't many command layers higher than his, only General Marshall and the President. The implication of approval of the mission by the highest national leaders had been a heavy consideration in their deliberations the past week. Even though their team already had done preliminary planning for the attempt on Hitler, the announcement to them of its imminence had a chilling effect on them.

Giles opened the session by stressing the critical planning constraint. "This operation will be a solo American effort. That decision is politically based. The British are inclined to allow Hitler some conditions for surrender. The U.S. has been set on Hitler's unconditional surrender all along. The elimination of Hitler will settle the matter decisively," Giles announced, "and should end the European war forthwith."

"The key ingredient, the *sine qua non* of this operation, is the man chosen to carry it out. I know the responsibility for choosing the right man to execute the plan has weighed heavily on you this past week. I too am humbled by the magnitude of this personnel decision. Not more than ten people know of the plan, and only a very few more will be let into the intelligence loop. Now is the time to make the critical screening decision.

"Time is short to process a candidate. In addition to his basic skills as a marksman, a paratrooper, and one who speaks German, the man chosen must have the capacity to operate alone and the psychological make-up to carry out a very difficult killing mission."

Giles nodded to Lt. Col. Alexander. Having chosen the team leader, he will rely on his and his selected team's judgment.

Alexander reviewed the procedure of assigning a screening task to each member of the team. Army Captain Frank Tobias reviewed the skills components required against those possessed by the six candidates.

"All six of the final candidates are military men whose records designate them as marksmen with a rifle. All speak German, some better than others. All have at least one jump. Only two have combat jumps. Only one has as many as three.

"My recommendation comes down to two people, an officer and a non-commissioned officer. One candidate is head and shoulders above the other on skills.

"I recommend Capt. Hayden Brooke. In addition to his combat jumps and many training jumps, he has superior weapons knowledge and proficiency with both rifle and pistol.

"He has been toughened by repeated combat situations for killing. He is highly trained in adjunct military skills, including map and compass reading for in-the-field orientation. He speaks German well, learned it mostly in conversations with a friend, and handles it well enough to be a prisoner-of-war interrogator.

"Sgt. Damon Anthony is my second choice on skills. He is qualified in the same respects as Capt. Brooke except for combat experience and known killing of an enemy. The Sergeant has one combat jump."

"The second team member asked to respond, Army Air Corps First Lieutenant Keith Raymond, a psychologist, emphasized the mental preparation and toughness required for the mission.

"The use of pertinent skills here is automatic once learned. You can jump with confidence based on past jump experiences. You can shoot a rifle well without even thinking about it because you have done it so often in the past. I'm less sure about German language skill as a second language.

"The ability to undertake a dangerous mission alone, surrounded by people you cannot trust or who are threatening, requires mostly a psychological disposition that is much less automatic. In some sense, you cannot be trained adequately for it. The best guide to that ability is the mental toughness found in having done similar things in the past.

"I would question the resourcefulness of several of the candidates since they have not operated in a hostile environment. We do have a man with proven ability to operate behind enemy lines. Captain Brooke has a great advantage over the other candidates there. He has, in my judgment, developed psychological fitness for this serious task by operating in very hostile environments. He has killed, virtually face-to-face, with a weapon aimed at people he intended to kill. He knew he had killed them.

"I believe Captain Brooke's attitude and commitment have been hardened as a paratrooper and leader in combat. I believe he is less likely to panic in an unexpected development. On a mission this perilous, I would venture that the unexpected might be commonplace."

The third team member, Major Bill Driver, an army engineer, discussed the negatives of each candidate and concluded, "I do not find a lack of willingness to undertake a dangerous mission in any of the six candidates. I stress the importance of combat experience in our recommendation. There are varying levels of experience in these six men.

"I do not disagree with the recommendation of Captain Brooke. Since he is the choice of Capt. Tobias and Lt. Raymond for the good reasons they have given, let me comment only on his personal situation. The issue of his wife's peace group involvement and their possible divorce would not affect his judgment, I believe. If anything, their differences suggest to me a level of imperviousness by him to her feelings. Nor do I see any problem in his relationship with Capt. Connelios. In short, I find in his personal situation no liabilities or risk to his carrying out this mission."

Lt. Col. Alexander summarized in stating his own preference. "I recommend Capt. Brooke also. I like his toughness. His record shows that he focuses on the mission at hand. He is adaptable to unforeseen circumstances.

"Our scrutiny of these men and their records this past week confirms an overall high quality of personnel. I believe also that any one of them could do the job well. However, I concur that Capt. Brooke is the best of the six for this mission."

Everett Giles seemed relieved that a consensus had emerged the first time the question went around the table. He asked, "Does anyone think we could do better than Capt. Brooke if we were to continue the search for another month or two?"

Lt. Col. Alexander answered quickly. "The sweep of prospects within the Army and civil service has yielded these six candidates with the highest overall ratings on paper. The preliminary screeners did their job well. I believe that another sweep would not find any candidates better suited to the task than those we have evaluated this week."

Colonel Giles nodded. He soberly stated his decision. "Here's what we'll do. Two of this team will accompany Capt. Brooke to New York and start two weeks of special winter training with him at Pine Camp. Then we'll give him a final field test on skills and resourcefulness under pressure. If he holds up under that test, he's our man.

"The other two team members will fly with Sgt. Anthony on a separate flight and work him through the same routine. All four of you should schedule time with each man over the next two weeks, of course.

"Hold off on Sgt. Anthony's final field test until we see how Capt. Brooke fares. If Brooke fails in a major respect, put Anthony through the same field test. If you should then feel that neither man measures up in some significant way, we'll re-think."

Chapter 15

Pine Camp, New York, Weeks of November 6 & 13, 1944

On Hayden's arrival at Pine Camp, Lt. Col. Alexander and his team met with him in the team leader's temporary office. It was immediately obvious to Hayden that the atmosphere had changed from Camp Springs.

The spacious and well appointed office was that of the deputy base commander who was on leave. The office easily accommodated five leather easy chairs drawn in a semi-circle around the fireplace. The room was paneled, carpeted, and lit with lamps.

The team members' demeanor had changed markedly. Instead of the hard, questioning, unfriendly stares that met Hayden at every meeting during the past week, the team members now stood as they introduced themselves. Hayden realized that their role had changed from examiners to preparers.

Lt. Col. Alexander spoke for the team. He had the look and demeanor of a showman today, comfortable in the spotlight.

"Captain, we are most pleased that a man of your abilities has come forward for a special mission. We can now put names on the interviewers. I'm Col. Alexander. Here is Major Bill Driver...Capt. Frank Tobias...Lt. Keith Raymond."

Major Driver extended his hand and shook Hayden's warmly. "You have given excellent service throughout your career, Captain. I'm proud to be at your side."

"Thank you, Major," Hayden smiled, though he wasn't entirely sure what the thirty-five year old slim, hawk-faced engineer meant by his compliment.

Captain Tobias seemed to be more Hayden's kind of man. He was maybe a year or two older than Hayden, grim, speaking little, smiling less. He seemed to say more with his steel-gray eyes. To Hayden he appeared hardened, probably by combat experience. His ribbons attested to several big campaigns. "Welcome aboard," Tobias said simply.

Lieutenant Raymond struck Hayden as the most outgoing of the team. Although he was the junior member of the team by rank, he was perhaps as old as Alexander, thirty-eight to forty, probably a draftee, not an army career man. Hayden recalled that psychologist Raymond asked a lot of questions in last week's testing. He gave the impression of a know-it-all, even though his observations often seemed shallow.

"I look forward to working with you," the Lieutenant said smiling. Hayden thought the "working with you" connoted something more than offering support. It sounded too much like Hayden was in desperate need of the Lieutenant's fatherly counsel.

"Thank you," Hayden said, and forced a smile.

They were all seated, Hayden on one of the end chairs farthest from the door. Lt. Col. Alexander sat in the middle chair.

Alexander spoke first after coffee was served. "We hope the questions last week were not too taxing?"

"I thought for the most part they were proper qualifying questions." Hayden would not relate his uncharitable feelings on the team's questions about Sarah and Jerry.

"The purpose of this meeting," Alexander went on, "is to inform you of your training sessions over the next two weeks. With this further instruction, you should be amply prepared to carry out the mission we have in mind.

"We will address three areas primarily. The first is the special weapon that you will use. Your orientation to that rifle and practice firings will take several days.

"Second, we believe a refresher course in the German language is in order. That instruction will be interspersed with your outdoor training. We have arranged for a college language instructor to come in to take you through that short course.

"Third, mixed in with several days of winter training, there will be special classes. We will conduct them like the round table discussions last week. The four of us and some experts called in will provide you some important guides to your operation as an agent behind enemy lines.

"I know you have questions. This team will answer all of them in due course.

For now, let's just relax and get to know each other informally with some food and drink."

Early on Monday, Hayden was introduced to the sniper rifle especially designed for this mission. It was a long range, semi-automatic rifle, .50 caliber, or capable of firing a bullet one-half inch in diameter. A scope magnificent in its clarity was fitted to the rifle. The craftsmanship was superb throughout. An armorer who helped develop the rifle told Hayden that the .50 caliber bullet had five or six times the power on impact as the standard U.S. Army M1 rifle. It was the finest killing weapon Hayden had ever seen.

The most remarkable feature was the barrel. It was cut in half, the end pieces threaded, with the pieces precisely machined for a perfectly tight fit when screwed into place. A locking device issued a barely audible click to inform the shooter that the barrel was properly assembled. The gas port to operate the bolt, ejection, and chambering mechanism was set toward the muzzle end of the first section attached to the breech. The aluminum stock could be telescoped to the size of the shooter's arm and then locked in place. It contained a buffer against its powerful recoil. The whole stock could be folded back against the first section of the weapon.

The total weight of the weapon without the ten-round side-fed clip was nine pounds. With the barrel unassembled and the stock in the folded position, the maximum length of any of the weapon's pieces was twenty inches. It would fit easily and unobtrusively into a German soldier's standard overnight bag, Capt. Tobias noted.

Lt. Col. Alexander later told Hayden that the practice firings would use "exploding bullets." The ammunition would also be tracer coated to allow him to track and correct the trajectory. Hayden would test the sighting and familiarize with the weapon under cold weather conditions. All the team members would observe his test firings.

The first practice firing was from great distances, starting at 1200 and working down to 1000 and 800 yards. The armorer cautioned him before they left for the firing range. "The round obviously will fade with gravity. But with the length of the casing and heavy powder load, the fade will not be as much as you anticipate, even at distances of over a mile. Observe the flight of your tracer shots and adjust. Don't aim too high. You can correct easier for a shot that is too short than one that is too long. You'll have trouble holding the rifle down during recoil, so you'll have to re-target after each shot."

After test firing several tracer rounds to set the rifle's windage and elevation adjustments, Hayden put five of the remaining seven rounds into the human-form plywood target at 1200 yards, nine of ten at 1000 yards with further adjustments, and all ten of the third clip at 800 yards.

The shooting exhibition Hayden put on for the team seemed to impress them all. They applauded politely when the target manager called the results to the team. Hayden felt like the first contestant in a shooting competition.

"This scope is a dream, Colonel," Hayden said to Barnett Alexander and Major Driver back at the team's viewing area.

"Any problems?" the Colonel asked.

"It takes some effort to settle it down again after each firing. Re-targeting takes a bit longer than I like."

"We had you on the stop watch at a fraction over twenty-six seconds getting off the last ten rounds."

"I wonder if we can find a three- or four-foot long rubber or elastic cord to tie it down to a tree or log. It should stay on line better that way and shorten the time for re-targeting after each recoil."

"Where would you fasten it?"

"Right here, I think, just in front of the scope mounting. The cord should be thin enough to pass between the scope and the barrel."

"See to it, will you, Major?" Alexander asked Driver.

"Also," Hayden continued, "we have no assurance that our real target will be standing still for a first or following shot. Will it be possible to rig a moving target for a later practice?"

Alexander was pleased, if not a little dubious. "Have you ever led a moving target at half a mile or so?"

"No, sir, but I think I can learn it."

Hayden felt comfortable in the outdoors training. He made three practice jumps in the two weeks. Two were jumps only, one in the day, the other at night, into a snow-covered clearing in the nearby forest. After landing the third jump early one morning, he hiked two miles to the firing range for a second round of practice firing on the moving target Col. Alexander had rigged. The tie-down elastic cord worked well to steady his aim as well as control the dislocation of the rifle from the target line after each shot.

His German lessons were with an elderly lady with the unlikely married name of Emma Sterling Silver. She taught German all her career at a nearby college. Her step was uncertain at her advanced age. She did several shuffle steps to maintain her balance whenever she changed direction. Her mind was still very sharp, however.

Professor Silver probed the weaknesses she detected in Hayden's speech patterns and worked with him intensely on those. She permitted no English during the day-long classes. Hayden was thoroughly brushed up on conversational German.

One of the most interesting discussions for Hayden occurred one evening in the second week of training when he and the team gathered for their twice-a-week evening meal together. Hayden was comfortable enough with the team members by then to ask several tactical questi0ons. "Why did the team decide on a solo shooter for this mission? Why was a strafing or bombing aircraft not used? Why couldn't an agent already in Germany be used?"

The questions went beyond Hayden's desire to know reasons for the team not using obvious alternatives to a single paratrooper. He hoped to draw them out on other matters of interest, especially the identity of the target.

The team members did not appear to be put off by the questions, although several glanced at each other before Major Driver spoke. "We may believe a target is located in a certain building or area on the day of the shoot. However, we do not know if he will be visible at an exact time. An attacking plane cannot lie in wait in the air for long without itself being detected, attacked, and destroyed. A team or person can lie in wait for a longer time, although not indefinitely, of course, without nearly as much risk of exposure."

The other team members deferred to Lt. Col. Alexander for the answer to the rather sensitive question of using an agent already inside Germany.

"The unfortunate truth, Captain, is that Allied intelligence services lately have been spending much of their time and resources validating their agents and the intelligence they provide. At the end of the validation process they are often still uncertain about what they have, given German deception, possibly turned agents, and inconsistent reports among agents in the field. Allied intelligence operates in a rather murky area here. Assigning any one of our inside agents to such a mission could be tantamount to informing the target himself and preclude a second, outside attempt."

Captain Tobias added, "An attack overland, from the outside, also has its limitations, of course. It is complicated by the greater vulnerability to mistakes of the agent operating in new and unknown territory, the problem of his getting through security checkpoints, and the risk of his being detected due to unfamiliarity with people and events in an enemy country."

"The same is true for a team effort, however that team is introduced into Germany," said Lt. Col. Alexander. "Logistics and cover are greater problems than for a solo job. Complications arise exponentially with an increase in team numbers. After a jump, for example, the travel and cover-maintaining problems are so great for a team that the SIP director scratched that option early on."

Hayden nodded his understanding. So the SIP director was that higher up who ordered this plan originally? It was reasonable to conclude that Colonel X had a hand in it, given his introductory overview to the recruits at Camp Springs and his presence there at the end of last week. He understood that the likelihood of higher echelons getting involved in planning a routine operation inside Germany was small. The intended target had to be very important to involve such high level planning and oversight.

The room was quiet while Hayden and the team worked on their steaks and baked potatoes. Lt. Raymond suddenly addressed Hayden.

"I think I know the answer, but I'll ask it anyway. What do you think is the advantage of a paratrooper undertaking a secret shooting mission compared to some other specialist?"

Hayden reflected for a moment, then explained the paratrooper's unique role as he had many times to trainees or replacements to his units. "I had the opportunity with other 82nd Division officers to interview two groups of surviving defenders against an airborne attack. In the first group were Belgian resistors to the small-unit German paratroop landing on the Belgian Fort Eban Emael in 1940. The second group was the British garrison on Crete in 1941 against the much more sizable German paratrooper attack that spearheaded the invasion of that island.

"The main problem for all those defenders was the same. It was an enemy arriving behind battle lines that seemed secure just hours or minutes before.

"In the confusion and hesitation among defenders, the paratroop aggressors can secure a winning advantage. If they survive the jump without serious injury, with their weaponry intact, and can find cover against counterattack against them, the odds for success swing in their favor.

"To be sure, there is a difference between a sizable unit of jumpers attacking in combat and a single trooper on a secret mission. But the result can be the same. Here's why. Suppose you are a defender, and someone drops behind you in your perimeter, let's say in darkness. What do you do? How do you react? Every movement out there is a potential threat to you. Your eyes strain to identify who it is. It could be a friendly. If you shoot, you could kill one of your own. More importantly, you would give away your position. You don't know how many attackers there are around you, in front of you, behind you. You may choose, therefore, not to stick your neck out. You may hesitate. In your hesitation, the aggressor has won half the encounter already.

"I believe those unknowns facing a defender are a distinct advantage in any paratrooper's mission. If a paratrooper, as landed infantryman, moves stealthily, offensively, conscious of danger, with the mission uppermost in his mind, he will succeed."

"That sounds like the paratrooper's combat creed!" smiled Col. Alexander.

"It may be a bit long for a slogan. But I have learned to live with it."

"You probably have deduced this already from several of our conversations, Captain," said Major Driver. "The plan is to drop you 'blind.' There will be no reception committee of underground operatives to take and shield you before and after your mission. Although the condition will change slowly as Allied armies move toward Germany, the same observation about our agents inside Germany that Col. Alexander made earlier applies here as well. The few Allied agents operating in Germany are no longer especially useful or reliable. Asking them for help in a mission invites more risk factors into the equation than we want to deal with."

"Gentlemen, I don't want to rush the ending of this pleasant and informative evening. I have some correspondence and calls to attend to, so I'll have to excuse myself." Alexander's rising to leave was the signal for all to make their departure.

In the round of hand-shaking that marked their exits from the dining room, Hayden made it a point to single out Lt. Raymond and put closure on the Lieutenant's earlier question. "I do believe the best schooling for operating behind enemy lines in combat is the actual experience of doing so," he said, conspicuously scanning the Lieutenant's ribbons for a hint of the psychologist's combat experience. There was none.

"*Touche*'," Raymond smiled at Hayden's successful put down.

In the remaining days of his training, the team members began to stress to Hayden the complications that could arise in his operation as a secret agent. They provided the same instruction that any American agent going behind enemy lines was given.

A veteran intelligence agent sent to Pine Camp instructed Hayden and the team on protecting an agent's cover. His main point was comforting to Hayden. "The best cover for an agent inside enemy-occupied territory is his own profession or trade. Your cover as a soldier is the best possible since you already have the mannerisms and reactions of a soldier."

"Continue to practice your cover story," Major Driver advised. "Believe in it. Insist on it in the face of any confrontation with hostiles."

Lt. Col. Alexander in another session offered Hayden some practical guides to protecting his cover. "As you know, the plan is for you to jump wearing the uniform of a German infantry captain. You may need to change uniforms and ID's regularly to maintain your cover and shake off those who might be tailing you. I recommend you change even when you do not suspect their agents are getting close. Don't be squeamish about getting rid of soldiers you contact for a uniform.

"There is merit in killing those soldiers. Don't leave anyone alive who can make life difficult for you. The more critical an enemy contact is for your cover, as in your obtaining a uniform while adapting to a new location or circumstance, the more important it is to eliminate that contact."

Capt. Tobias introduced a new perspective. "You will need to be ready to kill, of course, to protect yourself and the mission. However, your manner in normal, non-confrontational activities is also critical. Once in a German officer's uniform, don't slink or cower. Don't run or attempt to hide if you see a problem developing. You are there as a German soldier, a German officer. A German officer has an air about him. Don't act for a second like you don't belong there. Don't be too arrogant in your manner. But don't let on in any way that you are not who you are professing to be with your ID."

Lt. Raymond was equally grim in his advice. "You will be carrying a distinctive assassination weapon. If you are discovered carrying it, you will have a dicey situation on your hands. You may have to be ruthless. If you are trapped and exposed, you will have to use your wits or physical assault on your challengers to escape. Reciting a cover story in that situation would probably be futile."

Hayden grew increasingly restless and mildly irritated at the obvious, often redundant advice he was getting. Some of the team members needed to demonstrate they were contributing to his preparation, he thought. They may have been reciting bits of wisdom from manuals they had read or from personal contacts. He doubted any of them had operated behind enemy lines or participated in the kind of intelligence work they were planning for him.

Constant alertness to danger lurking in enemy territory was essential, of course. Common sense in good measure was even more critical to survival, he thought.

Hayden realized also that the killing he was being trained for and expected to do was of a different nature from the combat killing he had done. The practical killing advice being given by the team members invited unknowns that he and they could not yet imagine or plan for. His vision of the enemy to be eliminated was still the hostile, grey-clad warrior charging his position, bent on killing him and his comrades in arms. It was difficult now to visualize any other killing situation or enemy.

However, he did anticipate the unspoken issue the Lt. Raymond seemed to be broaching in his comment about being exposed, and the futility of his cover story if he were. He thought it was entirely proper to settle that serious discussion before it started.

"If my cover somehow is blown, or if I am confronted seriously, I will fight my way out or engage in what my comrades call a 'fighting suicide.' I'll take as many of the enemy with me as I can if it looks like I'll be killed. No poison capsule for me," Hayden said.

The absolute silence for at least a minute told Hayden he had divined correctly the intended direction of the Lieutenant's discussion.

Chapter 16

Off the southwest coast of Sweden, Friday, November 17, 1944

Bernadotte: "The designated hour of 10:00 for this meeting having arrived, let us begin the proceedings."

Ribbentrop: "Excuse me, Excellency."

Bernadotte: "Yes, Minister?"

Ribbentrop: "I am agreeable to conducting our discussions in English, although I recognize that the British Foreign Secretary has an interpreter available. My aides are also conversant in English."

Bernadotte: "Thank you for your offer, Minister. Secretary Eden?"

Eden: "That is gracious of you, Minister. We should not have to use our valuable time awaiting translations. The German I learned at Oxford faded rapidly since I did not later use it often enough. Please advise if we should slow down at any time."

Ribbentrop: "That should not be necessary, Secretary."

The crispness of von Ribbentrop's response was not confirmed in his demeanor or facial expression. It was simply a statement of language procedure they need not worry about.

Bernadotte: "Good. Let me first commend you and your governments for the courage to discuss peace. The cause of peace is always worth pursuing. Despite hardships, tragedies, and hostilities, there is this ray of light. We all recognize that there are past and present circumstances that cannot be changed. The future can be. I am at your service to assist you in any way that I can to make it more peaceful.

"I assure you that I have abided fully by your directions in setting up this meeting and facility," motioning to the luxurious yacht with a wave of his hand, "in the strictest secrecy. A minimum number of people know of this meeting at all...the crew of this vessel, of course, and the party who graciously lent it for our purposes.

"No one but I, outside of the two parties here and their heads of government, knows the reason for this meeting, however. The questions of others, I trust, can be deflected with a 'no comment.'

"I appreciate also the contributions by both governments to the Swedish Red Cross. The funds will be put to good use," he smiled.

Count Folke Bernadotte was effectively the head of the Swedish Red Cross although his 83-year old paternal uncle, Prince Carl, was nominally its head. Sweden was officially neutral in the war, and Bernadotte preserved neutrality in his speech and actions. He was internationally respected. He had helped organize the sending of thousands of food parcels to Jewish inmates of concentration camps beginning in 1943.

Eden: "We in turn thank your Excellency for the superb manner in which you have handled the preparation for this meeting. The choice of this location has allowed for accessibility as well as privacy. The British government is most grateful."

Ribbentrop: "The German government seconds the comments of the esteemed representative of the British government. The meeting preparations have been handled in a most expeditious and professional manner. Thank you."

Both Bernadotte and Eden nodded their thanks.

Bernadotte: "The introduction of parties will be somewhat limited. As per the request of the British representatives, their names will not be announced.

"They are identified as follows. To Mr. Eden's left is his military aide. To his immediate right is his political aide, and beyond him is his interpreter.

"I understand that the German representatives will announce their names..."

Ribbentrop: "Excuse me, Excellency. We will follow the same policy. My military aide is to my right. My political aide and economic aide are here to my left. Thank you."

Bernadotte: "Very well."

Eden had given each of his government service aides the option to have his name revealed or not. Each chose secrecy. Each announced forthrightly that he would prefer to avoid liability for any negative fallout associated with the meeting.

Eden saw now that the German aides may have wished to have their names announced. Could they be thinking that an open declaration might ensure their favorable treatment by the Allies later if recriminations were in order for any war-related reason? It was instructive to him that von Ribbentrop cancelled that option quickly, without conferring with them. It seemed von Ribbentrop was forcing his aides' acquiescence to a "sink or swim together" policy.

Bernadotte: "The pre-meeting agreement is that a proposal, response, and follow-up discussion on any proposal may be presented for no longer than five minutes each, for a total of fifteen minutes devoted to each proposal.

"To each formal proposal, the other party is asked to indicate a response that it agrees, makes no statement of agreement or rejection, or disagrees with/ rejects a proposal.

Eden had made this procedural proposal. Having this information should assist both parties to identify common areas of concern that might require lesser or greater negotiation effort in the future. It should also indicate the grounds for compromise or trade-off.

Bernadotte continued. "In a Second Category, there may be issues offered for discussion without a proposal being made, then discussed in a 'give and take' format, with total time of fifteen minutes allowed for that discussion.

"As the formal respondent to the offer of negotiations, the British representative has the option of choosing the first topic. Secretary Eden."

Eden: "Thank you. We would like to start with a Second Category issue. My government is most concerned about proof of compliance with any agreement that might be reached between our governments."

Ribbentrop: "Please continue."

Eden: "We have been disappointed at several actions whereby the German government ignored agreements between our countries.

"I choose as a prime example the 1935 Naval Treaty between our two countries. My government entered into the agreement in good faith, at some hazard to its alliances. It took some risk to accommodate what it thought were the legitimate concerns of the German government arising out of the Versailles Treaty."

Eden knew the sensitive issue of the Versailles Treaty had to come to the table sooner or later. Better sooner, he thought.

Ribbentrop: "Germany's claims indeed were quite legitimate. When the Allies violated the terms of the Versailles Treaty, Germany felt it was no longer bound by that agreement or any other pertaining to disarmament."

Eden was not sure what Treaty violations von Ribbentrop was accusing the

Allies of committing. He would not be side-tracked into thrashing through an argument that likely would end up going nowhere, however.

Eden: "The British government notes that the 1935 Naval Agreement was not part of, nor assumed in the substance of the Versailles Treaty. Its substance was, in fact, a departure from the overall tenor of the 1919 Treaty. It was between our two countries only.

"Our concern for fairness led us to believe that we could reduce or even eliminate one of the grievances Germany had with the Treaty. We frankly did not believe it appropriate or desirable for Germany to be relegated to second or third class military status." Eden paused for a moment to emphasize his conclusion.

"With our bilateral agreement, we believed Germany could feel more secure in its defensive posture.

"Again, the main concern of the British government is with verification of any agreement reached. The example of the German government's departure from the provisions of the 1935 Naval Treaty is not a comforting precedent for any new agreement our governments might reach. The existence of hostilities now makes verification even more difficult."

Ribbentrop: "With due respect for your views, Secretary, the 1935 agreement did not provide adequate relaxation or removal of restrictions on German military preparation…"

Von Ribbentrop stopped abruptly and leaned to listen attentively to his political aide who whispered and gestured in a rather animated fashion.

"Your objection is understood," von Ribbentrop said. Eden was not going to let the issue lapse entirely.

Eden: "Thank you. The British government will welcome any good faith demonstration of compliance by the German government, assurances that any new agreement will be binding on both parties and permanent."

Ribbentrop: "We understand, certainly."

Bernadotte: "Minister von Ribbentrop. A proposal?"

Ribbentrop: "The sign of good faith the German government asks of Great Britain is the immediate cessation of bombing attacks on German cities, homeland, and German-occupied territories."

Eden waited for further commentary the German Minister might wish to add. Hearing none, he responded.

Eden: "A British agreement to a ban on bombing of German territory would, of course, apply only to British forces, specifically its Bomber Command. And, while German forces are outside Germany proper, air attacks there would cease only with the signing of an agreement. The British government makes no statement of agreement or rejection now on the proposal. It will take the proposal under study, pending other understandings reached in these discussions."

Bernadotte: "Secretary Eden, a proposal?"

Eden: "The British government notes that the hundreds of thousands of inmates in German 'work camps' are designated 'enemies of the state' in name only, not in fact."

Ribbentrop: "The British and their Allies also incarcerate political enemies," snapped the Foreign Minister.

Eden ignored the feeble comparison.

Eden: "Are all German work camp inmates, without exception, 'enemies of the state'? Housewives? Children?

"Have trials been conducted for every person charged with being a political enemy? What evidence was admitted and weighed to determine the guilt or innocence of each person charged? Where is the trial testimony for each?

Von Ribbentrop was discomfited.

Ribbentrop: "Processing paperwork is always slow for defendants in a court of law…"

Eden: "Minister, is there any record or documentation you can provide revealing that any Jew charged and incarcerated was eventually found innocent of the charge of being an 'enemy of the state'? Just one?"

Ribbentrop: "I shall look into that," indicating to one of his aides to make a note as he spoke.

Eden: "There is no greater sign of good faith and sincerity that the German government can offer to further these proceedings than to free all the inmates of all the work camps.

"The British government sets that sign as a pre-condition to further meetings for negotiations between our governments. Let there be no doubt as to the resolve of the British government on this matter."

Von Ribbentrop was obviously unsettled at the prospect that further negotiations would stall over an issue that his superior had predicted would not be taken seriously by anyone at the table. He stared for several seconds into the distance at a spot above Eden's head, then met Eden's eyes.

Ribbentrop: "Secretary, the invitation extended by the German government to this meeting made it clear that the conversations between the British and German representatives were intended for military matters as they affect the people of both nations.

"The German government submits that the residents of work camps are not British prisoners of war. As this matter is one of internal state governance, it is beyond the purview of this discussion..."

Eden: "Excuse me, Minister. The non-combatant status of those inmates is all the more reason for including...no, for making it the centerpiece of these discussions. The British government notes also that there is no military advantage lost by Germany in agreeing to the release of these inmates.

"This sign of good faith demanded by the British government is not a selfish political ploy. My government must register the concern that the world must feel for the fundamental rights of all human beings. We respectfully but emphatically insist that the German government's release of work camp inmates is the pre-condition to another meeting."

Ribbentrop: "And what does the British government propose to do with these so-called inmates? Let them run loose to disrupt the orderliness of German civilian and military processes?"

Eden ignored the sarcasm in von Ribbentrop's manner.

Eden: "Not at all, Minister. Since their release would meet the pre-condition set by the British government, it would do all in its power to ensure that their movement out of Germany would be timely and efficient. It would join in asking the International Red Cross to administer the evacuation. It would persuade its Allies to suspend all military operations other than purely defensive measures during their departure. It would ask the German government to do the same."

Eden noted that Count Bernadotte was following every word closely, ignoring the clock for timing of proposals and responses. One of the German aides was shaking his head during Eden's comments.

Ribbentrop: "I am curious, Secretary. Where does the British government plan to move these inmates? What will it cost? Who will pay the expenses?"

Eden: "As a formal proposal, the British government asks the German government to demonstrate these signs of good faith:

> *(1) Admit the International Red Cross to every work camp with no hindrance or intimidation by German officials. The Red Cross will be asked to provide food, clothing and medical care for all inmates.*
>
> *(2) Allow these inmates to be moved by the Red Cross to Palestine under the joint protection of Allied and Axis powers. Once in Palestine, their welfare will be administered by the Red Cross.*
>
> *(3) Stop immediately both (a) the deportation of foreign nationals from German-occupied territories outside Germany to German work camps and (b)*

the movement of German nationals inside Germany to the camps.

(4) Pay twice the value of their business and personal property appropriated since 1933 to surviving inmates, up to one billion pounds sterling."

Von Ribbentrop smiled broadly, joining in the laughter of his aides.

Ribbentrop: "That is a preposterous proposal, Secretary."

Eden fixed the German Foreign Minister with a steely gaze.

Eden: "That is the pre-condition set by the British government. It will not be represented further at this meeting or attend any other meeting unless the condition is agreed to and verification started."

The Germans here and at home had to face the reality of the horror they had visited on millions by their inhumanity and aggression, Eden thought. The stand Great Britain is taking is on the high moral ground.

Von Ribbentrop's smile was now rueful. After some meaningless page turning in his portfolio and shuffling of note cards, he addressed Count Bernadotte.

Ribbentrop: "Excellency, can be break for fifteen minutes? Thank you."

As the German contingent rose to consult behind the table, Eden relaxed, certain that the discussions were over for today and forever. Both sides would offer regrets, shake hands soberly, and return to the grim business of diplomacy crippled by the scourge of war.

Eden turned his aides and whispered, "I think that will about do it."

Coffee, tea, and sweet treats were offered. The parties huddled at opposite ends of the conference room. Count Bernadotte strove to maintain equal distance from the two parties, showing no sign of being able to hear either whispered conversation.

When they resumed, Bernadotte nodded that it was von Ribbentrop's turn to speak.

Ribbentrop: "As a sign of its good faith, Germany offers cessation of V-2 rockets on British military targets."

Eden dropped his pen and sat back in his chair. His aides looked up as one in disbelief. In addition to the impertinence shown in ignoring Eden's clearly stated proposal, von Ribbentrop's offer came as a surprise. It was not the offer alone that irked the British delegation, however.

They were incensed that von Ribbentrop would suggest the targets of the V-2's were military. The German Foreign Minister knew better than anyone at the table that the V-2's were designed and used only as terror weapons against

British cities and civilian populations, not military sites. Moreover, the haphazard pattern of their impacts on London and elsewhere showed that their aiming was quite inexact, not suited to a precise military effect.

Nor would Eden bite on von Ribbentrop's implication of military targeting that the V-2's already launched had not reached the more heavily populated central London districts. British home defense personnel cleverly had been broadcasting bogus impact sites for the rockets. After each rocket's landing, they carefully and quickly calculated another, fake site as the impact site. Then they announced the fake site, hoping their misdirection would cause the Germans to aim future launchings at less populated suburbs.

The task was extremely distasteful to those calculating and broadcasting the misdirection. It put them in the tortured position of playing God, choosing what population districts would likely be hit and which spared. The deception had to be maintained to minimize human losses, however.

Eden could barely control his outrage.

Eden: "I remind the Minister that the good faith demonstration demanded by the British government is sought now."

It was the stiffest comment Eden had made all day.

Von Ribbentrop replied coolly.

Ribbentrop: "Germany agrees to stop V-2 rocket attacks when bombing of German cities by the Royal Air Force ceases."

Two of Eden's aides exchanged whispered comments. The political aide selected by Churchill immediately wrote a note and passed it to Eden. Eden nodded to his aide and said "Thank you."

Eden: "The British Foreign Secretary regrets that he can no longer represent his country at these proceedings."

Eden began to gather his belongings and close his portfolio. Whether von Ribbentrop was bluffing or could not respond intelligently to Eden's proposal was not known.

The dead-end reached on the issue was the kind of problem Eden had predicted would thwart any reasonable outcome of their deliberations. Eden was also aware that information of one kind or another was being passed across the table even when there was no item being seriously negotiated. He knew that the Germans were not above staging this exercise for the scraps of information they could gain for future use. Perhaps that was the real purpose of this meeting, after all.

He was sure, however, that the sentiment he expressed was exactly what Churchill believed, certainly what they had agreed to in preparation for today's meeting. Drawing the line in the sand on some meaningful, verifiable British demand had to come sooner or later. This was the issue chosen for that test.

Eden saw from von Ribbentrop's manner that the Foreign Minister was in an uncertain diplomatic area. He was reasonably sure that the Foreign Minister was not an architect of the death camps, euphemistically called "work camps" by the Germans. As a member of the Nazi Party and a confidant of Hitler, however, von Ribbentrop was certainly complicit in the atrocities committed.

Eden was also quite sure that the German was embarrassed to be in the middle on the issue, under instructions to push for a truce, but not clear how far he could go in negotiating an extremely volatile, life and death German program. Eden suspected that von Ribbentrop was now on his own. He probably had no instruction beyond downplaying the issue, and was surprised by the forcefulness of Eden's presentation.

The longer the silence from the German side of the table lasted, the more Eden believed that von Ribbentrop would not make an outright rejection of the proposal, regardless of his and his aides' immediate jocular response. He was correct.

Ribbentrop: "The German government makes no statement of agreement or rejection now on the British government's proposal on the release of work camp residents. It will take the proposal under study."

Eden could still see a possible German propaganda effort forthcoming, despite von Ribbentrop's pledge of secrecy. The German's response could also be another bluff, an insincere pretense, trying to appear reasonable about seeking agreement in order to extend the negotiations, perhaps to gain British concessions on other matters in a spirit of joint reasonableness.

Eden: "The British government reminds that German compliance must be demonstrated before it agrees to another meeting on other issues.

"With that pre-condition in mind, and in the interest of seeking resolution of other issues standing in the way of peace between our countries, we will continue this meeting."

Both Bernadotte and von Ribbentrop seemed relieved.

Bernadotte: "Thank you, Secretary Eden.

"Another proposal, Minister von Ribbentrop?"

Ribbentrop: "We would expect at some time that our joint discussions would include settlement of all territorial claims by combating nations. Those discussions would depend, we suggest, on the views of other Axis and Allied nations. Realistically, those views would not be finalized until all hostilities have ended."

Von Ribbentrop leaned back to signal the end of his contribution for the moment.

Bernadotte: "Secretary Eden?"

Eden was not going to respond to von Ribbbentrop's implicit suggestion that Eden speculate about Allied reaction to Britain's agreement to this first bilateral talk with Germany. He was reasonably sure that von Ribbentrop was reflecting the belief of Hitler that Germany could whip the other Axis nations into line, whatever agreements were reached with the British. Von Ribbentrop may have been inviting Eden's speculation whether Churchill might approach the Americans and Soviets the same way.

Eden recognized also the more subdued nature of von Ribbentrop's comments compared to his reaction on the inmate proposal. The air had gone out of the menacing balloon that had hung over the table. Churchill's position on the Jewish Question was not yet won. But Eden would not re-kindle the earlier confrontation now.

Eden: "The British government agrees with the sentiment of the German Foreign Minister's appraisal of territorial claims.

"We suggest also that standard settlement provisions would need to be drawn up regarding cessation of hostilities between British and German forces and the exchange of German prisoners of war."

Ribbentrop: "Of course. The German government agrees in principle to standard settlement provisions."

Bernadotte: "Minister von Ribbentrop, do you have further proposals?"

Ribbentrop: "The German government proposes the following items for acceptance by the British government:

(A) Germany will pay no reparations for the outbreak of hostilities.
(B) All colonies taken from Germany in 1919 will be returned.
(C) Germany will bear no guilt for the outbreak of hostilities in 1939.
(D) Danzig and the Polish Corridor will be governed as a German protectorate.
(E) The Sudetenland will remain a German Protectorate.
(F) The Rhineland will remain German territory.

The ghost of the Versailles Treaty is still very much alive in the German mentality, Eden thought. Moreover, these demands of Hitler are completely unrealistic, even delusional, in light of Germany's present military posture.

The reparations proposal is an implicit admission by von Ribbentrop and Hitler, despite Hitler's protestations to the contrary, that Germany is losing the war. For if Germany were to win the war, the question of reparations by Germany would never arise.

Eden: "On Item A, the British government, with one exception, agrees in principle. The exception is the payment for Jewish personal and business property. The British government will continue to insist that Germany pay into a fund equal to twice the value of properties confiscated. That fund would compensate surviving relatives and living Jews by paying for the establishment of Jewish settlements in Palestine. Those freed inmates must be sheltered, fed, and given medical attention."

Ribbentrop: Even if Germany were to agree to the proposal in principle, it would be impossible for the German government, or anyone, to establish what those values are."

Eden: "We suggest the German government can derive that information. Being always efficient, it has a source in transportation records over the years of those inmates from their homes inside and outside Germany to the work camps. It should also have records of home and business property transfers. Living inmates can also give an account of the property values surrendered."

Von Ribbentrop shook his head in silent protest.

"The British government agrees in principle to Part B of the German government's proposal, the restoration of German colonies."

Von Ribbentrop's facial response was positive. He opened his eyes wide in a modest display of diplomatic surprise.

"The British government rejects Parts C, D, E, and F of the proposal."

Bernadotte: "Further discussion, Minister von Ribbentrop?"

Ribbentrop: "Not at this time, Excellency. Thank you."

Bernadotte: "Further proposals, Secretary Eden?"

Eden: "As the Foreign Minister stated so well earlier, we would expect at some time that our joint discussions would include detailed settlements of all territorial claims and postwar areas of influence of Allied and Axis nations. Until all hostilities are ended, there cannot be a meaningful resolution of those issues.

"The British government notes, however, that resolution of those issues is critical to securing postwar peace. In light of the postwar diplomatic experience in 1919, it is incumbent on settlement negotiators to plan carefully their strategies, not to assure territorial aggrandizement or other advantages, but to further the cause of peace."

Ribbentrop: "Your concern and vision are well stated, Secretary. The German government certainly supports provisions for a just peace."

Bernadotte: "Anything further? Secretary Eden?"

Eden wanted to express the importance of speed in reaching any agreement, if one was to be reached, without appearing too eager. Both Churchill and he felt the Allied victory in the war with Germany could be finalized in a couple of months. Perhaps Hitler felt the urgency also, knowing that Germany could not sustain a three-front war much longer.

Eden: "With the start made here today, the British government trusts that more progress can be made soon. Would two weeks be too soon for another meeting?"

Ribbentrop: "Two or three weeks, perhaps. There is a weighty issue for the German government to resolve. That may take more time.

"I suggest also, Excellency," turning to Count Bernadotte, "that for the sake of security and secrecy, another meeting place might be arranged for the next meeting. These facilities have been most agreeable, and we thank you again. However, the repetition of site and vehicle might invite more questions and scrutiny than could be handled while maintaining secrecy."

Bernadotte: "I understand and agree. This is a worthwhile endeavor you have started. I believe you have made good progress today. Please contact me for any additional assistance I can provide."

Chapter 17

The White House, Friday, November 17, 1944

"I suppose we are both disappointed that more progress wasn't made in Europe in the last three weeks, General," said President Roosevelt to General Marshall in their regular Friday morning meeting. "We all had such high hopes that the European burden would be over with by Christmas. I heard that the Army postal service was considering the stoppage of Christmas packages to Europe since our troops probably would be returning home by that time."

Marshall shook his head in disbelief.

The President asked, "Is there anything decisive that we have not done that we can do, any aggressive initiative that we can come up with?"

"The Market-Garden operation seems to have drained the energy out of the Armies in France and Belgium and Holland," Marshall replied. "Everyone on the ground except Patton seems to want to pause and reflect rather than move."

"Is it fair to pinpoint Market-Garden as the source of the malaise?" the President asked.

"Things did stall after that mistake. And it was a failure, regardless of what Field Marshal Montgomery's staff publicists and the British press says. What we did achieve was at enormous material, manpower, and strategic cost. The same result could have been had by a much less dangerous massing of ground forces for a simple invasion in The Netherlands."

"Would not that approach have bled Bradley of resources also?" asked the President.

"Not as severely. The reduction would have been more gradual and less sizable overall."

"So, the whole operation was a double failure. The Arnhem objective was not taken. The American sector, especially Patton, was stalled," the President said.

"Montgomery has to realize at some point that his grand schemes have to be tempered by practicalities," Marshall said in continuing critique of the British military commander. "Of course, Eisenhower wanted to get things moving, too. He approved Market-Garden in that hope."

"General," the President said, "there is a serious question we have to face. How is our leadership there? Do we need to consider appointing new American and/or Allied commanders? Is General Eisenhower still up to the task?"

"He is!" Marshall responded quickly. "Ike is a great organizer. He is carrying many burdens and doing it well. I'm convinced the criticism of him as a tactician, especially in British circles, arises largely because he doesn't do everything the way they want him to.

"On the other hand, I've picked up a rumor that one of our general officers has accused Ike of being the best General the British have!"

"Patton, no doubt," the President said.

Marshall smiled without responding. He would not tattle further on the best tank commander the Allies had, knowing the President's rating of Patton had dropped in the last two years.

The General continued. "The politics inside and outside military decisions would overwhelm a lesser man than Ike. His diplomatic skills make him the ideal man for the job as Supreme Commander. He holds the alliance together. He is deliberate in his decisions, no doubt. If he has any fault as a leader, he may be too solicitous of his subordinates' views. But he has to convince widely divergent leaders of the merits of his decisions."

"Did you say 'widely' or 'wildly'?" the President asked. He burst out with his famous laugh, head thrown back, the smile instantly rearranging his face from the drawn, sober look he normally showed. The "ha-ha" was loud and vigorous in self appreciation of his witticism. Marshall joined in briefly.

"I'd like to think Patton would have learned by now how to shut up," Marshall said. "He's an outstanding leader. He gets the most out of his troops. But he is one of the worst at diplomacy. He seems to think diplomacy is his ability to sweet talk Eisenhower at times. He knows how to turn it on and off, showing a modicum of humility when he's talking to Ike. But he is as arrogant as anyone to subordinates, and a loose cannon on deck when he talks to the press."

"And Ike also has the heir apparent to God in Charles DeGaulle to contend with," the President said. "DeGaulle obviously thinks he knows more about a winning military strategy in France than anyone else. He does have the French people behind him. But he probably over-estimates the importance of his popular support. After the shameful experience the French had with Marshal Petain's too-willing collaboration with the Germans, I suppose anyone would look good by comparison.

"Winston told me the last time we met that the heaviest cross he has had to bear in this war to date is the 'Cross of Lorraine.' Winston is no pussy cat when it comes to military strategy. He is a bear. He can see through DeGaulle's self-serving pronouncements in a flash."

"Churchill is a good ally to have," Marshall said. "He's the right man for Britain now."

"He is, indeed. Winston apparently reminds Eisenhower regularly that he…and I…are his bosses in this operation. Rightly so, since Ike is the Allied Commander in Europe, not only the American Commander. Except Winston is close by and I'm not. So Ike, understandably, has to maintain deference to the Prime Minister."

"Ike is in a command position over Montgomery and Tedder and Ramsay and the rest of the British service chiefs," said Marshall. "I suspect they think that since Churchill is British and one of Ike's bosses that somehow Ike has to show deference to them, too. It's no secret that Montgomery and the rest go over Ike's head and suggest strategy directly to Churchill. I suppose Ike doesn't always know whether a challenge to his decisions by Churchill originated with Churchill or Montgomery or one of the others. It's a tough diplomatic hot seat to be on, and Ike handles it better than any senior officer I can think of over there.

"I certainly could not do the job Ike is doing. I would not even want to try," Marshall said. It was not humility that prompted the general's comment, but the need to assure the President that he was comfortable serving where the President needed him most.

The President now put the punch line on the discourse. "We need to get this European war over with as quickly and efficiently as we can for several good reasons, General. The most important is our need to shift manpower and resources to the war against Japan."

He leaned forward across the conference table and in a loud whisper referred to the deep secret shared by only a few.

"We don't know now when the super weapon will be tested and ready for use, or if it will be conclusive in ending the war in either theatre."

General Marshall shared the urgency spoken by the President, a now familiar refrain that sounded today like a complaint. The President's reference to the atomic bomb in development apparently was his ray of hope for a quick resolution of the war in either Europe or the Pacific.

Marshall confirmed the President's doubts about the weapon. "I don't think there is any chance that the bomb will be ready for use soon, if I'm reading the Manhattan Project progress reports correctly."

Marshall ventured to bring the subject back to the urgency of current decisions. "We cannot generate more manpower quickly or easily. We already have eight million people in uniform in the two theatres. Our ratio of staff and support personnel to front line troops in an infantry division stays at about two to one. Figuring about 15,000 men to a new Army division, effectively we need three new divisions to put that many riflemen on the line."

"Our military manpower requirements have been very taxing on this society," the President interjected. "I don't think the country is ready for more drastic draft measures. I doubt we can expand the range of the draft age, lower and/or higher, without jeopardizing war production and citizen morale. And without a significant change in recruitment policy, we simply cannot generate sizable manpower increases in the foreseeable future.

"General, you and I know that, despite our sizable manpower commitment, our contribution to the war that tips the balance in the Allies' favor is our production of material and technical support. God forbid, if our shores were invaded, we would have to rally every able-bodied person to our defense forces. But that's not where we are now. We need to continue to out-smart and out-produce our enemies. Those are our strategic military advantages."

After a long pause, the President returned to the question of strategy in Europe. "So, how do we get the Allied machine moving again?"

"I have two continuing recommendations from one of our intelligence agencies," Marshall replied. "One proposes a movement of all four American Armies, in a concerted effort all up and down the Western Front against the German West Wall, and possibly secure some Rhine crossings. Patton's Third Army could either spearhead that effort or move in concert with the other three armies. Significant supply and manpower shifts would be needed to make that happen.

"The more promising immediate action is continued heavy bombing of German industry by the Royal Air Force and our Eighth Air Force. That action won't show up in any immediate gain of territory by ground forces. The effort pays off in the intermediate future, however, certainly by the spring of next year. That campaign has already started."

The President sighed at the prospect of continued delay in winning the European war.

"As always, there's a lot to think about. I'll put my staff on overtime to see if there's anything more the several army commands can do, soon and effectively. And I'll call people myself to shake things up," Marshall promised.

The President extended his hand and forced a smile. "Thanks, General."

As Marshall left the Oval Office, he wished he had something more positive to reassure the President with. He was troubled also that the European conflict was taking much too long to resolve.

His call to Everett Giles was more perfunctory that usual this week.

"As you know, Everett, the bombing campaign is continuing. I don't think it is going to be possible to mount an attack all along the American 12th Army Group front. The state of logistics right now simply won't permit the movement of all four Armies at the same time, however much I'd like to show Montgomery it can be done.

"Patton's Third Army has the go ahead to continue movement up to the West Wall and penetrate it, if possible. Patton has told Eisenhower that with reinforcements and supplies he can go all the way to Berlin in a hurry. I don't believe that is realistic in a winter campaign."

"It probably isn't," Giles said. "But at least there would be some movement."

"Right now the President wants some movement. I suppose you know he is pressing for resolution of the issue in Europe. Don't stop looking for other options, Everett."

The most important direction Giles drew from his talk with Marshall was the General's continuing pressure to end the war in Europe soon. Giles was proud that his unit was now on the verge of striking a decisive blow consistent with Marshall's repeated urgency theme. We have the plan and now the prime candidate in the person of Capt. Brooke to execute it, he concluded.

Chapter 18

Vermont, Saturday – Sunday, November 18 - 19, 1944

Hayden was alone in the bay of a C-47, flying to his mission rehearsal jump from Pine Camp, New York. The designated jump site was within the perimeter of Fort Ethan Allen, Vermont. It was shortly after midnight.

Everett Giles and the planning team of SIP had stressed the value of a rehearsal for the assassination attempt. They wanted a test run in a controlled environment at the same time of night as the planned drop at Berghof. In choosing the New York training site and the Vermont jump rehearsal site, they also duplicated weather and terrain conditions as close to the Berchtesgaden setting as they could find in secure territory.

The plan was for Hayden to jump in full winter gear and hike to the target alone. He was told that he was to be tested on his ability to adapt. He would be challenged to use his resourcefulness to cope with unfamiliar surroundings and test his skill at finding a target and hitting it.

It was clear to Hayden from the wintry venue chosen for the rehearsal that Giles planned a go ahead for the actual attempt soon. The rehearsal, Giles told Hayden and the team jointly, would allow them to make any changes needed to conduct the plan. Hayden would be given a first-hand opportunity to learn what might have been overlooked in their planning, once he was told who the target was.

Hayden was given a map of the immediate environs of Ft. Ethan Allen and the four-mile square layout of the mountainous terrain west and north of the fort. The target was a man-shaped plywood figure in a small clearing halfway up the north slope of the middle of three small peaks. His firing position would be from a ridge north of and above the target. He would be firing south. In the team's plan, still unknown to him, that was the same direction as the planned firing at Berghof.

It was Hayden's standard practice before a jump to check out all his equipment, starting with the chute. As an airborne officer, and having led men into new battle surroundings, he was especially conscious of location and direction in preparing for combat jumps. He took the compass the team provided out away from all the buildings at Pine Camp and checked it for accuracy, at day by the sun, at night by the stars. He went to the Pine Camp library for a Fort Ethan Allen map, compared the smaller map the team gave him with a larger map, then scanned the fort perimeter and its outlying area. It all checked out.

He was carrying three days rations and one canteen of water. He would be on his own for re-supply of water. Being concerned about weight to carry, the few tools he chose were simple but essential. A .45 revolver and ammunition, a hunting knife, matches, clear goggles for the jump, sun glasses against the blinding sun on snow by day, a flashlight for night.

For the bitter cold predicted, he wore a hooded, white gabardine shell and pants as outer protection and camouflage. Under the shell he had on a standard Army winter woolen shirt and pants, all over long johns. He wore a white woolen stocking cap. He chose mukluks for his feet, soft leathery boots made of reindeer skin that could be laced up three or four inches above his ankles. They were made by Eskimos for use in very cold weather. He wore a pair of soft cotton socks inside longer, heavier woolen socks that extended above the mukluks and were tucked inside the bloused outer pants. The white gloves he wore were fur lined, specially adapted with a zippered flap for his right index finger. He felt he was sufficiently layered against the cold. He did not carry any personal identification or wear army patches or insignia of rank, as per instructions of the team.

In addition to the main chute in a back pack and the safety chute high on his chest, the pack strapped to his lower chest contained the disassembled rifle sections, the elastic cord, a clip of ten rounds of ammunition, his tools, and provisions. Since it was a specially made weapon, he was to pick up the brass after firing and return it for study by experts. The plan called for him to accomplish his mission in three days total or less. He would jump into the area in the dead of night. He would proceed to the firing position once he got his bearings. He could fire on the first morning if he could obtain the firing position by then and if the target was clear. He should fire as soon after 10:00 as possible, but no later than 11:00 on the day he reached the target area. After firing, he would hike the three miles or so to the fort on a route clearly designated on the map.

Sitting alone on the bench opposite the door of the plane, Hayden was lulled by the drone of the engines. He was reminded of his first combat jump, in Sicily. It was not nearly so cold in July in the Mediterranean, but all the troopers in the plane had chills of a different kind.

The invasion date was July 10, 1943. The drop zone for the 505th Regiment had been planned for just north of Gela, on the southern coast of Sicily, in front of the American Army's beachhead to be taken by the First and Third Infantry Divisions on the left and the Forty-Fifth Division on the right. These American divisions, Gen. Patton's Seventh Army, were the left wing of the invasion force. The right wing was the British Eighth Army of four infantry divisions commanded by Gen. Montgomery.

The Third Battalion of the 504th Parachute Regiment was to be dropped on July 11 and attached to the 505th Regiment. Thus the nucleus of the Regimental Combat Team in the invasion phase of the operation was formed.

The first rule of a jump is that nothing ever goes as planned. Minutes before takeoff from Tunisia the evening of July 9, the troopers learned that winds gusting up to thirty-five miles an hour, west to east, were hitting Sicily.

At jump time, when the red readiness light over the door came on, Hayden had a violent disagreement with the pilot as to the plane's whereabouts.

"You can't drop these men over water!" he shouted above the roar of the engines and the wind draft through the open door. "Look! The land mass is on our left only. The wind is causing us to drift too far east. Turn north!"

Hayden could see other planes nearby that might also be starting their jump run. He had the sickening vision of his weighted-down fellow troopers plummeting to the bottom of the sea.

The green jump light came on. Hayden immediately protested to the jump master that they obviously were still over water. He pushed back against the troopers close up behind him and told the pilot to continue on the same course as the other aircraft until they could identify landmarks. The pilot complied. They had to wait until there was land under the plane, fearful all the while of collision with other planes trying to find their course. Some shells were bursting below them over water. They had to be friendly fire from the sea-borne invasion force!

Then Hayden jumped first in his stick. He determined by the location of the moon and an occasional light from towns he thought were Gela to his left and Scoglitti on his right where north was.

Most recent intelligence had told them that the enemy, the Italian *Livorno* Division, was likely to be north of the planned drop zone, with invading American infantry behind it to the south. Hayden knew the wind had blown him and others in his stick considerably east of the drop zone, how far he couldn't tell. He soon learned that he and other troopers of his battalion had landed east of Scoglitti, among elements of the German Herman Goering Division, and were in for a tough fight.

His battalion captured San Croce Camerina and Vittorio before it moved northwest to link up with the main body of the 505th Regiment. The 82nd Division was less involved as it anchored the left wing of the invasion force along the coast all the way to the northwest corner of Sicily over the next two weeks.

The navigator interrupted Hayden's reminiscence as he came back to open the door of the plane. Frigid air flooded the cabin. "Five minutes," he told Hayden as the red readiness light came on.

Hayden immediately hooked up his static line and stood in the doorway to survey the terrain below him. It was a clear, moonless night with the light of stars too faint to allow him to recognize or distinguish the dark and still darker shapes in the forest below him. The piercing draft off the wing forced him to pull his goggles down to keep his eyes from tearing up and freezing. He could not see any of the map-established checkpoints or any landmarks.

The green light came on. The pilot and navigator were motioning and shouting for him to jump. His scan into the distance for a horizon yielded no clues, only unending blackness.

Instead of the planned eastern approach to the jump zone, Hayden had the distinct impression that the pilot had changed course over the last several miles and was now heading west!

He turned from the doorway and shouted to the pilot. "I don't recognize any check point. What's our heading? What's our altitude?"

As he shouted, he searched for the instrument dials. All but two were shielded from his view. He could barely make out from the compass dial that they were indeed heading west, with an air speed of 230 miles per hour. He recalled the similar green jump light experience in Sicily. He had the same kind of argument with that pilot.

The pilot responded angrily. "We've got our orders. Jump! Jump!"

Hayden now understood. "Nothing ever goes as planned," he swore. He was now inclined to believe that the current predicament was one planned by his handlers.

He made one last, quick scan of the skies and stars and the terrain below. There was still little light and no hint of the target area. He could not gauge the plane's altitude. He wrapped his arms around the pack containing the rifle, tools, and provisions, and stepped out into the black space.

His chute opened punctually. As his descent slowed, the air was not as frigid as it had been in the doorway of the plane.

His landing inevitably was going to be in a tree. It was a concern he had not expressed to the team. Jumping into a forest always contained danger. He could be impaled on a tree branch, killed, or seriously injured. The danger was worse in the dark.

There was no reason to attempt steering his decline since he could not see a clear landing spot anyway. He grabbed the lines above him to cushion the impact and tucked his head as much as he could into the safety chute pack to shield his face.

After a short eternity, he felt the slap of limbs against his feet, body, and head in quick order. He slipped through several layers of branches and jerked to a quick stop as the chute caught branches above him. The jolting stop stunned him for a moment. He felt some bruise pain on his legs and right hip. He pulled back his goggles and peered down. There were branches in his line of vision, but he could see patches of snow and ice faintly, perhaps fifteen feet below his feet. He pushed against the branches to twist completely around and confirmed his assessment. He could not pop the chute release for fear of falling too quickly onto a surface he could not see well.

The branches nearest him were about the thickness of his thumb. He reached out and felt for the strongest of them and determined from its resistance to his tug the direction of the tree trunk. He pulled on the branch and moved himself a couple feet. The aroma of the fir tree emanated from the squeezed needles. He held on with one hand and repeated the effort, hand crawling along the branch. The chute lines were drawing tighter as the caught chute resisted his movement. He would have to get to a higher branch initially to work it loose. In reaching blindly above him, he found one and tested it with one hand and most of his weight. He pulled himself upward and felt the lines loosen.

In ten minutes of strenuous work pulling his weight and the burden of his equipment, he reached the trunk and hugged it while he found some footing. He rested standing while his eyes acclimated a bit to the little light from the stars. He could make out the faint dark shapes of trees spaced from fifteen to twenty feet away, it seemed, in all directions.

He popped the chute release and wriggled out of the harness. He pulled sharply on the lines of the chute repeatedly with one hand to drag it free of the upper branches. He would need its cover against the cold night. He felt the chute drawing in closer to the thicker branches and soon he could not budge it further from his tree trunk position. He guided the lines below him down the trunk and descended to the last limb-step about ten feet off the ground. The lines fell three or four feet below the last spread of branches. He would be able to reach them from the ground. He hugged the tree trunk again and scraped and slid his way to the ground.

He untied his packs, propped them against the tree trunk, and found the flashlight. He removed a glove and felt for tears in his garments. He felt lucky that he could feel no damage, though he had some aching leg bruises from branches he hit on landing.

He reached to retrieve the suspended lines. While pulling slowly and steadily on the lines, he moved around what he determined to be the outer edge of the tree, back and forth, working to free the chute. It was caught from time to time in the lower, stronger branches of the tree he landed in and those of one or more converging trees. He yanked on the chute lines harder and cracked some branches. He could sense edges of the chute just above him. He cinched up his grip on the lines and pulled again. One side of the chute spilled down alongside the thickest branch Hayden could see. He grabbed a loose end and soon had the whole chute piled at his feet, broken branches and needles caught in its folds.

The snow cover was frozen hard. Hayden rummaged around, searching with the flashlight for exposed fallen tree limbs and found enough to make a wooden mattress at the base of a tree. He dragged the chute on top of it, doubling and re-doubling the thicknesses. He wrapped himself into as many folds of the chute as he could manage.

He realized he was very tired. He removed his knife and revolver from the tool pack and laid them beside him inside the bed with the flashlight. He pulled the rifle pack behind him for a pillow. As he rested his head against the pack, he felt a sizable lump in it. He pulled the pack around in front of him, turned the flashlight on it, and unzipped the pocket with the lump.

Here was a black box about the size of a cigarette pack taped to the canvas. In the stillness of the forest, Hayden could hear a very faint hum coming from the unit. It was a homing device. He remembered that Lt. Col. Alexander and an aide had come up to him as he was preparing to board the plane. The two had pushed here and there, front and back, zipping and unzipping pockets like doting parents sending a child off to school. They had gone over all the packs and harness, muttering about never being too sure in preparing for such an operation.

It had to have been Alexander who planted the device, Hayden concluded. He remembered thinking it odd that Alexander ordered a final check in the darkness of the runway, when Hayden had made a final check in his presence in the lighted control room just minutes before. Now he knew why.

It is thoughtful of my handlers to know where I am, he said to himself. He was amused that the team was concerned for his well being. Or were they? The bug might betray a lack of confidence in him. He tried to figure other reasons for the stowaway device, but nothing seemed to fit.

He had a lingering thought about the flight here. Could the changed flight direction have been simple inexperience of the crew? Sixteen months ago in the Sicily jump, when all the crews were inexperienced, that might account for the misdirection. Now he leaned toward game playing by the handlers as an answer. The pilot had shouted something about "we have our orders."

He dozed off wondering what other trickery his handlers planned to make his expedition more interesting.

Chapter 19

Vermont, Saturday, November 18, 1944

At daybreak, Hayden tried to make an appraisal of his location and situation. He climbed the landing tree again to get a good view. He took along his map, knife, compass, and rifle scope. He climbed as high as he dared on the smaller limbs, but still had too much visual obstruction. He shaded his eyes and looked in all directions to determine his position. In his second slow scan of the horizon, there was more sunlight against the forest to the north. Due north of his position, he was startled to see something quite different from the natural forested surroundings. Whatever it was, its shape definitely was man-made.

He cut off several branches to clear his view. Through the scope he now saw what looked like a ladder or stairs, mostly obscured by trees. "A forest ranger station!" he said aloud after some study. It appeared to be built atop a ridge, perhaps three miles away. He carefully took a compass reading. He then slid around to the east side of the tree to continue his scan of the horizon.

It was difficult to see anything against the rising sun. Hayden could tell something was wrong, however. Perhaps eight to ten miles distant, almost due east of his position, he barely made out three bumps in line west to east against the skyline. Could that be the target area?

The peaks were in the wrong location. He pulled out his map, the one he routinely compared to a regional map found in the Pine Camp library. It showed the mountain peaks, the highest, middle one anchoring the target, to be mostly east, but also north of his present position!

Had the plane crew dropped him on the back side, the south side of the ridge line and three mountain peaks, deliberately? He had been told that his hiking would begin from the drop zone on the north side of the target, possibly two or three miles distant. If Hayden's observations were correct, the target now was on the other side, the north side of the ridge.

The only way to confirm the target's location and his position was clear. He would hike the three miles up to the ridge line, climb to the higher view from the ranger station, and determine from a ranger or a map exactly where he was in relation to the landmarks. If he was correct, the hike due north to the station would not take him appreciably out of his line of march to the target. He would be going north and then east, as opposed to taking the shorter, northeast diagonal trek.

He climbed down, ate his morning rations, and prepared to move. As he folded up the chute and tied it into a separate backpack, he realized that while the plane was heading west just prior to his jump, the shouting disagreement with the pilot probably cost him several miles of backtracking.

He strapped the tool pack to his chest. He put the revolver in its holster and knife in its scabbard and attached them to his cartridge belt. The last thing he did before moving on was to anchor the homing bug in the crotch of a tree limb he could reach. He had thought a lot about what to do with the device this morning. Given the team-planned deception he had already encountered, he decided it was worth more to him for his handlers not to know where he was at any time.

While regularly checking his compass, Hayden in two hours trudged upward to the station. The small platform and room were deserted. There was a note on the door inviting any visitor to use the station. "Please, no fire of any kind," it read. Hayden appreciated what little humor there was in the situation.

The only items of interest to Hayden were the maps spread out under each of the four large windows facing each direction. He quickly determined on the East map that the three peaks he spotted at sunrise were indeed the target zone displayed on his smaller map, in line almost dead ahead to the east. It was not possible to find the firing position on the map. It appeared he could reach the vicinity of the target by following the ridge line on which the station was built. The ridge seemed to include the three peaks at its terminus. He would follow it to a position southwest of the target area, then cross a valley in a final northeast trek to a point above the designated firing line. He committed the view to memory and left the station.

Resuming the march, he decided to hike along the north face of the ridge line to get better traction in the snow. He planned to camp overnight on the ridge itself.

As a paratrooper, but basically an infantryman, he was used to long marches. The one milestone he crossed was the perimeter line of Fort Ethan Allen about mid-afternoon, a simple fence of three strands of barbed wire. He thought with wry satisfaction that he was now near where his starting point should have been with his jump, and was pleased he had not landed on the wire.

After the long day's hike, with few pauses, he had realized his morning plan. He spread the parachute again on a mat of branches. His rations were cold and tasteless. He was weary from the slipping and occasional sliding on the ice along the ridge line. The bruises he sustained on the drop into the trees ached and did not help his disposition. On top of all his other miseries, he did not sleep well his second night out.

Early in the morning of the second full day, he resumed his march, moving northeast off the ridge, down into a valley and up again to the higher ground above the firing position. The sunny day and the clear view of the valley, although snow covered in wintry Vermont, reminded him of the Dutch countryside. As he trudged along, he let his mind wander back to two months ago.

The Market-Garden jump was quite different from his jumps in Sicily and Normandy. For one thing, it had been a daylight jump. It was a beautiful day, sunny, with a very light breeze. The peaceful landscape, including the *Reichswald*, was visible clearly for 360 degrees. The *Reichswald* was a forest in Germany, on the very eastern edge of the 82nd Division's easternmost drop zone. Hayden had oriented quickly to the Grosbeek Heights, a wooded area on the north side of the zone. Several miles farther to the north he could see the Nijmegen Bridge, the main objective of the 82nd in securing an overland route for the XXX Corps, the land arm of the operation.

Within an hour of the drop, as the division was assembling by sub-units, shouts of alarm went up at the same time enemy rifle rounds impacted around them. Bodies hit the ground, some slumping in the throes of deadly wounds. Other troopers dodged and scurried for cover. There was no organized defense against the enemy troops pouring out of the *Reichswald*. Hayden didn't bother to look for battalion or regimental officers. Some of them had already departed to reconnoiter the smaller bridges that the 82nd was charged with capturing.

He grabbed a rifle and a belt of ammunition clips. "Get your weapons and fall in over here!" he shouted at the loose groups of men near him lying or crouching behind whatever cover they could find. He waved them in the general direction of the forest and waited for a moment as they responded, picking up weapons and ammunition as Hayden had, some from fallen comrades.

Hayden ran about thirty yards toward the forest to an overturned jeep and flopped behind its front end. He was maybe 150 yards from the enemy force emerging from the *Reichswald* to the east. To his left he could see troopers firing from the Grosbeek Heights. Their effective fire was causing the enemy to funnel in the direction of the thin line he was anchoring. The line to either side of him began to form behind whatever protection the troopers could find. There wasn't time for a thorough survey of his position, but Hayden knew it was precarious.

A steady rattling of rifle rounds pinged off the jeep. Fortunately, the enemy troops were short of heavier weapons. A few *panzerfaust* rounds were thrown in Hayden's direction with little effect. It was infantry versus infantry, and the enemy had a numbers advantage.

Hayden knew that the 82nd Division had several major tasks. Reports had come in earlier that the bridge over the Maas River at Grave on the southwestern end of the division's area of responsibility had been taken intact. That capture assured the division it would have a link-up with the armor of XXX Corps. Other units of the 82nd were probing German defenses at the four bridges over the Maas-Waal Canal east and north of Grave. Capture of at least one of those bridges was essential to bringing the XXX Corps tanks into attack position at Nijmegen.

The senior division officers were probably now to the north, Hayden thought, surveying from a distance the 1800 foot long highway bridge at Nijmegen. It was eleven miles from Arnhem, the final objective of the entire Market-Garden operation. The key to success of the plan was the 82nd holding its lengthy perimeter against German counterattacks.

Hayden shouted to a corporal some ten yards to his right. "Go back and tell battalion we need Browning Automatic Rifles (BARs) and mortars up here right now." He turned back to the front. Hundreds more of the enemy were charging wildly at the troopers' line.

He shouted again up and down the line for troopers to keep firing, even as he sighted the leaders of the enemy advance and squeezed off short bursts of fire at them. The troopers on the Grosbeek Heights saw the enemy concentration developing and focused their fire on the main enemy force attacking to their right, in front of Hayden's position.

Hayden was conscious of someone stepping over him and flopping to his right. The soldier began firing in sync with Hayden. Hayden emptied his clip, then glanced over while he fed another into his M1. It was General Gavin!

"Captain Brooke, we've got to hold here…and then force them back."

Hayden said "Yes, sir," between shots, enormously pleased that the General remembered his name, probably from the marksmanship classes Hayden conducted for the division in the pre-Sicily training in North Africa.

"We need to clear this zone for glider landings coming in soon," the General shouted.

Hayden knew that the rest of the division and the headquarters of XXX Corps led by British General Brian Horrocks, the Market-Garden ground commander, would be landing inside the 82nd's perimeter, dangerously close to the German border.

"Those do not appear to be front line troops coming out of that forest. But there are a lot of them, and there may be some veteran units in there behind them. We'll get you some help here. Hold on, Captain," the General shouted over the noise.

Hayden remembered the quick slap on his shoulder as General Gavin spoke and rose to leave. Without further comment, the young General ran off to his left, crouched and shouted orders and encouragement to the growing number of troopers—cooks, headquarters staff, engineers—coming into the fray.

Slowly the infantry battle changed character. Hayden heard and saw the blasts of mortar shells hitting within the enemy formation. Dirt and debris were kicked up in the enemy line. Some bodies were thrown aside as the mortar barrage launched from behind him gained strength.

He called for BARs to come forward and concentrate their fire on the front line of the enemy charge. "There!" he shouted to direct their fire. "And there!"

In a few minutes, the enemy attack began to subside. In a few more minutes, the remainder of the enemy force was scurrying back to the cover of the *Reichswald.*

Shortly after, the Corporal he had directed to contact battalion re-joined him.

"Good work, Corporal. Is your squad close by?"

"Most of my platoon is around, sir."

"And your officers?"

"I don't know, sir. I think some of our officers and non-coms went down in that first volley."

"Okay," Hayden ordered, "you take charge until an officer comes forward. Get your platoon together, and any others you can round up, and move them over there to the right, to that line…there," he pointed to the front. "Get those BARs up forward with you. We've got to clear this area for a glider landing coming in. We can't let the Krauts capture General Horrocks, can we?"

The Corporal seemed energized at the thought of reinforcements coming in and shouted, "No, sir!"

As the trooper ran off, waving and shouting the nearby troops forward, Hayden moved to his left and found two privates manning a mortar. "Good," Hayden said. He was gratified at their help in breaking up the enemy assault. "You men did all right. I want you to let those troops get forward," pointing to the advance forming to his right. "Then you and these other mortar units move up behind them and pour fire on the edge of that forest until our defense line gets dug in up there."

Hayden kept moving farther to his left along the line toward the Heights, urging men to move forward and then dig in. He directed lieutenants and sergeants from the mixed bag of squads and platoons and companies he encountered to take charge of the troopers along the line nearest them. He found two of his own platoon leaders and sent them to the right to coordinate the formation of the defense line nearer the *Reichswald.*

Hayden was startled to see Jerry Connelios. He was on one knee, directing troops around him. Hayden crouched beside him.

"Jerry! Glad to see you made it in okay."

"Hayden! Same to you, buddy. It looks like your company is intermingled with other units, too."

"Yeah, it is. Wherever all these troopers belong, they did a helluva job stopping that attack. It was touch-and-go there for a while."

Together they hurried along the left side of the original defense line, starting up the incline to the Grosbeek Heights, all the while ordering troopers forward. When they looked back from the Heights, they saw a solid line moving forward to clear the zone. Officers and non-coms were now directing the troops.

They saw as well the devastation the short enemy attack had caused. Bodies littered the plain below them, all the way back to the battalion's assembly area. Few were moving. Jerry commented that the enemy strength was considerably greater than had been predicted for the drop zone. The element of surprise the Allies had counted on had evaporated quickly. Hayden was proud of the 82nd Division and his and Jerry's role in organizing the defense of the landing zone on that first day of Market-Garden.

By 8:00 Hayden had traversed the valley a mile west of his planned firing position. He then turned east again along the south slope of the facing mounting to a spot less than a mile above the target.

He surveyed the area through his rifle scope. Below him, at what he determined to be his probable firing position about 800 yards from the target, he was surprised to see a small armed patrol. He was thankful that he had hiked a northeast route off the main ridge. Had he taken a true north route through the target area to reach the firing position, he would have been spotted immediately by the patrol.

He counted eight soldiers in olive drab field uniforms. They seemed very relaxed. He assumed they were "defenders of the site," ordered there by Lt. Col. Alexander on behalf of the intelligence team. He was quite sure they were not there to greet him with hot food and drink.

How would he eliminate their obstruction? There was no perimeter defense visible. Since he assumed they were there to intercept him about 10:00, he might have a few minutes to plan his approach.

Chapter 20

Vermont, Sunday, November 19, 1944

"Halt!"

Hayden was startled by the order from behind him. He had been caught off guard by a sentry. He was angry at himself, ashamed of his carelessness. He would later blame it on a restless night.

Still behind him, the sentry ordered in a voice with little emotion. "Hands up! Freeze! Turn around slow!"

Hayden turned as ordered. Here was a young soldier, Private First Class, Military Police. He had on a helmet liner but no helmet. Hayden read the youth's eyes and concluded that he was about Cpl. Jimmy Hartage's age. But I'll bet he's a whole lot younger in experience, he thought. He glanced at the rifle. The safety was on!

Hayden needed a distraction. "Good work," he smiled and extended his hand as if to congratulate the guard.

The young man instinctively raised the barrel of the rifle to refuse the shake. Hayden was on him in a flash, his weight thrown against the Private's chest, pinning the rifle and his arms simultaneously. They fell in a heap, Hayden keeping the upper hand by clapping his hand over the guard's mouth and punching his right knee into his groin.

"Ow!" The guard's cry was muffled by Hayden's hand. Hayden pulled his knife and pressed it against the Private's face. "Do what I tell you or you'll die."

The Private gave Hayden his total attention.

"Quietly now, where are the other sentries?" he demanded, slightly loosening his clasp on the Private's mouth.

Involuntarily, the Private glanced for a split second down the slope to his right.

"How many total?" Hayden insisted.

The guard hesitated. Hayden drew a few drops of facial blood as he pressed the knife closer. "I mean it!"

"Another guard down there." The Private's surrender was complete as he nodded in the same direction as before.

This was a close call, Hayden admitted. The Private could have fired a warning shot and Hayden would have had a tough choice to make...do some damage to these troops or disappear to make a second attempt later or even tomorrow. He did not consider giving up the project.

Less than a minute had passed since he was confronted. He listened for other sounds. Had the other soldiers heard the Private's order to halt? This guard has a hooded sweatshirt under his helmet liner to ward off the cold. He probably saw Hayden coming through the forest instead of hearing him. If the other soldiers are dressed the same, their hearing could also be limited.

"All the rest at the firing site?" Hayden demanded.

"The infiltrator! That's who you are!" the Private said, suddenly intent. Hayden was a bit amused at the title given him by the intelligence team.

"The rest of the patrol,..." he repeated, his knife again emphasizing the question.

"Yeah, at the site." The young soldier breathed out his admission reluctantly.

Hayden sprang to his feet, yanking the rifle from the soldier as he did so. He pointed the rifle at the prone sentry while he took a quick look down the slope.

"Stay there. Left hand...pull off your cartridge belt," he ordered in a loud whisper.

The Private loosened the catch, struggled to get the belt out from under him, and laid it to his side.

"Left hand. Unzip your jacket and take your belt off."

With considerable effort, the Private complied and pulled his pants belt out of the loops.

"Roll over, hands behind your back." Hayden knelt on one knee in the guard's upper back, fastened the belt buckle end around his right wrist and quickly tied his right wrist down against his left.

"Don't move," Hayden ordered as he rose. He leaned the rifle against a tree and removed his chute and tool packs. He cut a three foot strip of chute line. He cut off a small piece of chute and wadded it up.

"What time did you come on duty up here?"

The prone soldier refused to say.

"Look," Hayden whispered, "you made a slight mistake. That isn't going to lose the war." He knelt again beside the guard, bracing his left hand with his weight on the guard's back. "Telling me about the others will make it a lot easier on them…and you."

The young soldier seemed to regain a sense of duty, or at least recover from the fright of being threatened with death.

"To hell with you," he swore.

Hayden yanked the soldier's head back by pulling the hood of the sweatshirt. He pushed the wad of chute into his mouth. He wrapped a strip of line around his mouth and knotted it in back. He re-tied the guard's wrists and then tied his ankles.

"Up," Hayden ordered. He dragged the guard against a tree and tied him there facing away from the patrol.

The rifle was loaded. He moved two ammunition clips from the Private's cartridge belt to his own. He picked up his two packs in his left hand, the rifle in his right, and began to move down the slope slowly, using tree-to-tree cover. It was 9:20 and very quiet in the forest.

Taking his time, he moved silently, always conscious of the patrol barely recognizable through the trees. Soon he saw the next sentry some fifty feet away, about one-third of his body visible, casually leaning against a tree on its sunny side, the butt of his rifle held between his feet. The sentry was observing his unit's activities with some apparent amusement.

Hayden set his two packs down quietly and circled to the sentry's blind side, away from the main unit. He drew his knife, slid around the tree, and clapped his hand over the sentry's mouth. The startled sentry let his rifle fall into the snow. In a whisper, Hayden demanded silence with his knife against the sentry's throat. He quietly went about the task of muffling the sentry and binding him to a tree.

He circled down the slope to a level below the patrol to get the sun at his back. The forest continued to give him adequate cover. The patrol was not more than forty yards away now. He worked his way cautiously, tree to tree, to approach them.

Now close enough to see their faces, he observed several lounging on mats and folding chairs they had brought along for their comfort. They were bundled up against the cold, all with hooded sweatshirts under their helmet liners. Their rifles were stacked. None had weapons handy except the Lieutenant in charge who carried a holstered .45 pistol. Several were smoking, standing together and laughing.

When Hayden had crawled to within fifteen yards of the group, he jumped up and ran toward them, stunning them all with a crisp order, "Hands up!"

"Don't do it," he shouted as the Lieutenant tried to pull his .45.

"You wouldn't dare," the Lieutenant challenged Hayden.

Hayden fired a rifle round between the Lieutenant's feet and the officer of the guard withdrew his hand from the holster. Hayden pointed the rifle at two soldiers starting to make a dash for their own stacked weapons.

"Hold it! Don't do anything foolish. I won't aim to miss next time. All of you, hands over your heads! Now! Lieutenant, drop your cartridge belt and step away."

Hayden knew the Lieutenant's bravado was to impress his unit, recompense in some way for his guard detail and himself being caught off guard.

Hayden ordered seven of the soldiers to the ground, face down, spaced about ten feet from each other. He oversaw the belt removal and tying routine for them, one at a time, by the remaining soldier. He then secured the last soldier's hands.

He kept them all in sight on the ground while he retrieved his chute pack, cut more lengths of guide line, and tied each one's hands again with long tails to the bindings. Starting with the Lieutenant, he moved each in turn to a tree and bound him there, facing outward. The Lieutenant started to shout threats of dire consequences to come. Hayden gagged him as he had the two sentries on the slope. He asked if anyone else needed a gag, and they were all silent.

Hayden observed a black box on one of the mats. It was connected by wire to a sizable battery. The box was an electronic device of some sort, emitting a low volume hum. It had two dials. One was a compass. Hayden held the box and determined true north. The other, illuminated dial had an arrow pointing at about 230 degrees.

Hayden saw immediately that it was pointing to his drop site. The homing bug! These soldiers had been relaxed, thinking that Hayden was still at the drop site. He wondered how long Lt. Col. Alexander and the rest of the team would have let him thrash around in the forest before they came after him. If he had been injured or immobile after the jump, they presumably would have allowed him to suffer a while. Next to the box and battery was a field radio. Hayden could imagine Alexander amused at the periodic reports called in by the patrol.

He asked a Corporal where their transportation was. The Corporal said, "Up there," motioning with his head. Hayden barely made out a vehicle hidden by trees some seventy-five yards away.

"Keys," Hayden demanded. The Corporal nodded to his upper jacket pocket and Hayden fished them out.

It was 10:15. Hayden wasn't sure how important it was for him to shoot at 10:00 or shortly after, but he decided to follow the plan. The 10:00 – 11:00 scheduled firing window was designed mostly for the guard's interception plan, he concluded.

He assembled the rifle, found a fallen log for a prone firing position, tied down the rifle to the log with the elastic cord, and loaded the clip.

The report of the weapon sounded like a cannon in the stillness of the forest as he squeezed off ten tracer rounds at the human silhouette a half mile away. Through the scope he was pleased to see splinters fly from the target as the .50 caliber tracer rounds shattered the plywood.

"Stomp your feet once in a while," he called out to the patrol as he prepared to leave the site. "It will help circulation and keep your feet from freezing. It might also ease some of your frustration."

He decided to leave the direction-finding black box visible to remind them of their carelessness and false assumption about his whereabouts over the last thirty-four hours since his jump.

Chapter 21

Vermont, Sunday, November 19, 1944

On his way to the Fort Ethan Allen offices in the guards' two-ton truck, Hayden reasoned that the casual attitude of the patrol was an unintended by-product of the intelligence team's entrapment plan. The original assessment of the team arguably was that, in the harsh environment and on foot, Hayden could not make it to the target site at all in three days. The backup assessment presumably was that he could not make it on the second day for sure. Knowing the pre-arranged off-course drop site and the distance from there to the firing position, the Lieutenant and his patrol could conclude easily that Hayden would not arrive until the third day at the earliest. They would take up their guard posts on the second day as ordered, just in case, and spend the day relaxing.

The homing device was the second and conclusive reason for the patrol's lax attitude. If Hayden had not found the bug, the patrol would have been able to track his movements constantly. The guards would have been ready to capture him in their little war game once he got close to the firing position. He suspected that Lt. Raymond had a hand in planning the trap and would be thrilled to see Hayden captured in the exercise to put him in his place, especially after Hayden had embarrassed the Lieutenant about his lack of combat service. He blanched thinking how close the guards had come to capturing him, even without their ability to track him with their homing device.

Hayden drove straight to the Bachelor Officers Quarters where he was ordered to report after the exercise. He was surprised to learn that Colonel X was on site, presumably to witness the resolution of the miniature war game.

Colonel X had set up the intelligence team's headquarters in a conference room just off the main entrance. The intelligence team was assembled with a Captain of the Military Police, eating Sunday brunch.

As Hayden walked in, they all stopped their meals in a variety of stunned poses. Lt. Col. Alexander gasped at the sight of him. Major Driver and Lt. Raymond said, "He's alone!" in unison, incredulous to see him unaccompanied and so soon.

Alexander was the first to address him. "Captain Brooke! Our information was that we shouldn't expect you…" He had already given away too much.

Hayden reasoned that this morning's radio reports from the patrol had told the team that Hayden was still at the drop site. They apparently thought they would have to send a team to look for him later. Or the patrol would bring him in under guard sometime. What that scenario would have meant for Hayden's final selection for a mission Hayden couldn't tell.

Colonel X asked, "Did you complete the exercise?"

"I did, sir." Hayden dug into his jacket pocket and produced the ten shell casings he was ordered to bring back, and laid them on the table. "The target probably is not usable again," he said wryly.

He turned to the Military Police Captain and tossed the truck keys on the table in front of him. "It was nice of your boys to let me use their two-ton."

The Captain sheepishly took the keys. "Are they here with it?"

"No, I left them tied to trees, not lying on the frozen ground, mind you," Hayden said cheerily.

The MP Captain glared at Hayden.

Hayden was tired and hungry. He had faced more substantial threats in the last few days than a mean look from an MP Captain.

"If you start playing games, Captain, you had better learn to get your players ready. And be prepared to lose once in a while." Hayden scanned the intelligence team members meaningfully as he spoke.

The MP Captain, shaking his head, rose from his chair, possibly to call an aide to go collect the patrol.

Colonel X intervened quickly to prevent what he thought was further confrontation brewing between the Captains.

"Those men were just doing their assigned duty. I trust you have not mistreated any of them."

The gentle scolding by the Colonel invited a response from Hayden, whatever the cost.

"I would not have been able to complete the exercise if I had not acted as I did. I could have treated them worse. I suppose I was too easy on them."

Colonel X looked at Hayden as if he were seeing him for the first time. He chose not to comment further. The team members took his silence as the cue to follow.

Despite his disheveled condition, Hayden would not be put off by the niceties of the late morning meal. He pulled up a chair, asked "May I?" and joined them at the table without an answer. He poured himself some juice and called for a plate from an attendant.

The attendant glanced at Colonel X, who nodded his okay.

The man in charge now put the question to Hayden.

"Would you have wounded or killed one or more of the patrol to complete the exercise?"

Hayden answered slowly. "The idea did cross my mind. Those men were ordered into a potentially dangerous confrontation. They were armed. I thought I might have to wound the Lieutenant to convince him he could not stand in my way, whatever his orders…maybe one or two others as well."

He took a sip of juice before trying to make light of the whole matter.

"But then they all might get a Purple Heart, and probably a pension for life. I did not think that was fitting under the circumstances."

Hayden thought Lt. Col. Alexander was going to raise an impertinence objection to his comments. Colonel X made a non-committal grunt. Lt. Raymond shook his head for a reason Hayden could not fathom.

Colonel X pressed. "So you will kill, if needed, wherever you are sent?"

"Do you mean someone in addition to the main target?"

When Colonel X nodded, Hayden looked at him soberly and said, "Yes, I will."

The Colonel responded by squaring his hands flat on the table on each side of his plate as he sat up very erect. He studied each of the team members in turn with quizzical eyebrows raised. Each in turn nodded a go-ahead. Lt. Col. Alexander said "yes" to the silent question.

Colonel X got up from the table, went to the door and waved the attendants to him. "Leave us alone until we call for you again," he ordered. He closed the door securely, came back behind his chair and grasped its top with both hands.

"Captain Brooke, my name is Everett Giles, Director of the Special Intelligence Program. I have assembled this team to see you through preparation for a critical mission. I had planned that our decision about you would be made tomorrow, if you completed your recent exercise successfully by then. Your early completion of that task...against some daunting challenges, I should say...changes that decision to today. As you have just seen, we all agree that you are the man for the job. I am very relieved and pleased to learn that early reports of your possible immobility at the drop site were premature.

"We wish to start your final preparations tomorrow morning. We in the intelligence community cannot predict exactly what the political or military consequences of your successful mission will be. We do believe, however, that its success will at least change the course of the war in Europe.

"We cannot stress enough that all these deliberations and plans are top secret. Only the five people in this room, and now you, will know the details. The special instructors who will come in for classes with you will know only that you are being readied for some action with intelligence implications.

"We are telling you a few details this morning so that you can begin your focus, your mental toughening and preparation this serious mission will require. Do you understand and agree so far?"

"Yes, sir."

"Okay, here it is. Your target is in Germany. Your target is Adolf Hitler." Giles paused to let the announcement's impact sink in.

Hayden was not asked to comment, but he knew he was being observed closely by all the team members. Ever since Lt. Col. Baxter had conducted Hayden's preliminary screening in his office at Ft. Bragg, Hayden carried the suspicion that all the personnel requirements set out pointed to an assassination attempt on Hitler. That suspicion had been reinforced in all the instructions and training he had been given since. Nonetheless, he was momentarily overwhelmed by the revelation.

"Yours will be a solo mission. You are to jump into the Berchtesgaden, Germany, area and carry out our plan to kill Hitler at his Berghof chalet."

Giles had already considered Hayden's reaction and understood his reaching for help.

"Beginning Monday back at Pine Camp, we will jointly study the information we have on the Berghof compound and plan the specifics of the attack."

Chapter 22

Pine Camp, New York, Week of November 20, 1944

As with the first two weeks of winter training at Pine Camp, the classes now were mostly unstructured discussions with experts. The same format included Hayden, the four intelligence team members, and Col. Giles. Giles provided all of them the American intelligence community's rationale for the planned action against Hitler.

"After the elimination of Hitler, the prospects for achieving unconditional surrender of Germany will be improved greatly. Inroads can be made to negotiations with German generals. Several of them have indicated privately that the war is lost. The high political figures in Germany are not so inclined, however.

"Even without an immediate German surrender, Hitler's dominance as a strategic and tactical planner will be overcome. He is far too unpredictable. The Allies can plan the reactions of other German military leaders as strategists better than those of Hitler.

"Captain, we can also give you a more complete answer to the question you asked last week about using an agent inside Germany for the task. I believe the question involved either using an inside agent close to the target or inserting one already in Germany but not in Hitler's inner circle. We could not answer fully then without revealing the target." Colonel Giles nodded to Captain Tobias for the answer.

"Why not an agent already inside Germany? Discreet inquiries have been made about employing one of Hitler's staff for an assassination attempt. It simply is not going to be possible to get him or anyone in Hitler's entourage to do the job, especially with the increased security since the July 20 plot at *Wolfschanze* against him failed. Some useful information has been passed out by the underground agents who approached Hitler's staff member, however.

"It would be impossible to get anyone from outside his inner circle close enough to Hitler for a pistol shot. And even if possible, one of our agents inside Germany for a long time might not be as reliable now. The same is true for any rogue agent who is now ostensibly working for us.

"We cannot rely on an agent inside Germany for a rifle shot from a great distance for the same reliability reason. None of the agents inside Germany has that skill or weapon."

"You will be made privy to that underground information in a few minutes," Colonel Giles said. "As for our plan for a trained solo shooter from the outside, that is a different matter. We know for sure what we have in your recent record. On the other hand, we do not have information as usable or precise as a trusted agent with experience and already inside Germany would be able to obtain.

"The other personnel option, an assault team from the outside, is much more difficult to shield from scrutiny. An enterprising individual soldier, with proper papers, can be hidden or absorbed within a military unit or even into guards on duty. An entire unit of five or six would be less absorbable. We believe a long-range shooter inserted fresh from outside Germany is the most practical and efficient killing solution.

"Now that we are directly on the topic, it is worthwhile to note that Hitler has been the object of several attempts on his life since he gained power in Germany," Col. Giles continued. "Known past attempts on Hitler were planned as bomb or pistol attacks, where closeness of the killing medium to Hitler was required. We could not see you getting within handshake distance of Hitler, or surviving if you did the job that way."

"Hitler's surviving those attempts may have prompted him to think he was more and more invincible," Lt. Raymond said. "That ego might work to his disadvantage by not inspiring him to change his old routines."

"Let's turn to specific planning," Col. Giles said. "First, a final drop zone has not been selected. When we get to Paris, we will consult with local experts and choose a zone. We will also hear their recommendation on using an air field either in France or Italy."

Hayden was not pleased with the lack of decision on a drop zone and broke in to say so.

"Knowing a well-researched drop zone is a significant element in a jumper's mental preparation for a mission. It is also critical to his safe jump. Knowing and hitting the best possible zone sets the table for success of the project. He can even adjust to an off-target jump due to wind or weather, pilot error, even hostile fire, if he can orient to the mission's geographic base. A good, known drop zone is the first and most important step to a successful mission plan."

Hayden sat back in the leather chair facing the fireplace, confident that his point was so obvious that it would not be challenged. The other team members were already comfortable with their coffee and also leaned back.

"We will insist on the best aircraft and crew available to give you a safe landing," said Major Driver. "As you know, Captain, there are no guarantees in this kind of action."

Hayden leaned forward again and interrupted. "Excuse me, sir. I am confident of my ability to function in unforeseen circumstances and protect myself." Hayden let some irritation at Driver's disregard of his point seep into his voice. "The chances of mission failure have to be reduced by careful scrutiny of possible jump zones to find the most suitable one. On-the-spot corrections can be made best from that known reference point. A safe jump means the jumper is sound enough after the jump to complete the mission."

"Keep going," Giles urged. "We are still flexible in our planning."

"There is no perfect drop zone. We have to consider the tradeoffs, positive and negative, in planning for a successful mission. That decision should be made well in advance of other details. The risk of incapacitating the jumper on a rehearsal jump, for example, cannot be taken on a jump with a serious mission objective," he said pointedly.

"The outcome of a mission involves a series of bad case scenarios to avoid on the jump. Starting with the worst, I suggest they look like this for the jumper. A landing where (1) death or incapacitation is the result; (2) hostile fire is received on the descent, leading to injury, rendering mission completion impossible; (3) detection occurs without capture or injury; (4) exposure time increases without detection; (5) some delay occurs without detection.

"The objective of sound landing-zone planning should be to eliminate the least desirable outcomes. That is where the tradeoffs come in. A close-in drop may be in a heavily defended area where results (1) and (2) are likely. A drop in a populated area not heavily defended with troops would increase the chance of detection, as in (3). As the drop zone is moved farther away from the target area, exposure time increases, some of it potentially hostile, as in (4), or maybe not, as in (5), and simply causes delay in mission completion. The required tradeoff of delay against the loss of the mission, however undesirable that delay may be, is obvious."

All of the team members, now alerted to the depth of the problem, turned to Col. Giles. He, in turn, was silent and thoughtful for a long time. Hayden had a new admiration for the Colonel. He believed that Giles' willingness to consider a change in plans even now and spend the time necessary to get things right was a sign of his dedication to the success of this mission.

"This matter is very serious," Giles said finally. "Your concerns are quite valid, Captain. It makes no sense to plan thoroughly all aspects of the mission except getting you first, undetected and uninjured, into a location reasonably accessible to the target.

"Once we all get to Paris, it may be necessary to take an extra day or two and study possible landing sites with the intelligence people there. We'll try to get new data. Current aerial photos of the wider Berghof area might not be out of the question, though an over-flight is itself risky in the alert it may give to defenders."

Giles summarized with the need for soundness of preparations. "We've come too far on this project to get careless now."

Hayden nodded his satisfaction with the decision.

"Captain, do you have other questions?"

"There are a couple other things troubling me. The most important is, how do we know where Hitler is at any time? How do we know he will be in Berghof when we need him to be?"

"The answer is that no one knows anything to the contrary at any time," Col. Giles said. "There is credible information that Hitler is at Berghof. We have knowledge also that he is not at the other two locations he frequents, *Wolfschanze* in East Prussia and his Berlin headquarters. We have instructed all of our radio analysts to be especially alert to hints of his whereabouts. I am sure we will get immediate notice about any location change he makes. Anything else?"

"No sir. Nothing more now."

Hayden did not like the loose ends he learned about this morning. He was about to learn there were a few more.

"Okay, let's get to it," Giles said.

"Captain, this is top secret, protect-at-all-cost intelligence we are going to discuss. Over the years, we have provided the British information on data we intercepted, occasionally on what we learned about German V-2 ramp placement, U-Boat killing technology being developed, and so on. They routinely did the same for us. Once in a while we received some prime intelligence that was not necessarily military, or even useful at the time...political stuff perhaps...and passed it on. Again, they reciprocated with the same kind of material.

"The British recently passed us some interesting items on Berghof. One is a new aerial photo of the Berghof environs. Another is information on Hitler's daily routine. They got that from German defectors, dissidents, and turned agents. Some of this information has been confirmed by radio intercepts, agents, and German POWs held in the U.S. Moreover, some geographical data, especially on key points of interest around Berghof, has been verified by our scrutiny of the aerial photo the British gave us. So we feel comfortable with this intelligence."

"They thought about doing some hunting at Berghof themselves," Hayden said.

"No doubt," said Giles. "Some Brits are a bit strange on this point. We know that a vocal segment of their political and military leadership believes the Allies are better off with Hitler at the helm than someone else. In effect, they want to rely on his proneness to mistakes. That may explain their not taking any personal action against Hitler on their own."

"Better the devil you know..." Hayden suggested.

"Yes, even with Hitler's eccentricities. Exactly because of Hitler's eccentricities! However, back to the point. Col. Alexander?"

It seemed to Hayden that Lt. Col. Alexander was basking again in the spotlight of discussion, especially with a higher ranking official present. The confidence Giles has in Alexander by choosing him as team leader should quell any doubts as to his competence. Still, Hayden would keep an open mind on Alexander's mettle in a crisis.

"The attack site is Hitler's chalet called Berghof, a few miles east of Berchtesgaden on the Obersalzberg Plateau," Alexander began. "Berghof was purchased by Hitler in the 1930's. He had it renovated, re-decorated, and expanded. Berghof is not a mansion but a somewhat ordinary residence for that area. It is evidently large enough and impressive enough to receive diplomatic delegations, however. In pre-war pictures we can see a rather wide terrace along the building on two sides. It was then used for informal affairs and as a greeting venue for formal occasions.

"We know from the same sources that there are tunnels deep into the mountains connecting Berghof with nearby buildings. Bavaria is rumored to be the site of a national redoubt for Hitler and his close military and political leaders and friends to make a last stand when the end of the war nears for them.

Whether the plan for a redoubt is true or not, the deep tunnels and bunkers under the mountains make the killing by bombing or strafing unlikely.

"Several other prominent Nazis, including Herman Goering and Martin Bormann, acquired chalets near Berghof. You might note that Hitler has another residence a few miles from Berghof at the top of a mountain. It is called the Eagle's Nest. Hitler apparently does not go there often as he is rumored to be afraid of heights. In any event, those other locations are not in play on this mission.

"There are several critical timing issues to resolve. Given our need to scour the area for the best drop zone," Alexander said, looking at Giles, "we hope to drop you in darkness early one morning. The plan is to land you north of Berchtesgaden as close to that community as possible in a non-populated area. In the plan of attack, you should then be close to Berghof but not within its defense perimeter.

"After your jump, and as you approach the Berghof compound, do not use the Berghof Road, the main road connecting Berchtesgaden to Berghof…here," Alexander said, pointing to the greatly enlarged map taped next to the fireplace. "You might as well send an announcement of your intentions to the German security detail as walk up that road. It is too heavily guarded.

"We think you should plan to enter the Berghof perimeter using forest cover a couple miles north and west of the chalet. After your careful movement through the forest, your eventual penetration of the wire-enclosed Berghof compound should be west of the *Tee Haus*…about here.

"Why the *Tee Haus*? Given what we know of Hitler's routine, he retires late and sleeps perhaps until 09:30 or 10:00 in the morning. He has a known habit of then taking a little exercise, a ten- to fifteen-minute walk to the *Tee Haus* where he has breakfast. The word is that he walks alone, or with an aide or two at most.

"You can expect that he will be very well guarded by patrols in the forest and along the way, although there is a rumor that he does not like to see the patrols. Again, his ego may be at work here, his notion of invincibility," Alexander said, looking to psychologist Raymond in case any help was to be offered by him on Hitler's ego. "The word also is that he gets a ride back to the chalet after breakfast.

"This walk time to the *Tee Haus* is his most vulnerable time, and the only realistic time for a shoot.

"The *Tee Haus* itself is possible as a shooting site. However, if Hitler is coming there for breakfast, that means there are staff and many guards inside and around the *Tee Haus* that you probably would not be able to bluff or deceive. You would need to eliminate them. And there may be too many for you to eliminate safely and quietly.

"Your best firing position is not from the *Tee Haus* but here…in the elevated woods west of the building. You can expect guards there as well, fronting the woods or in the stand of trees itself. Maybe you should take along extra clips of pistol ammo." Alexander was only half joking. "You may get off only one or two shots at Hitler before you have to move on.

"Introduce a further complication into the plan, the changing of the guard. You probably will not be able to avoid detection entirely. So the timing of your disposal of guards will be critical. When you leave dead guards around, they will not appear for the changing of the guard. Their absence will prompt a full-scale search of the whole area. That would be extremely dangerous for you.

"This will be the trickiest part. You will need to get to your shooting position, shoot, and withdraw, all within one of those shifts. You will therefore need to confirm beforehand the length of the guard shifts and the timing of the shift changes. Also, the length and timing of shifts may change periodically as part of the security routine.

"Having worked your way into the compound, probably eliminating guards, if you do not get your shooting chance then, you may have to depart without completing your mission. You will not be able to erase the trail you have left. Bodies will be discovered. Security will be intensified. The Berghof perimeter will be impossible to penetrate again. You will not be able to repeat your attempt."

Hayden was bothered by another loose end being avoided. "The odds might be very low for all your stated events falling into place properly the day of the shoot. Hitler might oversleep. He might have a cold. The weather could keep him inside. He might take breakfast in the chalet for no reason other than a change in routine. The guard detail, out of his sight or not, might be increased in anticipation of his walk."

Col. Giles held up his hand before Lt. Col. Alexander could offer an answer.

"Any one or all of those are possible, Captain. As Col. Alexander said before, we cannot guarantee that the plan details and timing will merge neatly into place. Likewise, we know that you cannot guarantee success. You have indicated you are willing to give it your best effort. That is all we ask. With a bit of luck coming your way, you can succeed."

There was no denying the somber mood of the team when the talk turned to Hayden's escape after the shooting. Alexander sought to lighten the mood before addressing the topic.

"Remember that you are not visiting in Germany indefinitely on this trip. You can go back for sightseeing when the war is over." No one smiled. "You also have an advantage over our agents who are embedded there, who stay there to observe and report over an extended time at a constant risk of exposure."

"We believe your best route out is by train through Germany westward…perhaps to Cologne, Frankfort, Mainz, or Aachen. You probably will need to stay under cover, hide out while you await the advance of American forces into Germany." Major Driver seemed obliged to make some kind of contribution, Hayden thought. He offered no practical guidance, and his voice contained little conviction.

Lt. Raymond also tried to be helpful. "You will have to maintain the same aggressive posture afterwards as on your entry into Germany. You may need to eliminate German military or police personnel as before. Continuing to change your uniform should provide you with good cover."

The last team meeting with Hayden before the flight to Europe was for housekeeping. With Hayden's input, they all went over the equipment he would carry with him on his mission.

Most important in the checklist was the absence of an item, a radio. "There is nothing you will need to tell us and nothing further we can tell you once you're out of the plane," Col. Alexander announced. That meant there would be no call-back or re-direction.

Hayden did not want to carry extra baggage. A radio would be bulky. However, he felt the intelligence basis for his mission was suspect. There might indeed be something further for the team to tell him after he jumped. Last minute information on Hitler's whereabouts could be critical to the success of his mission.

Hayden expected that the conversation on the long flight to France would be the occasion for team reassurances and pep talk. Given the loose ends revealed in mission preparation, the team would have to realize the doubts created in Hayden's mind.

However, he did not have to be pumped up for his mission. He had not revealed to Col. Giles that he suspected Hitler was the target ever since his first meeting at Ft. Bragg with Lt. Col. Baxter. His suspicion was confirmed in the winter mountain training with a long-range rifle. He had begun concentrating on his task then.

He also knew all along that the mission would be very dangerous. The design of a plan so momentous had to be infested with unknowns and uncertainties. The absolute necessity to rid the world of Hitler and what he stood for had long been instilled in him, even in his early military training. Retribution furnished him more than sufficient motivation for carrying out his mission.

Chapter 23

Ft. Bragg, N.C., Friday, November 24

Jerry Connelios had been sure of the implications in the official message he received on October 2. He was then back with the 82nd Airborne Division in The Netherlands, helping to hold the perimeter created during the Market-Garden invasion. He had been given a week's leave after the initial stage of the operation was completed.

The message was from the Commander of the American Military Police in France.

> *To clarify some issues regarding your personal behavior as it may affect your performance as an officer, you are hereby ordered to Ft. Bragg immediately. Report there to the Office of the Judge Advocate General, Defense Counsel.*

The MP Commander in France apparently thought it best to handle the matter by not handling it in the European Theatre.

Documents were sent to the Military Police Commander at Ft. Bragg. They included signed affidavits from the Military Police Commander in France. Jerry and Lt. Zach Hanna had been observed together on several occasions. The witnesses had been interviewed and their sworn testimony also had been included.

One report stated that Jerry had frequented a steam bath in Paris. Several times he had gone in alone and come out with someone, a man fitting the description of Lt. Hanna. More important, a report from a bath attendant stated that they were seen naked, holding hands, hugging on at least one occasion.

Jerry departed France the day after the order. He barely had time to pack. Hayden was on special duty somewhere. Jerry left a note to him that he had been ordered back to Ft. Bragg for reasons he did not know.

Now, almost two months after reporting to Ft. Bragg, Jerry met Major Hugo Valerian, the defense counsel assigned to him. The Major began by explaining his role in the matter.

"I have been assigned to undertake your defense in this matter," the Major said formally. "I have represented all ranks of military personnel, officers and non-coms. I am not a newcomer to this job. I have been in the Army Judge Advocate General's Office since 1938, long before the war started. I have handled charges stemming from every kind of conduct, or misconduct, you can imagine. The volume of this activity has increased enormously in wartime as the numbers in uniform grew. I have handled my share of those charges.

"I need to tell you that routinely I have found some element of truth in practically all charges against my clients. Let me assure you also that I do not need to sympathize with the motivations of my clients or condone any wrongdoing in order to afford them my best representation," the Major said.

He waited for Jerry's response.

Jerry was silent, not sure what to say about this man's review of his past legal experiences.

"Indeed, I often find some actions of my clients to be personally reprehensible," Valerian continued.

Jerry waited again, now sure that the Major was challenging him to state his own convictions in the face of an uncertain endorsement of his cause by the lawyer. Could he trust his fate to this man? Did he have a choice?

"I appreciate your candor, Major. Apparently my friendships are the subject of this official inquiry. I assume I will have a chance to hear and refute any charges. Will I be able to see the detailed charges soon? Where does it go from here?"

"Since you apparently wish to contest those charges, here are your options," the Major said, puzzled at the front Jerry was attempting by minimizing some rather sordid activities. Of course, the Captain could not know yet the nature of the affidavits in the record. It was time to tell him what he was up against.

"A military trial is significantly different from a civilian trial. Here are the kinds of courts martial.

"A General Court Martial typically hears the most serious charges, including crimes punishable by death. A Summary Court Martial tries minor offenses.

"The offenses with which you are charged and would be tried fall in the middle category called a Special Court Martial. It handles serious, but not the most serious charges. This Court can order a bad conduct discharge, however.

"You have a choice. You can request trial by military judge alone or by the 'convened authority.' In this case, the Commander of the Military Police can convene a court of three members, one of whom is the presiding officer. I recommend the latter.

"An attorney such as I is supplied by the court at no cost to the defendant. Or you may hire a private attorney to defend you."

"When could I expect trial?"

"Obviously, each of the many army bases inside the U.S. and elsewhere has a different volume of case activity. Despite the sizable increase in the volume of legal activity during the war, the legal authorities here have moved cases along expeditiously. Since the docket is kept quite current here, you could expect a convening of a court in a matter of weeks, not months or years.

"Your choosing a court martial, as contrasted to admitting guilt and taking the consequences to obviate the trial, is an implicit agreement that you will answer any questions raised by the prosecuting attorney and the court itself. Those questions, I should tell you, likely will be brutally frank as to your conduct...what, when, where, with whom...with little or nothing on why."

"It sounds like you have made a judgment..."

"Not on your guilt or innocence. Only on the kinds of evidence we will have to confront. I try to be realistic. Are you prepared now to talk about some details with me, to see where we stand, given my experience and professional judgment in these matters? If you like, we can walk through the probable trial testimony, adding in the evidence that the prosecution is obliged to provide us, and let you decide?"

Jerry nodded, and Major Valerian continued.

"We have a report that you and Lt. Zach Hanna have been observed together on several occasions. After the Market-Garden operation, on your week's leave in Paris, you frequented a steam bath. You regularly went in alone and came out with a man, reportedly Lt. Hanna. More importantly, there is a report from an attendant that the two of you were seen naked together, holding hands, hugging.

"In addition to reports, these are these photographs from Paris," Valerian said matter-of-factly as he pulled them from a manila envelope in his file. "This one shows you hand-in-hand with Lt. Hanna checking into a hotel together in Paris. The report with it says that you and the Lieutenant seemed inordinately friendly. A maid was motivated by what she suspected and took another picture through the window. It is somewhat grainy, but as you can see, it shows the two of you together in bed."

"I am appalled that American Military Police will stoop to this disgraceful, contemptible practice, hiring non-military people to spy on their own..." Jerry blurted, frustrated by the damning evidence and aware that bravado in the face of it was futile.

"These people are not hired by the army or military police to follow military personnel around and spy on them. These free lancers realize they have a paying sideline. They know the value of this work and they get a payment for it in food or gasoline or whatever. What the pictures show is rather clear. Their value to the MP's is what they think cleaning up a dossier is worth.

"As to what is a disgraceful and contemptible practice...well, you could get some argument rather quickly from members of a court if that point were raised."

Jerry started to object, but Major Valerian stopped him with his upraised hand.

"The military pays locals in foreign countries for all kinds of information. Photographs are especially valuable for military intelligence uses. The kinds of pictures we have here are ancillary to basic intelligence gathering, of course. Officials other than the officers of a special court martial know their market value, and have no qualms about the army paying for such information. It tends to confirm and solve all sorts of problems that might otherwise get muddled in conflicting oral reports and testimony.

"An example of the latter is the recent incident in the Officers Club bar here. We have no pictures of that, only an oral report from a bartender of the things you and Lt. Hanna said to each other. But the court likely would agree with the prosecutor that your conduct stated in this charge is continuing, given the pictures."

Jerry suspected immediately that his old friend Hayden had to have revealed personal information to the authorities from their October 27 dinner meeting. Hayden had acted morally superior when he showed by his actions what he suspected was the sexual relationship between Jerry and Zach.

"Is there any report corroborating what the Officers Club bartender has stated?"

Major Valerian was puzzled again, now by the question of corroboration Capt. Connelios was seeking. He searched briefly through his files before answering.

"An anonymous tip put the MP's onto the bartender two days after your meeting with Lt. Hanna at the bar. Apparently, someone doesn't like you. Also, an officer the MP's sought to question has made no statement and is now beyond the reach of the MP's or the court. He is on secret duty, I understand."

"And he hasn't said anything?"

"Not a word."

"Could he somehow have made the anonymous tip?"

"I don't believe it was possible," the Major replied, now more curious than ever. "His orders rendered him totally incommunicado at least by the early morning following your meeting with Lt. Hanna."

Major Valerian did not want to say what he suddenly suspected. The anonymity of the tip had all the earmarks of retaliation by a spurned lover. Valerian knew that Hanna was also being charged. Could Hanna have thought that Capt. Brooke was his rival for Capt. Connelios' attentions, and then took revenge on Connelios with an anonymous phone call?

Connelios did not seem to suspect Hanna at all, but might later come to a different realization on that. He obviously suspected Capt. Brooke as the informant. The Major did not deem it worthwhile to pursue Connelios' suspicions.

"So, is there no defense worth presenting?" Jerry asked it weakly after a brooding silence of several minutes.

"Here's how I think the court martial dialogue would play out," the Major said. "I would argue that your conduct was not 'service-connected.' I might use the example of an off-duty service man, not in uniform and off base, getting into a bar room brawl. Our service man socks the other man, whether in self defense or as the aggressor probably is not material. The other man is not in military service. Our man is accused of assault by a person he had never met before the incident.

"I would ask the court why, in the first place, this assault is a matter for military authority, not civilian authority, to handle. Likewise, Capt. Connelios' private sexual conduct in all respects is just that, a private matter, while he was off duty."

"Good." Jerry smiled, pleased at the argument's strength.

"Not so fast, Captain. If the court is on the ball—and count on it, it will be—the response is most likely to be that the jurisdiction of the court is based solely on the accused, you, being a member of the United States Army, i.e., subject to military law. That jurisdiction is not based on any demonstration of the conduct complained of being service-connected in a strict sense. It is based instead on a serviceman's conduct not being 'conducive to good order and discipline'."

"They won't buy into your example, in other words?"

"I doubt it. I could argue that there is no allegation or evidence that Capt. Connelios' sexual conduct occurred while he was on official duty. There is no allegation, charge, or evidence that his conduct was ever detrimental to 'good order and discipline' of a military unit in combat or otherwise. I would point to your record and say, 'Captain Connelios' military conduct has been exemplary. There is no hint of misconduct offered into evidence by men under his command'."

"All that certainly is true," Jerry said.

"And two officers having a drink together at a private bar, the Officers Club, what precedent does that set for other officers relaxing after a long day?"

"Will they accept that argument, Major?"

"Here's what I think. If it were relaxation in the bar one time with a bartender overhearing something he didn't like, we would have no problem. But the total evidence is beyond what a lot of non-legal observers would call 'circumstantial.' Those pictures are kegs of explosives against any defensive wall we could build."

"Should I go ahead with the special court martial?"

"Your option, of course, is to resign your commission and leave the service. The advantage is that you will not have the trauma of trial to withstand nor the trial record to live with."

"You really don't think I can win?"

"Frankly, I believe you lost your case the day that camera shutter clicked."

Chapter 24

Paris and Strasbourg, November 26-30, 1944

Hayden left the U.S. late on the evening of November 26 with the intelligence team. They were taken aboard the Army cargo plane on Col. Giles' radioed insistence. Hayden's other traveling companions were high priority spare parts and six cases of "morale builder kits" for selected Paris military patrons. They looked a lot like scotch and bourbon to Hayden.

There was a break in the long journey at Thule, Greenland, for re-fueling and crew change at noon on the 27th, then on to Paris the next afternoon. On their arrival, Hayden and the team met with Col. Giles, who flew over a day earlier, and three members of the Army Intelligence staff in Paris.

Giles immediately announced a major change in the assassination plan. There would be no jump to enter Hayden into Germany. The local intelligence officers took turns explaining the reasons the air plan was being discarded.

"First, a single aircraft draws hostile attention. The enemy may not bother to send interceptor aircraft or man the flak guns for a single plane. But their reasonable assumption on seeing or hearing a single aircraft is that some threatening activity is occurring, even if a parachute is not seen by locals. Patrols are alerted. The surprise element is lost."

Hayden's handlers did not demur. They looked at Hayden, who asked, "That danger was known from the outset, wasn't it?"

One of the local intelligence officers nodded, and no one else answered. "In addition," the officer said, "a drop in the Berchtesgaden area was planned for night. Even minimum jump safety in a night drop there cannot be assured. A daylight drop has bigger problems. We know of no secure drop zones there."

Another Paris officer sensed Hayden's frustration. "We would be throwing away a plane, crew, and a trained agent if we proceeded with this plan."

Hayden was simultaneously vexed that this discovery came so late in the planning, especially after the dangerous night rehearsal drop in the Vermont forest, and pleased that his "safe drop zone" plea in the planning talks with Col. Giles and the team was heeded.

Col. Giles intervened. "Captain Brooke, there is some positive news that we believe supports the less risky land route into Germany. General Patch's Seventh Army fought its way to the Rhine just a few days ago, November 23, at Strasbourg. His army now holds a stretch of about twenty miles along the river. There have already been successful movements of agents across the Rhine, even in the face of the German presence on the east bank of the river. An entry into Germany across water and land is now entirely feasible with the help of the underground. It is dangerous but workable if a good time is chosen. We consider that option much less dangerous than a parachute jump into Bavaria."

Hayden agreed to the change despite some misgivings. "I'll see the plan through and make the best of it."

Team leader Lt. Col. Alexander followed with a flattering but correct assessment.

"The purpose of this mission has not changed. It is still of the highest military priority. True, a paratrooper is no longer essential to the plan. However, there is no other person available with your skills, specialized training, and mental toughness for this task, even if we waited a month, or six months."

The Paris chief of Army Intelligence, Colonel Braxton Belleau, spoke up. "This bit of information does not go beyond this room, you understand. I can tell you that there are going to be heavy American bombing raids against German defenses all along the east bank of the Rhine from the Black Forest northward the nights of November 30 and December 1 A raid should provide a good distraction and cover for a river crossing if you want to try it either night. The fireworks should keep the Germans hunkered down for a while."

"That settles the timing," said Giles. "We'll go when the bombing starts on the 30th. Let's move our operation to Strasbourg today."

Hayden spent the day preparing mentally for the mission while being transported to Strasbourg. He studied maps of the area between Strasbourg and Mainz, envisioning the route he and two agents on a separate mission would take through the Black Forest and Southwestern Germany. He then committed to memory the cities and rail junctions along the route he planned to take all the way to Berchtesgaden.

Once in Strasbourg, Giles and the team were put up in a public building commandeered for American military use. Hayden's temporary quarters were next door to Col. Giles. Giles told him to ask for any help he needed from the intelligence staff gathered there.

Giles called another meeting on the morning of the 29th. The newly appointed Director of Army Intelligence in Strasbourg, Major Jackson Pendler, had informed him that a group of about fifty German prisoners taken earlier in the morning were being held in a warehouse just down the street from where Hayden and the others were quartered. Giles had directed Pendler's aides to study the prisoners for suitable uniform and ID transfers to the three American agents. Several good prospects with fresh papers were identified, including a German Lieutenant of Hayden's height and build named Eric Klaysa.

Giles ordered several actions. "Set up a two-way mirror arrangement between the two offices at the prisoner warehouse. Tomorrow morning, let's interview the German Lieutenant. Captain Brooke can observe behind the mirror. Barney, can you line up the underground guides for tomorrow night? Major Pendler, let's get going with the uniform and ID changes. Get the POW uniforms cleaned. Go over the ID's and papers thoroughly. We can't be buying a pig in a poke."

On the morning of his departure, Hayden was shown to a room behind a two-way mirror in the office of the warehouse. It was learned from his papers that the prisoner, German Lieutenant Klaysa, was in German Army Intelligence.

Hayden's study of the German officer's mannerism led him to believe they were part of a planned deception. He whispered to Major Pendler, "The Lieutenant seems eager to reveal personal information, family, schooling, the region he comes from. But he turns very vague when he talks about military matters like what he was doing near the front line when he was captured."

The Lieutenant's interrogators later confirmed Hayden's assessment. The prisoner provided misleading relevant information interspersed with irrelevant correct information. He apparently hoped the bits of truth would give all his comments the ring of truth. Hayden decided he would ignore all of what the Lieutenant said and disregard all his mannerisms.

After lunch, final preparations for the mission were conducted in an assembly of SIP and local Army Intelligence officers. Hayden tried on the clean-but-not-too-pressed German uniform and it fit. His traveling rank would be Lieutenant, with ID and papers accordingly. The fake orders for Lt. Klaysa required Hayden to report to the regional security office in Munich.

He was provided a German officer's great coat out of the stock that Army Intelligence had accumulated. The Lieutenant's boots, watch, and other personal effects were given to him along with a Luger pistol. One of the intelligence officers matched a check list line by line to ensure that Hayden was not carrying anything "American." That list included captured laundered underwear, a spare shirt, and shaving gear.

Hayden was provided German marks, French francs, Swiss francs, and Eric Klaysa's rail pass. When he was given the most recent train schedules, Mainz to Munich, and Munich to Berchtesgaden, he was warned that delays were becoming more common with Allied bombings of rail junctions and equipment.

He slipped his own pistol with silencer into the inside pocket of his great coat. He told the checklist officer that it did not matter that the pistol was American made. If he had to use it, the receiving party would not have time to check its country of origin.

His German soldier's overnight bag to carry the rifle was emptied and he helped to re-pack it. As the heaviest item, the disassembled rifle was put at the bottom of the bag. It was wrapped in clothing to keep the other bag components from thumping against it. Included in the bag were two clips of pistol ammunition, elastic cord, a knife, wire cutters, a flashlight and a route map should he have to abandon public transportation. Again he had to fend off intervention of the checklist officer.

"If anyone should get into this bag," Hayden pointed out, "the cover game is over. How would I explain a .50 caliber, folded up rifle? I'm going moose hunting? This is the only bag I could find, so I sawed the barrel in half?"

He was given some pictures of himself, properly aged. He put them into his boot with other ID's and papers. He would paste one onto any new ID he assumed. The checklist officer reminded him to put one on Eric Klaysa's rail pass, and he complied without comment.

Major Pendler cautioned Hayden. "Captain, you will need to use your ingenuity to change uniforms from time to time as the locality and circumstances require. Don't be squeamish about putting on a used uniform. Remember that your cover is critical to your safety and the completion of this mission."

Hayden vowed silently that he would never tell Sarah of any uniform "exchanges." She had not been out of his mind for long in the bustle of the last week. The barrage of mission details did crowd the time he could give to other compartments of his life, however. The attention he had to give to preparation for the grim business ahead was effective in turning some thoughts away from the tension in his marriage. Sarah would see the seriousness of his mission if she knew it. And she would be concerned that her husband might not survive the mission. Would she deplore the mission for that reason alone? Or would her opposition still be fundamentally philosophical and moral?

He turned his attention again to the continuing pronouncements of Major Pendler. It had been easy to tune out the repetition and redundancy in his loud, expressionless voice as he talked of weighty matters.

"The cover you have in France by American ground forces, especially by Army Intelligence, will cease once you leave France. However, information as to your whereabouts will be limited to those selected few people in this room."

Hayden estimated fifteen people in the room and therefore in the know. The group included his four handlers and Col. Giles. He was seeing the others for the first time in this meeting. There was always a conflict between security for a mission found in fewer numbers knowing about it and the need to bring people with different expertise into the planning process. He was uneasy with the security loop being stretched by Major Pendler to touch all the preparation bases.

The insertion of Hayden and two Sergeants on other missions into Germany would be very secretive, of course. Two of the Strasbourg intelligence officers familiarized him with how the underground in France and Germany would get him through the front lines at an entry point not so heavily populated by German defense forces.

"Remember this is a no-recall mission. You cannot be contacted by radio since you won't have one. You will be on your own, with your only orders the ones you are given here, all the way to completion of the mission," one concluded.

"Let's go over the assassination plan one more time," Lt. Col. Alexander suggested. Hayden winced at revelation of crucial plan details to such a large group. He thought Alexander was showboating in talking about the assassination plan his team had developed. He looked at Col. Giles, who had a somewhat resigned look on his face. Further, the review wasn't needed. Hayden had etched it in his memory the first time it was revealed to him.

"The plan is to shoot on a morning when Hitler and entourage take a stroll to the *Tee Haus* for a morning meal after 10:00. The best site for firing probably will be the wooded hill to the right side of the *Tee Haus*. You should wait as long as you can to get the best possible shot at Hitler. The rest of the entourage does not matter. Once Hitler has been shot, you should make your way out of the woods and escape."

Hayden again did not observe any enthusiasm among the assembled officers for the un-detailed escape plan mentioned. Their demeanor was in sharp contrast to the spirited instructions they had given him on various aspects of his mission. Their attitude suggested to Hayden that they did not think an escape plan would be necessary.

At 16:00 Giles asked, "Anything else?" With no response, he continued. "Captain, you should get some rest and a meal, and meet back here at 21:00 tonight."

A few minutes before 22:00, the movement of Hayden and the two other agents into Germany started. The departure site was about midway between Strasbourg on the west bank and Karlsruhe on the east bank of the Rhine, due west of Baden-Baden, Germany.

Across the river a flashing light signaled the go ahead from the German underground. The drone of a large flight of approaching Allied bombers grew steadily louder.

Giles was lighthearted in his farewell. "Send pictures when you get settled in your mountain villa."

"I'll put them in a package to you with Hitler's personal pennant," Hayden smiled. He saluted and climbed with the others into the boat.

The two guides from the French underground seemed poised and confident to Hayden. Hayden had the greatest admiration for the underground. They took these operations very seriously. Every crossing they made was dangerous. They had crossed several times since the Seventh Army had reached the Rhine. They did not know the nature of the missions these agents were undertaking, and certainly they could not have guessed what Hayden was up to. They only knew these trips were most important or they would not be taking them.

In thirty minutes, amid the thundering bomb explosions up the river to their left, the underground guides managed to get Hayden and the two Sergeants rowed across the river undetected. Quietly and quickly, the French guides turned their charges over to three German underground guides. There were whispered comments, "good lucks" in French and German all around, and the boat left.

Hayden reflected on the fatalism of the situation. Three Americans were putting their lives, trustingly, for better or worse, into the hands of people they had never met. Indeed, they did not even know what these guides looked like. They probably were German. Hayden hoped they would continue their disenchantment with the Nazi regime over the next few hours.

The party formed up in the darkness. An underground point man started off into the cover of trees. A second fell in several steps behind. The three agents followed closely, one hand on the shoulder of the man in front, with the third underground man serving as the rear guard several steps behind. No one needed to tell the others to maintain strict silence. The trek seemed endless. Only once did they stop, frozen, awaiting a go ahead after a sudden noise somewhere in the trees in front of them.

Somehow, by 02:30 they had cleared the forest and reached a narrow, unpaved secondary road. As if by magic, a van appeared and the three agents piled into the back. The Americans' fatalistic trust was transferred to two new, unknown guides. Again there were quiet handshakes, whispered well wishing, thanks all around, and they were off.

The narrow road was also rutted. Tree branches occasionally brushed the sides of the van. The only smooth travel was the momentary slowdown for checking and crossing a major road. It was obvious these guides knew which less-traveled country roads and paths avoided military patrols. If they did contact a patrol, Hayden had no idea what would happen. He felt in his great coat to be sure he had his pistol.

The one positive was that, with each mile, they were moving farther and farther away from the scrutiny of German Army patrols. Despite the bouncing and rolling of the van, Hayden dozed off in sheer fatigue.

He and the other two agents were awakened several hours later in Mainz. The railroad station was close by. The guides gave them updated information on the train departure at noon. Hayden conferred briefly with the two Sergeants. They agreed that their security prospects were improved for each by traveling alone.

As he stepped from the van, Hayden confronted for the first time the full realization of where he was. It was Mainz, Germany, not Wichita or Kansas City or New York, USA. It was a German city, foreign ground, land of the enemy.

Hundreds of military in transit swarmed around him in the rail depot. In his anonymity, he could blend in with all of them, although he recognized them as potential threats to his safety. He had to be one of them, to think and act like them, even as he felt his throat tighten up as he worried about the many small ways he could betray himself. He could not draw attention to himself by a misstep or misstatement. He had to adapt quickly.

Hayden was pleased that his rail pass was accepted without question. He stored his bag on the rack above his seat and looked forward to the train ride providing a relaxing interlude from the tense and tiring overnight pace.

Chapter 25

Strasbourg, Thursday, November 30, 1944

German Lieutenant Eric Klaysa, German Army Intelligence, was in a group of prisoners confined in a warehouse on the outskirts of Strasbourg. His group of nine stragglers, without food and ammunition, out of contact with their units, had lived off the land and avoided detection for almost a week. They had tried to maneuver behind the lines as the French Second Armored Division of General Patch's Seventh Army closed to the Rhine and took Strasbourg on November 23. They had been captured west of Strasbourg the day before, November 29.

Klaysa was still frustrated at being captured. He had been near the front lines, trying to restore communications broken down among military units during their "orderly retreat" in the face of the Allied Seventh Army advance. He was angry about the defensive breakdowns in his immediate area among units of the German Nineteenth Army commanded by Gen. Wiese. That failure had led to his capture. Immediately to the south, however, the Nineteenth Army was holding a salient around the town of Colmar.

The warehouse holding prisoners was a temporary facility, loosely guarded by French troops. It was rumored the guards were awaiting military police to take charge of the facility.

Two important developments had occurred yesterday. A unit of four Americans in uniform arrived to survey the warehouse and its prisoners. Also, Klaysa and two sergeants in his group were taken under guard to a neighboring house and ordered to take off their uniforms. They were given poorly fitting fatigue uniforms of the American Army.

Klaysa understood the significance of the exchange. Similar exchanges had occurred when Allied soldiers were captured by Germans. The uniforms and ID papers were adopted by German agents for planned infiltration behind enemy lines. He had no doubt that the Americans planned to use the same deception to insert agents somewhere.

The only logical conclusion that Lt. Klaysa could reach was that the insertion would be near where he was. The Allies now held a stretch of the west bank of the Rhine. They could take advantage of that location to insert agents masquerading as German soldiers by water and land into southwestern Germany, and avoid hazardous parachute entry elsewhere.

This morning he alone was taken to a barren office in the warehouse. There was a table and six chairs, no other furniture. There was a large mirror on one side. The warehouse was old, but the frame of the mirror was new. There was no reason for the mirror to be there, out of place in the office.

Klaysa realized immediately what was happening. The man who would be using his uniform was behind the mirror. He was there to observe Klaysa and pick up anything of value he could to improve his cover in a clandestine operation.

Klaysa therefore tried to change his personality, all the while appearing to be cooperative to the interrogators. He tried to avoid giving away anything of intelligence value, mixing truths and untruths to confuse the enemy.

He learned later that the two sergeants whose uniforms had been exchanged were interviewed also, in the same room. He had not had a chance to warn them to be discreet. He hoped each would understand the purpose of the interview.

After their evening meal, Lt. Klaysa called a group of prisoners together, including the two sergeants. He sounded them out, learning how strong their commitment to the German military cause was. He learned a little of their political leanings as well. He was satisfied the group could be trusted.

"This uniform stealing," he began, "can mean only one thing. The enemy will use those uniforms to disguise agents they are planning to send into the Fatherland. They intend to do some damage. We don't know what it is, but activity of this kind often goes beyond military tactics. We have to alert the *Feldgendarmerie* of possible infiltrators."

Sgt. Eberer agreed. "We must do what we can to help our comrades. We must try to notify our Military Police as Lieutenant Klaysa says."

"How can we help?" another asked. "Shall one of us try to escape, rejoin our forces to the south, and alert our officers?"

"The danger is immediate. The need for action is immediate. It is better to communicate by radio. It is faster and has a better chance of success," Lt. Klaysa said.

Klaysa paused and looked over the group of twenty-five men. "I have a plan. After lights out, I want this group to rush the guards on my signal. Pin down as many as you can. Get past them if you can. At least provide a distraction. I have studied this building. During your charge, I will climb up, open a window, and get out."

"And then what?" one of the group asked.

"This morning while I was taken to be robbed of my uniform, I noticed that all the buildings along this street are being used by the Allied Army. There are jeeps parked all over the place. Most of them have radios. I will find one with a radio, drive out into the clear, and send a warning as often as I can."

The other prisoners enthusiastically approved the plan and vowed to help.

"What should we do if we get past the guards?" one asked.

"Try to escape, of course," Klaysa responded. "You can occupy the attention of the Allied personnel in the immediate area and maybe some of their military units. Make your way south, if you can, try to contact our people holding the Colmar pocket, and report what military information you have learned."

The escape began three hours later. The plan's progress was aided by an intense, thunderous bombing raid on the east bank of the Rhine muffling the noise of the prisoners' movement. With surprise, the plan went very well at first. Many of the guards were overwhelmed. Several prisoners made it into the street.

Lt. Klaysa, once out of the window, stayed off of the street until he was a hundred yards or more from the warehouse. While he searched for a jeep with a radio, he heard shots being fired, but not at him.

As he started up a jeep, he heard shouts of "Halt!" from several directions. He drove on. Other jeep lights came on behind him in pursuit. He sped to the only rise in the terrain he could find, doused the lights, clicked on the radio and dialed in the *Feldgendarmerie* frequency in the dim light the dial offered.

He began transmitting in the clear, over and over, without waiting for a response.

> *Alert! Lt. Eric Klaysa...escaped from Allies...my uniform and those of Sergeants Hans Eberer and Matthew Kleine are being used by American agents infiltrating across the Rhine.*

He had sent the message seven or eight times before a jeep pulled up and a gruff French corporal smashed a rifle butt into his face.

Chapter 26

Paris, London, Strasbourg, Friday, December 1, 1944

Early on Friday morning, a British intelligence agent in Paris pondered a very interesting tidbit. He had gotten it from an American, an Office of Strategic Services agent with whom he had been out drinking late the night before. The OSS man had heard the item from an Army Intelligence man just back from Strasbourg. It involved an American plan to assassinate Hitler. The British agent, Liam Paulding, immediately protested to the OSS man that there were always rumors of assassinations around...Hitler, Goering, Goebbels, General von Runstedt. "I hear about one of those plans every week."

"Well," the OSS agent insisted, "this rumored mission actually did start tonight. It took off at the start of that bombing raid."

"You mean a parachute drop into Germany?" Paulding asked. "No, a Rhine crossing, apparently."

"Forgive me, but what is your source?"

"A guy named Mike, American Army Intelligence, was at the planning meeting yesterday afternoon in Strasbourg. He told me not to say anything. You have helped me get hold of some data valuable to us in the past," the OSS man told Paulding. "I am doing the same now. This is a lone gunman going in, not a team. That's all I know."

The more Paulding thought about the information, the more plausible it sounded. He had to tell his section chief.

The Paris section chief was very interested also. His policy was to pass on any intelligence he received, even that classified as rumor. In his way of thinking, a rumor itself was an intelligence intercept, oftentimes the most useful kind of intelligence once it was substantiated. That it came from another Allied source did not diminish its value. By noon the message had been passed through the highest British intelligence level in London. The London bureau chief did not know what to make of it and passed the message, as top priority, to 10 Downing St.

Churchill had it immediately after his lunch. He was very curious and troubled. He asked for confirmation of the message, and received back within a half hour the response that agent Liam Paulding was one of the most reliable and resourceful agents in the Paris office.

Churchill was astounded. For one of the few times in his life he was speechless. The apparent brazenness of his American ally, keeping such a secret from him. He had to know more.

He soon had the London Intelligence Bureau Chief on the scrambler. "Chief, we need to confirm this beyond our own intelligence network. We may have to break down the territorial secrecy walls among Allied intelligence services. If this leaked information is true, we shall have to respond, for reasons I cannot divulge. What can you do to jostle a confirmation from American Army Intelligence?"

The Bureau Chief promised the Prime Minister he would give the matter his immediate and exclusive attention until he had an answer.

While he waited, distracted from other pressing matters, Churchill tried to think through an assassination scenario. He knew that his own intelligence service regularly considered similar plans against Hitler. Approval was denied for two principal reasons. Further information was always needed as to Hitler's whereabouts and his vulnerability to attack. And an attack plan could not be agreed on.

Churchill could not know the odds of the American plan's success since he did not know the plan at all beyond the vaguest overview. An assassination plan using a lone gunman had its strengths and weaknesses. So did every team plan British Intelligence had studied. What advantage did the Americans now see in a lone gunman executing an attack plan? What information could they possibly have gotten that made an attack plausible now?

The Prime Minister kept coming back to what bothered him most. He could not avoid considering the likely implications of this American action. If their plan succeeded, with Hitler eliminated, the major issue the British and other Allies would have to confront would be his successor, or successors. If the Nazi

Party structure took over policy-making, in the persons of Goebbels and Bormann and other party fanatics, they likely would continue on the present course. Those functionaries would feel obliged, as a memorial to the fallen Fuehrer, to continue his policies.

If Hitler were eliminated and more moderate elements came to power in Germany, they would have to address serious questions about the war's continuation. The American, Soviet, and French adamant demands for surrender would have to be tempered by the new realities. At a minimum, the Allies would have to listen to what certain German generals and political insiders would say in the open once Hitler was removed.

Have Roosevelt and his close advisers thought this all through? Churchill wondered. And if they have, and decided to go ahead with the plan, does that mean they are ready to accept the consequences, whichever way the power succession in Germany would go?

At the moment, however, Churchill feared the stronger repercussions would arise if the plan were attempted and failed. If Hitler survived and was still controlling policy, there would be hell to pay. Hitler in anger likely would blame all the Allies, denounce every diplomatic overture, and terminate the truce discussions. Churchill especially hated that knowledge of his approval of secret negotiations would come to light. Churchill would be exposed, not only for engaging in secret diplomacy behind the backs of his Allies. The worst outcome could be his failing in that attempt! He would get nothing but a black eye for the chances he took.

Churchill basically disapproved of the peace initiative from Hitler. Since he agreed to put the process in motion, however, he certainly did not want to be the one responsible for it being aborted. And the prospect of a grand diplomatic victory in obtaining release of Jews and other concentration camp inmates would be shattered as well.

His phone rang about 14:00. The bureau chief confirmed the message with the American Bureau Chief, Col. Braxton Belleau in Paris.

Churchill took a deep breath. "Chief, I need you to do one more, very important thing. I want you to contact Colonel Belleau again and ask that he recall their man. If necessary, mention that the Prime Minister is requesting it."

Churchill did not tell his Bureau Chief that he could not take the time to go through channels to Secretary of State Hull or President Roosevelt with his request. Nor would he mention that such an effort would be extremely awkward for the Prime Minister. The Americans might not see the urgency of stopping the attempt as he did.

When contacted, Col. Belleau did not know the political reasons behind the British Prime Minister's request to terminate Captain Brooke's mission. He did realize immediately that he had a hot potato in his hands. He would pass it off quickly.

The intelligence protocol between the two long-time allies was already breached in Churchill's request. Colonel Belleau could be excused for not trying to restore it from his end. He quickly passed on the order to the Strasbourg Army Intelligence Director, Major Pendler.

Pendler was most upset that there had been a security leak. In record time, it had reached all the way to London. The leak had to come from his own Strasbourg unit that assembled to prepare Captain Brooke for his mission. He regretted deeply that the leak was by an agent in his unit. He would have to do something about that soon.

Col. Everett Giles was not technically in Director Pendler's chain of command. Pendler knew Giles would not be thrilled at the leak or the order he would have to give to stop his man. But Giles had to be told of Churchill's request. And Pendler had to tell him. Immediately.

When located, Giles had just gotten back to Paris from Strasbourg. He was tired. He was already deeply troubled by the escape of prisoner Lt. Klaysa and his ability to send repeated messages before his re-capture. He could only hope that Captain Brooke was alert to his surroundings and potential threats. There was nothing Giles could do on his end to warn Brooke.

Major Pendler regretted his own need to call even more when he heard Giles' recounting of things gone awry in Strasbourg. "Colonel Giles, there's something else about our man's situation that I need to tell you. I hate to tell you, but I have to, since some action must be taken immediately. There has been a serious security leak about this mission within Army Intelligence."

"How bad?"

"Well, someone in my Strasbourg unit shot his mouth off at a bar. An OSS agent picked up the leak, repeated it, and it reached Churchill's office fast. He is not pleased."

Giles sighed. The agent doing the talking had to have been right there in the final preparation meeting in Strasbourg. Giles prodded, "The substance of the leak?"

"Word is out that it was a Rhine river insert, during the bombing raid last night, a lone gunman going after Hitler."

"Do you have any idea who the sieve is?"

"I do. I'll..."

Giles interrupted immediately. "I recommend that you do not discuss this unfortunate security breakdown or the action we probably will have to take against the guilty party just yet. There may already be too many in the British group who know about it. We have a responsibility to our own people, especially Captain Brooke. We do not need to make his presence behind enemy lines more hazardous than it already is. We can't have someone doing more damage out of spite at being threatened with the stockade, or worse. Isolate him for now.

"Major, you know that radio contact with Brooke is out of the question. Do you have anyone in your Strasbourg unit to pursue Brooke immediately, someone who speaks German well, someone trustworthy?"

"No. No one with that level of proficiency. And, regrettably now, no one who is completely reliable in a security sense, without my own serious internal investigation of this unit."

"Thanks for the call, Major. I'll take it from here."

Giles had to make up his mind, and quickly. He and his unit were exposed and embarrassed. The first rule of clandestine operations is that as few people as necessary should be privy to a project. They should be brought in only on a need-to-know basis. Giles regretted especially that he allowed almost a dozen Army Intelligence agents at the Strasbourg planning meeting for Brooke's mission. Some apparently were inexperienced. Telling of the assassination plan was a great way for a novice to impress people at a bar with his importance. Giles thought bitterly that a leak of this type was unlikely to happen back in the States, and certainly not in the front lines where life and death issues compelled secrecy.

He would now need to tell General Marshall before he heard it second-hand. Giles hoped that the general would see his plan as a bold master stroke to end the war.

But first things first. The best that SIP could do, without jeopardizing a lot of people, would be to send an agent into Germany to stop Capt. Brooke. Perhaps Col. Alexander and the immediate SIP team can handle the mechanics of a chaser's insertion into Germany as before, without the involvement of the local Army Intelligence group. Churchill does not know, and does not need to know, that the security of Brooke's mission was simplified by eliminating the possibility of a radio security leak or an enemy intercept. How pathetic that decision seems now, he thought.

He called Paris Army Intelligence Chief Belleau. "We don't have a lot of time, Colonel. Do you have someone, fluent in German, who can find his way around in Germany and, most important, someone who will be able to identify Brooke from pictures we have? I know it's a long shot, but we have to try."

"Let me say first, Colonel, that I have already contacted all our people in France and laid down the law in regard to security. I told them, in case they'd forgotten, there's a war on. I told them I would do my best to see someone shot for treason if another leak occurred in our house. That was a hell of a boost to my group's morale, I know, but it had to be done…it has to be done in all our intelligence units."

Colonel Belleau went on. "An agent with those skills and able to recognize Brooke from a picture…that's a tall order. I'll do my best to see, discreetly, if we have someone, soon."

Giles urged his immediate action. "If at all possible, we would like to insert a chaser in a matter of hours, not days. I'll send a picture of our man over to you right away. If the only thing one of your men does not have is the ability to recognize Brooke, I'll let him study other photos of Brooke."

"I'll do that when the picture arrives," the Chief said.

"I know the odds are against us, but if you can find someone at all suitable, we must make the attempt, Chief. If you do find someone, we can arrange moving him into Germany tonight. My team and I will fly with him to Strasbourg and brief him on the plane. It's now 15:30. Please do what you can."

To Giles' surprise and relief, he had a call back from Chief Belleau at 17:00.

"I think our luck is changing, Colonel. We located a recent addition to our cryptography unit. He is a German native, bolted from Germany in 1938. He knows his way around Germany. And, get this. He is quite sure from the picture you sent that he had a cup of coffee and a chat with Captain Brooke about a month ago at Camp Springs Army Air Field!

"His name is Frederick Penner. He seems willing to undertake the project."

"Great work, Chief! How about getting your man to the airfield at 18:00? We'll arrange things in Strasbourg with some phone calls. Please do not alert your unit there. Thanks for your help."

"It's the least I could do," said the chastened Chief.

The prospect of a special mission involving Hayden was as invigorating to Frederick at it was disconcerting. What was happening? When the chief passed the picture of Hayden among the agents, he suspected Hayden was in some kind of trouble. Frederick offered to help, but was cautious. He did not want their friendship in any way to jeopardize Hayden's situation, whatever that was.

Chief Belleau was pleased someone in his unit could recognize Hayden and was willing to help. To Frederick's questions, he was tight lipped beyond the need for a German-speaking agent who could recognize Hayden and was willing to travel. Frederick had been intrigued by his new front line work as a cryptographer over the past month. This new venture promised even greater excitement and the possibility of helping his friend.

On the plane, Colonel Giles handed him the other photos of Hayden taken at various stages of his special training. He studied them and said, not too quickly, "Yes, this is the man I had coffee with. He was very pleasant. I did not learn anything about his unit, nor he mine."

"That's okay…that's good." Giles smiled. "You're confident you could recognize him again?"

"Yes, I think so," Frederick responded. "I have a good memory of faces.

Giles paused before broaching the delicate leak problem.

"Mr. Penner, I don't know how much you have been told."

Frederick waited. Surely the SIP Director knew how he was recruited by the Paris Army Intelligence chief.

"Nothing," he said.

Giles seemed comforted by his answer. "We have a most secret mission underway as of last night. Captain Brooke has been inserted into Germany to attempt an assassination of a high level German official…"

Hitler, Frederick thought in mounting excitement.

"Adolf Hitler," Giles finished.

Frederick nodded thoughtfully, controlling his feelings.

"Now we have to stop that attempt. For security and other reasons, we did not set up a radio contact system with Brooke. We have no other means to reach him, except personal contact. We're hoping you can reach him to terminate the mission."

Excitement of a different sort flooded Frederick's mind. But he had a bad feeling about the director's use of "terminate."

"I have agreed to help, Colonel Giles. Where will I locate Captain Brooke?"

"That's another big problem we have," Giles said.

Frederick saw that Giles was now quite uncomfortable.

"Since the start of the mission about 22:00 last night, our team does not know where Brooke is at any time. We don't know his time schedule. In our planning, Captain Brooke suggested keeping things unstructured and flexible. We agreed. Our interest was not in a certain day or time for the attempt, only that it would occur soon, and with success. The other side cannot know his location either, of course. But the unstructured timing of the attempt is now a mixed blessing.

"About the same time as Capt. Brooke's insertion into Germany last night, an escaped German prisoner radioed the German Military Police, the *Feldgendarmerie*, that his uniform and papers had been taken. He sent his suspicion that an agent would be inserted using his identity."

"The escaped prisoner's radio broadcast puts Captain Brooke in some danger," Frederick said.

"It does indeed," Giles said. "What you should know also is that there was a leak from American Army Intelligence in Strasbourg about Capt. Brooke's mission and Hitler as the target. We do not know now how far that leak has been carried."

Frederick thought he saw a connection. His boldness might be understood in the circumstance.

"Is Captain Brooke's safety why I'm being sent? Or is there something else I should know?"

"Serious political considerations have surfaced over Brooke's mission since last night. I cannot reveal anything further," Giles answered.

"But the enemy knows, or logically can conclude, that Brooke is somewhere in Germany on his way to the attempt," Frederick said.

"Yes," Giles said. "We don't know where you can find Capt. Brooke, but we can tell you this. He has a rail pass, papers, and the uniform of German Lt. Eric Klaysa. His itinerary, once across the Rhine and out of the German military zone, was to be by train…Mainz, Frankfort on the Main, Munich, Berchtesgaden. That route may be suspected by the other side since they may have gotten wind of what we planned. But investigation of the leak so far does not lead us to believe they know any of the details we discussed in our planning sessions."

"I assume I will be furnished a cover identity, papers, rail pass."

"All of those," Giles said. "Plans are already in motion to get you across the Rhine tonight and into Mainz tomorrow morning. Two members of our group flew to Strasbourg earlier this afternoon to make preliminary arrangements, pending knowledge of an agent to be selected, of course."

Frederick nodded his understanding and approval.

"There is one other matter to consider," Giles added. "We think Capt. Brooke is a good soldier and will follow orders. He impresses us as very tough minded and reliable. We do not think he would reject an order to terminate his mission.

"It is of the utmost importance that the mission be aborted, however," Giles said emphatically, his eyes leveled on Frederick's. "Will you be able to eliminate Capt. Brooke, if for some reason he were to reject the order you are carrying?"

Frederick was astonished at the question. He searched a moment for the proper response. It was appropriate for him to take a minute and think carefully about such a request. He could not reveal the personal bond he had to Hayden. If Giles and the others knew of that bond, he might still be scratched from his chase mission. This question was what Giles obviously had in mind earlier in saying "terminate."

"I have never killed a human being. If it is a matter of extreme urgency, a matter of national security for my adopted country, I would do what had to be done."

Okay," said Giles. "Col. Alexander will fix you up with a pistol."

The two advance members of Giles team met the plane when it arrived in Strasbourg. They told Giles, Frederick, and the team that the only German officer's uniform in Penner's size they could find on short notice was that of an SS colonel. Other personal effects of the imprisoned German officer had been processed and were provided to Frederick. Once Frederick was in the colonel's uniform, a photographer took his picture and began developing prints for Frederick's use on his identify card and rail pass. Frederick chose to use the name Friedrich Freundes.

Frederick learned how and when Hayden was inserted. He overheard one of the advance agents tell Colonel Alexander that the underground did not like so much activity in a short time. It drew attention to the area and its operations. They agreed to help for the second night in a row, however, under the cover of the distraction provided by another Allied bombing raid.

Everett Giles was somewhat formal in his send-off of Frederick at 22:00 that evening. "Mr. Penner, I wish you good luck and a safe journey. You are doing an enormous service for our country. Your service record with Army Intelligence will be noted accordingly, with my personal letter of commendation."

As he found his place in the boat and felt the first pull of the oarsmen, Frederick was awe-struck by the realization of where he was going. He believed since his departure in 1938 that he would someday return to Germany. He hoped to live there peacefully, happily, and to die in the land of his birth. He had always assumed that his return would be at the end of the war. His antipathy toward the Nazi regime was not lessened by his leaving Germany, but increased in the daily reports of terror and death it inflicted on thousands of Germans and others. He believed that his setting foot tonight in his homeland should help to hasten the end of that hated regime.

Chapter 27

Frankfort, Friday, December 1, 1944

The *Feldgendarmerie* District Office in Frankfort on the Main picked up Lt. Eric Klaysa's call on the night of November 30. The lieutenant duty officer had debated for a while whether the message warranted a call to the home of the District Director, Lt. Col. Helmut Schwartz. He and the other junior officers in the office had learned to be sparing in their designation of breaking events as "urgent" or even "important." Their report would necessitate waking the Colonel or, worse, calling him away from a card game or drinking party. The duty officer made a note asking the attention of the Director to Lieutenant Klaysa's radio transmission. He inserted it on the Director's clipboard for action in the morning.

Lt. Col. Schwartz did not get out of a breakfast meeting and dull propaganda session until 10:30 the next morning. The Klaysa matter was not the highest priority today. The message was vague about identifying suspects. It didn't say what these American spies, if any, were suspected of planning or threatening.

He looked wearily at clipboards all around the office…lists of people sought by the *Gestapo*, the *Feldgendarmerie*, local police. They were evidence of an over-reaching police state, he concluded.

Why the *Feldgendarmerie* would give much credibility to Lt. Klaysa's transmission warning of a possible agent or agents being sent into Germany irritated him. He called the deputy director into his office.

"Major," he asked as he handed him the copy, "what do we make of

Lt. Klaysa's message? Was it a genuine call, or are the Allies playing games again? Has anyone checked whether this message was from Lt. Klaysa?"

"The lieutenant on duty last night personally heard three or four transmissions. He is confident the voice was Klaysa's."

"And Klaysa had been captured, and then escaped, and found a radio to send the message over and over..." The Colonel shook his head in disbelief.

"Look at all these lists," he went on. "They are all problem lists, countless hundreds of people we are supposed to find or keep track of, soldiers absent without leave," he said pointing, "possible deserters. Then here are some of our own people, intelligence agents and police, who have acted strange at times. How are we to keep track of all these?"

"Who knows what might be done with Klaysa's uniform and papers?" the deputy bargained.

"Consider this, Major. Since Lt. Klaysa broadcast in the clear, would not Allied intelligence—even if they had planned to use German uniforms and ID's for a mission—cancel any operation involving operatives using that cover? Don't you think they have uniforms and ID's of other German soldiers? Why would they decide to use those particular uniforms now?"

"Well, for one thing, these are recent captures. Their papers are relatively fresh. And I'm not convinced that the Allies are efficient. The guards there let at least one prisoner escape and use one of their radios," the deputy countered.

Lt. Colonel Schwartz was quiet for a moment. "Agents of all kinds are moving around inside Germany, more of them since the Allies have gotten closer to the Fatherland. There are probably hundreds of infiltrators now coming in each week. Why are these new ones special? What is their mission, if any?"

"I don't know that, Colonel. Perhaps this is another wild goose to chase. What are a few more names on the checklists?"

"This country is rife with people without proper ID due to bombings and other displacements. I can see an enormous problem with refugees soon." The Director sat back in his chair.

"Major, add Lt. Eric Klaysa's name to the list of people being sought—also Sgt. Matthew Kleine and Sgt. Hans Eberer. Put the word out to agents checking public transportation. Notify the local police chiefs in the district and the *Gestapo*. Why should they be spared the paperwork? The other intelligence agencies, too. We have to extend reciprocity to all of them, the same way they reciprocate us." He chuckled aloud at the thought.

The Director's sarcasm gets awfully heavy at times, the deputy said to himself as he left to post the messages.

Chapter 28

A Train in West Germany, Friday, December 1, 1944

Hayden was traveling by train from Mainz on the way to Munich and eventually to Berchtesgaden. He was in the first car behind the engine, three seats inside the rear exit to the car. The first car filled last since the seats in this car were less desired by passengers. Daylight air attacks on rail transportation by Allied bomber and fighter planes were aimed at the engine. Travelers preferred to stay away from the action and took seats in cars or rows farthest from the engine as much as possible.

The ravages of war and the shortage of materials and spare parts were evident in the condition of the car. Cardboard and wood panels covered half of the windows. Other panels, wood and tin, were fastened randomly around the car ceiling and walls. Presumably these panels covered holes made by air attacks as well. The car was unheated. Several seats were missing. The remainder were ragged and torn. The car had a musty, garbage smell. It needed a good cleaning.

Hayden had seen the two American Sergeants in German uniform board the train before him. He wondered how many other Allied military personnel were traveling free, courtesy of borrowed German rail passes.

The train made a half-hour stop in Frankfort in mid-afternoon. Hayden noticed two men boarding who took the seats in the very front of the car. Their civilian suits and hats were newer and better quality than the other passengers.

Once the train was underway, the new arrivals became inspectors. They moved down the aisle carefully checking papers, one agent checking either side.

Papers of civilians were checked casually against a clipboard list. German soldiers got much more intensive treatment.

Hayden observed that their most diligent examination was reserved for German Army lieutenants and sergeants. The inspectors together examined those soldiers. After reviewing their seemingly endless lists, one inspector thumbed through each soldier's papers and credentials carefully while both looked on, matching the person to the picture. Hayden had an uneasy feeling that he might be a focus of the search.

Something must have gone wrong. He would have to be very careful. When the agents came to his aisle seat, Hayden did not offer his papers. He got to his feet, leaned forward and whispered between them that he was on a "most secret mission." He motioned and asked them to exit the crowded rail car with him, telling them that he had to get away from so many ears. He would tell them what he could where they could talk more freely. The agents were very suspicious, continuing their demand to see his papers. Hayden kept moving the ten feet to the end of the car and its exit. One of the agents muscled his way past Hayden, not to stop him, but to keep in front of him. The other followed him closely. Hayden saw that the passengers, especially two lieutenants sitting together in the very last row of seats, were all looking intently at him and the agents.

Stepping out of the car door onto the narrow platform between cars, Hayden veered quickly to the left side of the platform to block the man following him from getting behind him. After the following man closed the door, Hayden quickly pulled his pistol with silencer from inside his great coat and killed both inspectors with head shots before they could respond.

He peered through the small door window of each car to see if anyone was moving. He took the papers from inside the agents' jacket pockets and their clip boards. He then quickly threw each body head first off the moving train to ensure they would be unrecognizable for a while. He ducked into the washroom at the front of the adjoining car to read their identity papers. They were *Feldgendarmerie* inspectors, German Military Police.

On the top page of each clipboard was a typed list of names of military personnel to be questioned. The hand-printed names of Lt. Eric Klaysa, Sgt. Hans Eberer and Sgt. Matthew Kleine had been added to the bottom of the list!

Hayden shredded the lists quickly and stuffed the paper in his pocket. He went back to the platform, sailed the clipboards as far away from the train as he could. He shredded each page further and threw the scraps into the wind.

Now he had to do something for the two Sergeants. First he had to retrieve his bag. He pretended nonchalance as he removed his bag, nodded to the passengers nearby, and sauntered back out of the car again. The passengers in the last two rows of the car, especially those in uniform, might be curious as to where the agents went before they completed their checking. Hayden did not have to explain anything. He doubted he would be asked. He hoped also they had a short memory for faces.

In the third car, he saw one face he recognized. He walked casually to the Sergeant's side and whispered he had critical information to relay. The Sergeant, now Hans Eberer, Hayden believed, followed him to the platform where Hayden told him the full story. The soldier was shocked to learn their cover had been blown so quickly.

"Find Sergeant Kleine and tell him what I've told you," Hayden ordered. "I'm moving to a new seat. Let's stay separated for safety. We should be okay for a while on the train, but we can expect more checks. We all will have to change identities soon in order to avoid detection."

The Sergeant started to tell him they were getting off the train "before Munich," but Hayden interrupted. "No. Don't tell me. I don't want to know." He wished them luck. He still did not know their real names, and did not want them to know his for everyone's protection. He suspected they were getting off at Nuremberg.

Sergeant Eberer went to find his partner. Hayden continued into the fourth car and found an empty seat, broken but usable. He had to get papers of another German lieutenant or a new uniform with a different ID somehow, and soon.

While Hayden mulled over the possibilities, the train stopped suddenly. They were in a small town. There had been an Allied bombing raid overnight. The tracks were still being cleared. A delay of about two hours was announced. Hayden took his bag and exited with all the other passengers.

In the confusion he saw spread around the train, Hayden was reminded of George Spurges' verbal essay on grinding wheels and the waste that war causes. There were hundreds of civilians in flight, seemingly not knowing where they were fleeing to.

Among the assembled passengers along the track Hayden spotted many German uniforms. He slowly wended his way through the crowd of travelers stretching their legs. He found an army lieutenant standing alone. He struck up a conversation, introduced himself as George Fox, and suggested they find a cup of coffee somewhere near.

They found an open coffee shop about three blocks from the track. It had been damaged in the bombing raid, but was open for business. It had no coffee, but did have beer. Hayden bought. He felt comfortable with the German lieutenant, buoyed by his conversational language lessons with Professor Silver.

The Lieutenant identified himself as "Julius." He then surprised Hayden, asking something he had not heard before. "I don't recognize your dialect. Where are you from?"

Hayden smiled disarmingly. "You have a good ear. I grew up in Cologne, but was studying in America for two years before war broke out. Then I came back. I suppose some of the American accent stayed with me."

"In Intelligence," Julius said, reading Hayden's insignia.

"Well, you know, we're not supposed to comment..." Hayden sparred.

"Of course," Julius agreed readily, some apology in his voice. "I did not mean to pry."

"No harm done," said Hayden. I won't ask about your unit or your destination." They both had a good laugh, and ordered another round of beer. If the war had not been going on, they could have had a very good time, Hayden thought, talking girls and soccer and their futures. However, the reality of the conflict was all around them in the sparsely furnished shop, its shabby condition, and the blank looks on the faces of its few patrons.

On their way out of the shop, Hayden led the Lieutenant down an alley as a suggested shortcut back to the train. Hayden let him lead for a moment through some piles of rubble. He chopped him across the back of the neck and Julius fell, stunned. Hayden took his papers, then killed him with a silenced pistol shot. He performed the act efficiently, but felt a twinge of regret. He dragged the body to the closest rubble area and covered it as best he could. He changed the ID picture, then shredded the ID and papers of Eric Klaysa and deposited pieces of the papers in trash cans along the way.

He returned to the train area as if nothing had happened and prepared to resume his journey in a different coach car.

His new name was Lt. Julius Osbert. His new papers assigned him to the Eastern Front by way of Munich. Hayden rationalized that he had saved the real Lt. Osbert the terror of combat against the Soviet hordes.

Chapter 29

Munich, Saturday, December 2, 1944

Hayden knew he had to change uniforms and ID again. It was shortly after midnight on the morning of December 2, in the train station in Munich. Lt. Osbert's papers officially would carry him only as far as Munich. If he were to head in a different direction, not toward the Eastern Front, he could be charged as a deserter if he were challenged.

The experience on the train with the *Feldgendarmerie* had been a close call. He was able to overcome the two challengers because he was aggressive and caught them off guard. He would have to assume in the future that German intelligence or police were only one step behind and that larger forces of opposition could be used against him.

Another serious concern was that he might assume the identity of someone well known among the local German military who would recognize Hayden as an impostor. One solution to that danger was to avoid taking the rank of the highest officers. The higher the rank, the more likely that the officer's name would be recognized. Still, he had to find someone his own size.

Adopting the successful tactic of his earlier adventure, he identified a German SS officer his size, standing alone in the waiting room of the Munich station. The cover of an SS officer, a Major no less, should give him sufficient authority to resist questions from any curious official or onlooker.

He had picked up some information on eating facilities near the station. With the proper deference of a lieutenant, he approached the Major. He concocted a story about good food and drink in a restaurant still open near the station and invited the Major to join him. The Major, stern and officious, didn't smile, but was induced by Hayden's promise of food and companionship.

The side streets off of the train station were sparsely occupied at 02:00. Hayden stayed on the street side of the walkway.

As they passed the doorway of what appeared to be a bombed out building, Hayden pointed suddenly to the Major's left and shouted "Look!" While he had the Major distracted for a split second, Hayden slammed him into and through the rickety door of the building with a blind side body block, driving the Major's head into the floor. Both their hats flew off in the scuffle. Hayden dropped his bag with a clunk as they fell.

Hayden was the first to his knees. The Major slumped with Hayden's chop to his neck. Hayden pulled his pistol and cracked the Major hard across the head for good measure to ensure his silence. He was quiet for several seconds, listening for any noise, cries, or footsteps. Hearing none, he began obtaining his new uniform and identity, leaving the Major in his underwear and socks. He was reluctant to kill another person, but felt obliged for safety's sake to do so. This close to his mission's objective, he could not afford to be the target of a security search.

He dropped Lt. Osbert's uniform into a sewer manhole on a different side street he took back to the station. He tore up his previous ID and orders into small shreds and periodically dropped pieces of them into waste containers he passed.

Back in the train station, he was reassured by the deference shown to an SS Major. His name was now Walther Moss. He had lucked out. The Major's papers identified him as a Regional Security Inspector with German Army Intelligence! He was carrying no specific orders. He concluded that the Major's position would give him *carte blanche* to go anywhere.

The Major had not been en route to a specific location. Why couldn't he go to Berchtesgaden? And who was going to challenge an SS intelligence Major?

While updating the Major's ID card with his picture, Hayden mused that Germany must be overrun with intelligence and security people. First Klaysa, two agents on the train, now Moss. Hayden accepted the danger that his new rank and identity could invite scrutiny. As in any army, there were fewer majors than lieutenants in the German Army. Moss would likely be known to many others, especially intelligence and police officials in the Munich district. Hayden would have to be extra cautious, resist having to identify himself, and be aggressive with the curious.

He boarded the delayed train at 4:00 a.m. and got an hour's sleep before it arrived in Berchtesgaden.

Chapter 30

London and Paris, Saturday, December 2, 1944

Lion Tamer was sent to England two years before the war in Poland began. Admiral Canaris, head of the German intelligence network, *Abwehr,* had foreseen the need for Germany to expand its spy operations against potential adversaries long before the British became actively involved in hostilities.

Lion Tamer spoke English well. He cultivated contacts in business and social circles easily. There were medium level government officials in his acquaintance.

The pre-war mood of Great Britain was isolationist. Even as war clouds approached, the hope of a sizable portion of the British populace still was for British non-involvement. His reports to Berlin included that information. The return instructions from Berlin urged him to continue to develop contacts.

With the German invasion of Poland on September 1, 1939, the mood of the British changed sharply overnight. His social contacts confided that Great Britain should not have been suckered into hostilities. The British were fighters, he reported. They would eventually get around to upgrading their defense forces. Meanwhile, they were vulnerable to attack.

Much to his surprise, Lion Tamer was approached by one of his social contacts in government shortly after the invasion. He was told that he seemed alert, politically aware, and a good candidate for government service. Would he be interested?

His entry into British government work seemed almost too easy. The falsified papers made up for him by another German intelligence unit in

England passed the routine check. His background check by security people was perfunctory.

His work in the political section of the Home Secretary's Office was not demanding. Two months into his new position, he heard through the office grapevine that X Section, the German Directorate of British intelligence, was seeking recruits. In his next communication to Berlin, he mentioned the recruiting and asked for instructions. The response from his handlers was immediate and enthusiastic.

They would help by shoring up his portfolio. They were certain that his acceptance into British government work already had paved the way for his continuing approval. The focus of his screening for intelligence work in fact was his past work in the Home Secretary's Office. It helped that Lion Tamer had an excellent work record in all respects. He was approved for the position.

Over several years, he had followed the instruction from his Berlin base to "listen, don't dig." It was his duty to pass along bits of information without exposing his position. He was to do his work well. Berlin's plan for him was to advance to higher levels of responsibility within the agency and then be available when he was needed for something really important.

In August, 1942, he was able to tip off the Allied commando raid at Dieppe, France, and felt he had contributed significantly to its failure. In January of 1944 he passed on confirmation of the Allies invasion at Anzio, Italy. Again he felt the intelligence he gained assisted greatly the German preparation for the rough treatment given the invaders.

The security leading up to "Overlord" in the spring of 1944 was especially tight. Plan details were available only at the top military and political levels. Opinion among the middle levels of the German Intelligence Service was that the attack would come in May across the channel at its narrowest point, the Pas de Calais. Lion Tamer predicted otherwise and went on record with his belief. His record later included a note that he was one of several agents correct in their predictions.

Recently, he was able to send his own knowledge of the locations of V-2 rocket bomb hits on London. His reports were again at odds with public reports given of their impact sites and prompted discussions among V-2 launching officers about probable British disinformation.

This afternoon he heard a commotion in the corridor outside his office. As was his custom, he moved to a filing cabinet near his door and pretended to be at work there as he listened. He heard some rather excited talk among several agents of an American assassination plot against Hitler having been put into motion the night before. He knew that security around Hitler was good.

However, this threat seemed different, the first one he had ever heard discussed among British agents. He had no way of leaving work early to report to Berlin without arousing suspicion.

Lion Tamer's radio was in his apartment. His schedule and radio frequency for communication with Berlin was determined by a mathematical formula. The seriousness of the talk he had heard justified his sending now on Saturday evening outside of that schedule.

He coded the message to be sent, retrieved the radio from its ceiling hiding place in a closet, and set it up.

> *Attention, animal control. Urgent. Report of an assassination attempt on the leader. Imminent. Entry into homeland by a single American officer, Thursday evening about 22:00, near Strasbourg. Name is Ivan or Dean Bruch. Lion Tamer.*

His handlers acknowledged. "Determine details—when, how, if possible."

Lion Tamer took the instruction to mean he was to dig more diligently than usual. He called the flat of an officer named Robert who worked in the adjoining office to his. He was quite sure that Robert was in the corridor this afternoon and may have been the principal informer. After some polite preliminaries, Lion Tamer admitted to Robert that he had heard the exciting news about the assassination plot and wondered how soon it was to take place.

Robert replied rather brusquely that their corridor conversation had been reported to the section chief. He and two others had been reprimanded for discussing the matter outside of channels. Their phone conversation ended soon afterwards.

Lion Tamer was reasonably sure that even if Robert did not suspect him to be a foreign agent, Robert certainly was in a foul enough mood to report his call. Robert might even interpret his call as a test set up by the section chief to determine compliance of the chastised agents with the strict secrecy order imposed on them by the chief.

Lion Tamer felt the rebuff as a kick in the stomach. For the first time in his seven years of work in London on behalf of the *Abwehr* he had crossed the line of exposure. Perhaps he had been too awkward in complying with the prodding by his handlers to take some risk due to the importance of his message.

Cpl. Lester Choles, a new man in the cryptography section of American Army Intelligence in Paris, was familiarizing himself with the radio equipment.

He was replacing one of the nine team members who just this afternoon had been selected for a special mission. For practice, Cpl. Choles was listening in on messages other than those sent by agents working out of the Paris office, recording them for further analysis. He picked two coded messages on the same frequency that he could read only partially with the German code book provided. He asked the duty officer for help.

"Ah, yes, Lion Tamer," the officer said as he recognized the fist of the sender on the recording. "He has an erratic time schedule, so it's been impossible to pinpoint his sending location. We and the British may be missing his traffic from time to time for the same reason."

"An important operator?"

"We're pretty sure he's German, underground in England, probably in London. He has sent some tips home in the past that suggest he's gleaning intelligence out of a government office."

"A mole?"

"Probably so, Corporal. The M16 bureau chief in London believes that the information Lion Tamer has sent over the years has often duplicated other agents' traffic the British have intercepted. So they have not made a big effort to find this guy. They think there might come a time they can use him for a major disinformation effort. Let's see if we can read what Lion Tamer has to say tonight."

The duty officer began unraveling the message. He interjected "Hmm" several times, and a final "Well, this may be very important. It seems our man has gotten hold of some loose talk about a current operation. Berlin wants more information. This could be a very delicate matter for one of our agents in the field."

Events moved quickly the rest of the evening in London. The X section chief was informed of the content of Lion Tamer's transmission by his American counterpart in Paris. British Intelligence would have urgent business to handle for the second time today on the same issue.

The X section chief had just had a call at home from one of his mid-level officers named Robert. Robert and several others had been indiscreet in talking about the American assassination plan. The British, and especially the Prime Minister, did not need further complications on that matter, and the agents were reprimanded severely.

Robert had reported that his office neighbor called him minutes before trying to pump him for more information on the American assassination plot. The German mole known as Lion Tamer had to be agent Lawrence Teegarten, the section chief concluded.

It was time to shut Teegarten down. The chief assembled the arrest team and gave the order to meet him a block from Teegarten's flat. After they had quietly gained access to the building, one of the chief's men forced the door lock and they all flooded in on Teegarten. Lion Tamer was reading a book, and did not seem much surprised by their visit.

Chapter 31

Germany, Saturday, December 2, 1944

Frederick Penner was traveling with the fake identity of SS Colonel Friedrich Freundes. The American Army Intelligence people in Strasbourg found just one uniform that fit him. It was in good repair, befitting a German officer of that rank.

His orders and ID, created by the experts at Army Intelligence, directed him to Berchtesgaden and the SS barracks there. Frederick and SIP Director Everett Giles agreed that the SS barracks was entered as a destination for purposes of the travel order only. The risk of exposure would be too great for Frederick to stay there.

Frederick had run into some mixed travel luck. In the Mainz train station, announcements and bulletin board notices stated that train service had been disrupted in several places along the line to Frankfort and thence to Munich. Departures were delayed. Travel schedules were uncertain.

For most of Saturday morning, Frederick asked around for information on other transportation options to Munich or beyond. One local suggested he try the air field. There was no regular commercial traffic originating there, he said, but private planes had been flying regularly.

It began to snow as he made his way to the air field. At noon, the field was not being cleared regularly. Things did not look good for any flights out today.

Over coffee with several other officers looking for rides, he learned that the pilot of a four-passenger plane was going east. Frederick found the pilot checking his plane in a hanger. He was indeed going to Munich. His two passengers had booked the flight for 13:00.

Frederick stressed to the pilot the importance of his getting to Munich. He showed his orders. He offered him money to pay half of the flight's cost. The pilot was sufficiently impressed. He would take Frederick. When the weather improved and the runway cleared, they were off. With any luck, Frederick could make it to the Munich train station in time for a 16:00 p.m. train to Berchtesgaden.

On the flight and train ride, Frederick had time to think through the implications of what he was doing. When he was shown Hayden's picture in Paris and asked by the Army Intelligence chief if he recognized Hayden, his guarded but positive response was prompted by his own curiosity. The fact that the chief was asking the questions, obviously with urgency, suggested that Hayden was in some danger. Wherever and whatever the trouble was, perhaps Frederick could help.

Frederick's initial suspicion was confirmed in his first meeting with Colonel Giles on the plane. Not only was Hayden in trouble. His mission was the assassination of Hitler! If caught and identified in that mission, Hayden would be subjected to unspeakable torture. Frederick's decision to volunteer was reinforced by his resolve to help Hayden in any new peril he might be experiencing. He hoped he could at least find his friend alive.

Another justification for his decision was the after-the-fact realization that he, not someone else, had to contact Hayden. Another intelligence agent likely would follow orders and kill Hayden if he resisted an order to terminate the mission.

For Frederick had decided when he first was informed by Colonel Giles of Hayden's mission that, if he could locate Hayden, he would not stop the assassination attempt. He thought of Giles' question to him whether "if necessary," he could 'terminate' or 'eliminate' Hayden. He left the impression with Giles that he could. He had lied calmly.

His hatred of Hitler and all that the Nazi regime had done to his people overwhelmed any of the "political considerations" mentioned by Giles, whatever they were. And even if he did not harbor that hatred, he certainly would not harm his friend.

Frederick decided he will tell Hayden of his work with Army Intelligence. His friend will no doubt wonder, probably even ask, what circumstances brought them together again. He will not tell Hayden why he is in Bertchtesgaden. He will determine if he can help Hayden in any way and then do what he can to ensure the success of Hayden's critical mission.

Hayden was having dinner in the restaurant of the hotel. He thought the back view of a German officer seated across the room looked strangely familiar, but dismissed the thought.

Shortly afterward, a waiter came to Hayden's table with a note. It said simply, "3...BKt5" and a brief note in German: "Show no surprise at this move." It was the opening to the Nimzo-Indian defense that he and Frederick had explored often in their chess games!

Hayden casually looked again around the crowded restaurant for the familiar form. He recognized Frederick across the room. He was in the uniform of an SS colonel. He was wearing glasses and a moustache. Hayden tipped the waiter and waved him off.

When Frederick joined him, Hayden properly stood at attention, then took Frederick's offered hand. It was a solemn, poignant moment for two Americans and old friends meeting again, alone in a hostile land, liable to torture and death if found out.

Hayden was overjoyed to see Frederick, but could not show it without calling too much attention to them. He motioned for Frederick to join him. In German, he started to ask his many questions.

Frederick stopped him. "Not here. You finish your food and I my drink and then we will walk. Let's talk patriotic war stuff now," Frederick whispered conspiratorially.

Later in their stroll along the frozen, snow-lined street in front of the hotel, Hayden asked the inevitable question, "Why are you here?"

"You see, I'm with American Army Intelligence in Paris," Frederick said.

At Hayden's look of surprise and likely question, Frederick continued.

"No, no, not in the army. I'm a civilian employee, doing radio work mostly. This is secret information, of course, and I know you won't pass it along. Once in a while it is necessary to verify that our agents behind enemy lines are sending straight information, that they haven't been compromised or are double agents. It was my turn to go into the field and observe an agent. It's delicate work, but there it is."

Frederick was counting on Hayden's lack of expertise in radio, Hayden thought. He apparently assumed Hayden could not know that verification was accomplished in a much less risky manner, and that field verification was almost never used.

"Am I the agent being verified here?" Hayden asked.

"No," Frederick said.

"It's good to know someone else on our side is around," Hayden observed somewhat hesitantly after an awkward silence.

Frederick smiled, "In a town in which Hitler lives part time, there is often a lot of idle information about military and political happenings that a person with big ears can gather easily."

Hayden wasn't buying Frederick's answers. His own experience with radio, added to what the SIP handlers had told him in his pre-mission training, meant that Frederick's answer was a thin cover-up. Frederick doubtless has a real mission that he can't talk about. Hayden had the brief chilling thought that Frederick might have been a German agent ever since he came to the United States, a role that Hayden never could have imagined for his friend. He dismissed the thought immediately. He could not seriously suspect Frederick of duplicity in so serious a matter. Frederick's forceful pronouncements on the plight of Jews, the savagery of the Nazi regime, and his demeanor when he stated them to Hayden, had to have revealed his true convictions.

Hayden also remembered the rumors that, towards the end of Hitler's regime, whenever that came, there would be a last stand made by his fanatic followers here in Bavaria. Perhaps Frederick was sent here to learn what he could about the plans for this "national redoubt."

Hayden could not now believe that Frederick, a German Jew, had agreed to undercover duty in this hotbed of Nazi sentiment. Or maybe he had volunteered to be put in this danger! He voiced concern to his old friend.

"What danger you are in, just being here, your background, having fled this country several years ago!"

"If the dangerous duty is not for those who have the most to gain or lose, then who is it for?" Frederick asked.

They had reached the entrance to the hotel again. Frederick turned to him, his back to the doorman, and asked quietly, "Hayden, is there anything I can do to help in what you are doing here?"

Hayden declined the offer, tempted for a brief moment to ask Frederick what he thought Hayden's mission was. They shook hands formally for the benefit of onlookers, and most sincerely wished each other good luck in their work before they entered the lobby together.

Chapter 32

Berchtesgaden and Berghof, Sunday, December 3, 1944

Before they parted the night before, Frederick asked Hayden if he could help in any way. Hayden declined, but was immediately curious. Why would Frederick ask that question? He admitted to being in Army Intelligence. Had he learned Hayden's mission? Why else would Frederick he here? Frederick's answer when Hayden posed the last question was thin and evasive.

Now, on Sunday morning, Hayden began to set in motion the plan he had been formulating since he saw Berchtesgaden for the first time yesterday. It was still dark at 06:30 when he dressed again in Major Walther Moss' SS uniform. He retrieved from his bag his pistol with silencer and spare clip and slipped them into the pocket of his great coat. In the other pocket he put his knife, compass, and a wire cutter. He strapped on his pistol belt and Luger. He emptied the bag of everything else but the disassembled rifle, scope, ammo clips, and elastic cord. He stuffed his shaving gear and change of underwear inside the uniform jacket under his great coat. He would dispose of them outside the hotel. He looked around one last time and then slid out of the room.

By leaving the hotel this early, he hoped to avoid anyone who had questions, especially Frederick. He might not be able to shake off Frederick during the critical early timing points of his mission. He paid his room bill and exited the hotel.

His plan for access to the grounds of the Berghof chalet was simple. As Lt. Col. Alexander predicted, scheduling was his problem.

He wanted to slip into the forest about two miles north and west of the Berghof chalet while it was still dark. That way he could minimize contact with anyone on the road bordering the forest. He had learned the guard change to be every two hours on even hours. He had to use the cover of the forest to sweat out the changing of the guard at both 08:00 and 10:00.

Meanwhile, he would have to work his way, undetected, to near the perimeter fence around the chalet by 10:00. He could not eliminate any human obstruction until after that hour. He could not risk an officer of the guard raising an alarm and starting a search in force when one or more of his detail did not show up for the changing of the guard at 10:00. If he encountered a guard or guards after 10:00, he would have to kill whoever was in the way of his gaining access to the perimeter fence around Hitler's chalet.

It was a little before 07:00 when Hayden began his trek up the street bordering the forest. After two miles of hiking, he crossed the street. He casually stopped to look intently at his German watch. Under the brim of his hat he took one careful searching look down the street and around the area. He was satisfied that he was not being observed. He strode slowly but steadily into the edge of the forest, then felt his way into the trees for another fifty yards. He stopped and sheltered himself behind a tree.

The immediate unknown was the existence of guards and guard dogs this far out from the chalet. Hayden stood perfectly still for a minute or more, listening, trying to detect movement in any direction in the blackness.

He made his way ever so slowly deeper into the forest, pushing in what his compass said to be a southeasterly direction. In effect, he would circle the east side of a mountain, staying at the same altitude. In the darkness, his eyes began to acclimate. He was able to distinguish the intense darkness of a tree trunk as he approached it as compared to the less intense darkness of its surroundings. It was much like a dream. Dark tree shapes that he couldn't see a second before suddenly appeared out of the deeper darkness behind them as he approached. He felt more than he saw this way, stumbling regularly, tripping several times over fallen branches or exposed tree roots.

Hayden adopted the tactic of taking a hundred paces and then stopping perfectly still to listen, facing in the same direction he had been moving. He checked the illuminated dial of his compass at the end of each segment to determine if he was straying from his planned direction.

He was also measuring distance with each segment. He was not covering a full yard with each step, more like a half yard. He estimated that he would cover about thirty-five segments per mile. If he could cover a forest mile in an hour, he should be above the intended point of the chalet perimeter, a bit over a mile from his departure point on the road, well before 10:00.

At the end of two segments, Hayden observed three things working in his favor. There obviously were no guard posts being walked and no guard dogs this deep in the forest. The first inkling of daylight was visible straight up through the trees. A light snow had begun to fall, flakes periodically working their way down through the forest branches onto his face. Any tracks he might make would be covered soon.

While paused at the end of a walking segment, Hayden thought he heard a whistle. It was very faint, some distance away. The whistle had been like no bird or animal call he had ever heard. He checked his watch and saw that it was 08:00. The corporal of the guard somewhere may have been assembling his troop detail for the 08:00 changing of the guard.

The planning by the SIP team for his last practice jump in Vermont was a reasonably accurate simulation of the Berchtesgaden area. The ground was frozen, and the layer of branches and leaves on the forest floor cushioned his steps. There was snow and ice, some patches three or four inches thick. In the faint dawn he could now see light filtering through the trees. It was like looking up a chimney overlaid with branches at the top. It might be an invigorating, even interesting, walk in the forest, he thought, were it not for the deadly mission he was on.

At 09:30 Hayden estimated he was close to the location for his descent down the mountain slope and out of the forest toward the perimeter fence. On impulse, he shed the great coat and shinnied up a tree. Perhaps a half mile away, the *Tee Haus* where Hitler routinely had breakfast was faintly visible through the falling icy mist. He could not see the perimeter fence between here and there. Hitler's chalet was well to the right of the *Tee Haus* and at a much lower elevation, perhaps three-fourths of a mile cross country, even less distinct from his perch.

He climbed down and moved lower through the trees, stopping more often now, being intently watchful for any movement around him, and especially conscious of his own.

Hayden was perhaps thirty yards from the edge of the forest and the perimeter fence ten yards beyond when he suddenly detected movement to his left and below him. He froze in his tracks immediately. A single guard was crossing his line of movement, north to south. He was dressed in a normal field uniform, no snow camouflage clothing. His rifle was slung over his shoulder, barrel down. He moved farther along the edge of trees down the slope to Hayden's right, almost totally obscured from Hayden's vision by the thick foliage between them. The guard stopped, waiting for something.

Again Hayden detected movement to his left. Six guards marched through the falling snow this side of the perimeter fence. They stopped to his right below him. One of them pulled out a whistle from his tunic pocket, checked his watch, and signaled for the guard. Hayden thought it unnecessary to make the noise, but it apparently was standard procedure, night or day.

The guard change took place. The corporal and his detail marched back to the north, soon out of sight.

Since the guard detail had turned around at this point, Hayden concluded that this guard change location was at the end of the line for one series of guard posts. He suspected also that each guard had a post of a mile or more to walk along the path next to the perimeter fence. The new guard had started to move slowly farther to Hayden's right, then stopped for some reason, facing the chalet, his back to Hayden.

Hayden gently set down his bag and crept along the forest floor, maintaining tree cover. He was still noiseless when, five yards away, he pulled his pistol. The pop of the silenced round seemed unduly loud. The guard fell immediately. Hayden quickly dragged the body ten yards or so into the forest. He brushed away all footprints with a tree branch. He checked the killing site for blood and covered with the tree branch what little he saw. The snowfall would obscure the rest shortly. He retrieved his bag and returned to the forest edge. It was 10:09.

The next part of his journey was going to be tricky. A chain link fence and a field of grass and scrub, occasionally broken by thirty foot tall trees, separated him from a small hill covered by a stand of forest immediately behind and to either side of the *Tee Haus*. Worse yet, the snowfall was diminishing, decreasing what little cover it could provide him.

Imbued with the spirit of staying one step ahead, Hayden cut into the fence vigorously, up and across from the bottom of the chain link to make a flap about three feet by two feet that he quickly bent back. He set the bag through the hole in the fence, crawled through, and stood up. He decided that running crouched would tell anyone who might see him that he shouldn't be there. He strode purposefully the 250 yards or so to the small stand of trees, conscious that he was very tall and alone in the field.

The SIP team had told him he would need skill, daring, and a lot of luck to complete his mission. So far, his luck was holding. When he reached the cover of the trees it was 10:26.

The tree stand was perhaps eighty yards deep. He plunged into it immediately, grateful to be out of sight of any roaming guard details, the *Tee Haus*, and the chalet itself. He followed his previous practice of stopping, standing completely still behind a tree once he had gained the cover of the trees on all sides. It was not as dark as in the early morning forest he had traversed. But the stand was so thick that he could see only occasional specks of light at the other end of the tree stand.

What Hayden did see was a dark movement ahead of him. He thought first it was a large animal. Then he made out the silhouette of a crouching guard, moving, it seemed, in his direction, perhaps fifteen yards away. Hayden knew that any movement of his own would be more visible against the gray daylight behind him. He waited, perfectly still, conscious of his breathing. It seemed a long time before he first heard the guard approaching slowly. Hayden slid his hat off, set his bag down, and withdrew his pistol. He slowly poked his head from behind the right side of his covering tree to take a look in the direction of the noise. The guard had stopped seven or eight yards away. His rifle was at the ready, pointed to Hayden's left as near as Hayden could tell.

Hayden slowly bent his knees, feeling the pain from the bruises he sustained in the Vermont rehearsal jump. Steadying himself with his left hand on the tree trunk between himself and the guard, he knelt on the ground, facing the tree. Again slowly, he shifted his weight to his right, crouching on elbows and knees, near to the ground, to get a different look. The guard was still frozen in his stance.

Hayden raised his pistol slowly and squeezed off two quick shots. The guard's rifle discharged with a loud report as he fell over it. Hayden stayed in his crouched position, peering from ground level for any new movement. He waited at least two minutes, hoping the forest had muffled the sound of the guard's shot.

At length he rose slowly, and with his pistol leading the way, approached the guard. He studied him for any movement, then gently pried the guard's fingers from his rifle before he pulled the weapon clear. The guard was dead. It was 10:34.

Hayden took the guard's rifle with him, picked up his bag in the same hand, and was shortly at the far edge of the forest, overlooking the *Tee Haus*. He had tree cover for the thirty-five yards or so to the back of the building. He then slipped around to the front door and immediately pushed it open, hearing a growling noise far behind him as he did.

There was music from a radio. One of the two SS guards immediately clicked off the radio and stood at attention with his partner. Hayden returned their salute. There seemed to be no one else in the building. The guards' rifles stood against a chair behind them.

"Will *Der Fuehrer* take food with his party here this morning?" he asked.

"No sir, Major," one replied, "the snow…"

Hayden nodded. That explained the absence of any staff.

He did not like this cold blooded approach to eliminating guards, but they were the enemy. They stood in the way of him completing his important mission. They would be able to identify him later. He drew his pistol and fired two shots before the guards fully realized what was happening. He dragged them to a small alcove, and followed with their two rifles and the one he had taken from the guard in the stand of trees.

Hayden then took a long look through the window of the *Tee Haus* with his rifle scope. He could see the flag staff and pennant, Hitler's personal pennant. It was flown to evidence Hitler's presence at any location.

The paved pathway curving to the left from the front door of the *Tee Haus* made a large loop before it met the chalet Hayden estimated to be a half mile away. Hayden could see from the tracks along the walkway that someone had recently been to the *Tee Haus.* A guard and leashed dog Hayden hadn't noticed on his quick entry to *Tee Haus* was stopped about a third of the way from the chalet, the guard's back to Hayden, peering off in the direction of a forested area to his left. The noise he had heard on his entry may have been the dog growling. Hayden assumed the guard had ignored it, perhaps thinking that the dog was responding to the *Tee Haus* soldiers' radio. Hayden waited until they continued along the path to the chalet and disappeared around the corner. Hayden was curious why there were not more guards patrolling.

The *Tee Haus*, though it provided excellent cover, was not a good firing site. The stand of trees through which he had approached the *Tee Haus* was situated on a hill. The front edge was perhaps thirty yards higher than the Tee Haus. That would be his firing site.

At 10:53, Hayden exited the Tee Haus and walked quickly to the back, into the stand of trees, then westward up the hill and away from the *Tee Haus.*

He found a good position for prone firing and assembled the rifle. The target would be about 800 yards away, as on his last simulation in Vermont. He tied down the rifle securely to a log with the elastic cord. The detail he could see in his first view of the chalet's terrace was amazing. He had a perfect view.

It was 11:02. Now started his wait for Hitler's appearance. Not being able to do anything to hurry the mission along was frustrating. The unknowns running through his mind were agonizing. Hayden hoped Hitler had not appeared outside the chalet earlier, before he was able to gain this shooting location. The *Tee Haus* guards' silence on Hitler's whereabouts made Hayden assume that he had not.

The information from the guards and the absence of staff in the *Tee Haus* clinched the fact that Hitler had not planned to come to the building for breakfast. Did he sleep in especially long today? Would a late breakfast force the shooting time frame dangerously close to the noon hour guard change? Or would he come out onto the terrace for a breath of fresh air after breakfast, if at all? Hayden's constant scan of the chalet revealed no movement.

Hayden worried most that, being behind in his routine, Hitler would not appear at all. He recalled the sober discussion when the team and he speculated about all the reasons why Hitler might not make his appearance on any morning.

It was already later in the two-hour time frame than any one of the team had anticipated. There was still no sign of activity around the chalet itself. He faced the prospect of a mission not completed, the disappointment of not even having a shot at Hitler, and the realization that he would still have to fight his way out of the perimeter.

Hayden had not really thought much about historical assassinations until now. His presence here on this site, for no other reason than to kill a major world political figure, brought them to his mind. Julius Caesar, U.S. Presidents Abraham Lincoln, James Garfield, William McKinley. How many kings and czars and emperors, dukes and government leaders had died at the hands of an assassin? Archduke Francis Ferdinand of Austria had. His assassination ignited World War I.

Hayden had no doubt that, if it occurred, this assassination would be added to the list. Maybe the destruction of Hitler would bring the end of this war, not start something terrible. He hoped it would be noted without his name attached, since that would mean he had not been discovered.

There was movement! A dozen or more workers came briskly onto the terrace and began working with shovels and brooms, clearing the snow and ice. Hayden thought this might be a routine cleaning operation after a snowfall. It could also be a sign that Hitler would emerge.

It was already almost an hour and a half into the 10:00 guard shift. Every additional second seemed an hour, and there were far too many of them in his dangerous, exposed position. There were dead German guards all around.

Precipitation was falling again. A mixture of snow and sleet turned the sky a dull white. There was no chance of the sun emerging for hours, maybe not all day. Hayden now feared the weather might keep Hitler and his entourage from coming outside at all.

It was 11:30. Several workers emerged to unroll wide swaths of what looked like tan carpeting onto the walkway. This could be the most positive sign of

Hitler's emergence yet. Snow was falling more heavily. Although he could not see it beginning to layer on the carpeting, he reasoned that it would soon build up, possibly canceling anyone's visit to the terrace.

Into his left field of vision, Hayden observed that the guard emerged again to walk his post along the curved path. A gang of sweepers came out to sweep the accumulated snow off the carpet. Through the scope, Hayden could make out the occasional tufts of snow flying to left and right as the sweepers worked. It was 11:39.

Suddenly, like magic, the sweepers disappeared around the corner of the terrace. Almost immediately afterwards, there was Hitler, flowing out of the chalet at the head of his entourage. He was in his brown jacket, distinctive military hat, black pants. He stopped, confirmed it was snowing with a gaze upward, gestured to the mountains in Austria beyond. He then began chatting with the small party, putting his hands slowly together repeatedly, as if silently clapping, beguiling his guests.

Hayden's moment in time was here.

The first tracer hit short of the group, on a flagstone. The round exploded in a puff. It splattered fragments into the group. Hayden saw Hitler and several of the party go down immediately. Others fled the scene. A few stayed, stunned, then crouched over the fallen Hitler. Hayden raised the barrel slightly and fired seven more rounds into the group, focusing on the brown jacket and black pants he could still see clearly through his scope.

There was no one moving now in the pile of bodies. Either they were mortally wounded, or were lying still to divert fire from themselves. Hayden had no camera equipment to record the results of his history-shaping shots. The picture would be etched indelibly in his mind forever.

The SS guard on foot patrol along the walking path to the *Tee Haus* was already running toward the *Tee Haus* with his pistol drawn. He had tethered the dog with a leash wrapped around his wrist. Hayden calmly brought the scope to bear on the guard and dropped him, the tied dog yelping and trying to free itself. Hayden swung back to the area of the chalet. He fired at another guard running toward the chalet, but did not hit him.

He swung the scope back to the killing scene on the terrace. There were two or three new arrivals on one knee, bending over the bodies there. Several in the group were pointing in the general direction of the *Tee Haus*.

Chapter 33

Berghof and Berchtesgaden, Sunday, December 3, 1944

Hayden rose from his firing position. It was 11:44. His work was finished at Hitler's Berghof chalet. He started to drop the rifle into the array of spent shell casings, but then thought better of it. He re-loaded his pistol and pocketed it with the last clip of ammunition from the rifle bag. He pulled the Luger pistol and began to walk north away from the scene, farther into the stand of trees. He paused to place the assassination rifle under the body of the guard he had shot in the stand of trees little more than an hour earlier.

As he emerged from the north side of the tree stand into the grassy field, Hayden saw three guards running toward him less than a hundred yards away to his right, from the north, rifles at the ready.

Hayden shouted to the guards when they were within hearing range, "This way…the assassins ran this way!" pointing to the West toward the forested mountains dominating the area. He waited just an instant to see if they were heeding his verbal deception. Then he began running, fearing that any moment he would feel the metal of the guards' shots. He found his own mostly covered tracks in the snow from over an hour ago and decided to run in them to the hole in the fence. No shots came. He slowed down to encourage the guards' haste. He could now see on his right periphery that they were buying into the deception and running as hard as he was in the general direction he was heading. They were some forty yards away, still to his right, and on a converging path.

He was enormously relieved the deception was working. He continued across the grassy field, the undergrowth slapping as high as his mid-thigh as he ran.

They met at the fence. He had to convince the guards of the fiction that there was more than one assassin and that he and the guards were now in hot pursuit. He also had to distract them from scrutinizing the scene too closely, the faint images of his earlier footprints, a single set of prints leading to the *Tee Haus*, not multiple prints leading away from it.

Hayden pointed to the hole he had cut in the fence.

"There!" he shouted. "They went through there."

The Corporal began cursing at his watch's lax security. Hayden looked him briefly in the eyes and saw no revelation of suspicion.

"No time for that now," Hayden commanded. "Quick, through the fence," he waved them forward. The Corporal fell to his knees and crawled through the fence. Hayden followed, then waited as the two privates flopped to do the same. He isolated the Corporal.

"Take this man and go there," pointing into the trees to his left, a path that would take the Corporal and his mate on a southerly route roughly parallel to the Berghof compound. More importantly, it would give Hayden the option of moving north and west, farther away from them and the compound, deeper into the mountainous forest. He ordered the remaining Private, "Come," and started off to the right.

The Corporal balked. "Major, Sir, should we not wait for more...?"

Hayden interrupted sternly. "They will follow. We can't let the assassins get too far ahead of us."

"I don't see any tracks," the Corporal wisely observed.

Hayden knew the body of the soldier he had killed on approaching the fence earlier was nearby. To distract the Corporal and the other two guards, he pointed to the faint snow tracks leading into the forest. "Look!" he said, and started to follow the tracks. Soon the guard's body came into view.

When the small patrol saw the body of a German soldier, Hayden had made his case. He repeated the order to the Corporal and one Private to split off and continue the pursuit.

Hayden made eye contact with the other Private, his companion to be, nodded in the direction of a deeper move into the forest, and began trotting in the lead. What served as a trail was increasingly difficult to follow as Hayden and the Private plunged deeper into the forest, climbing steadily onto higher and higher ground. Soon the other two guards were out of sight and sound in the thickening forest. His companion strained for breath.

Hayden stopped to let them both rest. He would not kill the Private yet. If confronted by another patrol, the idea of a companion seemed to make better sense as cover. As he stopped, he looked quickly back and down the thin trail. There was no indication anyone was following yet.

He peered ahead into the trees and asked the Private, a dark haired soldier with dark eyes, "Do you hear anything? See anything?" The Private's negative response was expected, of course. He knew the Private could not see or hear any more than he could, but he had to keep up the fiction. Hayden remembered from the map he had studied that he could eventually veer due west to intersect the road from Berchtesgaden he had used early that morning.

After a short break, they began to climb higher. They were no longer running but trudging, leaning into the steepening mountain. After a few minutes, Hayden pointed to the right and then led the way. The pair moved to follow roughly the route Hayden had taken earlier, now with more light. They walked more quickly now along their level path, circling the mountain. By 12:30, they emerged onto the road Hayden had walked in the dark early this morning.

Hayden saw that there was no movement on the road. He reasoned that the first inquiries into the killings at Berghof were being directed to the immediate area around the chalet.

He disliked eliminating the young soldier, but Hayden's face, voice, and manner were known to him. Hayden led him back into cover of the woods and shot him. He knew it might be rationalization, but he believed if the Private, or any of the guards he was forced to dispatch this morning knew he was an American officer, they would not have hesitated to do the same.

Hayden again felt exposed walking alone along the road. He would have trouble explaining what an SS regional security officer was doing alone and on foot in snow and ice this near to Berghof so soon after the killings.

His immediate plan was to go back to the hotel, find Frederick, and persuade him that they had to leave Berchtesgaden together. If Frederick hesitated, Hayden would now tell him the whole assassination story. If Frederick himself had a mission to complete, Hayden would offer to help him. Hayden would try his best to persuade Frederick that the morning events at Berghof made their existence in the vicinity extremely hazardous.

He was about to cross a side road. He could hear a vehicle approaching from around a bend. Hayden faded back into the edge of the forest. He saw a staff car, with impressive insignia on the right fender. The driver seemed to be alone in the car.

Hayden thought the time was right to take a chance. He stepped out in front of the car as it slowed for the intersection. The driver stopped, rolled down the window, and saluted Hayden. He was a sergeant, special services.

Hayden pulled Walther Moss' identification from his tunic pocket as he approached the car. "Sergeant, I'm the regional security officer for the SS. You may have heard about some negative news from the Berghof chalet in the last hour or so. I will need to see your papers and search this car. Turn off the ignition and step out of the car."

"Major, I'm on a special mission for *Reichsmarshal* Hermann Goering. I am carrying special supplies from his chalet near *Der Fuehrer's* Berghof to the *Reichsmarshal* in Munich. He needs them tonight. I do not believe he would approve of his vehicle being searched, or my mission questioned. Here is my signed pass from him on his stationery and under his signature."

Hayden pulled the Luger from his waist for the second time today. "Sergeant, I am under orders from SS Chief and German State Police Director Heinrich Himmler. You should know the latter office as the *Gestapo.* I do not believe Herr Himmler would approve my making an exception to his order for a special services Sergeant!" He waved the Luger menacingly and pulled the door open. "Out!"

The Sergeant complied, never taking his eyes off Hayden. He was the same height as Hayden, and about the same age.

"Open the back door, Sergeant."

The Sergeant obeyed, taking his time. He reached in to unlock the door and threw it open defiantly.

"Open those boxes," Hayden ordered, pointing to four boxes on the floor. "Pull out the end one."

While the Sergeant slowly bent to lift the box, Hayden took a quick look up and down the main road and the side road. They were clear of vehicles and pedestrians. He then cracked the Sergeant hard across the head with the butt of the Luger. He pushed the Sergeant as he fell so that he landed on top of the boxes. Hayden forced the Sergeant's legs onto the back seat.

He started the car and turned to the left along the main road. He shortly found a small drive-through park, probably used for picnicking during the summer. There were no tire tracks on the roadway. He stopped and checked the Sergeant who was very still.

Next was a difficult task, and Hayden had to do it quickly. He pulled off the Sergeant's great coat and uniform. He had to take his boots off to remove his pants. He then slid into the passenger side of the car and took off Walther Moss' uniform, including his own boots. He quickly dressed in the Sergeant's uniform and put his own boots back on.

Dressing the unconscious Sergeant in the Major's uniform took some effort. When the task was completed, he carried the Sergeant out of the car into some bushes nearby and used his own pistol with silencer. He did not regret killing one of Goering's aides, especially an arrogant one.

The double deception he had undertaken should buy him time and alibi, if needed. Two living guards knew of an SS Major a half mile or so from the Berghof chalet. Hayden's face and voice might also be recognizable to them. Major Walther Moss was now officially dead, and any blame that might be put on him for the killings at Berghof should divert attention from an outsider, at least for a few days. And the new Sergeant Bernhard Munsenn had a high-level pass through security checks and road blocks.

Hayden proceeded to the hotel to contact Frederick and persuade him to leave with him. There seemed to be a large gathering at the hotel. There were shiny staff cars, a few armored cars, and motorcycles in abundance. He had to park more than fifty yards away from the hotel entrance.

As he entered the hotel lobby, he realized immediately that things had changed from the night before. The room was crowded with military people, many of them standing near the fireplace excitedly discussing the news. Only a few were seated at tables. Four men with hats and suits, obviously security people, stood stiffly at the front desk, hands behind their backs.

Apparently no one had paid any attention to Hayden entering the lobby. But someone might think it strange if he left so soon after entering. He took a seat at a small table for two against a wall. He would wait a while before trying to contact Frederick.

As he waited, he overheard excited talk from officers standing near the fireplace. In short order, he was able to piece together the scenario. The officers passed the rumors that the *Gestapo* and *Feldgendarmerie* were pursuing a foreign agent. There was further talk about a mysterious officer, a German SS Major wanted for questioning. And, most chilling of all, one of them related, that German Major may have been in league with an American assassin infiltrated into Germany. A German spy in London even had the American's name! The *Feldgendarmerie*, and now the *Gestapo* and other police and intelligence units, were investigating other suspicious events of the last few days.

He chilled at the thought he might be recognized as the SS Major in a Sergeant's uniform. He leaned an elbow on the table, his hand partially shielding his eyes. There had been a leak, a serious breach in security, and he could turn out to be the victim. Hayden's coming into possession of a German staff car recently might mean more to his immediate welfare than simply getting out of Berchtesgaden.

Suddenly and loudly, there was a burst of activity coming down the steps beside the front desk. The stairway poured out a knot of a dozen or more bustling, uniformed military and police, pushing their way along.

In the middle of the pack was a German SS Colonel. It was Frederick! He had been taken. The security people at the desk joined in the parade of boots clacking against the hard wooden floor, marching their prey quickly out the front door. Hayden joined the rush of curious restaurant patrons out the door as the security detail piled into their vehicles. Frederick was being shoved into the back seat of a car. His hat was knocked off. He looked passively for a brief second at the crowd of thirty or more people in which Hayden stood. For the briefest moment, Frederick saw Hayden, widening his eyes as if inquiring, then nodding his head, as if in approval.

His eyes still on Frederick, Hayden started to take a step forward and pull out his weapon, to take as many of these obnoxious police and SS with him as he could, and to die with his friend. He saw Frederick now shake his head "no" in Hayden's direction.

Immediately afterward, Frederick's hand flashed to his mouth and he clenched his teeth. Frederick's head fell back as his body stiffened. Then his head fell limp to his chest as several German officers grabbed at Frederick and shouted simultaneously.

Hayden knew it was all over for his friend. There was nothing he could do to help Frederick. He would not do anything rash or stupid. The crowd stood there stunned as the vehicles roared away. Hayden hadn't prayed for some time. He now asked God to take his friend to the bosom of Abraham.

Hayden knew he was in danger of being recognized by anyone who was at the hotel the night before, staff or patrons. His one stroke of luck was that he was no longer in the uniform of an SS Major. He was sickened, confused, his mind racing to determine what he should do. He did not want to be pulled into the police machinery for grilling and probable torture that his friend had just escaped by suicide.

Hayden began moving slowly through the crowd and down the street toward the staff car, not sure of an immediate plan. Would the car itself be under surveillance?

The military of all ranks were still engaged in conversations around him. His leaving the crowd was not being noticed. Still, with each step, he expected someone to shout "Halt." Although he felt comfortable with the Goering pass, he did not want to go through the proof of his new identity in front of a throng of hostile officers. If stopped, he might have to fight his way as far as he could. He had noted when he went into the restaurant that only a few of the noncommissioned officers carried weapons, and the officers had their pistols. He was now separated by twenty yards or so from the conversing officers.

"Sergeant," someone called behind him. He turned quickly to see an SS lieutenant, alone, approaching him briskly. A fighting suicide might still be necessary, Hayden thought again.

Hayden strode forward and met the lieutenant, came to attention in front of him, and saluted.

"Relax, Sergeant," the lieutenant said, realizing he had surprised Hayden. "Do you have a vehicle?"

"Yes, sir, Lieutenant," he answered, thinking of no reason to give any other answer.

"Are you leaving now?" the officer asked.

"Yes, sir," Hayden replied.

The Lieutenant, apparently, was not now investigating anything. He, too, was leaving the hotel. His vehicle was disabled, he said, and he needed a lift immediately. He asked for a ride to the outskirts of town to re-join his security unit. Hayden said it would be his pleasure to accommodate the Lieutenant. There was no doubt that their meeting and conversing had been observed by the group outside the hotel.

When Hayden pointed out the staff car, the Lieutenant joked that he had never before been this close to a *Reichmarshal's* car, much less ridden in one. Hayden began to offer his identity papers, but the Lieutenant waved them off.

Inside the vehicle, the Lieutenant asked Hayden, in a non-threatening manner, where he was headed. Hayden told him the Goering story. The Lieutenant rolled his eyes at the thought of the *Reichsmarshal* using Army transportation for his personal desires at this time, but said nothing further.

At his drop-off ten minutes later, the Lieutenant stood at the open door of the staff car and talked for a moment to a corporal who hurried up to salute and report. Hayden regretted that he could understand the conversation. The corporal excitedly told the Lieutenant that the SS colonel arrested at the hotel had swallowed a poison tablet as he was being transported to the police station. He had died without talking.

Hayden had no reason to believe Frederick survived. The corporal's report gave finality to the sad hotel episode.

The Lieutenant turned to Hayden. "It seems like the excitement at the hotel is explained. Thanks for the ride."

Hayden shrugged a pretended indifference to the news, replied, "Yes, sir," and saluted. The Lieutenant waved to the guards manning the checkpoint to allow the car to pass. Hayden continued to drive slowly. The roadway was icy in spots. He would not invite any suspicion by seeming to hurry away from Berchtgesgaden.

What slowed him most of all was his deep sadness and melancholy. "Frederick," he said aloud over and over. The memory of the happiest year of his life would be forever darkened by the terrible scene at the hotel. The promise of other happy moments in the future with his best friend was gone also. Not one more chess game. Not a single laugh over a shared pleasure. Not one more comforting word of counsel.

Frederick had taken a big risk coming into Berchtesgaden, for whatever reason. Hayden wondered aloud. "Did he know all the morning news? I wonder if he somehow connected me with that news? His being here at this time...I wonder if he knew more about my mission than he let on?" He was more and more convinced that Frederick had to know. His recognition of him with widened eyes, his almost imperceptible nodding of approval told him Frederick knew something about his mission. And last night he was willing to help.

Hayden reflected also that his giving the Lieutenant a lift was only the last of several actions he had taken to date that were critical to his safety. He was deeply concerned about the animated conversations he had overheard in the hotel lobby.

Had he entered the hotel as SS Major Moss, he almost certainly would have been questioned and probably arrested, forcing his fighting suicide to take place then.

Nonetheless, his luck was holding. In other settings, with a difference of minutes or seconds in events, he might not have fared so well. His aggressiveness so far was being rewarded with good fortune. A new opportunity presented itself in this staff car. It was 13:30. A lot had happened in half a day.

On the highway to Bad Reichenall north of Berchtesgaden, Hayden considered his options. He had not thought he would make it this far. His pre-mission, barely defined plan was to go west in Germany, then to Switzerland, whatever was possible. Without a detailed plan at the time, he thought the simplest route would be the train to Munich, the train west to Frankfort, then somehow south to the Swiss border at Basel. He would get to Geneva, cross the border into France, already occupied by the Allies, and make his way to an American unit.

The information he had picked up at the hotel about a named American agent in the area cancelled that plan. All modes of travel would be more difficult. All travelers soon would be stopped. All ID's would be checked and verified. German internal security would be even more thorough now in its pursuit of suspicious persons. Even those mildly suspicious would be in for a severe grilling. Hayden knew that his regular changes of uniform and ID to this point had helped him cover any trails investigators might have started to follow. Passing as an officer had been a critical advantage to the execution of his mission. His former SS Major uniform, if not his personal identity and picture, could be the focus of a broad search in the next few days.

The pass signed by Goering did not have an expiration date. The irony was that it had an effective expiration time coming up very soon. When Sgt. Munsenn did not show up at Goering's apartment in Munich that afternoon, there would be questions. Sgt. Munsenn and the staff car would become the focus of a new and intense search by German police and intelligence services, a car known to have been in Berchtesgaden earlier that day.

Hayden calculated he had only this day, at most, before this staff car became his death warrant. He had to make and execute a plan quickly. He considered again his alternatives.

His obvious best option was to get into a neutral country. The only one near was Switzerland. Going south out of Berchtesgaden into Austria was out of the question. He would have to re-trace his journey through Berchtesgaden, and that was increasingly dangerous in the current sweep by the police and SS. Moreover, traveling in that direction would take him through mountains into the heart of Austria, a country as much Nazified as Germany. Limitations on movement were as tight as in Germany itself. Furthermore, he might then have to cross the Austrian border twice to get into Switzerland.

Going east or north beyond Munich would not work either. Traveling east meant more miles to cover, with an unknown terminus and an uncertain reception by Soviet army personnel. Traveling into Munich or beyond, into more heavily populated areas would invite more intense scrutiny. Allied bombing of population centers and transportation junctions was continuing, some of which he had already experienced on the train into Germany. That destruction might prolong his escape and make it more hazardous.

So it had to be west. He felt better with that option. It was in the direction of home and was closer in miles. How far west before he could safely turn south into Switzerland? That direction would entail solving a series of major problems.

There were two comforting positives evident. He was alive and not injured, thanks to his boldness and a lot of luck in how the circumstances had played out so far. And the original Sergeant Munsenn had gassed up the car before he left for Munich.

Chapter 34

Berchtesgaden Hotel, Sunday, December 3, 1944

Frederick regretted that he had to tell Hayden he was with U.S. Army Intelligence. He did not tell Hayden that he had been ordered to terminate the assassination mission with force if necessary. That alone might have caused Hayden to abandon his mission.

His excuse to Army Intelligence for permitting the assassination to proceed will be that he could not reach Hayden in time. He will, after the fact, tell Hayden the situation.

On the plane with Giles, Frederick had composed a scenario where he would somehow link up with Hayden and remain to help in any way he could until the assassination was over. Then, with Hayden, he would escape from Germany. Together they would find their way back to France and the U.S.

He had heard Hayden's door click open and close softly before 07:00. He was then quite sure that the assassination attempt would occur this morning. Otherwise Hayden would have sought him out for breakfast and conversation.

He decided to stay in his room until something happened. He would not interfere, not distract Hayden from his focus on his critical mission. He had gone down for coffee and a sweet roll to bring back to his room about 08:30. Hayden was nowhere to be seen.

He had brought with him a prized possession, a book of poetry by German poets. The volume was given to him by an elderly neighbor in Cologne when Frederick decided to leave Germany in 1938. The book had been at his side ever since, a constant reminder of the goodness and culture he knew still existed in the German people.

The excitement, the sudden shouting, the siren calling out the SS units from their barracks, all signaled by noon that Hayden's mission had progressed. He relished the point of Hayden's effort, although he then knew nothing of its outcome.

As the rumor of the killings was shouted in the hotel corridors, he alone was comforted in the news. Hitler was dead! His good friend had rid the world of its scourge. Frederick was pleased, proud to be a friend of Hayden.

Since he had not dared to ask Hayden about his mission, and especially its timing, without giving away a clue to his own mission, Frederick had not realized that the assassination would occur so soon after their meeting. He now had the uneasy feeling he should have left Berchtesgaden earlier. He could have arranged to meet Hayden outside the town, away from the spotlight that shortly would be focused on the community. All strangers would be questioned intensively. Hotel guests in Berchtesgaden, almost by definition, were strangers.

In the preparation for his mission to intercept Hayden, the discussion with his Army Intelligence handlers had turned grim. They had debated what identification he should carry. The team had put together a set of papers with the name Frederick had suggested, Friedrich Freundes. The team members had looked at him rather strangely.

One asked, why not take the name of an existing, captured colonel from an SS division? Frederick answered that if he were apprehended and questioned, any story he could develop probably would be challenged, getting him deeper and deeper into lies and attempted deceptions. His plan for survival after contacting Hayden, he told them, was to stay ahead of any pursuit and get out of the area quickly.

"Just in case," the Army Intelligence Chief in Paris had said, "you'd better take one of these. It will work in less than five seconds. It will be painless. It will save you a lot of pain if you're caught."

"I don't think I'll need it," Frederick said, pocketing the poison capsule. He had said it more to reassure himself that he would survive if he used his wits and was careful.

At the desk when he signed in late yesterday afternoon, he gave the same name, Freundes, "friends." If anything happened to Hayden in his mission, Frederick hoped that Hayden would know why he chose that name, and that one of Hayden's last memories would be of their friendship.

Suddenly there were two sharp knocks on his door. Even before he could get out of his chair, the door crashed in. Seven or eight men stormed in and surrounded him.

"Your identification papers," one demanded. Frederick had only an ID card, displaying a picture and a fictitious ID number. He had no military unit identification. He had already destroyed his travel orders since the contradiction of his presence in the hotel and his stated travel orders destination as the SS barracks would be a dead giveaway.

"What is your unit?"

"I am not allowed to reveal any information about my unit or assignment. I am on a secret mission I cannot reveal."

The interrogator scoffed.

"Where are your orders?"

"There are no written orders for such a mission," Frederick replied calmly.

Not at all politely, he was ordered, "Tell us what you know about the killings."

"I have been in my room all morning except for a few minutes to get coffee to bring to the room. I have no way of knowing what has happened outside this room."

The question about "killings" was a satisfying confirmation that Hayden's effort had succeeded. Frederick had been confident that if anyone could bring it off successfully, Hayden could.

Through the open door, Frederick could see uniformed men and others in dark suits and hats coming into the corridor to confer with the interrogating officers. In their conversation Frederick could overhear "restaurant" and "SS Major."

He knew he would be interrogated further after a check of his ID showed discrepancies. He decided then he would not be drawn deeper into the Nazi state police machinery, forced to reveal too much under torture. He reflected on what he had accomplished to date, and was satisfied with his small part in promoting the overall mission against the savage Nazi regime.

"Arrested for further questioning," the lead investigator snarled in Frederick's face.

Frederick was strong armed from both sides, pushed from behind. His last view of the room was of a policeman rifling through his book of poetry, looking for anything, shaking it by its back to loosen non-existent notes inserted between pages. They moved him brusquely down the corridor, then the steps into the lobby. As he scanned the crowded lobby quickly, he glimpsed a familiar face in the uniform of a German sergeant. Frederick did not give Hayden any sign of recognition.

That Hayden had adopted the disguise of an army sergeant was a good sign. He had to believe Hayden was staying ahead of the police network. Why was Hayden at the hotel? Hayden had to be coming to find Frederick so they could escape together.

Frederick was muscled out the door and jammed into the back seat of a sedan. As he faced forward he saw Hayden in the crowd gathered on the sidewalk outside the hotel. He nodded his approval of Hayden's heroic act quickly in Hayden's general direction. He could see Hayden start to move and shook his head no.

He had to stop Hayden's efforts to help him. Hayden deserved a chance to survive for Sarah and their future. And what was Frederick's own death compared to the death of the Nazi madman? He was content with the exchange.

In forcing him into the car, the policemen to his right had to release Frederick's arm. Frederick quickly found the capsule in his pocket, popped it into his mouth and bit down. They would get no further information from him. He had protected his friend.

He leaned his head back and began to recite his favorite poem from Goethe.

Über allen Gipfeln ist Ruh	*Over all the summits is Peace*
In allen Wipfeln spürest du	*In all the tree tops you feel*
Kaum einen Hauch.	*hardly a breeze.*
Die Vögelein schweigen im Walde.	*The little birds are silent in the forest.*
Warte nur, balde ruhest du auch.	*Just wait, soon you will be at Peace too.*

Frederick was at peace as he realized his personal checkmate.

Chapter 35

Southern Germany, Sunday, December 3, 1944

As Hayden entered Bad Reichenhall, he pulled off the road into a small park to ponder his immediate direction and destination. It was snowing again. Shops were on his left about a half mile ahead. Maybe he could buy a map. "Of course," he said aloud, and quickly opened the glove compartment of the staff car. He was elated at the contents. A map of the roadways in Germany, with special regional maps was his first interest. There was a compass. There were some packaged crackers and dried sausage. Hayden was almost sorry he had to dispose of Sergeant Munsenn so violently.

He plotted a route on the map as he ate. The drive along less mountainous roads would be about 200 miles to the Swiss border, two-lane roads for the most part. It was hilly country, with peaks in the 500 to 2500 foot range. The landscape was cut regularly by streams and rivers flowing north across his line of travel, draining the Bavarian Alps on the Germany-Austria border to the south. Those waterways flowed into the Danube River, north of his route and roughly parallel to it.

To enter Switzerland, he would have to travel to a point west of Lake Constance, a lake separating Switzerland and Germany. His uniform and ID made the lake crossing by ferry impossible.

The terrain past the lake area was increasingly mountainous and forested, more so the farther west toward Basel he traveled. He would need to turn south toward Switzerland once west of the lake. The reason was Germany's solid defensive line, the West Wall. It was built several miles deep behind the Rhine River as that broad waterway turned due north at Basel. The underground had gotten Hayden and the other two agents across the Rhine and through that defensive line less than a week ago, about eighty miles north of Basel, during a heavy bombing raid by the Allies.

Hayden could not hope to achieve a Rhine crossing there without someone's assistance. And he had no way of contacting anyone from the east side of the Rhine since he had no radio. The area would be swarming with German military personnel.

A further complication was simultaneously negotiating the Rhine River crossing and exiting Germany, presumably under German border guard scrutiny. He needed a plan to avoid that complication, to handle those problems separately, if possible.

He had to have an entry to Switzerland with a practicable Rhine crossing somewhere between the west end of Lake Constance and east of Basel. His close examination of the map showed such an option.

Along the German-Swiss border about twenty miles west of Lake Constance, a small piece of Swiss territory jutted into Germany. It was part of the Schaffhausen Canton. It looked to be about twenty-five square miles of land. Ramsen was a Swiss town on the rail line that crossed into Switzerland from Germany. The railroad then continued across the Rhine. Most importantly, the Rhine at that point was inside Switzerland. That meant a railroad bridge across the Rhine existed inside Switzerland. Hayden would make that small piece of land his travel objective.

Hayden knew his plan was not ideal. There were many unknowns. It was the only plan he could envision on short notice with any chance of success, however.

He quickly circled and committed to memory the towns and villages he would pass through from Bad Reichenall to the Swiss border. Rosenheim...Weilheim...Kaufbeuren...Memmingen...Saulgau...Menger...Sigmaringen on the Danube...Tuttlingen...then south toward Singen on the German-Swiss border. And from there across the border into Switzerland. The two hundred miles he had to cover now appeared to be the longest journey he would ever have to take in his life.

It was nearly 14:00 as he drove back onto the highway. He was keenly aware that Goering and his staff would soon be wondering when Sergeant Munsenn would return. If the guest list was headed by Hitler, Hayden surmised there would be a conspicuous absence. Would there be any dinner at all on the day

Hitler was killed? All such events certainly would be cancelled. Delivering his cargo in time for the evening's planned function was not relevant.

Even so, Goering's staff would wonder where the staff car and driver were. Goering was big. He could ask questions anywhere and demand immediate answers from hotel people or check points. A police radio request would go out within a radius of several hundred miles of Munich. The car's plate numbers would be broadcast.

For the same reason, the written pass signed by the *Reichmarshal* might be good until early this evening. Until then, he could buy a little time by lying about why he was not driving toward Munich or, as needed, resort to killing his questioners.

Hayden had passed through Memmingen in the last half hour. The small town of Saulgau should be coming up soon. "Damn this snow and ice," he said. "I can walk almost as fast." Fortunately, there was hardly anyone else on the roadway. He pressed harder on the gas pedal. It was nearly dark.

Even as he welcomed the absence of other travelers, he noted a car ahead pulled away from the road some twenty feet or so. It was stuck deep in the snow. Hayden pulled to the side of the road and found a pliers and screwdriver in the trunk of the staff car. He approached the stalled car cautiously. It was abandoned. He went to the rear of the car first, crouched and removed the plate. He did the same for the front. In short order he removed the plates from the staff car and replaced them. He sailed the staff car plates as far as he could into the snow drifts, one on each side of the road. He pulled the unique Reichsmarshal's insignia off of the right fender and pitched it into the snow. He looked for other identification on the staff car and could not find any. He did not feel totally secure, only that he had done all he could.

He could no longer suppress his curiosity. He had to know what Goering's Sergeant was carrying back to Goering in Munich. Hayden opened the four boxes on the floor. Candelabra. China and silverware. Olives, crackers and snacks. A case of wine.

At the next river crossing, Hayden hauled the four boxes of Goering's treasure and dumped them over the bridge, except for a bottle of wine, a large jar of rare olives, and special crackers. They would be his evening meal.

He had fiddled with the car radio dial earlier, but found only music and occasional propaganda pieces. He tried it again, hoping to get at least a hint of official response to the events of the day. There was nothing. He turned if off.

By 21:30 he reckoned his position to be about three miles from the border crossing. He picked what he observed to be an uninhabited area along the road and forced the vehicle into the forest, driving it as far as the accumulated snow and underbrush would allow him. He turned off the lights and the engine and sat quietly. After a few minutes, he got out of the car, retraced the tracks to the road, and began laboriously to fill and brush away the tire tracks he had made until he was safely back into the forest.

He ate his meal of wine, olives, and crackers. He would relax for a while, even doze a bit. He climbed into the back seat of the *Reichmarshal's* car and pulled the collar of his great coat over his neck as best he could.

Several events of the day troubled him, circumstances that he couldn't take the time to resolve in his mind when they happened. They surfaced now.

The corporal at the checkpoint had reported nothing about the assassination investigation at Berghof itself to the security Lieutenant. Was the assassination old news by then, shortly after 13:30, less than two hours after the killings? Or was an official net of silence dropped on it?

What kind of security net entangled Frederick? Had German intelligence simply run a fast sweep of contacts to learn that there were strangers in town? How many strangers did the police have to interview before they got to Frederick? Had they arrested everyone who seemed out of place?

The security agents from the *Feldgendarmerie* did have Lt. Eric Klaysa's name with them on the train between Frankfort and Munich. Was that information part of the same security breakdown that allowed identification of an American officer as an infiltrator, spoken about in the hotel lobby? And if someone outside the American Army intelligence loop had gotten that much of the plan, why hadn't Hayden been identified by name? Or had he been identified? Was there more than one security leak?

That security problem might account for Frederick being questioned so soon after the event. And if the same information was there to compromise Hayden, was it only Hayden's constant change of uniform and identification that kept him ahead of the police? Hayden dozed off with a headache forming.

He awoke with a start just after midnight, the early morning of December 4. Snow covered the windows of the car. His sleep in the back seat of the staff car had been fitful. He had nightmarish dreams in the cold. He was surrounded by wolves, their eyes glowing in the dark. All he had to fend them off was rocks. He threw, and threw again, over and over, and rarely hit a wolf. There were too many to chase away, too many grey monsters to kill.

Another nightmare had him run a spear through a young Roman soldier. When Hayden saw the youth's face, it was that of Billy, a high school classmate he had chummed with.

Hayden tried to shake off stiffness from his little sleep in the cramped seat with a vigorous twisting of his neck back and forth. He hoped it would also shake off the demons. He knew he had to be across the border before daylight. He had to clear his head to arrange his security and plan his escape.

No doubt there was a fence ahead. He pocketed the pliers and screwdriver and holstered the Luger.

He resisted the temptation to follow the road. Although much less difficult to walk on, it was too exposed. He proceeded along the edge of the forest instead, keeping the road in sight as best he could in the dark. By 02:00, he came upon a cleared area and the fence marking the Swiss border. A German checkpoint loomed three hundred yards ahead. He veered sharply away from the road, keeping the cover of trees. He also kept the border fence in sight.

When he was a mile or more from the road, he turned his attention to a chain link fence. As near as he could see, the fence was about eight feet high. There were three strands of barbed wire at the top, slanted away from the fence at about forty-five degrees, toward Switzerland. He could not tell yet if the fence was electrified. He advanced to the fence and tossed the screwdriver into it. Hayden was greatly relieved when the fence gave no reaction. He touched it again with the screwdriver in hand to confirm it was dead.

Suddenly, some distance away, Hayden heard the chilling howl of dogs. There would be a guard or guards following the dogs. His presence in the area had been discovered. He had to act quickly. The Luger pistol would not be a match in range or hitting power to the rifles guards carried. And he no longer had the advantage of surprise or concealment.

Hayden found the closest post supporting the fence and pushed hard on it, trying to rock it. It was anchored well, probably in concrete. That was good for his plan.

He pulled off his pistol belt and threw the Luger high over the fence. He took off his great coat, doubled it shut, and flung it as high as he could to cover the top of the post and post extension to which the three strands of barbed wire were attached. He reached to the top of the fence, dug his gloved fingers into the links, and pulled himself up, kicking his boots into the fence below him, trying to gain purchase.

His effort made a loud clatter. The dogs yelped louder, closer. He pulled himself up again, reached for the top strand of wire under the great coat, pulled and crawled onto the thick coat, astride the post extension. His right knee was penetrated by a barb as he did so. He pulled the top coat up to cover the ice at the end of the post extension. The coat should keep him from slipping off the extension. It also broadened the support the three strands of wire were giving his body. He then grasped the top of the extension pole with one hand to steady himself. He positioned his left foot, balancing it on the top of the chain link fence. Keeping his grasp on the end of the post extension, now with both hands, he raised his right foot, higher each second, until he had placed it even with his left foot on top of the chain link fence on the other side of the post. He was in a jackknifed position atop the post extension of the fence.

The dogs and guards were ever closer. They seemed to be converging on him from their separate guard posts along the fence. He could not stop now.

It seemed a long time since the rigorous physical challenges of basic training and jump school. He would have to improvise. He hoped his bruised legs and tired body would be up to the effort. Slowly, maintaining his balance, he moved each hand in turn to the top strand of wire either side of the post extension, to wire spacing free of barbs.

Still jackknifed, he quickly raised his left foot under his chest to step on the top of the extension pole, released his grips from the barbed wire, and in the same motion uncoiled and vaulted high over the fence with his right leg. He landed in the snow, knees flexed in a classic paratrooper landing.

He had to leave his great coat and hat, but found the Luger and belt. The guard dogs were now within rifle distance on both sides. He ran quickly over the cleared area of some thirty yards on the Swiss side of the fence, zigzagging in anticipation of rifle shots. He heard them and kept running, finally reaching the cover of a tree. He flopped in the snow to pause and survey the scene behind him as best he could. He could make out two guards. They were emptying their rifles into the trees around him. The dogs added to the commotion. After a minute or so, the guards paused, staring in his direction. One of them pulled on the bottom of his great coat and tore it down from the barbed wire.

He was alive and in Switzerland! He eased backward into the forest, crawling away until he was out of the guards' range. He would have to skirt the Swiss checkpoint also. The Swiss had to have heard the firing. Maybe they had gotten a call already. The Swiss checkpoint guards likely would be subservient to the German guards for a variety of reasons, and might try to escort Hayden back to Germany. That would be awkward.

He picked up the road a half mile behind the check-point but chose to remain under cover as he walked alongside it. The German military might use this road so close to Germany with little regard for Swiss neutrality, especially in pursuit of a fugitive. Soon he was at the edge of a town. It had to be Ramsen. He found a barn a couple hundred yards off the road, opened the door quietly, found a straw pile in the upstairs loft, immersed himself in it, and fell sound asleep.

Hayden was awakened by noise outside as the sun broke. There seemed to be no animals around. He climbed down the ladder, aimed the Luger at the door, but no one entered. Someone was using the outhouse. He peeked through a crack in the barn door and observed a man of fifty or so returning to his house. Hayden slowly emerged from the barn. The man seemed to sense Hayden's presence without turning to see him. Then he did turn. Hayden holstered the Luger, put his finger to his mouth to hush the farmer, and advanced toward him.

Hayden asked in German if he could buy food and clothing from him. He pulled out his wallet with a wad of German paper money.

The man said "no." Hayden insisted with his offer of money, not knowing whether the man wanted to avoid dealing entirely or that he didn't want payment. Or, perhaps the German money is worthless, Hayden thought ruefully. Maybe the man was a German sympathizer. Hayden tried again, speaking reasonably that he needed help and was willing to pay for it.

"A deserter?" the man asked. Perhaps he was afraid Hayden was testing his response on behalf of the *Gestapo* or *Feldgendarmerie.* He could later be apprehended and punished by German agents close to the border for assisting a deserter.

Hayden smiled, "No. I'm really not German." He held up his hands to ward off the man's suspicions, loosened the pistol belt and offered the revolver and belt, which was refused. He offered the man all his German marks and half the Swiss francs, which he took. As Hayden peered into the man's eyes, he could see a softening. Perhaps the farmer was trying to digest this unlikely event. He seemed to understand enough to act.

He waved Hayden out of the open, behind the barn to shield them from the view of any guards or agents who might be nearby. The man then smiled broadly and offered to shake Hayden's hand. Hayden laughed aloud in the joy of the farmer's good will and patted his shoulder gratefully.

Chapter 36

Berchtesgaden, Monday, December 4, 1944

Officers from several German police and intelligence services assembled in the Berchtesgaden police station to write a preliminary report on the Berghof killings. Hitler was demanding answers. Representatives of the *Gestapo*, SS security, *Feldgendarmerie*, the Berghof guard detail, and the Berchtesgaden police were there to provide them.

The senior *Gestapo* agent addressed first the confusion over interpretation of intercepted Allied intelligence. "We in the security community have assumed implicitly and logically all along that, if any organized attempt was ever made on *Der Fuehrer's* life, it naturally would occur where he actually was or was going to be. He actually was in Berlin yesterday, not at Berghof. One of his doubles was the unfortunate victim of the killings, along with several in the counterfeit entourage at Berghof. In short, have we assumed that Allied intelligence is better than it actually is?"

The Commandant of the SS barracks in Berchtesgaden chimed in. "Even the report from the German agent embedded in British intelligence in London about an American officer infiltrating to conduct a high level assassination plan could have carried the same assumption. Why would an assassin be inserted from southeastern France, just north of the Swiss border, if the attempt was to be made in Berlin? There are so many potential entry points into Germany in the North. Maybe the whole scheme was simply more misinformation contrived by the Allies."

The regional head of the *Feldgendarmerie* confirmed the confusion. "On any day, there are reports of infiltration into Germany. There has been a growing number of reports daily as the Allied armies have moved closer. All the leads must be followed up, but only a few are productive, that is, ending in arrests. For example, when captured army intelligence agent Eric Klaysa, from behind enemy lines at Strasbourg, France, alerted German intelligence across the Rhine, it was easy to conclude that a disguised Allied agent infiltrating Germany, if any, would have a localized task to perform instead of a task in Berlin or Berchtesgaden."

The Commander of the Berghof security detail continued. "There is also confusion in the dead ends we are encountering in this investigation. We have had all available personnel from all our offices," he motioned to the assembled group, "combing the area for the last twenty hours. What have we found? Practically nothing of consequence toward a solution. We have no living witnesses we can pressure for answers. The guards have only minor details to offer."

The Berchtgesgaden Police Chief added to the mystery. "The SS Colonel at the hotel…no one knew him." His observation was more a question to the SS Barracks Commandant than a statement. "He carried no orders or unit identification. What are we to conclude from that? What kind of lead does that give us? Was he here as an anonymous martyr to some cause? And all those guards killed, over a wide area. Who can derive a pattern from that? All individuals reported by surviving guards to be in the area or in the pursuit are accounted for in some way. Most of them are dead and cannot tell us more."

The senior *Gestapo* agent interrupted and took charge of the meeting again, impatient to get on with the process. "We need a report. We need it soon. I suggest we begin by first constructing the outline of a report. We can enhance with details as we go along, based on what we each know. We can adjust it later when new information arrives."

The senior agent went on to reveal the other benefits of haste in writing their report. "We certainly will learn something about the defective security that permitted this outrage to happen. The names of guards, staff, and others derelict in their duty during this atrocity at *Der Fuehrer's* residence will also be noted for subsequent punitive action. It is essential that we find the real perpetrators. It is not acceptable to find scapegoats and leave the real villains alive out there to repeat their treachery." The agent went to the door of the interrogation room and ordered a secretary to come in to take the transcript that followed.

PART ONE: Known Facts and Inferences

I. Seven persons were killed at Berghof about 11:40 on December 3, 1944: the Hitler stand-in plus six in the entourage accompanying him on the terrace.

There were another eight people in the terrace party at the time of the shooting. Three of those suffered wounds. None of the staff at Berghof was on the terrace at the time, and therefore none were victims.

II. After the first shot, several of the terrace party fell on the Hitler double, trying to protect him. Subsequent shots, perhaps as many as six or seven, were fired into the pile of bodies there, and some of the fatalities were the result of that firing.

III. The housekeeping staff at the chalet reports that all of the staff and several other aides on site had stayed inside the chalet when the party went out on the terrace.

The absence of the aides appears to be a violation of the protocol required of the stand-in party. All are obligated to participate in group functions within the chalet perimeter to keep up the appearance of *Der Fuehrer's* presence.

The names of those aides are known. They are being interrogated now to determine what they knew or suspected of the shooting beforehand.

IV. In addition to the seven persons killed on the terrace, two security guards died in the *Tee Haus.* They were shot in the chest at close range with a small caliber pistol.

The guards either were inattentive and therefore surprised at the entry of the assassin or assassins, or were deceived enough to allow their killer to approach them. Their presence inside the *Tee Haus* instead of patrolling the grounds may suggest they were delinquent in their duty.

Three standard guard rifles were found with the two bodies inside the *Tee Haus.* The presence of the third rifle is possibly explained by the circumstances in item **VII** below.

An official reprimand is the appropriate, minimum punishment for criminal dereliction of duty. Under the circumstances, notation on the records of these two dead guards will be made. It is recommended that all rights and privileges to their survivors be terminated.

V. One patrol guard was killed along the path leading to the *Tee Haus.* He apparently was responding properly to the shots heard coming from the woods behind and beside the *Tee Haus.* The size of the round that killed him seems to be the same as that used in the killing of the seven people on the terrace. The dog patrolling with him was constrained by a leash attached to the dead guard's wrist.

VI. Another patrol guard moving toward the *Tee Haus* after the initial shots reportedly was fired upon also. He, perhaps too cautiously, responded by proceeding to the point in the woods from which he thought the shots had been fired. He found ten shell casings behind a fallen tree, the site about forty yards from the *Tee Haus*. He did not disturb those shell casings. He saw no one present or moving at the site.

Within minutes, he discovered the body of another guard some twenty-five yards inside the edge of the woods from where the terrace shots were reported to be fired. He recognized the dead guard as a member of the patrol assigned to guard the inside perimeter of the chalet.

The dead guard was killed by two shots to the chest at close range by small caliber rounds. A specially made weapon, presumably the .50 caliber weapon used in the terrace killings, was lying beside his body.

VII. The circumstances of this private's death are initially incongruous. If the private was the assassin, who then killed him at close range?

This guard had only his holstered side arm and the .50 caliber rifle beside him. He did not have the standard rifle issued him. The corporal of the guard confirms that this dead guard was armed with a standard rifle at the 10:00 changing of the guard.

The connection of the dead guard to the killings is not made definitely here, and awaits further investigation. Could this guard, as assassin, have eliminated the two potential witnesses in the *Tee Haus* and then left his rifle there inadvertently? Or to deceive investigators deliberately?

VIII. This investigating group notes its disbelief that killing of the seven people on the terrace, the single guard with dog on the footpath leading to the *Tee Haus*, the two guards in the *Tee Haus*, and the guard in the woods beside the *Tee Haus* were all accomplished without any of the survivors seeing or hearing an assassin before, during, or after the shooting.

There is also a maxim that dead men do not talk.

IX. Three guards assigned to the Berghof perimeter security, a corporal and two privates, advanced from their guard house toward the *Tee Haus* upon hearing shots. They encountered an SS Major running from the direction of the *Tee Haus* just minutes after the killings. He ordered them to join him in pursuit of "assassins" whom they did not see then or later.

They joined the Major, and together the four found a hole cut in the chain link fence at the perimeter. Once through the opening, the Major pointed out in their presence the body of a guard just beyond the perimeter fence. The corporal and one of the privates were directed by the Major to search to the left into the forested, mountainous area west and south of the Berghof compound for assassins. The Major then ordered a private from the original group of three guards to accompany the Major to search to the right in a more northerly direction. Neither of the guards learned the Major's name nor saw his identification.

X. The corporal and private searching the forested area were intercepted by SS patrols about 14:30 yesterday afternoon about four miles into the mountains southwest of the Berghof compound. They had not since seen any suspects in the killings or the SS Major who ordered them into the search.

XI. A private, reported to be from the original group of three guards who met the Major leaving the *Tee Haus* area, has been found dead from a small caliber bullet wound to the head on the north edge of the forest. The location was just off of the access road to Berchtesgaden.

XII. A report by Berchtesgaden police states that a security patrol north of Berghof came across the body of an SS Major about 15:00 yesterday. The ID card was that of Walther Moss, but he had no SS tattoo. He had been shot in the head with a small caliber pistol. Moss was a security inspector in the Munich district. The Munich District Office reported he had not checked in for over twenty-four hours.

PART TWO: Analysis

Now, at 08:30 on December 4, after the Berghof killings about 11:40 yesterday, German intelligence officers can re-create most of the picture.

I. In its sweep and detention of suspicious characters, it arrested an agent masquerading as a German SS Colonel. Minutes after reports of the Berghof killings reached junior army officers assembled for a luncheon meeting at the Berchtesgaden hotel, a restaurant waiter reported to Berchtesgaden police that an SS Colonel registered there had been in the restaurant off the hotel lobby the evening before, December 2. The waiter had seen the Colonel upstairs in the hotel earlier. He thought his behavior peculiar. Why was the Colonel staying in the hotel, not the SS barracks? Also, he had brought a book of poetry to the bar and read it as he waited there over an hour.

When an SS Major entered, the Colonel wrote a short note and asked the waiter to take it to the Major. The waiter did so. He hesitated, thinking the Major might want to send a reply, but was tipped by the Major and waved away. He did see the Major immediately search the restaurant until he saw the Colonel. The Colonel, once recognized by the Major, then joined the Major at the Major's table. They finished their drinks and food and exited the hotel together about ten minutes later. The waiter thought it peculiar that the Colonel, after waiting so long, apparently for the Major, did not simply join the Major immediately without first sending him a note. The waiter stated that the note was not lengthy, probably not more than one line.

II. When the clerk reported this scenario to the Berchtgesgaden police, the police had just received the report of an SS Major's activities at Berghof. The Police Captain alerted the *Gestapo* and SS barracks chief. They ordered the nearest security units to the hotel about 12:30 to question the Colonel and Major. The Colonel was found reading a book of poetry when the police detail broke through the door to his room.

III. The Colonel was registered as Friedrich Freundes at the hotel. However, he carried no orders on his person, nor were any found in his room. That strange behavior is itself highly suspicious. The telephone operator at the hotel does not recall any calls to or from the Colonel's room this morning.

To repeated questions as to his purpose in Berchtesgaden, the Colonel responded that he was on a secret mission. He was evasive when asked about his military unit and function.

IV. The room of Major Walther Moss in the same hotel was two doors down from that of Colonel Freundes. It was searched thoroughly. It was empty of all effects. No SS Major was found at the hotel. Why was he also not staying at the SS barracks?

V. The police detail still believes it has caught the ring leader of the assassination plot in the person of the SS Colonel, whatever his real identity. His suicide, due to careless handling of the suspect by agents at the hotel, seems to confirm his involvement. Equally suspicious is that he was carrying no orders. His body had no SS ID number tattoo.

VI. The most plausible preliminary theory is that the SS Major, the guard found dead in the stand of trees near the *Tee Haus*, and perhaps one other patrol guard near the *Tee Haus* were in a conspiracy with the SS Colonel. The Colonel planned for his agents, once inside the perimeter, to kill the guards in the *Tee Haus*, and arrange for the shootings on the terrace. There are no reports that place the SS Colonel, a.k.a. Friedrich Freundes, on the site of any of the killings within the Berghof perimeter or beyond on Sunday morning.

VII. After the shootings, presumably by the guard in the stand of trees under the supervision of the SS Major, the Major could have escaped by pretending to be in "search of assassins."

The guard remained with the rifle, perhaps planning to make a separate escape. However, he was dispatched with two shots from a small bore pistol, presumably to ensure his silence. The guard's killer later may have covered the trail of the other conspirators by killing the guard just beyond the hole in the fence, the patrol guard who accompanied the SS Major, and then the SS Major as well.

VIII. Since the patrol guard near the chalet at the time of the killings (who alleges he was fired on by the assassin) was the person discovering the shell casings and the body of the guard with the .50 caliber rifle near his body, further intense questioning of him is mandatory. Interrogators may treat that patrol guard as a suspected co-conspirator. His opportunity to dispose of the two guards in the *Tee Haus* on his way to the stand of trees is evident. Being recognized by them, his ability to approach them without their challenging him is also evident.

PART THREE: Questions Remaining

I. In support of the analysis presented in **TWO.VIII**, it must be determined what happened to the small caliber weapon, presumably a pistol, after it was used for the two shots that killed the guard in the stand of trees near the Tee Haus. If it is later proved that the same weapon was used for the killings outside the perimeter fence, it will be necessary to document the transfer of that weapon to another perpetrator in order to connect the killings outside the perimeter fence to the killings inside the fence.

II. The patrol guard who found the body and rifle, and had opportunity to do the killings at the *Tee Haus*, reportedly returned to the chalet, called in his findings to the corporal of his guard detail at 11:57. He then remained in the presence of the security personnel who gathered at the chalet shortly after the shots were fired.

III. The patrol guard in **Part THREE.II** immediately above certainly would not have had time to travel so far as the access road, kill the private and Major, and return to the chalet before his report time of 11:57.

IV. The possibility of a second small caliber pistol in the hands of still another co-conspirator has to be considered. It could help to answer other questions on the locations of three bodies. The first private's body was found near the hole in the perimeter fence. The second private's body was located at the top of the access road to Berchtesgaden. The third was that of an SS Major over a mile from there, also near the same road. Preliminary examination indicates all were killed at close range by small caliber bullets.

V. The Major has not been identified for certain, although initial reports, and the ID he carried, point to him as the missing SS Major Walther Moss. His role in the killings and his death from a small caliber round to the head at close range remain unresolved.

VI. Other unanswered questions surround the timing of events related in this report. If the SS Colonel, registered at the hotel as Friedrich Freundes, was the chief assassin who directed his co-conspirators and then eliminated them, how and when could he have killed several people at close range with a small caliber weapon, most likely a pistol, to fit in the time frame under investigation? Those killings had to occur after 10:00, the changing of the guard.

The first killings with time certain were at the chalet about 11:40. The last, the guard with the .50 caliber rifle in the stand of trees near the *Tee Haus*, had to be completed before 11:47 when the patrol guard entered the tree stand.

VII. The hotel doorman and all the hotel lobby clerks are quite certain that Colonel Freundes did not leave the hotel this morning. Maids and janitors on the floor saw the Colonel return to his room about 08:30 yesterday morning and did not see him leave his room again until confronted by the security detail.

How and where could the Colonel have penetrated the chalet perimeter without being seen leaving the hotel?

Why would he kill himself if he had already eliminated others who could have implicated him in the killings?

Why did he choose to remain in his room alone instead of attempting to flee?

VIII. Although installation of a Hitler stand-in and entourage is part of the planned deception at Berghof to disguise the real location of *Der Fuerher*, the guards implicated in the killings had to know *Der Fuehrer* was not actually in residence at Berghof.

PART FOUR Security Measures Taken

I. Relatively few vehicles have passed through the road blocks quickly set up in and around Berchtesgaden after the assassination. The roadblocks are operational to this time and will continue indefinitely.

The continuing snowfall in the area has covered up footprints, vehicle tracks, and probably some evidence.

II. Officers at the SS barracks will be questioned as to their whereabouts yesterday afternoon and evening. A broad search is being conducted on all roads and public transportation facilities. All shifts of *Gestapo*, local police, *Feldgendarmerie*, and SS security have been called in to conduct searches. Search teams on public transportation have been doubled and tripled in most cases. Nothing immediately related to the killings has been discovered in routine checks of public transportation to this time. Questioning is also continuing of all the surviving witnesses to yesterday's events.

III. Cross checking of information is critical to answering our remaining questions. A central control has been set up in the interrogation room of the Berchtesgaden police station. *Gestapo* and SS agents will be on duty here until further notice. Field investigators are being instructed to call in anything that seems out of the ordinary. The group assembled here to write this report will meet twice a day for updates, at 08:00 and 20:00.

IV. All military personnel in the area are subject to questioning to determine if they were and are where they are assigned. If they were and are not, they will be questioned further, and their stories checked.

All general officers in the Munich district will be questioned as to their whereabouts in the last three days. There may still be some connections of yesterday's killings and the July 20 plot to be examined.

All SS Majors will be questioned. Information is being requested of all German military units to determine if any SS Majors are missing from their posts or duty.

Agents from all security and intelligence offices are being instructed to be especially watchful for the legitimacy of military travel orders. If military personnel being questioned are in transit, those personnel should know their previous posts, where they are going, and how long it is taking them.

V. Above all, secrecy will be required, and all documents handled on a need-to-know basis. Agents from all the offices represented here need not know why they are questioning people, or explain to those being interrogated why they are being questioned. They need to know only that they must follow the directives for the questioning that this group mandates.

ADDENDUM

Among routine checks of the movement and whereabouts of military personnel in the area, there are two interesting developments that may or may not be related to the assassination plot.

I. There is a report this morning that about 13:25 p.m. yesterday, a German army special services Sergeant in a staff car passed through a check point on the northern edge of Berchtesgaden after giving a security Lieutenant a ride from the hotel to that point. The Sergeant was on his way to Munich, on a mission for *Reichsmarshal* Goering. His pass and story were checked out affirmatively by an officer at Goering's chalet.

The housekeeper at the chalet has provided the Sergeant's name, Bernhard

Munsenn. Questioning of Sgt. Munsenn should now be made by Munich agents when he is located. We should know if he was ordered to pick up something at the hotel yesterday noon. Also, the Sergeant may have seen something in the Berghof or hotel area that he did not recognize at the time as significant to this investigation.

II. The most recent report of an infiltrator with a possible assassination objective is of an American officer being inserted into Germany from near Strasbourg, France. Discussion of this activity in the London bureau of British intelligence was overheard by an imbedded German agent code-named Lion Tamer.

It is unknown if that infiltrator ever made it into the Berchtesgaden area. If he did, and was one of the conspirators in the killings, he has avoided detection and apprehension. The possibility exists that he is in the disguise of a German Army Lieutenant named Eric Klaysa, as that cover reportedly was used for the American officer's entry into Germany.

The German agent who reported this infiltration heard the name he understood to be Ivan or Dean Bruch passed in connection with the infiltration. It is unlikely that an infiltrator bent on his task would use his real name. The infiltrator's picture is not yet available.

The *Gestapo* senior agent paused and asked if there was anything more to be added. There was nothing. He concluded the meeting with a warning.

"Don't think for a second that this investigation is not important since a double of *Der Fuehrer* was killed. It could have been *Der Fuehrer.* Our pressing this investigation has several important purposes besides finding the guilty parties. We will learn what security measures are defective. We will identify and cull out military and non-military personnel who do not express loyalty to *Der Fuehrer* by their actions."

He told the secretary to include his last comments in the report.

Chapter 37

Berlin, Monday, December 4, 1944

Adolf Hitler reacted to the killing of his double with an explosion of outrage. He stomped, turned alternately white and purple, and harangued his close aides.

Several top officials of the regime gathered in Hitler's bunker under the Chancellery with Hitler in the mid-afternoon of December 4. It was part of their implicit duty to show support for *Der Fuehrer* in difficult times. It was also the politically wise thing to do. Their presence helped to counter any hint of suspicion as to their own personal involvement in events contrary to Hitler's interests.

General Alfred Jodl, Chief of Operations of the OKW, Oberkommando *der Wehrmacht*, the high command of the German military, and General Wilhelm Keitel, Chief of Staff of the OKW, were the principal military leaders present. Foreign Minister Joachim von Ribbentrop and Propaganda Minister Josef Goebbels attended. *Reichsmarshal* Hermann Goering was absent. *Gestapo* and SS Chief Heinrich Himmler was absent.

Hitler spread his rage to include the German people for "not protecting him." Those around him tried to soothe his anger by observing that the security cordon at Berghof likely had been softer than when Hitler himself was present. The plot succeeded only because the natural inclination of the guards around Berghof was to relax if they knew Hitler was not in residence.

Hitler, however, while outraged and a little nervous that assassins had come so close, invading the sanctity of his Bavarian residence, nonetheless saw his survival as reinforcing his self-promoting and often-stated claim of invincibility.

The report of the intelligence team assembled in Berchesgaden to investigate the Berghof and area killings had reached Hitler an hour ago. It mentioned the mysterious role played by the SS Major, the German Colonel's suicide, and the pistol killings of German soldiers. The intelligence team, directed by the senior *Gestapo* agent in Berchtesgaden, had suggested since then that the killings probably were the work of one or more Allied infiltrators possibly aided by German security guard accomplices at Berghof.

The officers assembled with Hitler disagreed whether the killings were by Allies, by a team led by a disaffected German officer, or the result of another conspiracy by German generals. The memory of the July 20, 1944, bomb placement at Hitler's Field headquarters at *Wolfschanze* in East Prussia was still fresh in Hitler's mind. He believed that the Berghof perpetrator was a German officer, the SS Colonel, not an American. He was certain further investigation would find his connection to the aristocratic elite behind the July plot. Maybe the attempt was simple retaliation by those aristocrats and officers for the Hitler-ordered liquidation of many of their colleagues.

Hitler scoffed at the inexactness of the police report and threw it to the table in disgust after scanning the first several pages. He posed rhetorical questions criticizing the report. "What SS colonels were not at their assignments? What SS majors are missing? Has our vast, so-called intelligence operation gone blind and deaf?"

An aide came into the room bringing reports of afternoon calls from Munich and Berchtesgaden. "There are a few new developments to add to the mystery. The body with SS Major Walther Moss' identification was not Moss. His SS friends and colleagues in Berchtesgaden are certain of that. No one knows who this dead impostor was."

"*Reischsmarshal* Goering's staff car is not back from Berchtgesgaden, nor is the driver, Sgt. Bernhard Munsenn. He never showed up in Munich the evening of December 3. A search is underway for the car and the Sergeant."

Hitler raised an eyebrow and his voice at the news. "Goering's Sergeant? Was in Berchtesgaden yesterday? What's going on? Put that Sergeant under arrest and investigate him thoroughly," he ordered to no one in particular.

The aide continued his report of the phone calls. "The questioning of the guard detail at Berghof is yielding no results. Under intense interrogation and threats they all stick to their stories exactly as yesterday afternoon.

"The investigating team at the Berchtesgaden police station has nothing to add to their theory, except to suggest Allied infiltrators at work. They have not identified enough people actually within the Berghof perimeter, or outside the perimeter, to accomplish the several killings within the time frame of the 10:00 guard shift.

"The identity and role of SS Colonel Friedrich Freundes is a mystery. There is no SS colonel by that name on any roll."

Hitler responded with a loud "Hah!" and motioned for his aide to continue.

"The report sent by the German agent imbedded in X Section, the German Directorate of British intelligence in London, was helpful in one way, but complicating in another. Agent Lion Tamer reported that one possible perpetrator may have been an American officer named Bruch, infiltrated for that purpose in a German officer's uniform. That might account for the German Colonel's presence. However, other than being in Berchtesgaden and then departing suddenly via suicide, there was no involvement of the Colonel found except that he may have talked to the SS Major, Walther Moss. And Moss' connection to the killings is still not determined."

"Anything more?" Hitler addressed the aide impatiently.

"No, my leader."

Hitler waved him out of the room. He also motioned von Ribbentrop to follow him into a private office. "Cancel those talks with Eden! He can't be trusted any more than that dog-shit Prime Minister. They and their Jew friends in the work camps can all go to hell together!"

A distortion of recent events was inevitable in Hitler's anger. "I tried to be reasonable, to accommodate their desire for peace negotiations. And all I get is betrayal, a gross attempt to kill me and my friends!"

Von Ribbentrop, trying to see through the murky details, even contradictions in the killing scenario at Berghof, believed this plot was an American plan, with only incidental, if any, input from the British. He did not believe Churchill would jeopardize the diplomatic initiative to free the work camps that Secretary Eden had stressed in their meeting. Why would the British have invested all that time and effort, and gambled on a daring initiative, if they planned to sabotage their own work with an assassination attempt? And a poorly informed assassination attempt at that?

No, von Ribbentrop thought, the real crisis emerging could be in British-American relations, the future trust they would have in each other. If this was a solo effort by the Americans, as Lion Tamer's report suggested, there had to be some communication problem between the Americans and the British. The smart diplomatic play would be to ensure that split continued. The wrong thing to do would be anything that would force them to forget their differences.

He was afraid that Hitler's rage would cause him to ignore the effect on the

British and American alliance of a new hostile act by Germany. And that, the Foreign Minister concluded, was what Hitler was about to do. Von Ribbentrop decided to make one more effort to penetrate Hitler's rage with a scenario suggesting conspirators other than German aristocracy.

"My leader, is it possible that this heinous event was an American effort only, not a combined Allied effort? Our settlement negotiations were with the British only. What if the Americans learned about those negotiations, and wanted to thwart them for some reason? This crime against your person might be something they would do to de-rail the negotiations."

Hitler's response came after a brief, curious glance at his Foreign Minister. "I have always thought that we could exploit the mistrust between the British and the Americans. When Roosevelt hears about our talks with the British, that purpose might still be served. But an effort against me by the Americans alone to kill the talks? No, it is too clever…too clever by far."

Reading Hitler's body language, Ribbentrop could see that his suggestion would not be discussed further. Hitler in his paranoia did not believe all the perpetrators were outsiders. The July 20 assassination plot had not been cleaned up completely, he would say, despite his orders for the brutal elimination of hundreds of suspected active as well as knowledgeable silent conspirators.

They rejoined the assembled officials.

"We shall put into motion the battle plan *Wacht am Rhein*," Hitler announced abruptly and triumphantly. He turned to the generals. "Resume planning immediately for an invasion in two weeks. Keep this operation completely secret. Develop cover for all troop and material movements."

Hitler assumed the role of teacher to explain to the class why this initiative was necessary. "The Ardennes offensive will serve at least three purposes. First, we will re-take Antwerp, make the future supply situation for the Allies even more precarious, and ensure their defeat in the West.

"Second, we will punish the Allies for their complicity in these killings."

Hitler did not mention the break-off of negotiations that had been started with the British, von Ribbentrop noted, but he was certain this offensive was part of the payback to the Allies collectively. Hitler's expanding of the net involved in the Berghof conspiracy was not supported by any hard evidence to date. His satisfaction gained in accusing all the Allies would more than compensate for any inaccuracy, however.

"Because the Americans helped to promote this outrage, we will focus our attack primarily against the American divisions lining the Ardennes." Hitler was going to have it both ways in placing blame.

"Finally, the offensive will test the commitment of our senior army commanders to ultimate victory of the Third Reich." Hitler had long been closed to any criticism, especially from his generals, on his war planning. Any criticism, however innocuous, was treasonous. Von Ribbentrop cringed at the twisted, final rationale Hitler was offering for the Ardennes operation. It was the residue of Hitler's paranoia. It was also the only one of the three planned results likely to be realized.

Von Ribbentrop thought back to the battle for Mortain after the American break-out from Normandy. There, General Gunther von Kluge would have to prove his loyalty by following Hitler's orders to attack deeper into the Falaise pocket, even though Kluge and his successor, General Walther Model, thought it was a disastrous order by Hitler. The subsequent envelopment of the German salient by American and British armies in the Falaise pocket resulted in the loss of a quarter of a million German soldiers killed, wounded, or captured.

Despite the momentous defeat, Hitler's suspicion of von Kluge seemed justified. Von Kluge took poison and died on his way to Berlin after being recalled by Hitler. His Ardennes orders would provide a similar test of loyalty for suspect German officers. This outcome might also prove disastrous all around, the Foreign Minister feared.

"A brilliant stroke," said the lackey Goebbels to Hitler's plan. Hitler's official secretary, Martin Bormann, seconded the Propaganda Minister's enthusiasm. Von Ribbentrop only nodded with a non-committal stare. Generals Jodl and Keitel quietly turned to the map spread out on the work table.

Who in Hitler's inner circle of confidants would dare suggest the folly of this rage-inspired move on Hitler's part? Jodl? Keitel? Field Marshals Von Runstedt and Model had dared to argue against the original idea when Hitler presented it in September. What courage they could muster then was aimed at suggesting a limit to the plan's scope. Hitler would hear none of that. The two senior commanders' concerns abated when the plan was put on the shelf in late October, for reasons not explained to them.

Now the main theme of the resurrected Ardennes plan was precisely its strategic scope, a battle to turn Germany's war fortunes. A limited tactical engagement would not do. Partial results were not worthy of Hitler's strategic brilliance.

The practical implications of the killings still had to be handled. Goebbels and von Ribbentrop proposed that, to dispel any doubts and quiet rumors, Hitler should speak to the German people. What he said in his talk would not matter much. His live radio message would prove he was alive. He should not mention the killings. All should act as if nothing had happened.

Hitler agreed in principle. Not only would he not mention anything about the killings, he forbade its further discussion. Moreover, he would use the radio address to stress the need of the German people to fight on. He would prime his armies in the West to take on the unannounced Ardennes campaign. He would remind his listeners of his own determination and insight and brilliance as a leader.

Hitler indicated that the meeting was over with a gruff "Thank you." All departed except one secretary.

Hitler phoned Heinrich Himmler, *Gestapo* Chief and Commander of the SS. He ordered him to take personal charge of the Berghof investigation. He was to identify everyone involved, directly or indirectly. Himmler would provide Hitler alone the results of the investigation.

Punishments had to be administered to those whose vigilance had been lax. He ordered the entire Berghof guard detail arrested, officers and non-commissioned officers, the whole lot. They would be replaced with fresh *Waffen* SS troops. Security patrols would be doubled inside and outside the security fence.

He ordered Himmler to install another stand-in at Berghof, with an entirely new retinue. The routine of the household should be changed as well, with a new daily schedule and new safeguards.

Finally, he turned to his secretary to change his own calendar. He would be needed in Berlin or an advanced headquarters in the West all of December. His planned week of respite at the end of the year at Berghof was cancelled. He regretted that cancellation most. He had not been in Berghof since July 15, almost five months ago.

Chapter 38

Washington, Tuesday, December 5, 1944

President Roosevelt and General Marshall learned from communications between Berchtesgaden and Berlin heard by American intelligence services that an assassination attempt had occurred. Monitoring of the radio broadcast assured intelligence officials that it was Hitler himself broadcasting yesterday evening, December 4.

Roosevelt and Marshall had also learned of the aborted peace negotiations between Churchill-Eden and Hitler-von Ribbentrop. There had been a hint in an earlier radio intercept of something going on in Sweden about a month ago. That hint was supplemented by American intelligence operatives in Sweden reporting on a yacht anchored off the coast of Sweden on November 17. There had been a transfer of four officials from each of two frigates onto the yacht and then a transfer back later. No national flags were flown on any boat, only plain white flags.

Enough information was gained to substantiate the conclusion that some kind of negotiations went on between Great Britain and Germany. The President related his own impression of the events from the diplomatic perspective.

"So Winston was surprised about this assassination business. But he had a little surprise of his own, apparently. General," Roosevelt asked with a smile, "do you think he might be a bit sheepish the next time we talk? I would guess his secret diplomacy venture has already been torpedoed."

"I would imagine so. Of course, our action was kept pretty quiet, too," General Marshall replied, "even from the Chief of Staff."

"You didn't know?"

"I did not until Everett Giles radioed from Paris that the cover for our man undertaking the mission probably was blown."

"So you didn't approve it?"

"Not directly. I may have given the aura of approval to Everett Giles by not forbidding things of that type specifically. However, after the Yamamoto incident, who am I to say that the intelligence units could not feel that there was approval by precedent?"

"So they hit a double, according to the story picked up by State Department decoders," offered the President.

"Yes, sir, probably so. Hitler did not mention the killings on the radio last night. He obviously did think it is important to demonstrate that he is not out of the picture."

"Which unit of ours actually carried it out? An army unit, I understand?"

"Well, not a unit actually, sir. It was an individual. A paratrooper from the 82nd Airborne, acting alone. A Captain Brooke, I'm told."

"You don't say! So he jumped in and did his duty, thinking it was Hitler…"

"Well, that's part of the irony, too. He didn't actually jump in. Army intelligence changed the plan at the last minute. He moved by land somehow, all the way through southern Germany."

"And what has happened to that brave lad, General? Captured? Dead? Do we know?"

"I don't know yet. I've been trying to find out, but intelligence hasn't heard from him."

"Please let me know the minute…"

"Certainly. One other matter of interest on that action. There were two security leaks. One was fed by an escaping German POW. The second one came from inside Britain's X Section, a deep mole that they have since caught and arrested. Once our secret mission was known, Churchill made a frantic attempt to stop Captain Brooke."

"The negotiations."

"No doubt," the General said.

The President let his head rest back on his chair. "What do you think I ought to say to Winston? Do you think I ought to contact him now, or just wait and let things settle down a bit?"

General Marshall took it as a sign of the President's weariness that he would ask him about a diplomatic matter. Diplomacy had always been one of the President's strong suits, even when the fortunes of war had been in the enemy's favor.

"I suggest you wait a day or two. I don't think there's much point in raising issues we can't resolve anyway."

"Probably so," said the President. "I suppose we both have a little back-pedaling to do on this whole thing. I can't believe that the British, and especially Winston, would actually trust that Nazi bastard again after Munich. I suppose Winston's intentions were good, but he was leaving himself in for a lot of grief, especially if he had succeeded! Someday soon I'll have to find out what his bargaining chips were. What do you think?"

The General waited a minute while he thought through the implications of the President's comment. "Well, since Germany is not the only country fighting a war on more than one front, maybe the Prime Minister's intentions were strategically quite sound. I suspect Hitler was going to offer him the bait of peace in Western Europe, so that the British could finish their task of liberating their Asiatic empire. And, just maybe, Churchill thought he could sell us on the deal since we would be more than agreeable to go along with that effort to free our manpower and resources for the fight against Japan."

"And," Roosevelt broke in, finishing the General's thought, "Hitler could then turn his war machine in the West 180 degrees and go after the Russians full blast. Summer of 1941 blitzkrieg all over again!" The President seemed almost amused at the prospect. "I still can't understand why Winston decided to start down that road. You know, there apparently were some earlier peace feelers made between them."

"So I've heard."

"I don't suggest the two of them are cozy," the President hastened to add. "But I've often wondered why Hitler didn't finish off the British at Dunkirk when he had them helpless."

The General didn't interrupt while the President collected his further thought.

"It's strange, General, but from what I know of Churchill and Hitler, I find some similarity between them. They are both powerful speakers. They rouse their followers to action by their personalities. Each has a singleness of purpose. Each seeks to preserve his country's image and strength above all else."

"Yet they differ so drastically in their vision of the future," the General finished. "There obviously is a crucial difference. One regime is based on an appeal to followers through reason and the other uses an order supported by force.

"That difference is crucial," said the President. "That is another way of stating the fundamental difference between a democracy and a dictatorship. It is not that leaders in one kind of system exert power and those in the other don't. Of course both do that.

"The difference and the tragedy is that those who gain power by popular vote, as Hitler did essentially in the 1930's, turn their backs on, even destroy the structure that gives legitimacy to their power." The President was warming to his civics lesson. "Democracies provide a mechanism for lawful succession to those now in power, a mechanism for peaceful change. That mechanism ultimately is the mystery, and the glory, of true constitutional government. Those in power, when the electoral mandate is given, surrender that power peacefully.

"However, even in democracies, the constant threat is that those in power will use that power to corrupt and eventually destroy the electoral process itself, by deception at first, later by force. They thereby hope to retain power indefinitely. In uncertain times, they have evoked powerful images: God, Fatherland, Defeat of Despised Foes, and a Litany of Values to inspire selected audiences. Their ultimate justification for the power grab is that the powerful know better, or else they would not have gained power in the first place! They enjoy the result of that vicious circle of power reasoning.

"And their strongest supporters approve that tampering because they participate in that power and want to perpetuate it against any change. The leaders cast a country in the mold they believe is correct, not only for now but forever."

"Do you think the forces opposing that threat are unbeatable?" asked the General, not wishing to divert the President from the philosophical tangent he obviously was enjoying.

"That's the sixty-four dollar question, isn't it?" the President offered, removing his glasses to clean them. "Standing against that threat at times historically have been church leaders, academics, and private spokesmen. Ultimately, however, the best challenge is made by informed citizenry, abetted by a free press. When those forces all fail, or when some or all of them throw in with the powerful, the only defense of the process is by force, inside as in revolution, or outside by invasion. That raises an interesting question for another day, the purity of purpose of the opposition to renew, re-invigorate, or re-establish the constitutional process democratically, or institute their own dictatorship.

"So, I agree that the difference between leaders is in their vision for their countries, General. The difference is not so much in the leadership style of world leaders as it is in the strength of their commitment to a constitutional process that permits orderly change."

"And Hitler obviously is not committed in that direction," General Marshall concluded, "and Churchill is."

Marshall didn't want to raise the question, but it was hanging there ominously. "So, now what?" recalling the topic of their special meeting.

"I won't pretend to know the mind of Hitler, but I'll wager he's more than angry right now. What has he got left to hit back with, General?"

"Recent intelligence reports tell us that his western divisions are operating at half strength. His losses in the Falaise pocket in July were about a quarter of a million men. That would be a staggering loss even if he had had no serious manpower shortages elsewhere before and since. Logic tells us that he has to go on the defensive on all fronts.

"Their prepared defenses on the Rhine are quite formidable. I don't expect anything significant offensively from them until spring. The German armies have not been fond of winter campaigns historically."

The President acted for a brief moment as if he would disagree. Instead, he mulled over Marshall's scenario for a long time before he asked, "What about our ability to move our forces? Has this assassination episode changed anything?"

"Well, not directly. Since Allied logistics have been re-balanced after Market-Garden, Patton can be urged to straighten out his front and move the whole Third Army to the Rhine by the end of the year. That may be all we can accomplish by spring."

The President sighed. "After the breakout from Normandy at St. Lo, I felt we were so close to getting that business over with in Europe. Now it looks like, well..."

General Marshall could see that the President was tired, weary of the war and recent events. The General rose to leave, went around to shake the sitting President's hand and said, "I'll keep you posted the minute anything further comes in on the assassination business. And thanks for the lesson in constitutional government."

"Thanks for coming by," the President smiled broadly.

Chapter 39

Washington, Wednesday, December 6, 1944

Director Everett Giles was preparing SIP's preliminary assessment of the assassination mission results. The results were mixed. A Hitler stand-in was killed. He had died with several others in the Berghof entourage.

The presence of a stand-in at Berghof, not Hitler, was a major disappointment. SIP's own intelligence on Hitler's whereabouts had been incomplete and incorrect.

The lack of specific information about Penner and Brooke caused some consternation within the SIP office. Giles concluded that Penner's mission to overtake Brooke in time had failed. There had been no contact from either since the attack. SIP's report to reach General Marshall and the President would depend to some extent on whether either or both were captured, and if so, if SIP could learn if either talked under pressure.

German communications intercepted by American Army Intelligence reported that "one assassin" had died. That report introduced further confusion into SIP's assessment. The American intelligence operatives with Giles in Paris probably would not know the whole story for some time.

How could the Allied human intelligence sources inside and outside of Germany miss so badly on Hitler's whereabouts? Was it simply faulty intelligence? Certainly, the combing of intelligence from the underground could always be improved. Or was some specially contrived enemy misdirection injected in this instance?

The failure of the mission to eliminate Hitler apparently was not due to poor execution of the plan by Captain Brooke. Somehow he accomplished the plan that Giles and others knew beforehand had only a middling probability of success. Only the change in German personnel at Berghof prevented complete success.

In planning the mission, Giles had contemplated the strategic benefits only if the mission resulted in Hitler's death. SIP relied for its planning on Hitler being at Berghof. No one discussed the consequences of killing a double, since that possibility never came up. There was no serious consideration of any alternatives except Capt. Brooke's failure to reach Berghof or his inability to shoot in the time frame planned.

None of the projected military advantages were realized with this outcome. German generals will not succeed to power and cannot introduce their more predictable strategies. Likewise, the generals now are not given the chance to consider surrender in what some of them might consider a lost cause. No other impetus to end the war occurred. No end to atrocities resulted.

The mission realized some unplanned positives, however. Giles saw a likely political result of the mission in the sowing of doubt, a weakening of trust by and among the Nazi leadership. That doubt within the German military and general populace could now be encouraged more effectively through the Allied propaganda mission radio, leaflets, and press notices.

Some German insiders might not believe that it was a double killed. The German people are accustomed to handling official lies. Will they accept the inevitable rumors of Hitler's death growing out of Brooke's mission? Germans generally have no way to confirm the genuineness of Hitler's voice. Will they come to believe that the re-appearance of Hitler after the assassination is also a lie circulated by the Propaganda Ministry? The gist of the rumors would cause more defeatist talk. If Hitler is dead, why continue his war?

Allied intelligence operatives are also skillful at blending news of true events with damaging fiction. Reports have surfaced of German Army battalion commanders relying on the situation reports Allies printed to misdirect them. Newspapers and leaflets dropped into German lines are used regularly to demoralize German soldiers in battle units. Allied intelligence services milk confusion in its fake German newspaper, *Soldatensenser*. For example, *Soldatensenser* once wrote of the "decrease in diphtheria deaths" among German children, suggesting a slightly positive development in very negative, devastatingly bad news for German military fathers away from their families.

Even though the military objective was not realized, if there is encouragement given to the German military leadership to take a more independent stance from Hitler, that would be a positive result. Himmler and Goering and possibly some generals have been deemed approachable by Allies, although not necessarily by Americans. The prospect of real negotiations with the military could be improved.

Hitler also has to be aware of his increased personal vulnerability. His heightened suspicions might also limit his willingness to discuss promising military and political options openly with his advisors.

Some experts, mostly British, have argued that Hitler's unpredictability is a positive. His past recklessness led him into mistakes. Hitler stalled the development of more sophisticated weapons early in the war by his resource allocation decisions. The weapons his forces had then were successful, that is, sufficient to the task of winning military victories. He got around later to stimulating development of the V-1, V-2, and jet aircraft. His continued presence as the German leader could augur further hesitation in his moving dwindling resources to new weapons.

Giles thought if Hitler does anything except stay on the defensive as a result of the assassination attempt, it will be a plus for the Allies in the long run. His manpower and resources are too thin for anything but a defensive effort.

Giles reviewed finally the general intelligence operation questions raised in this mission. He had been intrigued by the intelligence gathering process for some time, especially the verification of information. Giles contemplated specifically the mystery of information flows in the intelligence business in the light of the assassination mission.

The question he was prompted by the mission to examine was the reason why some vital information gets into the intelligence loop and some does not. How was it, for example, that the German mole embedded in British intelligence for several years was eventually shut down because of one transmission he made? At the same time, the intelligence error that guided SIP planning, the assumption that Hitler was at Berghof, was not revealed until after the actual killing attempt was made. Why does such an anomaly happen?

Perhaps there is a lesson in paradox to be learned from the overall experience, he thought. Routine security measures are adopted in all intelligence operations, military and diplomatic. Not all projects receive the highest possible security protection, however. The radio transmissions of the German mole, Lion Tamer, were not worthy of Germany's top secret Enigma encoding process. In fact, many of Lion Tamer's transmissions in softer code had been read by American cryptographers, and presumably the British, for some time.

The low and mid-level quality of intelligence being sent warranted the same level of security assigned to those messages.

However, the more secret endeavors attract the most intense enemy attention. The paradox is that the wall of secrecy constructed to provide security for top secret activity itself invites the most serious enemy scrutiny and eventual penetration into the secrets. Such was the case with the diligent, successful effort of British cryptanalysts at Bletchley Park to crack the German Enigma code.

No extraordinary security measures seemed to be in place at Berghof at the time of the mission, although the security at Berghof arguably would have been even tighter had Hitler himself been there. Nor was anything known about pre-mission security changes at Berghof to prompt SIP to conduct a special investigation. Giles himself had ordered only a closer listening to radio traffic for any signs of Hitler's movements. No American intelligence operative in Germany was directed to inquire seriously into Hitler's location.

Hitler's whereabouts at any time presumably were known inside official German circles. Wireless communications continued between Berghof and Berlin. A double with a counterfeit retinue gave the impression of Hitler's presence. No compelling evidence indicated that Hitler was anywhere but Berghof. An American investigation into the real identity of the man wearing the brown jacket and black pants therefore did not seem necessary.

Overall, Giles was dissatisfied with the mission's results. The mission's principal objective, the elimination of Hitler, was not achieved. The secondary results still to be realized were long term. They were not likely to have the decisive impact on the war's outcome that Giles had hoped the elimination of Hitler would have.

Chapter 40

London, Thursday, December 7, 1944

Prime Minister Churchill was reviewing quietly the events of December 3. The American assassination attempt on Hitler had been uppermost in his mind since he learned of it. It triggered termination of the secret peace talks between Great Britain and Germany.

His reaction was mostly annoyance at the news of the stand-in killed at Berghof. He was miffed at the Americans for not confiding their plan to him. He tried to thwart the assassination plan. He regretted that his request to American Army Intelligence in Paris had to be hurried and forced, however. The potential complications in revealing the truce negotiations kept him from making the request directly to Roosevelt. In that request, he certainly would not have made a brief for Hitler's sincerity.

He had no qualms about killing an enemy, even a major world figure. His own intelligence service had offered plans to do the very same thing in the past year.

However, in a war that had brought dishonor to the fore in countless diplomatic, social, and military engagements, he still felt the need to try to do the honorable thing. He had agreed to the peace overture. Some progress had been made. He did not want to be on the side that sabotaged the process.

He was upset that the timing of the assassination plan was all wrong. Accomplishing Hitler's assassination a year ago could have brought enormous relief to the world when it mattered most militarily. Now the war was winding down.

Worst of all, the American assassination plot did not succeed. The Allies now had to contend with an unpredictable military strategist in rage. The revenge Hitler might take against other innocents or Allied POWs was a very serious concern. The only hope was that he would turn his rage inward against other Germans as he did after the July 20 plot against him. At some point, efficiency in the house of German officialdom could be affected adversely by the suspicion and fear that Hitler engendered.

The one silver lining he saw in a wretched episode was that the Americans had uncovered a mole in British intelligence. We must be grateful for all favors, he thought.

The termination note to the negotiations Foreign Minister von Ribbentrop sent was undiplomatic and rude. Its tone was uncharacteristic of von Ribbentrop, denouncing Jews somewhat gratuitously and questioning the motives of Churchill and Eden in rather gross language. Churchill suspected Hitler looked over the Minister's shoulder in its drafting.

Secretary Eden raised the question whether he should reply that von Ribbentrop's poison dart was fired against the wrong target. Churchill told him that such a response would suggest to the Germans that the British were indifferent about souring their relations with the Americans. Moreover, the attempt and its aftermath of blame placing might precipitate more internecine warfare inside German officialdom. The British leaders agreed to let the matter drop with no response.

Churchill thought all along that the peace overture was a very cynical move on Hitler's part. It was clear that Hitler's planned strategy was to free Germany's forces in the West to fight an ultimate knock-down battle with the Soviets on the Eastern Front. Stalin certainly was not blameless. He had already shown his true colors by holding up the Red army outside Warsaw while German soldiers killed an estimated 200,000 Poles in the Warsaw Uprising. Churchill saw that action as indicative of Stalin's already intransigent attitude in regard to Poland. Poland was scheduled by Stalin to be one of the Soviets' postwar private preserves.

Churchill knew also that Hitler in time will realize it is to his advantage to let Stalin know of the British-German peace talks. What will Stalin say and do when he learns of Churchill's complicity in the peace plan? Churchill was troubled that he would have to sort out Great Britain's relations with the Soviets anew. The Russian bear had a short recall of Allied material assistance he received at the time of his great peril three years ago. However, he had a very long memory of grievances, alleged or real, suffered at Allied hands.

For better, and increasingly for worse, Stalin was still an ally. The peace plan would have alienated the Soviets and made the other Allies' lives more miserable. In that respect, and out of regard for the Americans especially, Churchill was relieved that the peace plan had failed.

In assessing the impact of the Americans' assassination action and its consequences over the last four days, the Prime Minister kept coming back to Anthony Eden's strongest objection to the proposed truce. "If Hitler should prevail, either against the Soviets or the Americans or both, let us say after a peace agreement was reached with us alone, would he then turn back to his initial objective to subjugate Great Britain? And what stronger guarantees against that eventuality could the British obtain in an agreement with Hitler than the ones given to Czechoslovakia and Poland? How ready would the British be, with or without its current Allies, to start hostilities all over when Hitler reneged on his agreement?"

The 1940 experience for Great Britain was a close call. The Battle of Britain was a battle for its national life. September 15 of that year found the sky over Britain full of German attackers and British defenders. There were no reserves of British planes or pilots. All were committed. In the weeks that followed, had the *Luftwaffe* continued its attack on Britain's air bases and planes, instead of switching the attack to its cities, it could have won the air battle, with invasion of the islands following.

Churchill would not have to awaken from the nightmare arising from a broken peace agreement. He could return to the task of destroying the Nazi regime decisively. Eliminated also were the prospects of increased tensions with the Americans over the peace plan. The difficulties, especially between some senior military commanders, likely would have been exacerbated had the truce been reached. Churchill would have had to get American approval for the plan eventually, of course. That might have been difficult. Churchill had counted on a *fait accompli* that the Americans could not refuse in the interest of peace and saving concentration camp inmates' lives. However, had the Americans learned of the peace plan as a work in progress, they might well have reacted as quickly to foil it as he did to stop the assassination plan.

Churchill was deeply troubled by the loss of his initiative on the Jewish question. He did not want to negotiate with Hitler. The only motive for him to overcome his intense distrust of the Germans was the possibility of saving many lives. He had been encouraged in the Sweden meeting that von Ribbentrop had not rejected his proposal outright.

Churchill still believed in his basic proposal. That proposal to Hitler was so strong that the Americans, and maybe even the Soviets, would have seen its merit immediately. Even if they did not join in it formally, it could have led to a positive outcome.

In his final analysis, Churchill could not downplay the likelihood that the German peace overture was designed to achieve something other than Hitler's stated intent. Was Britain's consideration of the plan or the British agreement to negotiate itself planned as a German diplomatic victory? It could alienate Britain's major allies, the United States and the Soviets, even if no truce ever came of it. Alternately, Hitler's offer of a peace proposal may have been only an attempt to test the strength of Churchill's insistence on unconditional surrender.

Churchill knew that the Hitler confronted in the peace proposal was the same duplicitous aggressor who produced the world's agony of the past decade. Historians, Churchill thought, are left to debate whether there was a date or event when a firm response from other world powers would have stopped Hitler. Without knowledge gained in hindsight, how they then would have handled Hitler's aggressive intentions and preserved peace is a second interesting debate topic.

He will call Roosevelt today. He will remind the President on this anniversary of the Japanese attack on Pearl Harbor how far their countries together have come since 1941.

Chapter 41

Paris and Washington, December 11-14, 1944

Hayden had been sheltered in a barn the day of December 4 while he rested. He ate decent food and reveled in his new, non-military clothing. He had given the Swiss farmer and his wife over half of the Swiss francs SIP supplied him, probably worth over $200 in American dollars.

They took him to a bus station the following morning, and for two days, with several transfers, he made his way to Geneva. There, the morning of December 7, he entered the office of the American consul. He told a deputy that he was an American Army officer. He gave his real name and ID. He stated he had been doing undercover work in Germany. He did not relate any details of his mission.

Hayden urged the consulate to contact American Army Intelligence in Paris. It did. There was a lot of back and forth on his status for reasons Hayden did not understand fully.

Two days later, Hayden was approved to cross the western Swiss border and re-enter France. He contacted French, then American military forces. He eventually reached Paris on the evening of December 11. He went straight to the office of American Army Intelligence and was provided a room.

Hayden contacted Everett Giles on a secure phone line. Only then did Hayden learn the real results of his mission.

"You hit a double and a bunch of phony aides, Captain." Giles also told him that the SIP team was on the way to London from Paris. He would have them return to Paris the following morning to assist in Hayden's de-briefing.

"Captain, there was a leak in Army Intelligence at Strasbourg. Your name got into the intelligence network somehow, and it appears the Germans have it too."

"That's sweet," Hayden said disgustedly.

"For some time after you get back here you will have to live under an alias for your protection."

"Okay, sir. Colonel, this revelation only adds to my lack of confidence in the Army Intelligence unit here."

"The advice I give you is to answer their questions with care, with discretion. Since that unit was in on the planning and preparation, it's hard to keep them out of the loop now." Everett Giles paused. "Is there anything else on this mission you can think of to do while you're over there?"

Hayden thought it was a very curious question. Giles had not mentioned Frederick Penner. Neither would he.

"No, sir."

"I look forward to seeing you back here in a few days, Captain."

Hayden's de-briefing started at 08:00 the following morning. There were eight operatives in the room, seated in a semi-circle on wooden classroom chairs in front of Hayden and Colonel Braxton Belleau. Hayden wanted to ask again that the de-briefing not start before the SIP team arrived, but held his tongue.

The first question from one of the group was about Frederick Penner. When asked if he had seen Penner in Berchtesgaden, Hayden answered "Yes" without hesitation. From the quick, meaningful glances of staff people to each other, he knew immediately that something strange was going on. Obviously, one of the principal questions on the minds of the Paris Army Intelligence group was answered.

Hayden took the initiative without being asked. "What was Frederick Penner's role in the mission?"

Chief Belleau tried to wave off the question. "It doesn't matter."

Hayden was not pleased by the answer. "That is still a mystery. Its solution is important to me. I would like my questions on Frederick Penner answered before I respond further."

"Go ahead," Chief Belleau said.

"In my conservation with Penner, I got the distinct impression that he was working in your intelligence unit. He said he was in Berchtesgaden gathering whatever incidental information he could in the town of Hitler's second residence. I thought that answer was thin. Was Penner supposed to have assisted me in some way that he did not? Had Penner turned and sought to betray the Allies? What was his mission?"

Hayden didn't know yet that the intelligence people had learned after Penner was sent to find Brooke that the two had worked at the same time at Boeing in Wichita. They knew the two were better acquainted than Penner had let on. In their minds, that might account for some things turning out as they did.

"Do you know where he is now?" the Chief asked.

"He is dead. He took a poison capsule when he was arrested by the Germans. I know that because I saw it happen from a distance." Again there were glances and more than a few whispers as members of the group leaned to each other.

"But my question is still relevant," Hayden persisted. "What was Frederick Penner doing in Berchtesgaden? If someone planned for him to contact me there, why was he contacting me?"

The Chief would not yield. "I'm not going to reveal that now."

"It seems everyone else in this room knows what was going on. And I don't." His frustration at the non-response to his question caused him to raise his voice. "Let me ask also how the German *Feldgendarmerie* got so interested in German Army Lieutenant Eric Klaysa's ID and papers, the cover I was using my first day in Germany."

"The Lieutenant escaped from the Strasbourg holding area and radioed that his uniform and papers were taken," the Chief answered somewhat indifferently.

Hayden's astonished reply was almost incoherent as he sought answers to more fundamental questions. "And what else did he tell his German contacts? Did he implicate anybody? Did he mention my name? That's a great send-off on a top secret mission, having your cover blown as soon as you start."

"You obviously have survived that mistake," the Chief replied. "Klaysa did not know your name, then or now."

"Then how did the Germans get my name?"

"You're now into an area under investigation by this unit."

"Colonel, before we proceed. May I have a word with you privately?"

Colonel Belleau stood and asked the other members to take a fifteen-minute break. This tall, thin officer had eyes that could not be read easily behind his wire-rimmed classes. He was maybe fifty years old, with graying crew-cut hair that was also thinning.

After the others had cleared the room, the Colonel said simply, "Go ahead."

"With all due respect, Colonel, I request that no more questions be raised about my mission except by the SIP team."

The Colonel dropped his pen and note pad on the arm of his chair, took a step aggressively toward Hayden, and stood erect before him. "And if I order you to answer our questions?"

"My request stands. This whole matter obviously got out of control in Strasbourg."

The Colonel shrugged. "Unfortunately, those things happen."

Hayden's temper flared. "Those things should not happen! Have criminal charges been brought against the people who leaked the mission plan, and my name, and jeopardized the whole mission? Has the Paris Chief of Army Intelligence been reprimanded for allowing it?"

"You're insubordinate!" Chief Belleau shouted, his face reddening as he thrust it another foot toward Hayden.

Hayden had confronted far worse than a bureaucratic superior trying to cover his unit's errors in the last ten days. He did not back up. He shouted his response.

"I'll be a hell of a lot more than that if you press this matter, Colonel. The mission and my life were on the line. Your people behaved like this was a radio soap opera. I'll bet even a mediocre Army lawyer can make a strong case that your unit is responsible for a national security breach! I'll be damned if I'll give your people the opportunity to screw things up again with another leak. That's all I have to say."

Hayden saluted and left the office.

Two hours later the four SIP team members arrived. Lt. Col. Alexander talked briefly with Chief Belleau, then drew Hayden into a private room.

"Captain Brooke, I've just been told by Col. Belleau about the little flare-up. I don't disagree with what you said, Captain, only with how you said it."

"I tried to do it diplomatically. I requested that the de-briefing include the SIP team. The Chief denied my request and then pressed too hard. I didn't have much choice but to refuse, given the recent performance of his team."

"Then you know about the security leak in Strasbourg that got to London and then to Berlin?"

"I did not know the path for certain until just now. I suspected something disastrous had happened in the intelligence network from what Colonel Giles said and how Col. Belleau tried to flit around my questions."

"He may still try to make some trouble for you. We intelligence people can get very sensitive, even vindictive, when we're crossed."

Hayden was shocked at Alexander's comment. The intelligence people were closing ranks. So be it.

"Colonel Alexander, under the circumstances, perhaps my de-briefing should be conducted by Colonel Giles alone. I'll ask his guidance in how much is revealed to others. My identity and my career are at stake because of some people's negligence and mistakes. And it smells like a cover-up is underway. I don't want to fuel that activity by anything that I say today."

Lt. Col. Alexander was quite sure that the Captain had the backing of Colonel Giles, obtained in their phone conversation last night, in order to make that statement. Or Brooke was an awfully good bluffer.

"Captain, that may be the best course. Any further problems are not going to land on my doorstep. I'll arrange for all of us, you and the SIP team, to get on a flight to the States soon. You're in the custody of the SIP team until we turn you over to Colonel Giles."

The flight, stopping in Thule, Greenland for refueling before proceeding to Camp Springs Army Air Field, was luxurious compared to the journey Hayden had with cargo as his main companion on his trip to Europe two weeks ago. There were actually seats for the twenty or so passengers in the C-47. Several of them bore medical paraphernalia indicating wounds. There wasn't much talk among the passengers. Lt. Col. Alexander apparently had warned the other SIP members that talk with Hayden should be limited to the essentials.

Hayden dozed off on the second, longer leg of the journey, and was soon sleeping soundly. He was again confronted in his dream by many wild animals. He strained in the darkness to see them. They were grey wolves. He had only a steel pipe to fend them off. He swung the pipe back and forth vigorously at them but they kept coming on.

He tried harder, and hit a few. Their yelping brought even more wolves into the pack. There were simply too many to fend off or kill. They continued to attack, surround him, confronting, threatening. One of them locked its teeth on his left arm, and Hayden desperately tried to shake him off.

Hayden awoke with a start. Captain Tobias seated beside him was shaking his arm and shouting, "Captain! Captain! Wake up! You are having a nightmare," he said as Hayden opened his eyes and quit struggling.

"Thanks," Hayden murmured. He stretched his arms over his head. He could not recall ever having a dream so vivid. He replayed the episode in his mind several times before the plane touched down. He was troubled by the little sense he could make of it. He was sure this dream and others like it underscored the tension he had experienced in the past weeks.

At Camp Springs, he was taken to the same fenced compound where he had spent his first week of screening for his mission. He would again be under guard day and night.

He found a phone and called Sarah.

"Sarah, I need to tell you at the beginning that this call is being monitored by our security people."

"Can you tell me where you are?"

"I'm just outside of Washington. I've just completed a project, so I'll be in a somewhat quiet phase for a while."

"Will you be able to visit us?

"I'd very much like to, but that is not going to be possible for a while. The army won't give me a leave just yet. Do pass along my best regards to your parents."

"I'll do that. They think very highly of you."

"I hope that they are not the only ones in your family who think that way."

"I don't think they are," Sarah teased.

"Sarah, if you get a letter from a strange man soon from this part of the country, don't simply throw it away as a crank letter without opening it. I likely will have to operate under an alias for a while."

"You must have done something really bad." Her lighthearted jest could not cover completely the concern in her voice.

"Some people think just the opposite."

"I talked to someone who works at Boeing the other day. She couldn't say much either. I mentioned you and Frederick working there. It seems like a lifetime ago."

"Yes," he said quietly, "a lifetime."

Chapter 42

Washington, Saturday, December 16, 1944

Hayden was given the alias of Lucian Randolph. His army personnel record was put on hold, pulled from normal review and statistics-filing channels.

Everett Giles was more professional than personal in the official de-briefing on December 14. He wanted first to know Hayden's route, procedure, and actions. The discussion then turned to the killings at the chalet and elsewhere. The Director made no judgment on his actions one way or another. However, Giles questioned Hayden for over three hours on how the plan went, what deviations from the plan were required, and how Hayden had improvised. He sought the lessons Hayden learned that could be applied to similar missions conducted by SIP in the future.

At the end of his questioning, Giles first complimented Hayden on his ingenuity in getting out of tough situations and when circumstances or events forced him to change his procedure. Giles was especially impressed with how Hayden handled his confrontation with German police after the two security leaks occurred. He then asked Hayden if he had any questions.

Hayden was hoping he would be asked. "Yes," he said, "four."

"Did SIP and Army Intelligence realistically expect me to come back from the mission?"

"No, we didn't. I will say also that I felt if anyone could do what you did and come back, you could. We knew, as I think you did, that penetrating the Berghof compound and getting off your shots at the right time, with the tight security cordon, the weather, the timing problems…we all knew it was going to be extremely difficult. And your escape. Well, that was going to take a lot of skill and luck and perseverance. Your manner, your resolve, and your ability to adapt, provide a textbook example of how a professional should function under extreme pressure."

"Thank you. Can something be done to recognize the selfless, heroic act of Frederick Penner? His name should not disappear into a void after the danger and death he accepted to protect me."

"I agree wholeheartedly. I'll look into it. That is all I can promise now. I learned after the fact, of course, that he and you were close friends. Had he returned, I suppose I would have had a difficult, philosophical, moral issue to resolve. His friendship and political convictions overrode the order he was given."

"Excuse me, Colonel. I don't understand."

"No, I suppose you don't with the information you have been given. You see, the security leaks caused several reactions. Apart from the danger they put you in, the most serious one was letting one of our Allies know the mission was underway. That Ally had some delicate negotiations going on. It was thought by the Ally that an assassination attempt on Hitler would torpedo those negotiations. Once it was learned that the assassin to be was an American Army officer, that Ally tried to stop your mission by appealing to American Army Intelligence. There was a lot of very high level clout behind that appeal, to be sure."

"Appealed to Army Intelligence in Paris?"

"Yes, the Paris office was contacted. And, of course, your friend Frederick was located there. Eventually he volunteered to chase you into Germany to halt your attempt."

"So Frederick found me, but made no attempt to stop me, and didn't even tell me what his real mission was."

"That is correct, given what you've told me today. I can't say that I disagree with that part of the result. By his refusal to deter you in any way, by not mentioning the real reason for his mission, he was ensuring that your attempt would be made on Hitler. I supported that objective from the beginning, and still do. From what I can gather, his decision was based on his own convictions opposing the Nazi regime."

"I'm certain that was his reason. And, Colonel, I think I'm beginning to see something else here. He volunteered because he knew then he would not try to stop me…"

"And he no doubt concluded quickly that if someone else were sent, that person would try to stop you, even with force, if necessary."

Hayden sat back, somewhat shaken by Giles' revelation that fitted another disturbing piece into the puzzle. For he realized that the man who had given the conditional termination order to Frederick to apply to Hayden was now sitting across the table from him.

"On orders from your office," Hayden said.

"Yes, Captain. Believe me, an order I issued with profound reluctance. I planned the mission, you know. I certainly did not relish aborting it. Only a request from the highest office of one of our Allies caused me to issue the order. I am greatly relieved that my order was not carried out. As I said, I supported the objective of your mission from the beginning, and I still do."

Hayden was quiet for a moment, contemplating the grave decisions he and others had to make as circumstances changed during his mission. His best friend had carried a verbal order to kill him if necessary. It was issued reluctantly by Col. Giles, a man Hayden respected for his determination to do whatever was necessary to resolve the European conflict in our favor. Giles, in turn, had been checked in his attempt to change the course of the war with Hayden's mission by another order from a higher authority. Both orders were nullified only because Hayden's best friend was, in the end, the best of friends.

"But why was Frederick apprehended by the enemy? He wasn't assigned his own hostile mission in Berchtesgaden, was he?"

"No, nothing assigned. I guess we'll never know if he did some free-lancing that got him into trouble."

"He did not give me even a hint that he was contemplating anything else in our meeting the evening before," Hayden said.

"And the schedule of his movement from Strasbourg into the Berchtesgaden area did not give him much time for planning something else," Giles said.

"So, it might have been nothing other than blind chance that the Germans caught Frederick...maybe pressure on someone who looked out of place?"

"Maybe so. And his personal priorities were clear enough when he saw the danger you were in, even after your mission seemed accomplished. He had to be a very good friend to do what he did."

"He was. I shall miss him every day..."

The Colonel looked at his notes and maintained a respectful silence before continuing.

"You had other questions?"

Hayden asked the same, plaintive question he had asked himself over and over since he learned of Hitler's absence from Berghof on December 3. "How could Allied intelligence know so much, and not know where Hitler actually was?"

"There is no doubt a long, technical answer about how official secrets are made and kept. The short answer is it did happen, and we don't know how for sure," the SIP Director replied.

"The last thing is right there in front of us. What does my future look like? Under an alias forever? Can I go back to the part of the country I am from?"

It was clear to Hayden that he was a problem for SIP. At some point, German intelligence will put two and two together on the role of the American officer who entered Germany from Strasbourg in the killings. Sergeant Munsenn will be the man identified in the uniform of Major Moss. The body of Major Moss will be found and identified. Goering's staff car will be discovered. The German border guard detail will confess to an escapee in German uniform getting over the fence in their zone. Hayden's killing pistol will be matched to slugs found in several German bodies. Some clever non-com in German intelligence will earn another stripe by connecting the clues correctly.

Hayden will then have a target on his back for any German underground operatives in the States for the rest of the war. And after that, any number of rabid followers of the Nazi pack might consider it a badge of honor to take Hayden out of the picture in retaliation.

"All things considered, Captain, I don't see how you can return to active duty. Your personnel record is in your real name. You could not function in your real name without some continuing danger to yourself and to those around you. If we set you up with an alias, your personnel record would have serious gaps that could invite suspicion and questions for someone with an evil intent. If we reconstructed your actual record with your alias, someone really motivated could find out that your alias really wasn't here or there at some time or that the events stated in your record really didn't occur. Then what?"

"For the immediate future, what alternative is there for me?"

"I suggest that you go to Ft. Bliss, Texas, under loose protective custody for a year or so. Continue to live under the alias, Lucian Randolph. No one there will know any name for you other than that name. Only you and I and persons you tell will know your real background. There will be no personnel record accompanying you for anyone to snoop into, as befits someone in loose custody. There will be no official duties for you to perform.

"You may already know that the Army has a facility where other men in similar circumstances are housed. There is a cordoned off, fenced area containing several barracks. No cameras are allowed. Only American or Allied personnel are permitted in that area. You will be free to go anywhere on the base, but only by pre-arrangement, and accompanied by two guards. You will find the barracks very comfortable, I believe, bedroom, sitting room, study, and bath. Good food on site. Daily newspapers, magazines, and so on. You'll continue on the payroll, paid out of SIP funds.

"For a year, you suggest?"

"At least a year, Captain. Our intelligence services will monitor all radio and other traffic to identify any interest from anybody in pursuing leads flowing from your mission. With a reasonable prospect of the European war being over by next year, we will do the same monitoring for a while after things quiet down."

"Will I be allowed visitors at Ft. Bliss?"

"Of course. They will have to understand the identity rules. You may want to limit visitors for that reason. Idle talk can destroy the cover provided you in a minute."

"How well I know," Hayden said.

"Any problem—anything except that your steak isn't done to your specifications—here is a phone number and a code number to verify it is you. If I'm not here I'll call you back when I can, and do what I can. Don't hesitate."

"Okay, I accept," said Hayden.

As he prepared to leave, Hayden paid respect to the job Everett Giles was doing.

"We've had quite an adventure, haven't we?"

"We have, indeed. The sad part is that nothing you do the rest of your life will match the intensity, the excitement, or the uncertainties you have experienced in the last six weeks."

"The last four years have had their highlights for me also. One of them is meeting and working with you. You have been honest with me, and I appreciate that."

"Well, thank you. We have all served as best we could. Your record is as good as anyone's. I know it, even though the rest of the world can't know, if that's any satisfaction to you."

"Thank you, Colonel."

"One more thing. The army cannot officially recognize your contribution publicly, of course. And I must stop calling you Captain. What I have been able to do, with the approval of the Army Chief of Staff, is jump your permanent rank to Lt. Colonel."

The SIP Director reached in a drawer and produced the silver oak leaves. "May I?"

Giles removed Hayden's Captain's bars and pinned on his new rank insignia.

"I am stunned, Col. Giles. Thank you so much for your kindness."

"We can't have a war hero taking orders from some washed-out major at Ft. Bliss, can we, Colonel?" he smiled.

"I look forward to a more quiet life for a while," Hayden said, "now with much more satisfaction."

"Just don't use your real name when you write your memoirs."

Chapter 43

Ft. Bliss, Texas, December, 1944 – November, 1945

Hayden's life at Ft. Bliss in protective custody was pleasant in most respects. Thanks to Everett Giles, Hayden was the highest ranking officer in the compound. It was a dubious distinction, given that rank didn't mean much in this setting. He was consulted on barracks rules early on, one time on how late radios and phonographs could be played without disturbing others. He was relieved that the decisions in the compound were no longer on life and death matters.

Accommodations and amenities were all that Col. Giles had promised. The mess hall food was better than any Hayden had experienced on an army post. He quickly grew weary of the bleak surrounding desert landscape, however.

Biggs Field was nearby. Planes were constantly flying over and around the compound. Hayden was reminded regularly of his wartime combat experiences.

Most important to Hayden, no questions were asked by the guards or officials. He wondered at times how many of the compound residents conducted killing missions as he did. It was also not proper for residents to ask questions, however.

After a week of lounging and settling in, Hayden began an exercise routine. With several others he ran daily in the compound. There were regular shuttles to the library, post exchange, theatre, and playing fields.

The presence of two armed guards hovering around him on his excursions out of the compound became a nuisance. The guards' constant presence with a compound resident seemed to evoke accusatory feelings toward the resident from people outside the compound. The guards were all good humored and efficient, however. Hayden asked one guard if he had ever needed to draw his weapon to protect a resident. He admitted "not after my first day of duty."

Hayden's personnel records were locked up in the office of the Army Chief of Staff, off limits except to the Chief. Hayden's record joined others in tightest security with other records containing American military secrets too volatile to allow into normal channels.

Hayden's settling into a routine allowed him to review his recent experience and current condition regularly. He felt he had been relegated to the status of a non-person with his alias, an exchange of higher rank for virtual anonymity. He had not expected awards or medals. He certainly did not expect this official oblivion.

He had never thought much about a post-army career because he had not planned for it to end so abruptly. His record was clean and meritorious. He had followed orders. He was not ashamed of the orders or the way he had carried them out. His decisions often had been clouded in the uncertainty of poor information, but he did not let down the men he commanded when the going was rough.

Without his performance of the mission, his career would have been drastically different. A regular advance in rank could have been expected, leading to command of a battalion or regiment some day. However, he knew the West Point grads probably would have the advantage there.

War produces countless ironies. One of the several twists in his own experience was his choice for the Berghof mission. As a trained paratrooper, Hayden's selection by SIP was a natural fit. His training in the States was constantly geared to the team's plan to drop a trooper near Berchtesgaden for the assassination mission.

In France that plan changed abruptly. Hayden's training as a paratrooper was suddenly irrelevant to the mission. He might have missed the show, not even been considered for it, had paratrooper not been part of the original job requirement, however.

He did not consciously regret being cast in his assassination role. The ironies were what haunted him. His struggle with those ironies, he was coming to believe, led to the constant tension and nightmares he was experiencing.

Hayden did not know why Frederick had been sent into Germany until Colonel Giles fitted in the details at the de-briefing. It was a mystery how Frederick had been implicated in the assassination plot in the first place, and so quickly. Why Frederick did not make it back and he did was possibly the difference of a few minutes in timing of events, a change of clothing, or unknown random circumstances loaded with risk.

Hayden liked to believe that Frederick had done the honorable thing, willing to die for what he believed in. And in dying he ironically as a Jew had expressed the ultimate of Christian love, giving up his life for his friend.

The nagging question remaining about his mission was on the vagaries of Allied intelligence. How could our people know so much about Hitler's routine at Berghof, about the stoppage by Himmler of the deportation of Hungarian Jews, how Hitler had assumed control of the military both as to strategy and some tactics, and not learn that Hitler was not present at Berghof late in November or early December of 1944? Or did Army Intelligence, and possibly other intelligence agencies, know that Hayden would be shooting at a double, and choose to go ahead with the mission for some reason?

The double, not Hitler, had to be in Berghof for the obvious reason of planned deception. Berghof was arguably the only site where Hitler's double could deceive people not in the inner circle as to Hitler's whereabouts. It was the only other place known to be frequented by Hitler besides the Chancellery in Berlin and the military planning post at *Wolfschanze* in East Prussia where the July 20, 1944, assassination attempt on Hitler took place. The double could perform ceremonial functions in Berghof's leisurely setting. He could not substitute for Hitler's executive functions at a military site or at the Chancellery without the risk of serious mistakes being made.

Identifying the one most likely site for Hitler's double to operate should have facilitated the process of locating Hitler by Allied intelligence groups. Hayden learned late in October of 1945 from post-war documents that Hitler left Berghof in the middle of July, 1944, and never returned there.

Hayden was curious about the lives who had crossed his path. He often wondered about the two Sergeants who took off on their adventure across the Rhine in the boat with him. The likelihood was that he would never know their mission or its outcome or see them again.

Hayden had lost contact with Jerry Connelios. Jerry was one person with whom the old wartime experiences could have been discussed. Appeals to the 82nd Division's Information Officer and to the Department of the Army for Jerry's whereabouts met dead ends. Hayden learned eventually in calls to old friends and acquaintances that Jerry had disappeared from their circle of contacts after being dishonorably discharged for "conduct unbecoming an officer." Hayden saddened to think that his old friend and colleague through officer training and several tough campaigns might have become a non-person also, another casualty of the war.

The toughest personal issues remaining for Hayden to resolve were his growing doubts over his need to kill so many in his recent mission and his destabilized marriage to Sarah. More and more those issues were intertwined.

He realized soon after his arrival at Fort Bliss that it was not good for him to be alone. While active in the 82nd, he learned that soldiers troubled by their role in knowingly killing an enemy, one on one, were able to talk things out with their comrades in arms. In the justifications their mates provided they were able to find some emotional resolution of their doubts. He had heard all the explanations and promptings and, as a platoon and company commander, had used many himself.

"This is war, man. Killing has to be done."

"If you don't kill them, they won't hesitate to kill you or the other guys in your unit. You don't shoot, and someone else pays the price."

"This is a fighting unit. Each of us has to fight to protect all of us."

"You can't let your buddies down, can you?"

Other approaches were often more successful in motivating riflemen to pull the trigger and kill people. Anger could motivate them. There were reported instances, real or fabricated, of the enemy shooting unarmed prisoners. The enemy was described as sub-humans or animals who kill and rape and plunder innocent people and, in turn, need to be killed to prevent their further crimes.

The support for the wavering soldier found in these discussions within the unit was based on the recognition that no one can understand the personal doubts generated by such killing unless he also has done so. Soldiers with their own killing experiences were powerful influences on their uncertain fellows.

Hayden sought to justify his recent violent actions in the same way now. He had tried to do what was necessary and ordered. His duty was clear to him at the time. Killing in war was required.

Those justifications still worked for Hayden's combat killings and the terrace killings at Berghof. The problem he had was with killings up close. The justifications from combat experience weren't as convincing to him for the face-to-face killings he felt he had to do on his assassination mission.

He was harassed by troubling questions. What good did the killings do? How did they change anything? Those dead soldiers and police, whatever their circumstances and past behavior, were also following orders, doing their jobs. Like American soldiers they were bakers, craftsmen, teachers, and farmers in their civilian lives. They were also fathers, sons, brothers, and husbands. When

Hayden had looked in their eyes and even gained the confidence of several, killing them was different from shooting at a shape many yards away, a human form de-personalized by the distance.

There was no one Hayden identified in the barracks or compound who might be amenable to a discussion on the morality of killing. The residents were not much good for any talk but the small. As Hayden did, they were either adhering to gag orders they had been given or were not disposed by personality to be talkative.

It probably was unfair of Hayden to lay the burden of his doubts on Sarah. Her questioning prompted his gradually revealing details of the assassination mission, however. With doubts plaguing him about the moral calluses he developed in the war, he gradually unloaded on her his own emotional war.

He had opened the door to that dialogue in his first call to Sarah the day he arrived at his new residence.

"Sarah, darling. I have some good news. I've been promoted to Lieutenant Colonel."

"Isn't that unusual? Don't soldiers get promoted one grade at a time?"

"You're right, it is different. There are some people who think my recent service has been worthwhile."

"Well, congratulations. More pay and such?"

"Indeed. My new boss assured me it is a permanent rank. When I retire, I'll have that level of retirement pay and benefits, and you will too as a dependent."

"And when will that be? Please tell me that is going to happen soon. Or are you off on another military adventure?"

"Not likely. There is almost no chance that I will be returned to a regular army unit." Hayden wanted to tell her more. Instead he asked for her indulgence again. "Maybe in a year, Sarah. My boss in Washington, not the President, told me things should be cleared up in a year or so. It's not that I wouldn't like to get out sooner. But it's probably for my own good to stay here at Fort Bliss for a while. And yours, too."

"Oh?"

"I wish I could give a more exact date," he said, ignoring her uncertainty. "It depends in part on when the European war is over. That could be sooner than anyone believes. A matter of months, maybe."

Sarah's quiet for a while worried Hayden.

"That sounds good…good," she said finally. Her matter-of-fact voice spoke vividly of her lack of enthusiasm.

Hayden dreaded the answer that might be given, but he had to ask the question.

"Sarah, where do we stand? Did you file for divorce?"

"Of course not."

"I'm so glad to hear that."

"How about you? I haven't asked how you are. You're not wounded or anything? Is that the reason they've got you there? And given you a new boss?"

"No, no. Nothing like that. No physical injuries." He already regretted his comment about a new boss and would not highlight his career change by trying now to explain it. "I'll admit to some bad dreams lately. Nightmares, really. Maybe it's just the reaction, the adjustment a person's mind has to make after a lot of tension."

"Has someone told you that?"

"No, I'm just speculating, really."

"I've always worried about you not coming back, of course. I also feared what you would have to do. I dreaded what you might become."

"I'm still the same old Hayden," he laughed, hoping to reassure her. "I would love for you to see for yourself. Sarah, can you come to visit me?"

"Is that possible, where you are?"

"Of course. Many of the men here have female visitors...wives, mothers, sisters. There are a few details that will have to be worked out. I can handle those from here."

"Yes, let's plan for that. I'll let you know what days I can get free from work. Would Christmas be too soon?"

The date was December 17.

"That would be lovely. Outstanding! You know, I proposed to you just three years ago on Christmas Eve."

"I know. And I accepted without hesitation. If we can start over, that would be a good day for it."

"Sarah, there's one other thing. When I make these arrangements, you should know that your name will be entered on the visitor's book as Sarah Randolph, because now my name is Lucian Randolph."

"Sarah Randolph. Isn't that one of Winston Churchill's relatives?" For the first time in over two years, Hayden heard Sarah laugh.

The Christmas weekend was all that both had anticipated in happiness and pleasure. Sarah did not seem at all uncomfortable in the military atmosphere. She was surprised at how spacious and neat Hayden's quarters were. She said that he had more space than she had in her Wichita apartment.

The guard detail installed and decorated a large Christmas tree fitted into the angled ceiling at one end of the mess hall. Hayden and Sarah were served at one of the special tables set up for residents with visitors. Hayden was impressed anew by the admiring glances other residents and their guests gave to Sarah.

He had made a special request of the compound Commander to be allowed to take Sarah to the base Officers Club for the Christmas Eve dinner and dance without the ubiquitous guards. The commander agreed to a compromise. The guards would take them to the club and back, since they needed transportation anyway. The guards would stay discreetly out of sight during the evening, however.

After reservations were made, Hayden arranged the purchase of a white evening gown, corsage, and his Christmas gift to Sarah of diamond necklace and earrings. Her dark hair and trim figure stunned the party. They entered to a noticeable buzz among the assembled. Hayden was never prouder of Sarah and his being with her. That they did not know anyone else there did not matter to them in the least. They reveled in the intimacy of the special time they had together in their reunion.

Hayden was able to turn aside the questions of several busybodies who happened by their table to introduce and be introduced. He did not reveal anything but his name. "War time, you know," was all he would say. He was even a little smug in telling that story, so like the one he had to use before under much more secretive circumstances.

Hayden had feared the awkwardness that might ensue in his reunion with Sarah after so much negativism in their communication over the several months leading up to his return. It never happened. They both agreed to adopt the mindset of starting over. They later spoke of their life together after he retired from the service. Yes, they would have children, Sarah agreed.

Sarah told Hayden that her work with the peace group had decreased. She and her father were no less passionate in their belief. After much soul searching, however, and not a little official pressure from authorities, they had relented in their public pronouncements. Sarah confided that their being related to a fine paratroop officer played a large part in their decision.

For his part, Hayden revealed his own doubts. "Killing is a horrible thing to do, Sarah, even when it is official. I know that same belief drives what you and your father have tried to do in the peace movement. I try not to think about the people I had to kill. But I have these pictures in my mind of the men I killed. I don't consciously want to dwell on them. At night they keep coming back. I can't get rid of them. I don't know what to do with them.

"Worse yet, being sorry and having doubts are signs of weakness in a militarized culture. And the secrecy I still have to maintain about some things limits my access to professional psychological help."

Sarah seemed to understand. "That is an awful thing to handle. Are you saying you were close enough to know the faces of people you killed?"

"Some of them, yes. Mostly young fellows."

Sarah grieved at his revelation. "No matter how right the cause, the wrong people die."

She turned back to the practical reality. "Are you in some danger, Hayden? I mean, besides that terrible emotional burden you are carrying? Am I also in danger?"

"This much I can tell you. Your official name change probably would be advisable."

Sarah now was more curious than ever. "It's something you did—an official military secret—not just killing young enemy soldiers, but something so colossal that after you did what you did, they had to change your name. Is that about it?"

"That's about it."

"And your name change is for your protection, against retaliation or recrimination by someone?"

"You've always been very quick at putting clues together. The same possible vengeance against me by someone out there could reach you too. I'm somewhat protected now by this location and my name change. These changes are a basic precaution."

Sarah was silent for a moment. "The irony of an American war protester being made a target by an Axis power."

Hayden nodded. "I haven't told you a lot of things, my love, because I was forbidden to tell anyone. And I still can't tell you everything. These recent changes in my life require secrecy still. But you have to be told enough to protect yourself."

"Because you feel guilty about any harm coming to me?"

"No, because I love you."

"I'll change my name," she said simply. "The change will drive the girls at work insane with curiosity. They'll think I've married again."

"That isn't such a bad situation for us to be in, is it? The two of us, in effect, starting a new life together?"

Sarah visited again on the weekend before Valentine's Day in 1945. She called Hayden on April 12 in a very somber mood to see if Hayden had heard the news of President Roosevelt's death. She called again on May 7.

"The Germans have surrendered. Does that make any difference in your discharge schedule?"

"My boss said earlier that he would have to check a few things after the end of the war in both theatres before that can happen. I'm encouraged, however. I'm anxious to see if the 82nd Division is going to be sent to the Pacific."

"You could still go?"

"I doubt it. The 82nd might not have a place for me now."

Sarah visited again on July 4. It was a glorious day. They picnicked with others on the lawn of the Officers Club. In place of fireworks, the chorale from a local university sang to the group in the twilight and early darkness.

Later in July, Winston Churchill was unseated in British elections and no longer was Prime Minister.

The news of Japan's agreement to surrender on August 14 prompted Hayden's call. "I think the clock starts now till my discharge," he told her.

The days and weeks began to drag. He called Everett Giles twice a month and left messages. Each time the SIP Director counseled patience.

The situation in Germany was tense, and the Four Powers in Berlin were being swamped with post-war intelligence gathered on suspected war criminals. De-Nazification would take a while. Until the hard liners were identified in Europe and South America, it was still too risky for many in protective military custody in the U.S. to be assuming normal lives.

Hayden asked Giles finally if the same would be true if Hayden agreed to keep his alias indefinitely. Giles said he would consider that.

The anniversary of Hayden's first meeting with Lt. Colonel Baxter on the then unidentified assassination plot came and went.

The preliminary, grim statistical estimates of the just completed war began to filter into the news. In the six years between September, 1939, and September, 1945, an estimated ten million Allied servicemen and six million Axis military were killed. The total military and civilian deaths were estimated to be as high as fifty million. The total civilian wounded and injured was unknown as were the total displaced, refugee, and homeless populations.

George Spurges would not deplore the horrible numbers any more than Hayden would, Hayden thought. In addition, the number of hearts broken and lives ruined by the war was incalculable.

Chapter 44

Wichita, November 15, 1945

Martin Pake, an ex-Army Air Force Lieutenant, was traveling along a country road southwest of Wichita on November 15. He had been troubled by persistent headaches, sleepless nights, and nightmares when he did doze off. He did not understand at first why those problems arose. He had no physical injuries from his recent wartime service as a B-29 bombardier in the Pacific.

Lately it had begun to sink in that all the bombs his plane dropped had killed people, soldiers and civilians alike. The photos released post-war of the air strikes confirmed the slaughter. Newspaper accounts and a few pictures on the ground brought the faces of the victims up close. Pake had been troubled by ghostly figures appearing in his dreams, pointing an accusing finger at him and his killing machine.

He had taken to drinking to dull his memory of the horrible images. The drinking quickly became excessive. He had been drinking with friends the night before and was returning home in the morning, bleary eyed and out of control. He was using side roads to avoid being arrested. He was speeding to get home quicker.

Pake did not see the car entering the country road from a farm. He had crossed over into the path of the oncoming car. When he did see it, he could not react fast enough. He hit it as it was barely accelerating. Pake was knocked unconscious.

*　　　　*　　　　*　　　　*　　　　*

Later on November 15 Hayden received two phone calls. The first was from Everett Giles. He still had not reached a decision on the advisability of Hayden's resuming normal activities under an alias. Intelligence signals on the location of German agents who had gone underground around the world and who possibly were seeking to continue the war were not yet decisive.

The other piece of news Giles gave was that SIP would close down and he would retire at the end of 1945. The records of Hayden and other army personnel in protective custody would be housed permanently in a special, secure office of the Army Chief of Staff.

Hayden reflected over lunch on the limited options he had. When he returned to his room, there was an urgent call to return to the Wichita operator. In a few minutes he was connected with Sarah.

She was crying, almost incoherent in her tragic message. "Hayden…Hayden!… They're gone…!" She broke off in a fit of wailing.

"Who's gone, Sarah? Tell me."

"Father and mother."

"Are you saying…Sarah, please try to tell me clearly what has happened."

"They're…they're…gone…dead in a car accident."

"My God! I'm so sorry, Sarah. Is there someone with you?"

"Yes, some friends from the office are here."

"Sarah, I'll work things out to be there as soon as I possibly can. Ask one of your friends to take the phone."

Hayden confirmed with the co-worker that someone would stay with Sarah around the clock until he got there. He knew that he now had to force a decision from Colonel Giles. His second conversation with Giles today might plot the course of Hayden's life for the foreseeable future. The indication of an emergency prompted Giles' return call within the hour.

"Colonel, I have a crisis. My wife's parents were killed in a car accident this morning. I must go to her immediately. I need several favors."

"My sincere sympathy to your wife, and to you, Captain…Colonel. You are owed some favors."

"Thank you. Of course, I need to be released from protective custody. I would also like to retire from active service right away. I am willing to keep this alias indefinitely."

"I see. There are several loose ends that need to be tied up. Where do you need to go now, and how are you planning to get there?"

"Wichita. I don't have transportation worked out yet. I am packed, for a permanent departure from here, if that can be arranged."

Giles paused only briefly. "Consider it done. Also your discharge. Call me in a few days with your wife's residence and other data and I'll have someone set her up for your retirement benefits under both your new names. Hold a minute..."

When Giles came back on the line, he had already begun to solve problems. "I've got one of my people here on another line to the Base Commander at Biggs Field. We'll get you on a flight as close to Wichita as we can and as soon as we can. Go ahead and arrange your ground transportation to Biggs Field. That should be your quickest way out of there. Good luck. Again, my sympathy."

The air lift Giles arranged arrived in Wichita after stops in Dallas and Oklahoma City. It was 22:00 before Hayden's whirlwind air trip was completed and he was on the way to Sarah's apartment.

Sarah was a scene of personal devastation. Hayden held her for a long time while she sobbed out her grief. He had to choke back his own emotions as he tried to soothe her. He had the greatest respect for George and Beatrice Spurges. He had never met kinder people. There was nothing not to like about their personalities, attitudes, and life styles. They were warm, friendly, devoted to each other and Sarah. He loved them both.

Sarah vented her bitterness toward the drunk driver. Martin Pake had survived the crash with minor cuts and bruises. She spat out epithets against him. Hayden had never seen her like this, but understood this up-swelling of emotion. He would rather see her voice her feelings than sit sullen in a corner.

Sarah also directed her venom at the war that created this monster who then tried to hide his life in a bottle. Hayden could not disagree. He tried to steer her to look beyond this terrible event, to look to the better future when the pain was not so immediate and searing. Some day, Hayden feared, Sarah would realize that her hatred of the driver could lead her to thoughts of violent action against Pake.

The funeral was somber and very sad. Hayden physically supported Sarah through the church and graveside services. The view of the Kansas plains, the vastness of the flat fields of wheat stubble and yellow-brown weeds and grass extending to distant horizons in all directions, brought home to Hayden the insignificance of any one or two humans in the overall scheme of things.

Many people who identified themselves as farm neighbors of the Spurges family said their condolences and offered to help in any way they could. Sarah's co-workers turned out in large numbers to support her. Everett Giles sent a beautiful flower wreath and a personal note. The newspaper account and memorial cards listed the survivors as daughter Sarah Randolph, son-in-law

Lucian Randolph, two sisters of Beatrice from Pennsylvania, and a brother of George from New York.

Hayden knew it was critical for Sarah to grieve, to get through the ceremonial trappings of grief and loss. She needed to realize closure, to get on with letting time heal the deep emotional wound she had suffered.

In the week that followed, the deaths of Sarah's parents had serious consequences for Sarah. Hayden saw his fear of her changing emotional condition realized as she underwent a change of heart. She seemed to abandon her lifelong opposition to killing, as she now swore vengeance against Martin Pake in the name of justice.

Hayden was distressed that her mood swing was so violently opposite to what she had espoused previously, her adamant opposition to the taking of life violently. He had to bide his time in pointing out to her the inconsistency of her attitude with the war-long crusade against violence by Sarah and her parents. He knew their renewed relationship might still be too fragile to introduce now his concern over her changed feelings.

After arranging with one of her co-workers to stay with Sarah, Hayden for the first time since her loss took an afternoon away from her side. He went to see the minister who conducted the funeral service. Hayden told of his fear that Sarah's pacifist personality was changing in her hatred of the driver Pake. He admitted that he hesitated to intervene for fear her hostility would again be turned against him for his military service. He needed to know what he could say or do.

The minister was very explicit from the outset. "The therapy to achieve healing is forgiveness. Gaining justice gives satisfaction, but not healing. Justice in these matters is often motivated by vengeance. Getting even does not solve the problem. It does not bring real closure, even if vengeance can be obtained quickly. Only forgiveness brings closure."

"That seems like impossible therapy for Sarah right now," Hayden said.

"The more forgiveness needed, the more difficult the therapy is. You would forgive me quickly, I'm sure, if I mispronounced your name. That is easy because it does not matter much. If I slapped your face, your forgiveness probably would take longer and would be more difficult for you, even if I asked your forgiveness. However, you would get over your emotional injury from that slap only if you forgave me.

"If I killed your parents, by accident or other, your feeling of injury, your hurt, would get all mixed up emotionally with your grief. The hurt would go on and on indefinitely, maybe suppressed or forgotten at times, but always there while you contemplated what you could do to get even, to gain vengeance, to get justice done. Even if I asked your forgiveness, you might not be willing to grant it.

"Until you forgave my transgression…not necessarily forget it, you understand…until you forgave me, you would not achieve true closure. You must convince your wife that any act against the driver will only prolong the healing process, probably even subvert it.

"Her complete recovery to what you would consider a normal condition may take a long time. Her hurt is deep, deep enough to cause her to abandon, only temporarily, we hope, some of her basic religious and social principles."

"I hope I can deliver your message as convincingly to Sarah as you have to me," Hayden said.

"You have advantages in that direction, of course. You know how she listens. You can choose the right time to present this message. And you love her more than I do."

They both had a good chuckle.

"In any event, she is always welcome to come here and talk things over with me."

As he rose to leave, Hayden thought of one more question. "By the way, does that same therapy work for oneself?"

The minister's eyebrows flashed upward for only a brief moment. He had counseled returning servicemen and he could guess where the question was coming from.

"Most certainly," he said. "A person has to forgive himself to gain peace from any injury he might have inflicted on others." The minister waited to see if Hayden wanted to pursue the question.

Hayden nodded and thanked him again.

His second visit was to the Spurges rural home and farm. The debris from their fatal encounter had been removed from the gravel road. Someone had placed two white crosses along the road opposite the entry to their farm. Several neighbors had left messages and flowers on the porch. One left a box of home baked cookies. A large printed message informed whoever came to the house that the writer had taken the Spurges' dog with him to ensure his food and water, and left his phone number.

The door to the house was unlocked. Hayden wasn't sure why he had come here, perhaps a vague belief that something might have to be done before Sarah saw the house again. He rummaged about for any especially troubling reminders of her parents to shield from Sarah. He emptied the refrigerator of perishables and carried them to the car. He took the flowers, messages, and cookies along to Sarah. Otherwise he left the home as it was.

Sarah would have to come to grips with her feelings again when she visited this house with its pictures of her loving parents, herself at various ages, relatives in Pennsylvania, even a few photos of Hayden in uniform. Hayden hoped her visit there soon would also help to bring her closure. She could then see her parents were no longer in the place where she had the fondest and most enduring memories of their place in her life.

Hayden gave the messages, flowers, and cookies to Sarah. She cried again at the kindness of her once alienated neighbors. Hayden took the opportunity to relay the forgiveness message from the minister as carefully as he had learned it. He stressed that she should consider visiting the minister herself. She was non-committal to the message and suggestion.

"I'm not sure I am up to that yet."

"That's okay. He is a good, wise man. You ought to write down the questions you have, and keep him in mind for answers. I can't pretend to know many of the answers."

"You've been very helpful...Hayden." She gave him a small smile. "I just can't get used to calling you anything else right now."

"You have the benefit of keeping your first name.

"Sarah, tell me when you're ready to go to your parents' home. Well, it's your home now. I think it would do you good to see it again. Don't you think it would help to be close again to where they were?"

"Is there anything that has to be done there now...house or farm?"

"Nothing pressing, I suppose. The crop has been harvested. Shep is being taken care of at a neighbor's house." He pondered a moment his next suggestion before stating it. "Another thing, I want you to come with me to the stone works to pick out headstones for your parents."

"Maybe one day next week we can do both," she agreed. "Let's think about that the week after Thanksgiving, okay?"

Hayden had a hunch that fixing a date to resume normal activities might be a fortuitous development to change Sarah's morbid mindset. It might work as if she had agreed to allow herself grieving to that date, and then to start the process of living her life again despite the pain. She had displayed great inner strength on many occasions when the odds were against her.

He was therefore impressed but not greatly surprised on the Monday after Thanksgiving when she rose early, got dressed in a nice outfit, put on makeup, and announced, somberly to be sure, that she was ready to take care of her parents' unfinished business.

At the stone works, Sarah chose a memorial stone for their side-by-side graves. She asked Hayden to help with the wording of the engravings. They agreed on simple language.

<table><tr><td>George Fox Spurges
Husband of Beatrice
Father of Sarah
A Man of Peace
July 5, 1898 –
November 15, 1945 –</td><td>Beatrice Grace Spurges
Wife of George
Mother of Sarah
Love is Thy Name
October 10, 1899 –
November 15, 1945</td></tr></table>

They stopped next to see the family attorney. After reading the will, they started the legal process to transfer the estate to Sarah.

Then they began their trip to the Spurges farm. Sarah hadn't volunteered any information about her parents' final days till now.

"I last saw them about ten days before the accident," she started. "I came out to see them, and it was great, as usual. They were going to come see how I had fixed up my apartment. "Maybe that was where they were heading…"

Sarah teared up as she recalled it. "We planned for me to be home for Thanksgiving and let me go to see you for Christmas."

Hayden patted her shoulder in understanding.

Sarah's tears flowed again as they entered the house. "Just as I always remember it," she said. "Somehow I never gave a thought as to how it would be with both of them gone."

Sarah was quiet for a long time on the road back to Wichita before she asked Hayden suddenly.

"Have you planned or thought about what we might do now?"

"Not much, really. Why, do you have something in mind?"

"I'm torn between getting as far away from here as I can and staying here with them. I know I can't sell the place. It would be like betraying them."

Hayden was silent, not suggesting, knowing that the decision Sarah made was the one she could live with best.

"Would you consider running the farm with me?"

"I was hoping you would come to that," Hayden responded enthusiastically. "I would love to. I did a summer of farm work before I came back to Wichita in 1941."

"I remember," she said brightly.

"A gentleman farmer, a working gentleman farmer. Who'd have thought it?"

"You'll be very good at it, I know."

They stopped for lunch at a roadside cafe. As they ate, Hayden suggested they go back to the farm to find any business records her parents kept. He would like to study them for insights into how the farm had been run in the past.

Once there, and the records boxed up, Hayden asked Sarah to sit out on the sunny porch with him while he told her some important things.

"Your father and I sat in these same chairs almost five years ago. He told me his strong feelings about war, the terrible consequences of war, and how nothing got settled by war. He talked about the detritus, the corrosive waste of war. The waste came home to me in what I saw in Europe—the devastation, the refugees, the ghastly wounded, and the dead. There was way too much horror for any person to have to see.

"I did not understand all of war's destruction your father talked about until I came back. I know now that a war's destruction continues long after the last shots are fired. I suspect the deaths of your parents, however indirect, are a consequence of war. There are countless millions in this country and around the world who are scarred physically and mentally and emotionally by war. I believe my own awful nightmares and the unease I feel are direct consequences of what I was required to do. My dreams likely will continue, a murky reflection of what I saw and did."

"Is it more guilt or remorse that you feel?"

"I'm not sure I can distinguish. The guilt I feel is shared. I'm not rationalizing by spreading guilt around for all involved, you see. But I was under orders. I would not have killed had it not been for my orders. And in no case did I kill randomly, outside of a combat or ordered situation. Still..."

"I can't give you any professional help on that since I don't have any. It sounds to me like the combat violence is not what's haunting you. I've heard about a lot of returning soldiers where killing in combat is the guilt problem, as with that devil, Martin Pake. I sense you are anguished about something else. The colossal what?... Effort you made? Was it a project?"

"A mission, really, inside Germany."

"I thought we had spies to do things like that."

"Well, they said they needed a trooper and a marksman and someone who spoke German well and who had operated behind enemy lines by himself and was resourceful. I think that was the language they used. Oh yes, they also needed him soon."

"Let me see. You were selected because the job required a marksman. So you went after somebody important, a German big shot! How big?" she asked, confident that she was close to the mystery's solution.

"You understand, you can't tell anyone about this."

"No one to tell anymore," she said.

"The Nazi regime personified. Hitler himself," he said matter-of-factly as he dumped onto a civilian the enormous secret he carried.

"No!" She paused to gather her thoughts through the excitement she felt. "You, Hayden Brooke, my Hayden Brooke, out of the thousands that could have been chosen, you were chosen for this history-making task…"

She let her excitement run out before she asked, "Why would you anguish over taking a crack at Hitler? I might have been persuaded to do that myself."

Hayden suspected she was conflating the images of the German dictator and the American bombardier Pake, but said nothing.

"That is a big secret, Hayden. I'm overwhelmed by the very thought of it. I understand why you couldn't tell me.

"It was tough not being able to tell you. I thought you'd have understood if I had been able to tell you at the time."

"I think I would have too." She was silent, thinking.

"You obviously did not kill Hitler. Unless there was a massive cover-up," she said.

"No, I didn't. Our intelligence people were not aware a double and his entourage were in place at Hitler's Bavarian chalet at the time."

"I still don't get it. You're not agonizing because you shot at a Hitler double and some actors, are you?"

"No, those deaths were the consequence of their own participation in deception. And I shot them from about a half mile away, so we weren't face to face by any means. But you see, dearest, I didn't just stroll into Bavaria and start popping away at Hitler with a rifle. I had to fight my way in and out of Germany. I was very lucky, too."

"I think I'm beginning to see."

"Yes, I had to fend off several serious challenges—evade discovery on the train, change identities regularly, gain entrance to the compound at Berghof, acquire a good shooting location, and get out alive."

"And those challengers were who? Civilians? Soldiers? Police?"

"No civilians. Both soldiers and police. All of those challengers forced me to choose. They were close. Most of them knew my face and clothing. I could have disabled them, of course, but I would have run the risk of being identified by them later. At the least, they could have related the story of their being attacked by a person they could describe. That revelation would have jeopardized my mission and my life, I thought. The only real choice was to kill them.

"How dreadful that you had to make those decisions."

"The worst part was that I actually got to know several of them, drank with one, talked for some time with several of them. Now, in looking back, I realize that those killings were a lot like cold-blooded murder."

"Here am I," Sarah said, "a war resister, telling you to justify your actions, serious as they were, by the need to kill! The awful truth is that the only other choice you had was to put yourself in peril by not killing those who threatened you."

"Several of them were little more than boys," said Hayden. "But the other soldiers, even the police, weren't they much like me, ordinary men doing their job? And at the time, weren't they also as unknowing and unconcerned about the consequences of what they did on their own mental well being as I?

"We were trained and readied to kill. No one warned us that we would have to live with that reality for a long time afterward. We were trained to think that dropping an enemy is no big deal. But it is a big deal. I had to condition myself not to feel it, since the people coaching me seemed not to be bothered by it.

"How could I have become so hardened to kill those men, while they were so unaware, so close? I still dream about bodies of children. I feel once in a while that I am an evil person. At Fort Bliss I had doubts about most things I was trained to do."

Hayden went silent, shaking his head.

"Don't beat yourself up constantly over your past, love," Sarah said. "I was once your harshest critic. I can't blame you, and you shouldn't blame yourself for the circumstances you were forced into.

"You have a conscience, a moral compass. You felt obliged to turn off or ignore the compass while you did what you thought was needed for the greater cause. You naturally wanted to protect your existence under the stress of war. Large groups of people, sometimes whole societies, did the same thing.

"Now you are free from that pressure. You feel some compassion for the people you encountered and killed. That is a good reaction. It is sad that there is not a more widespread, global return to compassion now."

"You are your father's daughter," Hayden said and smiled. "He was proud of your moral convictions. As I am. You are also wise beyond your years."

"Someone very wise told me something profound in the last few weeks," Sarah said. "You told me to look forward to our life ahead, our life together. My believing that is possible began to restore some balance for me."

"Sarah, do you think it would be worthwhile for me to re-visit those sites in Europe some time, maybe after we put in a crop and harvest it next year? I'd certainly want you to go along. I would not go without you. We can re-trace my mission. Maybe I can talk it out as we go along. Without the pressure that was once there in those same settings, maybe I can understand some things better, and shake off these emotional demons."

Hayden related to Sarah a radio program he had heard long before any of its content was relevant to his present situation. That discussion among psychologists centered on the belief that with the right trigger, suppressed memories that are causing anxiety to an individual can be reached and released. Hayden observed that this might still be experimental psychology for World War II veterans. He also thought it would be a much better course of action than simply being encouraged to get over those nightmares somehow.

"In any event, coming to terms with those past killings might be worth trying," he concluded. "The minister told me that forgiveness of oneself is also part of therapy."

"An interesting idea," Sarah injected. "Instead of your trying not to think about people you have killed, you should stop trying to forget and try to remember instead, and then forgive yourself for what you had to do in the pressured circumstances.

"It probably would be good for me to have something to look forward to also. A holiday, really," she said.

"Yes, let's plan it. I will listen, though I fear the talk will be grim."

Chapter 45

Kansas and Europe, 1945-1946

Hayden and Sarah began re-building their lives on the farm before Christmas in 1945. Two weeks after Hayden moved into the farm home and renewed the farm's routine, Sarah quit her Wichita job and moved in also. They dug eagerly into the mystery of the land in both its physical production and emotional senses. They learned as much as they could about the business of farming and soybeans in particular.

Hayden had never mentioned to Sarah since his return to the States anything about his lost contact with Frederick. She thought it odd, but concluded that his silence was due to the absence of further information about his best friend.

Over coffee on their first weekend together in their farm home, Sarah was reminded of Hayden and Frederick working together before the war by a newspaper article about Boeing's postwar aircraft contracts. She knew that Frederick had left the Wichita area soon after Hayden went into the service. Hayden mentioned that a letter to Frederick had been returned. He asked Sarah to check at his old residence in Wichita. Frederick had moved without a forwarding address. Hayden had not mentioned Frederick's whereabouts since and Sarah had not asked about him. She thought Frederick might return some day to this area.

"You never heard from Frederick again, I suppose?"

Sarah could see immediately that her husband was surprised and troubled by her innocent question. He gently placed his coffee mug on the table, paused a minute, leaned to her and took her hand in his. He expressed a sadness that Sarah had never before seen in his eyes or heard in his voice.

"Sarah, the worst day of my life was seeing Frederick die."

"No!" she said loudly as she grabbed his arm. "How? Where? He wasn't in the Army, was he? What happened?"

Slowly he told her the story as he knew it of Frederick's involvement in Hayden's mission. He paused at length several times, gathering his emotions, especially as he related the awful scene that took place in the hotel lobby and on the street in front of the Berchtesgaden hotel. He related details later filled in by Colonel Giles on Frederick's agreement to his "termination" mission and how he then abandoned it, with plausible reasons for Frederick's action being filled in by Hayden and Giles in Hayden's de-briefing.

At the end of the sad story, Sarah sat back in her seat, sipped her coffee, and looked straight ahead. She was suddenly certain that Frederick's tragic death was the wellspring of Hayden's emotional problem. He had kept Frederick's death from her for over a year now. He had not told her, the one person who would understand their close friendship and the depth of his loss. She thought she now knew why. His failure to achieve closure had to be related.

Hayden's nightmares were explainable, she thought, as the release of his horror at the repeated vision of Frederick dying without him doing anything about it. Hayden was able to kill young men he had come to know briefly. He did not act to try to save the life of the man he most respected and knew best in his life.

Frederick, with his powerful moral and political convictions, volunteered to try to reach Hayden. By refusing to intervene to stop Hayden's mission, she now understood, he approved its purpose. Hayden and Everett Giles both believed Frederick's timely suicide saved Hayden's life. Frederick finally chose to die for Hayden, rather than be forced to reveal Hayden's identity and details of his mission.

Hayden believes he owes Frederick his life, she thought. He believes that he was the one who should have died, or that he should have died with Frederick, defending him.

And he does not know what to do about it. He admits to remorse at killing several enemy police and soldiers he saw face to face. He believes that self-forgiveness is the answer to those killings. The minister probably is right on that.

However, Hayden began only today, in the last few minutes, to verbalize the anguish he feels over the circumstances of Frederick's death. That is his fundamental emotional challenge, she believed. His subconscious mind is mixing that with his killing of wartime enemies.

Sarah reached for his hand, pulled him toward her and kissed him. "It's all right, dearest. We will work it out."

Over the winter months, Sarah came to view the family farm as sacred property. It was where her parents had lived, and from where they left for the last time, coming to see her.

With the onset of another growing season, she and Hayden, as beginners in this new venture, faced the enormous challenge of conducting the farm business in all its components. She did the business end of the operation. She kept the books, handled all the correspondence, and ensured supplies were available. She was proud to be a new director in the enterprise George and Beatrice had founded.

She also made lunch to share with Hayden each day he was in the fields. He did the scheduling, plowing, sowing, weed and pest control, and harvesting.

As all farmers did, they gambled. They hoped for nature's cooperation in providing the essentials of sunshine and precipitation, both at the right time.

Martin Pake's insurance company paid a reasonable settlement after Sarah and Hayden threatened a lawsuit. Sarah did not insist on her pound of flesh from Pake, but her hostile feelings toward him had not moderated. Both were relieved that they would not have to go through the trauma of a trial.

Their trip to re-trace Hayden's wartime mission was planned throughout the summer of 1946. After a good soybean harvest was completed and sold, they made arrangements for the care of the house and farm and departed on October 20.

Hayden's thoughts on the flight to London, he told Sarah, were bounded by the anticipation of seeing those war sites again with Sarah and some apprehension at the awful scenes he would re-visit and remember. It was Sarah's first flight of any significant length and her first journey out of the country, a history-geography lesson for her.

She was enthralled with all the sights. London was being re-built, but enough of the old city was there to confirm her knowledge of it. Casablanca displayed a culture she had only dreamed of before, the embodiment of Bogart and Bergman and mystery.

They followed the coast along North Africa, then went by boat to Sicily and the troopers' landing sites. The mountain and sea views all along the western coastal highway of Sicily, the invasion path followed by the 82nd Airborne Division in 1943, were spectacular. The cities of Palermo and Trapani, the destinations of the Division's expedition in Sicily, were scenic, warm, and comfortable.

The same was true of Naples. Hayden's entry into Naples with the 505th Parachute Regiment had not been by air, but followed mountain fighting to the south and east after the Anzio landing. They rented a car and re-traced the rugged terrain, then swung north toward the Volturno River and Rome beyond.

Local residents were courteous throughout their Mediterranean excursions. They seemed to recognize and appreciate why Hayden was there, one of many Americans returning to visit the scenes of their wartime trials.

After the flight from Rome to Paris, Hayden and Sarah traveled by bus to the French northwest coast. Most of the debris had been removed from the coastal invasion sites and the area behind the bluffs on the Normandy beaches. The cemetery and memorial to the dead were awe-inspiring in the solemn memories they evoked. Although some of the site was still under construction, the row upon row of Crosses and Stars of David were the most memorable images of their whole trip.

Hayden found the landing zone of his company near St. Mere Eglise. The 2nd Battalion of the 505th Regiment had the task of holding the road north of the village. Then it captured the town of Neuville-au-Plain to block German movement southward. Hayden stood for a long time envisioning, re-creating the noise, the immediacy, the shock of the battle. He told Sarah it was not difficult for him to hear the sounds of the intense exchanges and see the bodies crumpled and strewn about on this site.

The Dutch countryside they visited two days later, once so fraught with the commotion and danger of battle, was now peaceful also. They spent one night in an inn on the Grosbeek Heights, overlooking the grounds of the frantic struggle of the 505th Regiment to gain a lodgment so close to the *Reichswald* inside the German border.

Then it was south to Strasbourg. Hayden related to Sarah the escape of the German Lieutenant Eric Klaysa after Hayden had adopted his uniform and papers. He also mentioned the intelligence leak picked up by the German mole inside British Intelligence that could have been very costly to him.

"You were fortunate to be able to sense the danger points developing," she said.

"Yes, very fortunate, here and elsewhere."

They took a ferry across the Rhine into Germany at Karlsruhe, then a bus through the same country Hayden and the two Sergeants had traveled at night in a van over rough and unpaved roads on their way to Mainz.

On the train from Mainz to Frankfort, Munich, and Berchtesgaden, the litter and devastation of war from time to time punctuated the historic, picturesque beauty of Germany. Hayden related the close call with the *Feldgendarmerie* inspectors on the train. He held her arm and simply pointed to the various piles of uncleared rubble in the small German town where he had disposed of Lieutenant Jules Osbert and obtained his identity.

"The Lieutenant seemed like a decent enough chap," Hayden said. "In different circumstances, I think we could have been friends."

While Sarah marveled at the impressive countryside, Hayden occasionally reflected aloud on the changes since he left Europe after the Market-Garden operation.

The 82nd Division had been called up out of reserve to help form the American defensive line against the initial German breakthrough in the Ardennes in mid-December. The Division did not take part in the massive Varsity jump into west Germany in 1945, but was in on the drive to the Elbe River and the end of hostilities there.

Hitler had underestimated the ability of the Allies to recover from the surprise of the *Wacht am Rhein* offensive through the Ardennes. He miscalculated the effect of using up the divisions in the offensive on his own defense of the Western Front. In leaving his western defenses to deteriorate, he committed a strategic blunder. Although Allied losses were severe, they could be replaced. Hitler did not have the reserves to replace his Ardennes offensive losses.

The political changes resulting from the war were far-reaching. Roosevelt, Hitler, and Mussolini were all dead. Other military and political war leaders in Germany and Japan were facing the death penalty in war crimes trials to be conducted. Churchill had been voted out of power in 1945. Only Stalin of the Big Three Allied leaders remained in office.

Old alliances were ruptured and new ones formed. The Soviets were a key departure from the war-winning combination. They went off by themselves, looking for new partners in the international socialist movement. They now suspected everything the Western powers did. They were held in check mostly by the United States possession of atomic weaponry.

Everett Giles was in retirement. Hayden regretted that he had lost contact with the others: Wyatt Baxter, Jerry Connelios, his own Corporal and Sergeant, and many other acquaintances made over his three years of active service.

The Munich train station and surrounding buildings had been bombed heavily in the months after Hayden's stop there. He mentioned, without humor, that he had obtained a temporary promotion to SS Major in this setting. Sarah by now understood a reference to his need to kill without his elaboration.

The high point of the Berghof visit for Hayden was his ability to stroll unhurried and without fear of detection through the grounds surrounding the compound. The *Tee Haus* had been heavily damaged in the bombing of the whole area and was no longer usable.

They were able to convince the American guards at the chalet to let them enter for a closer look. After admiring the captivating scenery around her to the south, she found

Hayden kneeling to feel a scratch on a flagstone.

"What is it?" she asked.

"I think I did this," he said matter-of-factly, retracing the elongated mark. "I think this is where my first round impacted. If so, isn't it remarkable that this scratch would survive all the bombing and devastation? The Hitler double must have been standing about there," he pointed as he spoke.

Hayden expressed his sadness and anger when he saw the Neo-Nazis coming to the "Hitler Shrine at Berghof." The American guards would not allow native Germans into the Berghof chalet remains, but pictures and crude memorials to the fallen German dictator were placed along the roadways and trees in the area. "People like Frederick Penner and millions of other who sacrificed and died should be the ones with shrines," Hayden said bitterly.

Hayden's apprehension grew as they approached the hotel. He told Sarah it was painful but easy for him to recollect the awful happening outside the hotel since he had seen it every day since in his memory. He related the details of Frederick's arrest in the hotel and suicide in the police car. Sarah stood by him, her arm around his waist, murmuring words of disbelief and sorrow occasionally. He recounted the entire episode as if it were happening again right in front of them.

Eventually they turned and entered the hotel. Hayden asked the manager if there was any way he could see rooms 417 and 421. There was nothing exceptional or revealing about either room. He tipped the man for his help.

As they turned to leave the hotel, Hayden asked suddenly, "Do you have a storage area for guests' baggage left behind?"

"Why, yes," the manager answered, and led the way, explaining, "all baggage and items left are marked with the guest's room number and held in this room."

"Hayden and Sarah scoured the musty room with him and found nothing with room number 417 on it. The police no doubt had seized and kept Frederick's effects from his room.

Hayden thanked him again, and started to leave.

"Wait!" the man fairly shouted. "Come with me. I always save some of the things that are left behind in the rooms." He led them to a sitting room containing several shelves of books. He scanned the room numbers printed on the spines of books, found one marked with number 417, and pulled it out.

"I remember this one especially," he said, "from about two years ago. It was the day there was a rumored assassination attempt on Chancellor Hitler at Berghof. We knew he was not at Berghof. The people in this community always knew. Before I came on duty that day, a squad of police arrested an SS Colonel in his room early in the afternoon. They were always curious when an SS officer stayed here overnight and not at the SS Barracks not far from here."

Hayden whispered to Sarah the danger both Frederick and he had been in by staying at the hotel, and how it was Frederick's fate to still be there after Hayden did the shooting.

"Later I went to the room of the SS Colonel," the manager continued. "I found this book of poetry lying on the floor behind the window drapes, as if it had been thrown there. I saved it," he said, and showed it to Hayden.

"Yes, I remember it," Hayden said with excitement, a strange feeling of being very close to Frederick as he took the book. Even though the book had no name on the inside front cover, Hayden said he knew it was Frederick's. "He often had it on his desk when I visited his apartment," he said.

Hayden moved quietly to the better light from the window and began to flip through the book. It fell open to a page that startled him.

"Look!" he shouted to Sarah, "Look!"

There, above the poem on peace by Goethe, was a note.

"Show Hayden."

Sarah gasped as she took the book, "I don't believe it! Frederick left a memento to you. What a find!"

Hayden could not control his feelings. While Sarah marveled at the discovery with the manager, Hayden walked quickly into the corridor. She let him weep, probably most for his dead friend and for the loss of his lifetime companionship. She guessed he was remembering George and Beatrice Spurges also, and those who had fallen around him in four battles, all the young soldiers he had to kill, all the victims and the devastation.

Sarah came up behind him in the corridor, turned him toward her and hugged him close. After a minute, she spoke softly.

"It does not lessen the important, heroic things you did over three years to regret now that you had to do them. You can put your bad memories back on the shelf. Keep the good ones active, especially of Frederick. Be grateful, without remorse, for what he did for you.

"We both have to let go of the belief that our bad memories are too important to put aside. Our wanting to grasp at the past, as if we could somehow still change it, poisons our dreams. It wastes our energies. It doesn't yield answers, only more questions and anguish.

"We have to accept and savor what others have done for us without worrying that we cannot repay them. We have to accept love as well as give it. Frederick wanted you to accept the gift he was giving you...his friendship over part of his life, and then his life itself. He would want you to take it without regret. He would want you to pass on his gifts of friendship and love and life itself to others."